$\mathcal{O}$NE KISS
IN... $\mathcal{H}awaii$

DEBBI RAWLINS

JILL MONROE

WENDY ETHERINGTON

ONE KISS

IN... COLLECTION

April 2015

May 2015

June 2015

July 2015

August 2015

September 2015

ONE KISS IN... *Hawaii*

DEBBI RAWLINS
JILL MONROE
WENDY ETHERINGTON

MILLS & BOON

Published in Great Britain 2015
by Mills & Boon, an imprint of Harlequin (UK) Limited,
Eton House, 18-24 Paradise Road, Richmond, Surrey, TW9 1SR

ONE KISS IN... HAWAII © 2015 Harlequin Books S.A.

Second Time Lucky © 2011 Debbi Quattrone
Wet and Wild © 2009 Jill Floyd
Her Private Treasure © 2010 Wendy Etherington

ISBN: 978-0-263-25390-0

025-0615

Harlequin (UK) Limited's policy is to use papers that are natural, renewable and recyclable products and made from wood grown in sustainable forests.The logging and manufacturing processes conform to the legalenvironmental regulations of the country of origin.

Printed and bound in Spain
by CPI, Barcelona

Second Time Lucky

DEBBI RAWLINS

Debbi Rawlins lives in central Utah, out in the country, surrounded by woods and deer and wild turkeys. It's quite a change for a city girl, who didn't even know where the state of Utah was until four years ago. Of course, unfamiliarity has never stopped her. Between her junior and senior years of college she spontaneously left her home in Hawaii and bummed around Europe for five weeks by herself. And, much to her parents' delight, returned home with only a quarter in her wallet.

This is for all the working mums
who need a spring break more than anyone.
Women with dogs and cats totally count.

Prologue

SHE WASN'T THERE. Disappointed, Mia Butterfield shaded her eyes against the bright sun and scanned the crowded park, her gaze quickly skipping over the noon-time joggers and past the rows of nannies, whose concentration was split between children and gossip. With it being unseasonably warm for January, she'd felt certain Annabelle would be here walking her dog, or rather being walked by the oversize part St. Bernard and part Rottweiler she'd affectionately named Mr. Muffin.

Barely five feet tall and close to eighty, Mia's new friend should have had a nice little Yorkie or toy poodle as a companion, but no, not Annabelle. She preferred the big moose of a mutt that she'd found at the local shelter. Mia had only met Annabelle Albright six weeks ago when Mr. Muffin had spied a rabbit and pulled away from the older woman. Mia had been walking back from the courthouse to her office when she encountered the runaway dog. He'd literally run into her, costing her a pair of forty-dollar pantyhose and the three-inch heel of her new Jimmy Choos.

The upside was that Mia had made a new friend that

day. A much-needed friend. Her two best buds lived thousands of miles away, but the truth was, Annabelle served a need neither of Mia's college friends could. The woman had an unbiased ear. She listened, her gaze clear, her smile knowing, her rare questions about clarity, not judgment. Sometimes the silence frustrated Mia. Here she was twenty-eight and all she wanted was someone to tell her what to do. She hated that streak of vulnerability.

From the time she was a kid she'd always been a take-charge person, fully in control, absolutely clear on what she wanted. Her younger brother and sister had come to her for advice, as had her friends. When she'd graduated from law school with honors, no one had been surprised. Not even when she'd been recruited by one of the most prestigious law firms in Manhattan. She hadn't bothered explaining to her family what an incredible opportunity that was for a young lawyer.

In retrospect, it was a good thing she hadn't made a big deal of it because then for sure they wouldn't understand why she wanted to quit. All of it. Just walk away. Start fresh. No, they wouldn't get it. She barely did herself.

The mere thought of what she wanted to do twisted her stomach into knots. She stared down at the white paper bag in her hand and sighed. She didn't care about the apples and yogurt she'd bought at the corner bodega. The main reason she'd taken a lunch break was in the hope of seeing Annabelle.

"Mia!"

At the sound of the familiar voice, she turned around to see Annabelle being dragged toward her by the big dog. Prepared for an onslaught of large paws and sloppy kisses, Mia knew better than to crouch.

"Hey, Mr. Muffin." She held out a firm hand for him to sniff. His attention immediately switched to the paper bag. "Seriously, I don't think you'd be that interested."

"If it's food, he's interested," Annabelle said with a throaty laugh, her remarkably unlined face artfully made up. "Come on, Mr. Muffin, don't be a mooch." She tugged on the leash to get his attention, and with her other hand reached into the pocket of a smartly tailored burgundy jacket that had once been elegantly in style. "Here you go, you big lug." She produced a plastic bag of treats and made him sit before passing him a MilkBone.

"I was hoping I'd see you here today." Mia straightened, anxious to take advantage of the dog's temporary distraction.

"It's marvelous weather. Can you believe it's January?"

"I know. I can't afford the break but I couldn't help myself."

Annabelle waved a gloved hand. "You work too hard as it is." She saw that the dog had finished and quickly gave him another MilkBone. "He shouldn't have so many treats," she said absently, looking over her shoulder. "Where is that young man?"

"Young man?"

"Oh, there he is. Good." Annabelle signaled to a blond teenage boy on a skateboard near the fork in the sidewalk.

He zoomed toward them, skillfully avoiding a strolling couple before pulling to a stop in front of Annabelle. "Hey, Mrs. Albright. I'm not late, am I?"

"Right on time." She handed him the leash. "A half

an hour should tire him out." She crouched to nuzzle the dog's bulky neck, her fluid movement that of a much younger woman, a tribute to her early Broadway days. "Isn't that right, Mr. Muffin? You be a good boy, you hear?"

With hopeful eyes, the dog watched her pass the treats to the teenager, and then happily trotted off alongside the boy. Annabelle continued to watch the pair disappear while Mia found a bench partially shaded by a bare but huge old elm.

"Who's the boy?" Mia asked, as she brushed off the bench seat.

"Kevin, my neighbor's son." Annabelle joined her. "But you'll walk Mr. Muffin while I'm away on my trip?"

"What trip? You didn't tell me you were going anywhere."

"Oh, it's this cruise." Annabelle waved a dismissive hand, looking less than thrilled. "I'd promised a friend a few months back."

"Good for you." Mia rubbed her friend's arm. "It'll be great to get out of the city. Where are you going?"

"I don't actually know. Hamilton—" She cleared her throat. "—my friend, is in charge of all that."

Mia hid a smile. So, Annabelle had a gentleman friend who wanted to sweep her away. Which was made all the sweeter since Mia doubted the woman could afford a vacation of any sort otherwise.

Mia opened her bag and gave Annabelle an apple.

"Thank you, dear." The woman smiled. "You never forget that Granny Smith is my favorite. But I already ate my lunch."

Mia shrugged. "Save it for later. I bought yogurt, too."

Annabelle searched Mia's face, making Mia avert

her gaze in case her intentions were too obvious. She guessed the woman was struggling financially, but was too proud to accept charity. Her clothes and shoes were well made and had probably cost a few bucks new, but most of her wardrobe should have been donated years ago. Still, she was always impeccably groomed, her white hair and makeup tended with great care, even her short buffed fingernails were nicely maintained. She clearly took pride in her appearance and even greater pride in remaining self-sufficient. Mia had made the mistake of offering to help buy food and hiring a dog walker for Mr. Muffin, and was abruptly shot down.

"So, tell me what's on your mind," Annabelle said with her usual forthrightness.

Mia hesitated. "I hate my job." There, she'd said it out loud. "I do," she insisted when Annabelle twisted around to narrow her faded blue eyes on Mia.

"What brought this on?"

"The hours are long. I have no social life." She shrugged helplessly. "It's sort of a combination of things."

Annabelle's expression softened. "Are you thinking about changing firms?"

A sudden chill breeze made Mia pull the lapels of her suit jacket tighter. "I don't know that I want to practice law anymore," she said softly.

Annabelle settled back on the bench and stared off toward the children riding the swings. "That's a big decision." Her voice was calm, reasonable, but Mia had seen the alarm flash in her eyes.

She thought Mia was being impulsive. Crazy, really. Who went through three grueling years of law school, was lucky enough to work at a firm like Pearson and

Stern, and then walked away from it all? Certainly not a sane person. Her parents were going to have the same reaction. God, she dreaded telling them. This was good practice.

"You're right. It's a huge decision. Not one I'm taking lightly."

"I should hope not." Annabelle frowned thoughtfully. "What would you do?"

"You've heard me mention my friends Lindsey Shaw and Shelby Cain. In college we'd talked about starting a concierge and rental business. Our sorority participated in a fundraiser where we all rented ourselves out for a day to run errands, cook, babysit, host a dinner— whatever the client needed for a specific occasion." She shrugged. "Not only did we have a blast, but we also could see the potential for some sort of full-service business in Manhattan."

"Sounds rather dangerous."

Mia smiled. "We'd make sure our clients are properly vetted. Besides, I figure the larger part of our business will be about renting designer purses and bridal gowns, that sort of thing. If kids from the local colleges want to sign up, we'd hire them for the concierge side. Our motto will be 'You can rent anything at Anything Goes.' Hey, maybe you'll want to rent out Mr. Muffin."

Annabelle smiled, but her expression remained troubled. "Your friends, they're willing to quit their jobs and move here?"

Mia sighed. That was going to be tricky. "I haven't discussed any of this with them yet."

"Oh…" Annabelle seemed relieved. "So you truly haven't made up your mind yet."

The reaction shouldn't have bothered her, but Mia

couldn't ignore the sense of betrayal she felt. For some reason, she'd thought Annabelle might understand. Here was a woman who'd shunned convention, turned her back on marriage and children in pursuit of her career when women simply didn't dream of forging their own path.

"No," she lied. "I haven't made up my mind."

"Good. This is a very big decision. You mustn't be hasty and do anything while I'm gone." Annabelle reached over and squeezed her hand. "Don't walk away because of David."

Mia jerked back and blinked. "David? Why would you— He has nothing to do with this. I don't understand why you'd bring him up."

Contradicting Annabelle's gentle smile, her eyes gleamed shrewdly. "Of course. Forgive a doddering old lady."

"David's my boss, nothing more."

The woman nodded.

"The only reason you ever heard about him was because we worked a few cases together." She paused, frustrated that she was feeling defensive. So, she talked about work sometimes. It was only natural that his name had come up. It wasn't as if the man noticed her. She was just one among the many, a useful tool, a worker bee. He hadn't even so much as shared a pizza with her when they'd been stuck late at the office. As if there could ever be something between her and David. The idea alone was laughable.

Annabelle lifted her face to the sun, her eyes closed, an annoying smile tugging at the corners of her mouth.

1

MIA WAITED UNTIL the waiter had poured the champagne into her friends' glasses before she raised her flute. "To us," she said, grinning at Lindsey and Shelby. "We did it."

"Yes, we did," Lindsey agreed, her mouth twisting wryly and her expression not looking quite as enthusiastic as Mia's or Shelby's. "We now owe more money than any three twenty-eight-year-old women should owe in their lifetimes."

Shelby laughed and downed her champagne.

"You're such a pessimist." Shaking her head, Mia elbowed her. "If we didn't think we could make a go of this, none of us would've signed on the dotted line, much less have quit our jobs."

"You did?" Lindsey's eyes widened. "Seriously? You've turned in your resignation already?"

"It's typed up and will be on my boss's desk tomorrow morning." Mia swallowed around the lump in her throat, the one that seemed to swell every time she thought about pulling out all of her savings and having no income until their new venture turned a profit. She glanced at Shelby. "What about you?"

"I was just waiting to sign the loan documents. I'll turn in mine on Monday as soon as I get back to Houston." Shelby snatched the pricey bottle of Cristal out of the ice bucket and refilled her glass. "We might as well enjoy this. After tonight, it's gonna be the cheap stuff for us until we make some dough."

Lindsey made a small whimpering sound, her blue eyes clouding. "Don't remind me."

Mia set down her flute, prepared to give the pep talk she'd been rehearsing for the past few weeks. Once she'd made up her mind that she wanted to leave her firm and take a chance on starting the new business, she'd leaned hard on Lindsey and Shelby, so to some degree she felt responsible for the other two taking the plunge with her. Plus she already lived in Manhattan. Her friends had to make the move, but they missed one another, and wanted to live in New York together.

"Oh, it won't be that bad," Shelby said, urging her to take another sip. "We'll eat and drink well when we go out on dates."

Mia cleared her throat. "About that…"

Both women looked expectantly at her.

"Unlike the glory days of college, Manhattan isn't exactly teeming with eligible men."

"Well, neither is Chicago." Lindsey sighed. "I haven't had a real date in seven months." She lifted her brows accusingly at Shelby, who never seemed to lack company of the male persuasion. "Maybe we should've moved to Houston, Mia. If things got too bad, at least we could count on leftovers."

Shelby waved dismissively. "Oh, sweetie, you're delusional if you think I've had any better luck there."

Lindsey snorted. "Right."

Mia eyed her friend. "Really, Shelby?"

"Really," she answered defensively, and then shrugged. "I can't remember the last time I went out a second or third time with the same guy and those are the dates that count." She sniffed. "And no, it's not because I'm too picky."

"You have every reason to be damn picky. We all do," Mia said and meant it, even though she was in the middle of a particularly long dry spell. It was mainly her fault. All those ungodly hours spent in the office hadn't helped. And if she were totally honest with herself, she'd spent too much time hoping David would finally man up, ask her out, share one lousy dinner with her. Despite what she'd told Annabelle, despite what she'd told herself, she'd honestly thought he'd been attracted to her, at least in the beginning. Sadly, she'd clearly been fooling herself. No use thinking about him now.

"Amen." Lindsey downed a healthy sip. "Still would be nice to have an assortment to be picky over." She narrowed her eyes at Mia. "What ever happened to that guy you worked with? David, right?"

Mia nearly choked on her champagne. "There was never anything there."

"Yeah, I remember him," Shelby chimed in. "When you first started with the firm you thought he was hot."

"He is hot. Unfortunately, he's taken."

"Married?" Lindsey observed sympathetically.

"To the job. His father and uncle founded the firm, and the guy still puts in more hours than anyone else."

Mia shook her head. "Anyway, there's a rule about fraternization. God knows David Pearson would rather be strung up by his thumbs than step one toe over the line."

Lindsey giggled a bit, which told Mia the bubbly was getting to her friend, then grabbed the champagne and topped up everyone's glasses. "This is what I don't get…when we were in school there were all kinds of guys around. If we didn't have a date, it was because we didn't want to go out."

"I know, right?" Shelby frowned thoughtfully. "Even when we went out in groups, guys always outnumbered us. So what the hell happened to them? They can't *all* be married and living in the burbs."

"You have a point." Mia sipped slowly, worried that the alcohol was getting to her, too. Usually she wasn't such a lightweight, but she hadn't eaten anything all day. "Even during spring break, I swear, there were two guys to every girl."

"I'm the accountant," Lindsey said. "I'd say more like three to one."

"Junior year. Fort Lauderdale." Shelby slumped back in her chair, her expression one of total bliss. "Oh, my God."

"Are you kidding?" Mia stared at her in disbelief. "Come on. Senior year, Waikiki Beach, hands down winner."

Shelby's sigh said it all.

Lindsey smiled broadly. "Yep."

Along with the other two, Mia lapsed into silence, enjoying the heady memories of that magical week. She sipped her champagne as a notion popped into her head.

"Hey, guys," she said, her pulse picking up speed as the thoughts tumbled. "I have an idea."

"Oh, no." The ever cautious Lindsey glanced dramatically at Shelby. "I don't know if I can take another one."

"No, this is good." Mia grinned. "There's no law that says spring break is just for college kids."

"Okay." Shelby drew out the word.

Lindsey just frowned.

"We're going to be working our asses off until we get Anything Goes off the ground, right? If we want to take a vacation, this is the time. Probably the last time for years. Who knows, maybe we'll even get laid." Mia saw the interest mount in Shelby's face.

Not Lindsey. Her frown deepened. "Hawaii?"

"Why not?" Mia noticed the empty champagne bottle and signaled the waiter.

"Because it's too expensive, for one thing. Are you forgetting we've just signed our lives away?"

"I don't know." Mia sighed, not quite willing to give up the idea. "Maybe we can go on the cheap, pick up one of those last-minute deals. And none of us has officially put in our resignations. I'd be willing to work another two weeks at the firm if it meant enough money for Hawaii."

"It wouldn't hurt to see what's available," Shelby said.

"I suppose not." Lindsey set down her glass, not looking at all convinced. In fact, she stared at Mia as if she were a traitor. "But we'd have to set a budget first. A firm budget."

Mia nodded in agreement. The whole thing was ridiculous, and even if they did stay at their current jobs a bit longer, a Hawaiian vacation was pretty extravagant for

three women who were about to give up their incomes
and live on hope and dreams until they got their feet
planted again. It shocked her that she'd even thought of
it, let alone was actually considering such a crazy thing.
She was normally far more sensible, for God's sake.

But damn it, she'd worked hard for the past six years,
first in law school and then at Pearson and Stern. She
deserved the break, and right now, with the cold March
air whipping around outside, Hawaii sounded like a slice
of heaven.

"You know what would be really cool?" Shelby's eyes
lit up as she leaned forward. "Remember those three
guys we met at that party on our last day on Waikiki
beach?"

"Uh, yeah," Mia said. "Smokin' hot."

Lindsey stiffened. "What about them?"

"What if we could get them to meet us?" Grinning,
Shelby darted a mischievous look between them. "In
Hawaii."

"How would we do that? We don't even know their
last names." Mia snorted. "Not to mention they're probably married or in prison."

Shelby gave Mia a look, then ignored her completely.
"We know what university they went to, so we use
Facebook."

"Huh." Mia thought for a moment. "We could send
a message to the alumni group. It couldn't hurt."

"But they'll have to have signed up as alumni to get
the message." Lindsey didn't seem thrilled.

Shelby shrugged. "Lots of people do. I have, haven't
you?"

Mia shook her head. "Look, they answer, they don't,
so what? It's Waikiki. We're bound to meet some

gorgeous surfers who'll be ready to party," she said, warming to the idea.

"I like it." Shelby dug in her purse and produced a pen. "Anybody have a piece of paper or a dry napkin?"

Mia pulled her day planner out of her leather tote and tore off a used page. "Here."

"Oh, my God, they still have those things around. Why don't you use your BlackBerry?" Shelby found a clean spot on the table and started writing.

"I do both," Mia said, and glanced at Lindsey, who understood about being careful. She did not look happy.

"Okay, how about something like this…" Shelby squinted as if she were having trouble reading her own writing, which was awful. No one could ever read it but her. "Here we go—'Remember spring break? Mia, Lindsey and Shelby will be at the Seabreeze Hotel during the week of whatever. Come if you dare. You know who you are.'"

"Not bad, but we'll have to be more specific." Mia did a quick mental calculation. 'Remember Spring Break 2004.'"

"Right." Shelby scribbled in the correction. "Lindsey, what do you think?"

She shoved a hand through her blond hair and exhaled a shaky breath. It was dim in the bar, but Mia could see she was blushing. "I think you'll have to change Lindsey to Jill."

Shelby blinked. "You didn't give him your real name?"

With a guilty smile, Lindsey shook her head.

Mia and Shelby exchanged glances, and burst out laughing.

DAVID PEARSON PASSED Mia's empty office on his way to the conference room where he'd been summoned by his father and uncle.

He still couldn't believe she was gone. The day she'd handed him her letter of resignation had been a shock. Now, two weeks and three days later, he still couldn't come to grips with Mia no longer being with the firm. That she wouldn't be stepping off the elevator each morning, early, before anyone but himself had arrived at the office, her green eyes still sleepy, her shoulder-length dark hair still down and damp. By eight, she'd have drunk three cups of coffee—no cream, a little sugar—and pulled her now dry hair back into a tidy French twist. He'd known her routine and habits almost as well as he knew his own.

"Good morning, Mr. Pearson."

He looked blankly at the receptionist. Only then did he realize he'd stopped and had been staring at the plant Mia had left behind that was sitting near her office door. He silently cleared his throat. "Good morning, Laura."

Smiling, the pretty young blonde continued toward the break room with a mug in her hand.

"Laura."

"Yes?" she said, turning back to him.

"Will Mia be picking up this plant?"

She blinked. "I don't know. I don't think so."

"Well, something has to be done with it," he said more gruffly than he intended. He never got involved in such petty matters. Even more annoying was the unexpected hope that he'd see her again. "Either have it sent to her or if she doesn't want it, let someone take it."

"Mia's going to Hawaii. I'll keep it watered for now."

"Hawaii?" His chest tightened. "She's moving?"

"I bet she wishes." Laura grinned. "According to Lily, she'll be gone for a week."

"When is she leaving?"

The curiosity gleaming in the young woman's eyes brought him to his senses.

"Never mind." He shifted the file folders he'd been holding and started again toward the conference room. "Just do something with the plant."

"In a couple of days," Laura called after him. "She's leaving in a couple of days…I think."

David didn't respond, but kept walking. What the hell was wrong with him? It was none of his business what Mia did. She'd quit. Thanked him for the opportunity to have been part of the firm, told him she would be pursuing other endeavors, and that was it. He hadn't tried to talk her into staying. She was a damn good attorney, and he should have. But mostly he'd been too stunned.

The conference-room door was closed, and he knocked briefly before letting himself in. At one end of the long polished mahogany table sat his father, his uncle Harrison and Peter, one of the equity partners. Odd enough that his father would be in the office instead of on the golf course on a Friday, but all three men looked grim.

"Good morning, gentlemen."

"David." Peter nodded.

"Have a seat, David" was all his father said.

His uncle poured some water from a carafe on the table and pushed the glass toward David. "You'll want to add a shot of Scotch to that in a minute."

"What's going on?" As he slowly lowered himself

into one of the sleek leather chairs, he looked from one bleak face to the next.

"We've lost the Decker account," his father said, his complexion unnaturally pale.

David felt as if the wind had been knocked out of him. Thurston Decker was their second biggest client. "How?"

"That's not all," his uncle added, his features pinched. "It looks as if Cromwell may jump ship, as well."

Bewildered, David looked to Peter, who was staring at his clenched hands. "I don't understand." David shook his head. "They've both been with us for two generations without a single complaint. We've done an excellent job for them."

"They don't dispute that." His father removed his glasses and carefully began cleaning the lenses. "They're citing the economy."

"That's bull." Harrison angrily ran a hand through his graying hair. "It's Thurston's grandkids who're responsible. Those greedy little bastards. They're edging the old man out of the company and making a bunch of jackass changes."

"No point in getting steamed," David's father said wearily. He rarely got angry or displayed much emotion. David was much like him in that way. "We need to focus on bringing them back around."

"I doubt that's a possibility," Peter opined. He was a quiet, studious man, who'd joined Pearson and Stern a year before David, and arguably knew more about what was going on in the firm than either of the two senior partners. "I heard that Fritz Decker, the oldest grandson, has already hired one of his former prep school buddies who bought in to Flanders and Sheen. And for a much smaller retainer."

"How reliable is that information?" David asked.

Peter's mouth twisted wryly. "We can forget about Decker's business."

"Jesus Christ, what the hell happened to loyalty?" Harrison exhaled sharply and eyed David. "You might not know this, but your grandfather had just started this firm when Thurston Decker got into the booze business. He started out with one store and a bar. When he got tangled up with a moonshiner, your granddad took him on as a client for next to nothing."

David had heard the story and just nodded. "What about Cromwell? Did we screw up, or is he playing the economy card, too?"

Peter shrugged. "We didn't do anything wrong."

"Do we have a chance of wooing him back?"

"Good question." His father put on his glasses. "We've lost a few smaller clients in the past couple of months, legitimately as a result of the economy, and nothing that would ordinarily concern us, but at this juncture, throw Decker and Cromwell into the pot and we're in trouble."

David sank back in his chair, his head feeling as if it weighed a ton. He never thought he'd see this day. Pearson and Stern had been a reputable, prestigious firm his entire life. "What happens now?"

"We cut back," his father said. "No more weekly fresh flower deliveries, and the daily catering for the break room and conference rooms are to stop. You'd be as shocked as I was at how much those two items alone will save us."

"What about layoffs?" Peter asked.

The question startled David, especially when neither his father nor his uncle balked. He hadn't dared allow his imagination to go that far. Naturally he understood this was serious, but there had been other lows in Pearson and Stern's history and they'd always taken pride in keeping every one of their employees. "Layoffs? Surely we're not at that crossroad. We haven't tried to drum up more business yet."

"Not quite true. Your uncle and I have made some calls, but we've come up empty."

David stared at the defeated look on his father's tired face, and the heaviness in his chest grew. It wasn't just his reasoned approach to business that made David admire the hell out of his dad. He'd always been a fair employer, a dignified member of the bar association, and David was glad that he'd recently been able to pull back from the office to spend some much deserved time on the golf course. "I can make some calls, too," he said, withdrawing his BlackBerry from his pocket. "A couple of my old law professors from Harvard should be able—"

"David. Wait."

He glanced up.

"There is something you can do. That sharp young attorney, Mia."

"Mia Butterfield," Peter clarified.

"Right." Lloyd Pearson leaned forward. "There is a potential new client considering our firm. A very big client, who requires the administration of a rather large charitable foundation. That means a hefty retainer and billable hours for two to three full-time attorneys."

"What does this have to do with Mia?" David asked, confused. "You do know she no longer works here."

"Sadly, yes, because the new client has stipulated that Ms. Butterfield be in charge of the account."

"That makes no sense. Mia never did estate planning." David exhaled. "We have a stable of extremely talented tax and estate-planning attorneys. Or I could take on this new account myself."

His father shook his head. "I'm afraid not having Mia Butterfield handle the account is a deal-breaker, and no, there was no further explanation. You worked most closely with her. You'll have to convince her to come back."

"I doubt that's possible." He vividly remembered the day she'd delivered her letter of resignation. She'd stayed while he read it, then without hesitation on her part or even a trace of regret she was out the door.

"Offer her a bonus, a promotion, certainly a raise. Whatever it takes. We need this business, David, or we bring out the chopping block."

David loosened his tie and sank back. It was no use denying he wanted to see her again. For an instant he had wondered if her leaving would end up being the best thing that could've happened.

Damn it. Yeah, he wanted to see her again all right. But not like this.

2

THE HOTEL HADN'T CHANGED much in six years. Which was a very good thing because why mess with perfection? The lobby was airy and open, the fragrant scent of exotic flowers and salt water carried on the breeze that never failed to cool Mia off no matter how warm and humid the air.

She and Lindsey were headed to the Plantation Bar—by way of the sundry store to pick up a pair of sunglasses Lindsey had forgotten to pack—when they spotted Shelby walking through the lobby, alongside a bellman who carried her two designer bags.

"Look at her. She's already tanned," Lindsey said, shaking her head. The short pink sundress bared her shoulders and most of her legs, and a few more highlights had been added to her tawny-colored hair. She looked relaxed and happy, as if she'd already been here a week. So Shelby.

"Tanning salon," Mia murmured and lifted a hand to get their friend's attention. Mia had planned on using a tanning bed, too, but there had been no time. Up until her final day at Pearson and Stern she'd worked feverishly to make sure all loose ends were tied up and her one open case had been seamlessly turned over to one of the other junior associates. Then there had been some advance orders to place for the new business. Life had been hectic.

"Shoot, I worked up until the last minute," Lindsey said. "I didn't even have time to pick up some bronzing lotion."

"I'm just glad we got some sleep on the plane." They'd met up in Chicago and flown together directly to Honolulu. Since Shelby left from Houston, she'd come on her own. Having company, though, hadn't mattered much to Mia or Lindsey. After chatting for half an hour, they'd both crashed for most of the flight.

"Aloha." Shelby greeted them with a grin, her teeth particularly white against her tan face.

Mia noticed that she'd gotten a manicure, pedicure— the works—while Mia had been lucky to squeeze in a hair trim. "I hate you," she said, eying Shelby's strappy gold sandals and pretty pink toenails. "I really do."

"Thank you." Shelby glanced down at her tanned legs and feet. "I found the sandals yesterday. On sale, too."

"We've already checked in," Lindsey said, exchanging a glance with Mia. They both still wore their travel clothes, jeans and light sweaters, because Chicago had been nippy when they'd left that morning. "We scored adjoining rooms but they won't be ready for another hour or two."

"A whole hour? Bummer." Shelby made a face, and then smiled prettily at the bellman. "Kimo, do you think we'll really have to wait that long?"

His brown face split into a grin, and then he winked. "The assistant manager is my cousin. Let me see what

I can do." He put down the bags and set off on his mission.

His uniform included white shorts, and the three of them ogled his fine ass and muscled calves as he walked unhurriedly toward the front desk.

"I forgot how disgustingly healthy everyone looks around here, even in winter," Mia idly observed.

"And how everyone seems to be related," Lindsey said, and then turned to Shelby. "What a shameless flirt you are. Not that I'm not totally jealous."

A smug smile curved Shelby's lips. "Do you know if any of the guys showed up yet?"

Mia shrugged. "We were headed to the bar. If they're here, they might be hanging out there or at the pool."

"Oh, God." Alarm widened Shelby's hazel eyes. "You can't go on the prowl dressed like that."

"The prowl?" Mia laughed.

Lindsey rolled her eyes.

"Too bad we don't know their last names," Shelby said, "so we could see if they checked in." Her gaze drifted past her friends. "Although if they don't show, I see a couple of damn fine consolation prizes coming this way. No, don't turn—"

Lindsey whipped her head around, and then abruptly turned back to Mia, her cheeks red when the two buff dudes wearing only swim trunks smiled at them.

"Subtle, sweetie. Real subtle," Shelby whispered, her gaze averted, her lips barely moving.

"I'm going to get sunglasses," Lindsey muttered.

Mia elbowed her. "Wait, here comes Kimo."

The bellman approached, holding up three key cards.

"You're a doll, baby," Shelby told him, taking the

cards from him and flashing one of her trademark
smiles, before passing two cards to Mia and Lindsey.
"Um, Linds?" Shelby whispered, leaning close to her
friend, "you might want to get some bronzing lotion
along with those sunglasses."

FRESHLY SHOWERED and feeling rested from her nap
on the plane, Mia left the other two to unpack and
stake their territories while she went in search of an
umbrella drink. The pool bar was packed with half-
dressed people, lots of couples, but the Plantation Bar,
which featured a view of the ocean, was shady, breezy
and perfect. She slid onto a stool and studied the tented
menu of exotic drinks.

The three of them sharing two adjoining rooms with
a small parlor had sounded great in theory. It meant they
had only two bathrooms, and while that setup had been
fine in college, she was so not used to sharing anymore.
But it was only for a week, and she wasn't planning on
spending much time in the room. Especially if spring-
break Jeff showed up.

And if he didn't…oh, well. She'd promised herself
she wouldn't be bummed if their Facebook shout-out
went unanswered. Even if Jeff did show up, he might
not be as tall as she remembered, or broad and hunky
with thick sun-kissed hair. She couldn't recall if he'd
told her what his major had been, or if he'd shared his
interests or much of anything else. They'd both been
tipsy that night they met at the pool party—him more
than her—and there had been a lot more kissing than
conversation.

The swarthy, smiling bartender approached to take
her order, and she settled on a blue fruity concoction,

based solely on the pretty picture, and then swiveled around to gaze toward the beach. Aside from more couples stretched out on beach towels, there were a few groups of guys, but they looked young. One dude wearing a pair of red floral swim trunks and no shirt caught her attention. He was standing at an outside table where the bar met the sand. He had the same build as Jeff, except this guy's hair was a bit darker and shorter.

"Here you go," the bartender said, and she twisted around to find the tall, frothy drink garnished with a cherry, pineapple wedge and yellow paper umbrella. "Do you want to sign this to your room or keep a tab open?"

"I'll sign for it now." She grinned at the fancy cocktail. She wouldn't be caught dead ordering something this froufrou in Manhattan.

She plucked the cherry first and popped it into her mouth before using both hands to pick up the odd-shaped glass. The only other people sitting at the bar was a couple huddled at the far end who'd been talking to the bartender. As she struggled with her first sip, determined to leave the pineapple wedge undisturbed, she noticed a man pulling out a stool at the other end of the bar close to the wall. Tall, short dark hair, cream-colored shirt.

Frowning, she set the glass back down. Even though she hadn't actually gotten a good look at him, there was something oddly familiar about the way he moved, the way he...

Her heart somersaulted.

David.

Ridiculous, of course. It wasn't him. Couldn't possibly be. Not in this universe. Damn it. She had promised herself she wouldn't think of him once on this vacation, and she'd blown it in the first two hours.

For peace of mind she had to take another look. Trying to be inconspicuous, she used her cocktail napkin to wipe up an imaginary spill and slid a sidelong look at him.

It couldn't be. Except…it was.

Holy crap.

David smiled, and lifted his hand in a wave.

She blinked. Hard. He was still there. She'd never seen him in anything but a suit before. Certainly never seen him smile like that. David Pearson actually looked a little nervous. But that was impossible. In fact, this was nuts. What could he possibly be doing here?

"Mia?"

She blinked again, felt the heat of someone close behind her. A hand touched her shoulder, and she slowly turned.

"Mia, right?" It was red-swim-trunks guy.

She stared blankly at him, her mind still on David. "It's Jeff."

"Jeff. Right. Of course." She looked into his familiar blue eyes and forced a smile.

He gave her a lopsided grin, ducked and zeroed in for a kiss on the mouth.

She turned her head just in time. The wet sloppy smooch landed on her cheek. His beer-saturated breath nearly knocked her over.

"Sorry," he mumbled, taking a second to right himself. "I wasn't sure you'd show up. I couldn't believe it when I read your post on Facebook. That was wild."

Mortified that David had seen what had happened, she leaned back, trying to put some distance between her and Jeff, who took the hint and sat on the stool beside her, fortunately not too close and blocking her view of David.

"When did you get here?" she asked, scrambling to concentrate.

"Yesterday morning. Me and two of my buddies. We got too much sun yesterday and spent more time than we should have at the bar today." He smiled sheepishly. "You just get in?"

"A couple of hours ago. My friends are still unpacking."

The bartender came for Jeff's order, and she was relieved when he asked for a soft drink. Though she was disappointed that mentioning her friends hadn't prompted him to volunteer whether his two buddies were the ones Lindsey and Shelby were expecting. She glanced at his friends and pretty much figured it out on her own. They didn't look the least bit familiar, and boy, were they not the right type.

Her gaze went back to Jeff and she found his bloodshot eyes fixed intently on her. "You look the same," he said, sounding relieved. "Your hair is shorter."

"Yours, too."

"Yeah." He self-consciously rubbed the back of his neck. "Good ol' corporate America."

"Jeff."

His friends hollered from across the bar, and when he turned to acknowledge them, she shot a look toward David. His seat was vacant, his glass half-empty. Her gaze shifted in time to catch a glimpse of his back as he left the bar.

"Look, we've rented surfboards," Jeff said, signaling for his check. "You wanna come?"

"Maybe another day."

"How about dinner?" Jeff lightly touched her hand and gave her the boyishly charming smile that had gotten to her six years ago. "You have plans yet?"

Her wistful gaze drifted helplessly toward the stool where David had been sitting only seconds ago. What was he doing here? It made no sense. Whatever the reason, it couldn't have anything to do with her. He probably hadn't given her a moment's thought since she'd left. As soon as it was announced that she'd given her notice, nearly everyone had tried to talk her into staying with the firm. But not David. He hadn't said a single damn word. This was simply a coincidence. A bizarre crazy coincidence. "No," she said finally. "No, I don't have plans."

"I'll make reservations someplace nice, and call your room when I get back. Okay?"

"Sure. I'm looking forward to it." She didn't even mind when he kissed her cheek.

DAVID HOPED HE WASN'T hanging around the lobby like an idiot for nothing. He checked his watch, then for the second time in five minutes, looked at his BlackBerry for messages, while mentally cursing his own stupidity. For God's sake, he knew why she was here. He'd overheard the ladies talking in the break room about Mia and her friends' plan to organize a reunion or some such thing relating to their senior year spring break.

Frankly it had sounded odd to him, not at all like something Mia would be involved in. He thought back to his own spring break, the last one before going to law school, and smiled. He and three friends had gone to Barbados for the week, where there had been a lot of women, too much drinking and not a shred of common sense among them. Twice they'd had to buy their way out of sticky situations with the local authorities.

Though nothing to be proud of, he wouldn't have traded that wonderful, reckless carefree week for anything. Everyone needed that rite of passage. A few months later, he'd been firmly embedded in law school, studying his ass off, and doing the Pearson name proud. He hadn't veered off course since, and he certainly wouldn't pull an adolescent stunt like trying to recreate the week.

Hard to believe Mia was part of this at all. She was a damn fine lawyer, a sensible, focused woman. He admired that about her, and so much more. She was poised and sexy and had the most incredible green eyes that had the damning effect of turning his insides to butter. Which made him twice the fool for having followed her here.

No one at the firm knew he was here, except his father and uncle, and neither had said a word about him taking off in search of Mia. In fact, they had breathed a sigh of relief that he was on the case. Only David had known that he wasn't in Hawaii to gain a client, no matter how desperately the company needed the influx of cash. He had come to see Mia for himself.

In the short time since she'd given her notice, too many of his thoughts had been regrets. He'd hidden his feelings for her for so long, he'd almost convinced himself that she didn't fill him with want. He'd cursed the fact that she worked for his firm, which made her off-limits. Now, when his opportunity was finally here, when there would be no negative repercussions if he asked her out, he couldn't. Not if he wanted to save a lot of jobs.

He didn't even know if it mattered. She might have no interest in him. He was boring, serious, a drill sergeant. He'd heard the nicknames too often when his employees had thought they were alone. David had no reason to think Mia would want to see him now.

But he needed to know. Once and for all. If she laughed in his face, it would be a good thing. He'd be able to stop thinking about her, fantasizing about that beautiful body. That quick wit. What might have been. Sure it would hurt, but not forever.

He needed to know before he asked her to come back to the firm. Before it became a moot point. Again.

He checked his watch. If she didn't show up within the next three minutes, it meant she was still hanging out at the bar with her new friend, and David would be wise to think about taking the next flight back to New York.

As soon as Jeff left, Mia drained her drink, and headed through the lobby toward the elevators. The first thing she was going to do was find out if David was registered at the hotel. If not, she'd call Suzie, an admin assistant who'd started with Pearson and Stern about the same time as Mia, and find out what the woman knew about why David was here. She was older and married with two children, and unlike most of the associates and admin staff at the firm, she had a life. Mia could trust Suzie to be discreet.

She didn't make it to the elevators.

"Mia." Suddenly David was right in front of her, a couple of feet away. If she'd turned left instead of right...

"David." Her breath caught at the wedge of exposed chest hair where his tennis shirt came to a *V*. She'd never seen him without a tie. Not once. He was always impeccably dressed in his tailored suits, with his black hair perfect, his eyes so serious. "What are you doing here?"

"Vacation."

"You never take vacations."

"Not true."

"Four-day weekends occasionally."

He shrugged. "I needed some time off."

"You're right. This is good." She cleared her throat as she looked away. Of course she *felt* discombobulated. That didn't mean she had to show it. "Are you here with someone?"

"No, alone." He smiled, faint lines fanning out at the corners of his brown eyes. "Not counting you."

She tried to hide her unsteady hands in her pockets, fumbling with the folds of material until she remembered she had no pockets, not in the short halter dress she wore. So instead of disguising her nervousness, she'd drawn his attention to her legs. Her very pale legs.

"How about you?" he asked, lifting his gaze to hers. "Are you here with that guy in the bar?"

"Him? No." She laughed dismissively. "With Lindsey and Shelby. I don't think you know them."

His mouth curved into another smile, and it stunned her how much it changed his face. The man had incredible dimples. His eyebrows lifted along with his grin, and he looked ten years younger.

"No, I don't think you ever mentioned them," he said.

She didn't roll her eyes, although she wanted to. Of

course he didn't know them. Had they ever once discussed anything personal? Not for one hot second.

"Have you ever been here before?" he asked.

"A long time ago. For spring break."

"Ah." His slight frown confused her. "So you'd know some of the good restaurants? Hot spots?"

Mia pressed her lips together, wondering what straitlaced David Pearson considered a hot spot.

He was still smiling, and she was still trying to get used to it. "Assuming you were in any condition to remember."

At that, she laughed. "Me?"

"Come on. Anyone who took off on spring break wasn't there to crack the books."

"Not even you?"

"Let's say I have a few stories I won't be telling my grandchildren."

"Well, well, Mr. Pearson, I see you in a whole new light."

He paused. "Good." The slow sensual curve of his lips made her heart trip. And his eyes, good God, the way he looked at her, as if she were the only person in the lobby. She couldn't speak. Could barely think. He was here alone…could that mean…this wasn't real… she was making stuff up…

"Hey! I thought I'd find you in the bar."

Coming from behind, Mia barely registered Shelby's voice.

"Mia? Oh, I'm interrupting. Sorry."

Mia blinked, glanced blearily at her friend. "Shelby. Hi."

Shelby smiled. "Hi." She swung a look at David, her

eyes full of amused curiosity as she sized him up. "I'm Shelby."

"David." He politely offered his hand as if he were meeting a new client for the first time.

The moment was gone. What was left was the same David she had known for three years.

"You're not interrupting. I was on my way up to the room," Mia said with a small shrug.

"Yeah, um…" Her gaze skittered briefly toward David then back to Mia. "Someone left you a message."

"Who?"

"It's about dinner."

"Already?" The word slipped out as she was unable to contain her surprise. Refusing to look at David, Mia's eyes met Shelby's. "This couldn't have waited?"

"Lindsey's out shopping and just texted." Shelby's mouth lifted in a sly smile. "She may be having company."

"Oh." Mia frowned, paused. "Oh," she repeated with enthusiasm. Lindsey had been certain her guy wouldn't show up. "Good." She sent an apologetic glance at David, and then a more probing one at Shelby, who gave a small sad shake of her head.

"Look, I'm the one who's interrupting," David said, taking a step back. "Maybe I'll see you around."

"No, wait." Great. Now what? They both faced Mia, waiting expectantly. "Let's all have dinner," she said, shocked at what had just come out of her mouth. Yet she'd feel awful deserting Shelby on their first night here. "David, Shelby, join Jeff and me. I'm sure he won't mind."

3

"ARE YOU SURE ABOUT THIS?" Shelby asked when she and Mia approached the designated restaurant two minutes early and saw that David was waiting outside. "He's absolutely gorgeous."

"If you ask me one more time, I swear I'll…" Mia finished with an exasperated grunt. The closer they got, the yummier he looked in crisp khakis and a white button-down shirt open at the neck. She hoped tonight wasn't a mistake, but she couldn't stand to think of Shelby being left alone, especially knowing that her guy wasn't coming, and that he was married with his first child on the way.

Shelby hadn't seemed particularly disappointed; of course, the girl always landed on her feet. She'd undoubtedly have men lining up in no time. Besides, David wasn't her type. But Mia had opened her big mouth, so too late. End of story.

"Still, I know you used to have a thing for him."

"Used to. Now shut up," Mia murmured as they got within hearing distance.

They both pasted on smiles, and the moment he

spotted them his smile came so easily that Mia had trouble believing this was the same guy she'd worked with for three years.

She'd always considered him attractive, with his dark hair and intense brown eyes. The first day they'd met he'd sent her pulse skittering, but his rare smiles and overall serious nature had bothered her. She'd understood to some degree why he'd kept up the barrier. He was a supersmart guy and one hell of a lawyer, but his high-ranking position with the firm at only thirty could have easily been interpreted as nepotism. He was thirty-three now. Time to relax. He'd proven himself many times over.

"You ladies look lovely," he said, giving them equal attention as he took in their new sundresses. "Would you like to be seated at our table, or wait out here for Jeff?"

"Let's sit down," Mia said, never having had trouble being decisive. "We should be able to see him when he gets here."

"Good." David gave the host a slight nod, and the man gathered menus and indicated they should follow him.

Shelby went first, and then David lightly touched the small of Mia's back for her to proceed. A triangular cutout at her waist exposed bare skin, allowing his fingertips to graze the sensitive area. Her entire body reacted. The tingling started at her nape and slithered down her spine. Goose bumps surfaced on her arms and back.

She picked up the pace so that contact was quickly broken, but he'd have to be blind not to see what his touch had done. The restaurant was outdoors, and even though it was twilight, strings of white lights were woven through the surrounding palm trees to illuminate the walkway—and reactions Mia preferred weren't so obvious.

They arrived at the table, an excellent one, private yet affording a breathtaking view of the water. She'd bet an expensive bottle of wine that David had greased the host's palm to get this baby.

The host pulled out a chair, and so did David. Shelby and Mia exchanged secret smiles as they settled in. David's manners didn't surprise Mia. Not once had she seen him sit or enter an elevator before a woman. He probably opened car doors, too, but she'd never had the opportunity to see him in action.

"Your server will be Cole. He'll be here shortly to offer you cocktails." The host passed out the menus, leaving the wine list with David. "In the meantime, is there anything else I can do for you?" he asked as he shook out Shelby's white linen napkin and draped it across her lap.

Shelby smiled and shook her head. Mia didn't bother. She knew the question was mainly addressed to David, who said, "I think we're fine for now. Thank you, Ryan."

"Oh." Mia stopped the man. "If you could be on the lookout for the fourth person who's joining us—"

"Of course." The glance at David told her he'd already taken care of that, too.

The situation was kind of weird for her. When she and her friends were out, she was usually the one in charge, or at least they automatically deferred to her.

"I could get used to this," Shelby said, surveying the other diners, mostly dressed in subdued aloha shirts and lightweight floral dresses. "Houston can be casual, especially in the summer when it's so hot, but this rocks."

David followed her gaze. "I'm practically overdressed."

Shelby grinned. "Feel free to take your shirt off."

Mia chuckled when David blinked, his normally expressionless face slightly startled. Nothing that came out of Shelby's mouth surprised her, but she doubted David was used to being teased. That's why she didn't feel threatened by Shelby, who looked too damn cute in her strapless yellow dress. She simply wasn't his type.

There. She'd acknowledged the evil little thought that had consoled her after she'd foolishly suggested David and Shelby come to dinner.

"Think I could get away with it?" David asked, his eyes filling with warm amusement.

Shelby laughed. "What's the worst that can happen?" She shrugged her bare bronzed shoulders. "They'll ask you to put it back on."

"I think I'll let a braver soul than me test the boundaries of their dress code." His gaze met Mia's.

She forced a smile. How could she have underestimated Shelby? It wasn't that she blamed her for being so charming and irresistible.

"So, Shelby—" David set the wine list aside "—I understand you went to school with Mia. Are you also an attorney?"

"No," she said with a startled laugh, as if that was a joke. "No offense. Nothing wrong with being a lawyer. I'm in PR. As soon as we get the business off the ground I'll be handling the publicity, advertising, networking, that sort of thing."

His brows went up, and Mia cringed inside. She

hadn't told him about Anything Goes. It wasn't as if it were a big secret. But David would never understand how she could walk away from the law to start a business like that.

He didn't ask the expected question, but rather stared past Mia. "I believe your date is here."

She swung a gaze toward the entrance, and there was Jeff headed toward them. He'd cleaned up nicely, having changed into white jeans and a blue Hawaiian shirt. He waved, acknowledging them, and then stopped to talk to a waitress carrying a full tray of food. With her chin, she gestured to a passing waiter, and after Jeff had a word with the guy, he finally joined them at the table.

"I'm not late, am I?" he asked, kissing Mia on the cheek before taking his seat beside her.

She immediately smelled the booze on his breath. Great. "We've only been here a few minutes."

Frowning and totally ignoring David, who'd gotten to his feet, Jeff's gaze skimmed the table. "They haven't served drinks yet."

"Our server is coming," Mia said tightly. "I don't know if you remember Shelby, and this is David."

"Jeff." David extended his hand. "Thanks for allowing us to join you."

Jeff half rose and accepted the handshake. "No problem. I should've brought my friends, too."

Mia tried not to shudder. She tried even harder not to look at David, who'd reclaimed his seat. Though maybe she was the only one who knew Jeff was slightly off.

"How did the surfing go?" she asked.

"Shit. I nearly broke my neck. Check this out." He yanked up the hem of his shirt to show where the skin across his ribs was beginning to bruise. "I banged up my back, too."

Oh, God. They didn't need to see that. "Bummer," Mia said, and picked up the leather-bound menu. "We should look at the menus."

Jeff dropped his shirt in place and craned his neck. "Where's our waiter? I gave him my drink order."

Mia glanced at Shelby and David. They both had taken her suggestion and were studying their menus. Neither of them seemed put off by Jeff, but they were probably just being polite.

The waiter arrived with Jeff's Scotch and an apologetic look for the rest of them, then he took everyone else's drink order. While they waited, Mia quickly decided on an entrée and urged Shelby with a pointed look to do the same. David diplomatically handled the selection of the wine, something Mia gladly would have skipped altogether.

Other than Jeff reaching under the table to squeeze her thigh, an attempt that was immediately rejected, the rest of the meal went smoothly enough. David and Shelby got along fabulously, chatting away as if they'd known each other for ages. Mia should've been grateful they were distracted, but their rapport only helped to darken her mood. She was jealous, and she had no one to blame but herself. And Jeff. Rational or not, she totally blamed him. Why did he have to turn out to be such an ass?

When the bill came, there was a brief struggle between David and Jeff. No surprise to her, David won. Any other time, Mia might have offered to pick it up herself since she'd invited Shelby and David, but all she wanted was to get back to her room. No way was she spending another minute with Jeff, who'd had a glass in his hand throughout dinner. Only one thing could make the night worse—if Shelby stayed out with David.

"Well," Mia said, after giving Jeff a firm send-off, and he'd started weaving his way toward the lobby. Or more likely, the next bar. "I'm beat."

Neither Shelby or David responded, and a lump swelled in Mia's throat. They'd gotten along much better than she'd anticipated. Who knew David could be that social and charming, damn him. She wouldn't be surprised if they wanted to spend more time together.

She swallowed hard. "Guess I'll catch up with you two tomorrow." Mia's gaze involuntarily flicked to David. He'd been watching her intently. She blinked at the sudden awkwardness. "Thanks for dinner. I should've foot the bill. I owe you one."

His warm chocolate-brown eyes stayed level with hers. "I'll remind you," he said, his voice a seductive murmur in the semidarkness.

Shivering with awareness, she rubbed her bare arm. She couldn't seem to look away. With a jolt of regret, she remembered Shelby was standing there watching.

Mia stepped back, avoiding a glance at her friend. And David. "Okay. I'm off to bed. See ya," she said breezily, knowing she wasn't going to sleep one lousy wink.

"Wait for me," Shelby said, and Mia stopped and cautiously turned. "I'm pretty jet-lagged myself. David, it was so nice meeting you. You're staying here, too, yes?" He nodded, and she added, "Then we'll see you around."

David's gaze briefly shifted in the direction that Jeff

had disappeared. "I wouldn't mind walking you to your rooms."

"We're fine, really." Shelby looped an arm through Mia's. Not a Shelby-like thing to do. "We're staying in rooms seven-twenty and seven-twenty-two. Give us a call tomorrow."

He nodded. "I just might do that. Good night, ladies."

Shelby gave Mia's arm a small tug, and they headed toward the elevators. "Do not turn around," Shelby whispered sternly. "I promise you he's watching."

"What?" Mia jerked her arm away. "Why would I turn around?" Any remorse she'd felt for stepping on her friend's toes disappeared in a flash. "You could've stayed out with him. I don't need an escort to my room, for God's sake."

Shelby only grinned.

"I should warn you. He's not always that charming. Frankly, I didn't know he had any personality. He's usually stuck in Neutral."

"Uh-huh." They'd arrived at the elevators and, still smiling, Shelby pressed the Up button.

"I'm not trying to discourage you. I'm not," Mia muttered. "I say go for it. I can see why you might be attracted. I was once."

Shelby laughed. "For being a brainy chick, you're such a dope."

Mia scowled at her, but kept her mouth shut when the elevator doors opened, and two couples exited.

"Get in there." Shelby pulled her into the car, and then waited for the doors to close. "Sweetie, he is so into you, it's pathetic."

"You're crazy. He was all Mr. Charming with you."

"He is charming. But you didn't see the way he was looking at you."

"No, he wasn't."

Shelby rolled her eyes. "You were too busy being embarrassed by Jeff. David wasn't obvious, he's too gentlemanly. But he didn't miss a single eyelash flutter. Trust me." She sighed. "Seriously, if he'd been eyeing me like I was a juicy steak, I'd be all over him."

Mia thought about it for a minute. "Then why wait and come all the way to Hawaii?"

"Yeah, Mia," Shelby said with a hand on her hip. "Why would someone, who never takes vacations, suddenly come all the way to Hawaii for a week? Tell me."

Excitement fluttered in her chest. "It is odd," she admitted. "All he had to do was pick up the phone while I was still in New York."

"Hey, hopping a plane at the last minute is a pretty grand gesture, don't knock it." The doors opened, and Shelby walked out first, her key already in hand. "And for God's sake, don't blow it."

DAVID PACED THE PARLOR of his suite. His body recognized East Coast time, where it was three in the morning and not 10:00 p.m. Hawaiian time. Add to that the twelve hours he'd spent in the air, he should've been exhausted. But he was too keyed up to sleep.

Even dinner had been draining. Shelby had been great company—witty, refreshingly open and quite beautiful. But it was Mia's attention he'd wanted, when her green eyes had locked with his. Instead he'd watched her helplessly act as buffer for that idiot Jeff. He'd pitied them both. Jeff, because he was too drunk to realize what he'd screwed up, and Mia, well, her evening had virtually been ruined.

David smiled ruefully. The upside for him was that he'd come out the victor. Or so he hoped. He still didn't know where he stood, whether he was a fool for showing up. Damn it, he should've stopped her from going to her room, asked her to have a drink alone with him.

He wasn't worried about hurting Shelby's feelings—it wasn't as if they'd been on a date. She was clearly a bright woman and knew what was what.

He slid open the glass door, walked to the balcony railing and stared at the city lights. Getting this last minute suite had been lucky. The corner unit provided both a view of the ocean and the Waikiki skyline. It also came with a well-stocked bar, or he could've ordered drinks from room service. Either way, Mia should've been enjoying this view with him right now.

Rooms 720 and 722. Weren't there three of them? Which room was Mia's? He could call the front desk, but they wouldn't give him her room number, only connect him. He had no desire to talk to her on the phone, he decided as he closed the balcony door behind him. He'd done enough talking. Enough dodging and evading for the past three years. Enough denying himself.

He grabbed his key card off the bamboo console table, and let himself out.

Enough was damn well enough.

TIRED OF PACING, Mia lay back on the queen-size bed closest to the bathroom, locked her hands behind her head and stared up at the ceiling. Occasionally she could hear Shelby rattling around in the next room. Mia knew she wanted to stay up chatting, and Mia felt only slightly guilty for not indulging her. The need for privacy won out.

Lindsey hadn't been in the room when they'd returned, and they suspected she might not show up again until morning. Good for her. Mia was dying to meet the guy Lindsey had been so tight-lipped about, but this was the first moment's peace she'd gotten since arriving, and she had a lot to think about.

David.

Good Lord, it still didn't seem real. Him. Here. Thousands of miles away from New York. To some degree it pissed her off that for three years he'd given her not one itty-bitty hint that he was attracted to her. Talk about cool, dispassionate, stoic. Great qualities if you're in the courtroom, but damn it, they'd spent far too many nights working late for him not to have cracked just a little.

So there was a "no fraternization" policy at the firm? So what that he was the heir apparent? He could've been human, showed a trace of emotion toward her. Then she could have decided what was more important, staying with the firm or seeing him. Who knew what could have developed by now?

What a coward. She had a good mind to go knock on his door and make him spell out why he'd come to Hawaii. Had he come for her or not? If not, fine. There was plenty of trouble she could get into all by herself. But if he had come for her...

She had to know, she decided, swinging her feet to the floor, even if it meant they had only this one week. In fact, if they reverted to their former relationship once they returned to New York, that would be perfect. All her focus and energy would be invested in the new company. She'd have no time for a relationship. All the more reason not to waste a minute now.

Her key wasn't where she'd thought she left it. Impatient, she dumped the contents of her purse onto the bed, then found the key card tucked safely in the side pocket, where she now recalled putting it. She checked her reflection in the mirror, applied some lip gloss, drew a brush through her hair and adjusted the bodice of her coral-colored dress. When she twisted around to inspect the back, her gaze snagged on the skin exposed by the triangular cutout. Where David's warm palm had been, had lingered until she'd pulled away.

Reliving the few seconds in her mind, she shivered. His hand hadn't been as soft as she expected. She knew he was an avid tennis player in his spare time, and that his mother was fond of arranging dates to accompany him to company dinners. Mia knew nothing more about his personal life. Among the paralegals and clerical help, there was some gossip and the occasional rumor, but she made a point to stay clear of the whispers.

Smoothing down her dress, satisfied that it wasn't too wrinkled, she palmed the key card and opened the door. And stopped cold.

David stood in the hall, staring at her. He seemed as surprised to see her as she was to see him. He wore the same clothes he'd worn at dinner, only his sleeves were rolled back, exposing his muscled forearms. Definitely a tennis player.

"I was about to knock," he said. "If you're on your way out—"

No way she'd let him weasel out of this. She opened her mouth to tell him just that, but he hadn't finished.

"I'll keep it brief." Without hesitation, he took a step

toward her, his lips twitching into what could only be described as a predatory smile.

"Okay," she said, trying to keep her voice from shaking.

Then he crossed the threshold and closed the door behind him, sending her scurrying backward with the inelegant grace of a beached whale.

4

"I HOPE YOU WEREN'T on your way to meet Jeff," David said. "If you are, it's a complete mistake."

Mia backed up another step, stopped, gave him a good long look, then laughed. "You came here to tell me that?"

"I did."

"For an overpaid attorney, you're not every observant."

He lifted his brows.

She hid a smile. "I meant high-priced."

"I know you were embarrassed at dinner, but that doesn't mean you wouldn't give him another chance." Again he advanced on her, and her pulse skittered. "The guy's a drunken lout. He's not good enough for you. Even if only for a week."

Heat crawled up her neck. He was right, of course, and she had no intention of doing more than exchanging a greeting with Jeff should she see him in the lobby. But David had no business butting in. "Since when are you an expert on my personal life?"

"Touché." He took her hand, slowly rubbed her palm with his thumb.

She tensed, but in a good way. Jesus, this was David touching her, his face so close that she could see the light flecks of amber in his brown eyes. Funny, she'd always thought they were much darker, more serious.

She straightened, tried to ignore the disturbing sensations his thumb caused. "In fact, Mr. Pearson, you really don't know anything about me, do you?"

His gaze touched her mouth, lingered and then leisurely moved up. "Don't I?"

"In the three years since we met, you haven't said anything more personal than 'Have a nice weekend.' And that was on a Saturday afternoon, after we'd worked most of the day together."

"You exaggerate."

"Not by much."

"You think it was easy, keeping my distance?"

"I honestly have no idea." Her breath caught at the flicker of amusement in his eyes. "You should've been a poker player, instead of a lawyer. You could've made a killing."

He wrapped his fingers around her hand and tugged her closer. "My intentions must be fairly obvious now," he said in a low, gravelly voice.

She tilted her head back, refusing to be the first to break eye contact as he slid an arm around her waist and pulled her against him. He was hard behind the fly of his khakis, the knowledge shattering a bit of her control. His hand splayed across the exposed skin of her lower back, and his palm felt hotter than it had before.

The tingling began there, traveled all the way up her spine and settled in her braless breasts, tightening her nipples, making them so sensitive that she could hardly stand to have them touch the light sateen material of her dress. Only a knot of fabric at her nape kept the halter in place. The gentlest pressure, the smallest tug...

He put his mouth on hers, his lips soft and supple, his breath minty. She moved against him, laid a hand on his chest, finding a surprising wall of muscle beneath the cotton fabric. When he drew his tongue across the seam of her lips, she parted them, inviting him inside.

David knew how to kiss—he was even better than she'd imagined. He smoothly dove in, but took his time, tasting, nibbling, touching his tongue to hers, giving her just so much, and then holding back until she trembled from wanting more. She pressed herself against him, pushed up to increase the pressure of his mouth. Her aroused nipples rubbed against his chest, and she thought for one dazed, hopeful second that he was about to untie her top.

But he only stroked her back, made a final sweep of the inside of her cheek. When he retreated, lingering long enough to touch his lips to hers one last time, she nearly whimpered in protest.

"I've wanted to do that for three years," he said, his voice husky, his eyes smoldering with a hunger that stole her breath.

"I didn't know," she whispered, her whole body weak. "You never showed it."

"No." With his thumb, he stroked her cheek. "I couldn't."

A part of her resented his ability to exercise that much control. She herself had struggled to keep her feelings in check, and too often she'd failed. How many times had she worried that other people in the office had noticed the lingering looks, the longing in her face? Especially that first year when she'd been too naive to understand that David would never breach company policy. Or finally to accept that he simply wasn't interested in her.

He lowered his head again, and brushed his lips across hers. Gently, almost too gently. Surely he didn't need a push. She was about to make it clear they wanted the same thing, even if she had to strip off his clothes, when he broke contact, moved back, out of reach.

"I've rented a car," he said, "and I plan on driving around the island tomorrow. I'd like for you to join me."

Her arms hanging loosely at her sides, her chest still heaving, she could only stare mutely at him. He'd reverted to the old David. Just like that. His face was unreadable, his eyes filled with that dark intensity that both excited and frustrated her. But the thing he couldn't hide was the bulge behind his fly.

"Naturally I understand if you already have plans." He stuffed his hands into his pockets and backed toward the door.

"No, um, not yet." She really hadn't had much to drink, maybe it was jet lag, but her head was fuzzy. She didn't get what was happening. "I'd love to go."

"Would nine-thirty be all right?"

"Nine-thirty. Sure."

"Let's meet in the lobby."

"Okay."

"I'm looking forward to spending time with you, Mia," he said. "Tomorrow, then."

"David—"

"Good night." He barely smiled, then left the room.

Mia stared at the closed door, wondering what the hell had just happened. Her lips weren't the only place still damp from his kiss. And he'd been as aroused as she. Ten more minutes and they would've been locking the adjoining door and diving between the sheets. She wanted it, and she knew he did, too.

Was he giving her time and space to consider what she was getting into? That would be totally like him. Sighing, she kicked off her sandals, and glanced at the digital bedside clock. Damn, she hoped she could get to sleep and not spend two hours replaying the last ten minutes.

She undid the bow at her nape, pausing to massage the tense muscles underneath when she heard her Black-Berry signal that she'd received a text. In her haste to grab the phone, she jammed her bare foot into the corner of the dresser and nearly broke her little toe. All for nothing. Disappointed, she read the text. It was from Lindsey—she didn't know if she'd be coming back to the room tonight. Good for her.

Mia muttered a mild oath and limped to the bed. What a waste. She had the room to herself, and David, the coward, had slunk away. That was the last time she'd let him off the hook. He'd already shown his hand by flying all the way to Hawaii. Tomorrow he'd better plan on doing more than sightsee.

DAVID ARRIVED IN the lobby fifteen minutes early and made arrangements for the car to be brought around before Mia showed up. He'd blown it last night, and didn't want to waste another minute of the six days he had left here.

No, he hadn't really squandered last night. He could easily have gotten her into bed. They both wanted it. They both knew it. Especially after that kiss. Which he also didn't regret, but couldn't think about now or risk embarrassing himself in front of a lobby full of Japanese tourists. He watched them, dressed in their aloha shirts and muumuus, cameras hanging from around their necks, chatting with their guide near the koi pond filled with orange and gold carp.

He envied their carefree excitement, their sole purpose as vacationers to enjoy the sparkling blue ocean, the balmy March air that came off the water. Ordinarily he never would have considered traveling this far for a vacation, or for that matter, staying away from the office for longer than three or four days unless it was work-related. But then, this wasn't actually a vacation.

It could have been, and God knew he wanted this time alone with Mia where they could forget about work and family obligations and get to know each other on a personal level. But hooking up with her wasn't that simple. Not now, not since his father had asked him to convince her to return to the firm.

He had to make her understand that he wanted to be with her, that he wasn't here just to lure her back. He could have talked to her in New York, offered her a nice bonus and promotion that she would've had to think twice about turning down. But he needed this break because by the time they returned, he wanted her to be clear on what she wanted, him or the firm.

Only problem was, it was a fine line. Once he extended the firm's offer, she'd have to trust that his motives were pure.

"David?"

He snapped out of his preoccupation. She stood right in front of him, and he hadn't even seen her walk up. "Mia."

"Bet you were thinking about work."

"Oddly, no."

She grinned. "Right."

He frowned at his watch. "I haven't even called the office, and it's what, one-thirty there."

"Go ahead. I'll wait."

"Nope. If they have a problem they can call me," he said, ignoring her skeptical expression and appreciating her brief white shorts and the long expanse of legs even more. "The car is parked right over here." He gestured at the red convertible, uncomfortably aware of how much he wanted to kiss her.

"Sweet." She took her sunglasses out of her bag and slipped them on as they walked toward the BMW. "Do you know where we're going?"

"I have a list of places."

"That's not an answer."

Unable to help himself, he touched the small of her back with a guiding hand, even though it was completely unnecessary. "I'll let you know when we get there."

She flashed him a smile, her teeth white, her lips a pale glossy pink. "I don't know how to navigate, so if you're counting on me…"

"The car has a GPS system."

"Ah." She lifted the hair off the back of her neck. "It's warmer than I thought."

Tempted to plant a kiss at her nape, he had to look away. "Only in the direct sun. We can put the top up if you want."

"No, I want to feel the wind in my face and in my

hair. It's Hawaii. I'm on vacation. I want it all," she said, giving him a look that made his cock twitch. "It might be a rumor, but I heard that what happens in Waikiki, stays in Waikiki."

"Right," he muttered, uncomfortably aware that he suddenly felt awkward. He never had trouble with women. No, it wasn't even that. He had a plan. Sex wasn't supposed to come first, but if she kept up the sly smiles and sultry looks, it was going to be murder keeping his head.

The valet who'd brought the car around trotted up and opened Mia's door before David could. "Need directions, sir?"

David shouldn't have been annoyed. The man was only doing his job, but David had missed out on watching her swing her long bare legs into the car. "No thanks," he said, slipping the man a ten before climbing in behind the wheel.

"I could get used to this." Mia adjusted her leather seat so that she partially reclined, and then tugged at the hem of her shorts.

He turned away and fiddled with the navigation system. "It drives well. I picked it up at the airport instead of taking a cab."

"I'll take your word for it. I have my license, but I've only driven twice since college."

He wasn't completely surprised. In Manhattan, he mostly took cabs himself. "What about weekends? Don't you like getting out of the city?"

Her eyebrows arched over her sunglasses, a cynical smile curving her lips. "Weekends? Is there such a thing at Pearson and Stern?"

"Point taken." He took out his sunglasses and slid them on before pulling out of the lot. "Is that why you left?"

"I never minded the work."

He cursed himself for bringing it up. Not so much because she sounded defensive, but the subject only reminded him of his unwanted errand. Luckily traffic was heavy and required all of his attention. So did the GPS. He already knew from studying the map earlier that Hawaiian street names were difficult to differentiate. Too many vowels.

She apparently got the message that he was focusing on driving, but as soon as they stopped at a red light, she asked, "The day I resigned…why didn't you ask why I was leaving?"

"I was too shocked."

"You had two and a half weeks."

David sighed. "I don't know why. Denial, maybe."

She didn't respond, but tied her hair back into a ponytail with something she'd found in her purse. "The light's green."

"Thanks." He started to proceed, but two pedestrians darted into the crosswalk, and he jammed on the brakes.

Mia gasped softly, her hand shooting out to brace herself. "And they say New York is bad."

"No kidding." He waited until it was clear, and then accelerated. "I keep forgetting you've been here before. I should've asked if there's someplace in particular you wanted to go."

"Uh, I didn't get too far out of Waikiki. Or off the beach, for that matter. I had the worst sunburn."

"I did the same thing freshman year, and I knew

better. When I was a kid we spent a lot of summers in Aruba and St. Thomas."

"Yeah, I know what you mean. That Caribbean sun is killer."

"Where did you summer?" he asked conversationally, then heard an odd strangling noise coming from her. He glanced away from the road long enough to see her burst out laughing.

"The backyard in a small blue inflatable swimming pool." She patted his arm. "That's where we Butterfields summered. On special occasions we went to our neighbor's backyard."

"All right." He felt like an idiot. "Consider me duly chastised."

"You get a pass, but only because you're not spoiled or a snob." She paused. "Contrary to what I thought when I first started with the firm."

He took his gaze off the road long enough to shoot her a look of disbelief. "Totally unfounded."

"Not from where I sat."

"On what grounds?"

"Oh, my God, you sound like a damn lawyer."

He smiled. "Guilty as charged."

"Okay, no more of that kind of talk."

"Or what? You'll fine me for contempt?"

Mia groaned. "The upside is that you do have a sense of humor, corny as it is. It wouldn't be enough that you're pretty."

He choked out a laugh. "Pretty?"

"Oh, come on." She drew a finger along his jaw. "You know you are."

All he knew is that if she didn't keep her hands to

herself, he'd end up rear-ending the Jeep in front of them. "Where did you grow up?"

She withdrew, though chuckled softly as if she knew he was trying to distract her. "Upstate New York. Ithaca, not too far from Cornell."

"But you didn't go there as I recall."

"Too expensive. I went to NYU." She'd moved her hand, or at least she wasn't touching him. "I'm surprised you know anything about my undergrad studies."

"I read your résumé."

"You weren't there for the interview process."

"I was in Atlanta overseeing a case." Good thing. He clearly remembered meeting her on her first day at the firm. One look into those sexy green eyes and he knew he wouldn't have hired her. "But I was the one who initially flagged you as a candidate."

"Hmm, I didn't know." She shifted, angling her knees toward him. "Why me? You probably had a dozen Harvard and Yale graduates nipping at your heels."

"We did."

"So what was it about my résumé that caught your attention?"

He cocked a brow at her. "You were only second in your class, but the top dog had already hired on with another firm in San Francisco."

"Thanks," she said dryly. "I happen to know you're full of it because Lance Heatherton went to work for his father." She sniffed. "And just so you know, he barely inched past me."

David smiled at her competitive streak. "Frankly, being second in your class obviously got our attention, but what impressed me more was that you were there on a scholarship, working a part-time job and volunteering with the ACLU and the Legal Aid Society. To me, that shows a lot of character and ambition."

"Ambition nothing, I was exhausted. But I also learned a lot from volunteering."

He thought for a moment. "I'm going to tell you something that I've never admitted to anyone." He glanced over at her to reassure himself. "The first four years at Harvard, I did the typical spring break things, traveled abroad during the summer, screwed off like the rest of my friends. When I started law school, my father told me I had to start spending break times at the firm, sort of like an intern. I resented it. I figured I'd be working my ass off soon enough. He knew how I felt, but he didn't say anything.

"That first week during Christmas break I showed up like I was supposed to. I was given a small office, and I mean small. In fact, now it's that storage closet the admins use."

Mia issued a short laugh. "Seriously?"

"Oh, yeah. I couldn't believe it, especially since there were a couple of empty offices with windows."

"I can see your dad trying to teach you a lesson."

"He never said a word about it, and I didn't, either. I thought, screw him. I wouldn't give him the satisfaction of complaining. It took me a couple of years, but I figured out that he'd saved me a lot of grief. Ended up, respect was more important to me than being the boss's son. It never would have mattered how good an attorney I was if I hadn't earned my place in the firm."

She stayed quiet for so long that he finally took his gaze off the road to look at her. Had he revealed too much?

Her lips curved in a soft smile. "Thank you for

sharing that with me." She touched his face, innocently enough, but he tensed, because with Mia, there was no innocent touch. It was crazy how easily she got to him. "You missed a spot." She circled the side of his jaw with the tip of her finger and then moved her hand to the tightness at the back of his neck.

"Good thing it's a straight shot to Diamond Head, or we'd be lost already," he murmured.

"Oh, am I distracting you? Sorry," she said, with a sly smile in her voice. "I'll try to keep my hands to myself." She folded them primly in her lap, then slowly, deliberately crossed one shapely leg over the other, effectively snaring his attention.

So that was how it was going to go down. Him trying to put on the brakes, and her doing all she could to make him crack.

5

THEY SKIPPED THE scenic lookout where several groups of people were already stationed, and chose a spot off to the right. Mia inched closer to the edge of the cliff and stared down at the waves slamming the jagged black volcanic rock below. She'd long given up on trying to tame her thick, unruly hair. Between riding with the top down and the stiff breezes that swept off the ocean, the best she could do was keep it secured in a ponytail so that her hair wasn't whipped into her face.

"Look at those two." With her chin, she indicated a couple who'd left the lookout and were picking their way down toward the water.

"Did you want to go down for a closer look?"

The words were no sooner out of David's mouth when water shot out from the blowhole, jetting a good twenty feet into the air. The scene was spectacular, the white spray fanning out in every direction. Though they stood a safe distance away, Mia reflexively leaned back and bumped into David. The adventurous pair below shrieked and scrambled backward, trying to avoid getting wet. Or worse.

Mia shuddered. "The view from here is just fine, thank you."

He casually slipped an arm around her shoulders, and she sighed and relaxed against him. His skin was warm on hers, his scent spicy and all male.

"Yeah, I wouldn't get too close," he said closer to her ear. "Apparently the spray is unpredictable. There's an underground lava tube that extends into the sea and when the waves crash into it, pressure builds inside the tube. The water can shoot up to thirty feet. Certainly enough to knock someone over."

Mia pulled away to look at him, disappointment pricking at the pleasure of being held. She'd had the impression this trip had been a last-minute decision. That he'd pulled it together for her. "How do you know all this stuff?"

"I read a few guidebooks."

"When?"

"Last night."

She frowned. "You were in a rush to leave my room so you could read guidebooks?"

His mouth twisted wryly. "Right."

She was instantly sorry for bringing up last night, especially when he lowered his arm and they were no longer touching. Did he think he was rushing her? "I wouldn't have minded if you stayed," she said finally.

He kept silent for too long as he faced the ocean. That his sunglasses hid his eyes meant nothing—David was an expert at masking his emotions. "I know, and I wanted to stay."

"But?"

Sighing, he rubbed the back of his neck. "I was trying to give you some time."

"You've been doing that for nearly three years."

"This isn't the same."

Mia hated that she couldn't read him. Hated it even more that he had the ability to shut everything out, including her. She stared at his familiar profile, her gaze taking in the proud strong chin, the perfect nose, the sculpted jawline. He was from Pearson stock all right, cultured, reserved, confident.

Maybe what she'd seen at work was all she'd get. Maybe she'd been wrong to think there was another David beneath the layers of breeding that prevented him from being more human.

But then there was last night. That kiss.

No, she wasn't wrong.

At the memory of his hot, wet mouth covering hers, his tongue plunging in and taking no prisoner, her insides fluttered. He hadn't been guarded then or reserved. Definitely confident though. He'd be that way when he made love to her.

Damn him, he made her want more. She wanted him naked and sweaty and vulnerable, all of his defenses gone. She wanted him inside her.

She hesitated, but just for a second. "Remember," she said, "I don't work for you anymore."

He'd straightened, suddenly alert. "Look." He slid his arm around her shoulders again, brought his cheek close to hers and pointed.

Her first reaction was annoyance that he'd ignored her comment, or was trying to distract her. Not that she disapproved of his methods. She snuggled a bit closer and squinted in the direction of his outstretched arm. "What am I looking for? I see some kind of boat—"

"No, to the right. Farther out. Just watch."

She stood still, barely able to think about anything but his slightly beard-roughened cheek pressed against her skin.

"There." He hugged her. "Did you see?"

"Only for a second. What was it?"

"I'm pretty sure it's a whale. Let's keep watching. It might surface again."

Her gaze transfixed on the spot, she waited, thrumming with excitement. Their patience paid off. In a matter of seconds, not one but two animals arched out of the sea, making their mark with a jettison of water that echoed the blowhole.

She gasped. "Wow."

"We're lucky. I read that this was a good spot for whale watching, but only in the winter. This is the tail end of the season for them to be passing through."

The reminder that he'd wasted last night reading nearly threatened her improved mood, but she decided she wouldn't allow it. They *were* going to talk, but perhaps this wasn't the place. For now she planned on enjoying the fact that he still held her and that she could feel the steady beat of his heart against her arm.

"I see something else," she said, keeping her sights on the horizon. "It almost looks like another island. Is that possible?"

"Yep." He didn't move, which suited her fine. "I see it, too. When it's clear enough they say you can see any one of three other islands—the Big Island of Hawaii, Lanai and I can't pronounce the last one. Starts with an *M*."

"I know. These names are crazy. I have no idea how to pronounce the highway we're on."

"You mean Kalanianaole?" he asked smugly.

"Like I would know if that's right or not. That sounded pretty good, though. What's up with that?"

"I cheated. I listened to the vocal part of the GPS directions earlier."

"Sly, Pearson, very sly." She turned enough to rest a palm on his chest, then tilted her head back and gazed up at him, daring him to kiss her.

A tiny twitch at the corner of his mouth was the only reaction she got. But for him, that was something. In his dark glasses, she saw her reflection, saw what a mess her hair was, and sighed.

He nudged her chin up a fraction. "What's the matter?"

"I just caught my reflection in your glasses. My hair. Yikes."

He gave her ponytail a light tug. "I like your hair. Especially when it's down." His warm moist breath bathed her cheeks, made her heart skip a beat. "You used to start out with it down when you came to work in the morning. It would still be damp."

She was blown away that he'd noticed that minor detail. It seemed he'd barely spared her a glance unless they were working together on a case. "Your hair would be slightly damp, too, sometimes."

"Mia, I want—" He closed his mouth, gave his head a small self-deprecating shake. "We'd better get on the road. We have a lot more to see."

She stopped him from drawing away. "David, please."

"Look, you're only here for a week, you've made plans with your friends, and here I am butting in."

"That's not what you were going to say."

"No," he admitted, clearly conflicted about something. "This is more complicated than I anticipated."

"This? You mean, us?"

He nodded.

Mia didn't try hiding her frustration. "We're in Hawaii. I don't work for you anymore. We're obviously attracted to each other. What's complicated about that? It's only one week, David, and then we go back to our respective lives."

He flinched slightly, something she'd never expected. Had she hit a nerve? Was he worried that she'd want more from him than he was willing to give? His life was already full, between work and social obligations that went with being a Pearson. If the rumors were true, his mother not only fixed him up with dinner companions to attend company functions, but family gatherings, as well.

A sudden and truly awful thought struck Mia.

"We both know what I'm going back to," David said, his voice bringing her out of her dark thoughts. "But what about you? What's life going to be like for you now that you've left the firm? Shelby mentioned something about a business?"

This time, she drew back and focused on the waves that had gotten choppy, spewing whitecaps toward the rocky shore. There was one huge reason why he'd be hesitant to engage in no-strings sex.

Without looking at him, she asked, "Are you seeing someone?"

"What? Jesus, no." He made a sound of disgust. "Of course not. Where did that come from?"

"I figured that's why you'd backed off last night. Why you seem kind of skittish."

He snorted. "Skittish?"

"Poor choice of word maybe, but I'm pretty sure you know what I mean."

"Come here."

At the way his voice lowered to that sexy rasp, she sucked in a breath and shot him a sidelong glance. Her heart started to race as she slowly swiveled back toward him. Taking her hand, he drew her close. His arms went around her, and he locked his hands at the small of her back. She was certain he was about to kiss her. Instead, he moved his mouth near her ear.

"If I told you what I want to do to that body of yours," he whispered, his jaw grazing her sensitive skin, "you'd run as far and as fast as those long sexy legs could carry you."

Her brain went numb. She had no clever retort. The rest of her body sprang to life, blazed with excitement. There was no place for her arms except to loop them around his neck. Leaning into him, she felt the beginning of his arousal.

He took her lobe between his teeth, nibbling lightly, and then briefly pressed the flesh between his lips before nuzzling the side of her neck.

A stiff wind whipped off the sea and buffeted them. Already mentally off balance, Mia pressed her entire body against him, trying to steady herself. He was broad and solid, so much more than she would have guessed a week ago. With a deep inward sigh, she relaxed her hand and dragged her palm over the contour of chest muscle beneath the green tennis shirt.

"Ah, Mia," he murmured against her warm skin.

There were still people using the lookout, cars whizzing past them on the highway. Did he even remember where they were? Did she care? How could she? This was David. This was what she wanted.

Her lips parted, and he pushed his tongue inside, kissing her with a sweeping thoroughness that made her forget everything.

They broke apart only when a noisy minivan full of children pulled off the highway and parked not far from their rental. David straightened and finger combed his hair. Feeling like a guilty teenager who'd been caught making out, Mia tugged at the hem of her shorts and adjusted the front of her blue tank top. It didn't seem to matter that she wore a bra. Her nipples were tight and hard and testing the elasticity of the fabric.

"We should go," she said, averting her eyes so that she didn't have to meet with the white-haired van driver's disapproval.

"Just a minute," he said, concentrating on something on the horizon.

She swung her gaze toward the open sea. "Another whale?"

David noisily cleared his throat, sounding as if he were trying not to laugh.

"Oh." She spotted the problem. They really were going to have to do something about that swelling.

They waited until the gang was clear of the van and headed for the lookout before David used the remote to unlock the BMW's doors.

"Where to next?" she asked breathlessly.

He stuck the key into the ignition. "You have a swimsuit under that?"

"I do." She had on bottoms, anyway.

"Good." He exhaled a long breath. "Maybe we can find someplace to cool off."

So MUCH FOR STAYING in public to prevent him from stripping off her clothes and kissing every inch of her. David mentally shook his head as he guided the car onto the highway. He hadn't checked the GPS but he already knew that as long as he stayed on the coastal road they wouldn't get lost.

He was acting like a damn kid, unable to curb his libido. Hell, he had more pride and self-control than to put himself—or Mia—on display. In fact, he took pride in his self-control. How messed up was that? And acting the way he had in front of a carload of children? He wasn't himself. He was never reckless. It didn't matter that no one here knew him. That wasn't the point. He knew. Worse, Mia knew.

"Why are you scowling?"

He tossed her a glance, noticed the gaping neckline of her top, and gripped the steering wheel tighter. "I'm sorry about back there."

"I'm not."

He shook his head. "That was inappropriate."

"Wait," she said. "I want to be clear. Do you feel that way because somebody saw us, or because it's me you were making out with?"

He cringed at the term. "Both."

She made a low growling sound. "You do not get to say that. Not after that kiss last night, or for that matter, after what you whispered to me earlier."

"I know. I know. I'm sorry for all of it."

"First, I'm pretty sure you're speeding," she said, and he checked. She was right.

He eased his foot off the accelerator, even more irritated now. The highway was starting to wind, and he had no business being distracted from his driving. Having Mia sitting beside him was dangerous enough.

"Second, you're here in Hawaii, not at work. You've already shown your hand. You can't run hot and cold on me. It's not fair."

He smirked at that. She was inarguably right. Her impeccable logic was part of what made her a good lawyer. "I didn't think I should jump your bones without taking you out on a date first."

Mia chuckled. "Okay, now we're getting somewhere." She sighed. "For God's sake, I hope today qualifies as a date."

He cocked a brow at her. "This is an interesting new side to you."

She laid a hand on his thigh, close to his crotch. "Back at you."

He hissed in a breath. If she was waiting for a come-back, she'd be disappointed. She hadn't actually put her hand where he'd like it, but his body reacted anyway. "Um, for the sake of our well-being, I think you might want to keep all your body parts on your side of the car while I'm driving."

"So, pull over." She chuckled again, sounding completely satisfied with herself as she tucked her hand into her lap, wiggled around—more to drive him crazy, he suspected, than to get comfortable—and laid her head back against the headrest. "I'm ready for a swim."

"So am I," he muttered, and steered them off onto a turnout. "So am I."

She quickly straightened, her lips parting in surprise, her eyebrows arching above her sunglasses as she stared at him through the dark lenses. Good. She thought he'd called her bluff.

Ignoring her and trying to quash a smile, he consulted the GPS.

"Are we lost?" she asked.

"Nope. I think there's a beach nearby where it's not too rocky to swim." He turned on the GPS's audio, and they listened to the voice pronounce the odd-sounding Hawaiian street names. "Did you get that?" he asked.

Mia started laughing. "If you're counting on me, we're never going to get back to Waikiki."

Her cheeks and nose were pink, and although he'd applied sunscreen earlier, he figured he probably had gotten too much sun himself. He reached over to the glove box, his arm grazing her breasts in the tight confines of the car. Hearing her sharp intake of breath, he smiled to himself.

"Here." He tossed her the tube. "You can use some on your face and shoulders."

She squirted the white cream onto her palm, then removed her glasses and slathered the sunscreen on her face, shoulders and arms. Looking over at him, the sun shining in her face, her green eyes so beautiful, they sparkled like emeralds, robbing him of oxygen. "You, too," she said, her gaze lowering to his mouth and lingering. "Take off your sunglasses."

She waited for him to do as she asked, then squeezed more sunscreen into her palm. Using her fingertips, she smoothed the cream across his chin, dabbed it over his cheeks and down to the tip of his nose.

"Thanks." He rubbed in the leftover white spot on her chin.

"I'm not done with you," she said in a throaty voice that got to him in a not so surprising way. "Look down."

He frowned, automatically glanced at his fly, then smiled to himself when she applied the sunscreen to his exposed nape. When she was finished, he asked, "Done with me now?"

"Not even a little."

He looked up. Their unguarded eyes met. Something so primal stirred inside him that he didn't know what to do.

She was wrong about one thing. He hadn't shown his entire hand. He hadn't told her the firm wanted her back, and that he'd been ordered to do anything to make that happen.

But he'd been wrong, as well. Wrong not to tell her up front. He knew what he had to do. He didn't like it, and didn't much like himself for agreeing to do it. But his feelings changed nothing. The firm needed her.

6

THEY STOPPED BRIEFLY at Sandy Beach, aptly named
because the rocks were fewer and a long stretch of white
sand left plenty of room for sunbathers, picnickers and
children building sandcastles. The problem was there
were too many people for David's taste, and even if there
weren't, the waves were too big for a pleasant swim or
any other water activity that interested him.

A few people rode surfboards and kept safely to the
left of the swimmers and kids using boogie boards. He
and Mia mutually decided to move on.

Makapuu was the next beach, different than Sandy
in that it was a bay surrounded by rocky cliffs that kept
it somewhat hidden. Again, the main drawback was the
number of people, mostly bodysurfers testing their skills
against the powerful waves, or the spectators sunning
themselves.

"Let's stop for a while," Mia suggested just as he was
about to pull onto the highway again.

Although David preferred going elsewhere, he cut the
engine. "No swimming here. The way the waves break

in the middle of the bay makes it too dangerous. That's why there are only bodysurfers in the water."

"I do want to swim, but I'd like to have a better look at the bay and those two islands out there. Wish we had binoculars."

He squinted at the pair of barren islands not too far from the coast. "Not much to see. One of them is called Rabbit Island. No rabbits left, though. It's a seabird sanctuary now."

She grinned at him. "You're just a fountain of information. Did you get any sleep at all last night?"

"Not much," he muttered, as he watched her get out of the car, the hem of her shorts riding up high enough that he caught a glimpse of her peach-colored swimsuit. Grudgingly he climbed out behind her. "I'm thirsty. Supposedly there's a small town about ten minutes from here."

She smiled over her shoulder at him. "I just want a quick peek. I doubt I'll ever make it out here again."

He stood alongside her, their shoulders almost touching. "You mean to this side of the island?"

"No, Hawaii."

"Too many other places on your list?"

"I wish. More like too much work and no time for anything else. Not to mention no money," she added ruefully. "This is kind of a last hurrah."

"Ah, the business Shelby mentioned." After he'd returned to his room last night, he'd belatedly wished he'd asked questions during dinner with Shelby as a buffer. Find out if their new venture would be a further complication for him. "I understand now why you felt you had to leave us," he said casually. "With the hours you worked, starting up a business would have been nearly impossible."

"Nearly?" She chuckled. "Not a chance I could have done both effectively."

"I didn't catch what kind of business it is."

"Sort of a concierge service."

He waited for her to elaborate, and when she didn't he said, "Good thing you have a PR person."

"Look at you being all funny." Mia gave him a wry smile. "If I thought I could nab Pearson and Stern as a customer, I'd be all over it. We're going to rent out everything from power tools for that small one-time do-it-yourself project to designer handbags in case you want to impress your future in-laws."

"I'll keep that in mind."

"Or if you need a wife for the day, we'll provide that, too."

He choked out a laugh. "Pardon me?"

Mia's teasing grin made her eyes sparkle. "To do errands or plan or help host a party, that sort of thing. Our sorority held a fundraiser when I was in college, and Shelby, Lindsey and I rented ourselves out for a day. That's how we came up with the idea. But we never had the seed money until now."

"Should I even ask what service you rendered?"

"Oh, just use your imagination."

"Right." That could get him in trouble. "So I assume the new firm you're going to work for is smaller and won't swallow up your time."

She looked startled. But when she said, "I don't want to talk about work or anything related," he understood. She looped an arm through his and leaned her head on his shoulder. "This week will go by fast enough."

Briefly closing his eyes, he deeply inhaled the exotic scent of her spicy shampoo. His initial instinct had been right. Maybe it was wrong to tell her about the offer now and ruin her vacation.

This was insane. He'd never in his life been this indecisive. Or cowardly.

No, business would wait. For once, he was putting himself and Mia first.

"Come on. Let's get out of here."

Mia HAD DONE THE RIGHT THING. She'd spent enough sleepless nights expounding on the pros and cons of quitting the firm. If her decision disappointed David, then too bad. No "if" about it. A third-generation lawyer like him wouldn't understand that she simply didn't want to practice law. Neither would her family and her former coworkers. That's why she'd withheld that small detail. She couldn't help it if everyone assumed the new business was a sideline. Eventually she'd have to tell her parents and siblings, but she figured the shock would be easier to overcome once Anything Goes was a success.

She finished off the last of her ice-cold strawberry slushy just as they found Bellows Beach Park. Unlike the other beaches, there were trees. Lots of them, providing both shade and privacy. Fortunately, there weren't many people there: a small group of surfers, a few teenagers who probably should've been in school. But that was it, and the white sand seemed to go on forever, which meant they weren't likely to be bothered by newcomers.

They easily found a secluded spot where someone had recently been camping, if the charred remains of a small cook fire were any indication. Nearby, palm fronds had been used to erect a makeshift shelter. The lean-to wasn't much, probably helped to block the breeze, but it also provided privacy. Privacy she had no intention of wasting.

She glanced over at David, who'd just cut the engine, and found him watching her. Was he thinking the same thing? "I wish I had thought to bring a beach towel from the hotel," she said, "or picked up a couple of those straw mats I saw people using."

He gave her an amused smile.

"What?"

"Did you enjoy that slushy?"

"I did. You can't say I didn't offer— Oh, crap." With a swipe of her tongue, she'd figured out why he was still smiling and pulled down the visor. In the mirror, she regarded her clownish reflection with a sigh. "You could've said something earlier."

"I shouldn't have said anything at all. It'll fade soon enough." The way his voice dropped told her he had the same idea about how to use their lucky spot.

She dabbed ineffectively at the red stain that made her lips look as if they were twice as big as they were. "How did I manage to do this?"

"Fortunately I love strawberry." He leaned over and kissed her briefly before sweeping his tongue across her lower lip. "Hmm, very good."

"I dare you to do that again."

"Plan on it." He winked and opened his door.

She *really* wished they'd done more kissing before he got out, but she quickly changed her mind when he stepped out of the car, removed his sunglasses and yanked up the hem of his shirt. After exposing his flat belly, he paused to unfasten another button at his neck before pulling his shirt off altogether.

Mia blatantly stared. It was rude. Definitely embarrassing because she couldn't quite close her mouth. And she didn't give a damn. He had a gorgeous chest, tanned and lightly muscled. But how? He worked all the time.

"I'm not stripping," he said. "Not here. No matter how much you beg."

"Even if I get on all fours?"

He gave her a long, studied look. "You get down there, and I'm sure we could come to some kind of agreement."

"Oh, wow, if the ladies in the office could hear you now."

A flush tinged his cheeks. "What happens in Hawaii stays in Hawaii, remember?"

"I'm just saying…" She opened her door and slid out, unable to drag away her gaze. "How do you have time to go to a gym?"

"I don't." He shrugged. "I have a few routines I do at home every morning to keep in shape for tennis."

"Plus, you're tan." She narrowed her eyes. "It's March. You used a tanning bed."

"Right," he said dryly. "I had to be in Florida recently." He stuck his head inside the car, and fiddled around, the fluid movement of his shoulder muscles holding her gaze prisoner. "Do you play tennis?"

"Badly." She was dying to ask what he'd been doing there, why he hadn't been home licking his wounds because Friday had been her last day. Obviously it wasn't all business that had taken him south, or he would've had no time for the outdoors.

She heard the trunk pop, and met him at the rear of the car to see what he had stashed.

There were a pair of folded blue beach towels and two rolled-up straw mats that seemed to be a favorite of tourists crowding Waikiki beach.

"Should have bought a cooler and drinks." He grabbed the towels, passed them to her and then got the mats.

"I'm impressed you thought to bring these, although not surprised. You're thorough, if nothing else."

He closed the trunk and pocketed the keys, watching her the whole time, a wicked glint of amusement in his brown eyes. "Yes, I am, I'm thorough in everything I do."

Somehow the amusement melted into a promise that made her skin tingle with yearning. If this were a dream, she'd be hitting the snooze button, loath to wake up. Good God, this was David. In Hawaii. With her. Sure, she'd known him for a long time, but that was some other David, who in some ways she'd gotten to know quite well.

This version brought back the old feelings she'd struggled with early on, day after day.

"Why are you staring at me like that?" He rubbed her upper arm, as if she were a child that needed soothing.

"Like what?"

He frowned, the tender concern in his eyes nearly her undoing. "As if you're afraid."

"That's crazy. What's there to be afraid of?"

His mouth curved into a thin smile. "I hope not me."

She sucked in a breath when she realized he was right. Fear had tucked itself in a small corner of her heart. But that wasn't on him. It would be her own fault if she tried to make more of this week than it was. "Nope. I just want to have a good time, no regrets, no expectations."

"I want that, too."

"Perfect." So why did his agreement hurt a little? Now that she'd had a small taste of him, was she getting soft? Getting greedy? She had to stick to her cheesecake rule. She could only indulge when she ate out. Not even a sliver was allowed to reside in her refrigerator since one bite was impossible for her. It invariably led to a minibinge.

Thinking something might come of this week would be a mistake. If David had seriously wanted to pursue her for a real relationship, he could've done that in New York. No, she'd seen the women his family deemed appropriate, and while she was no slouch, she wasn't on anyone's social radar. Now that she wasn't even going to practice law, she could just imagine his parents' horror. But that was good, right? All she wanted was a one-week fling—that's what this trip had been about from the beginning. That it was with David didn't change the game.

His hand closed over hers, and she snapped out of her musings. "We don't have to stay," he said quietly. "Say the word, and I'll take you back to the hotel."

"No, I'm having a great time. I spaced out, I know." She shrugged. "Sorry. It's just that— Nope, not talking about work."

"No argument here." He let go of her hand, and used the car to balance himself while he kicked off his deck shoes.

"Mind opening the trunk again? I want to leave my purse and sandals."

He did as she asked, then frowned at the peach-colored bikini top she pulled out of her bag.

"It's my top," she said.

"I know." He glanced at her breasts. "Where are you going to change?"

"Here."

He didn't seem thrilled with the idea, but then he didn't have a say. He squinted through the trees at the pair of figures walking close to the water at the south end, far enough away that their genders were undistinguishable. "I saw a sign for the restrooms about a mile back."

"It'll take two seconds." She reached under the tank top and unsnapped her bra. "You can warn me if anyone's coming."

"Okay," he said, doubt reflected in every syllable of the word.

She smirked. "You do have to turn around."

"Right." He surveyed the area once again before he slowly gave her his back. "You might feel more comfortable changing in the car."

"It's a convertible."

"I meant that I'd put the top up," he said dryly.

"Okay. All done. You can turn around."

He wasted no time in doing just that. His gaze went unerringly to her breasts, which were barely covered by two skimpy triangles of fabric. The way they were thrust out while she tied the bow in back made her a bit self-conscious. Made her clumsy. The task seemed to take forever.

He finally dragged his gaze away, looking slightly embarrassed.

She nervously busied herself with wiggling out of her shorts, being careful not to pull the bikini bottoms down with them. Then she took her time folding everything, trying to get rid of the jitters.

After depositing her clothes in the trunk beside her bag, she did a quick check of her front to make sure everything was in place. She cringed when she noticed a spot on her upper thigh she'd missed covering with the bronzing lotion. Unfortunately, she also noticed the slight roundness of her belly because she never made time for the gym, nor had she done crunches in forever.

Sighing, she gathered the towels she'd set aside while she changed, and strategically held them up in front of her. Only then did she realize that David had slipped out of his khakis to reveal a pair of red swim trunks. His thighs were nicely muscled, though not overly so, but his calves surprised her with their bulk and definition. They didn't belong to a casual jogger, but more like a serious runner.

He closed the trunk, and they followed a grassy path through a cluster of trees that bordered the pristine white sand. There was no need for discussion as to where they'd plant themselves. They stopped at a spot that was half-sunny, half-shaded, and shielded them from the north side of the beach by the leafy lean-to.

David untied the straw mats, and then shook out each one, placing them side by side, so close together they almost touched.

Mia dropped a beach towel on each mat before focusing her gaze on the water gently lapping the shore.

She was painfully aware that David was staring at her. It was weird that she would feel more self-conscious in a bikini than being naked. But then, this was full, unforgiving sunlight. Not the same as a dimly lit hotel room. On the upside, she got to eye him, too. She looked over at him.

He gave her a guilty smile. "I feel like the proverbial kid in the candy store."

She grinned and lowered herself to the mat, positioning herself so that she could lean back, giving the illusion of a flatter tummy. Giving the illusion that she was cool and composed when her insides were doing somersaults.

He got down beside her and tossed the car keys on the mat, and mirrored her position, so that the upper halves of their bodies were both in shade. The sun burned down on their thighs and calves. She stared at the pesky mole near her knee that she'd hated since grade school. Had she been smart, she would've had it removed while she still had health insurance.

"You've been out of law school for eight years now?" she asked, turning to meet his eyes. She was pretty sure he was thirty-three, past the age a lot of guys started getting married. No way she'd bring that up.

"Yep. It feels like twenty." His brows drew together to form a slight crease. "You have the greenest eyes. I used to wonder if you wore contacts to get them that color."

"Maybe I do."

He shook his head.

"How do you know?"

"I've had almost three years to figure it out."

She snorted. "You barely spared me a glance."

"Think so?" A slow, sly smile lifted the corners of his mouth as he looked so deeply into her eyes that her entire body flushed. He leaned over and pressed a gentle kiss to her lips, then touched the corner with the tip of his tongue.

"Oh, God, I still have clown lips, don't I?"

David stopped her inane muttering by kissing her again, this time coaxing her lips apart and kissing her long and hard and deep. She felt herself start to slip backward, and his arm was suddenly behind her, guiding her back until their kiss broke and she was lying supine on the mat and staring up into his warm brown eyes.

"No one's coming," he whispered as he trailed a finger from her chin down between her breasts, his touch so light she couldn't be sure she hadn't imagined it.

He kissed her eyes, kissed her nose, brushed his lips leisurely across hers. Then he touched her breast. She automatically arched up, filling his hand. Her nipples tightened, communicating their need. He found one through the fabric of her top and circled it with the pad of his thumb.

"We shouldn't have stopped," he whispered huskily. "We should've gone straight to the hotel."

"You said no one's coming," she reminded him in a weak voice.

He groaned, and pushed aside one triangle of her top. For a second he just stared at her bared breast, his eyes dark and hungry, and then he put his hot mouth on her puckered flesh. His moist heat bathed her skin, and she shivered, squeezing her eyes closed when his teeth scraped her hard nipple.

She blindly reached for him, found his hip and slid

her hand around to cup his firm, round ass, urging him closer until his erection pressed her thigh. She moved her leg so that she rubbed him just right, smiled when she heard his soft groan, groaned herself when he sucked hard at her nipple.

He cupped her other breast, inched the fabric over until he'd exposed the other nipple. He rolled his tongue over the crown, stopping briefly to nip at the hard tip. But when he simply breathed on it, Mia shivered.

"Do you know how long I've wanted to do this?" David whispered. "How much I want to kiss you everywhere." He kissed the spot between her breasts, and then moved to the heated skin between her ribs. When he got to her navel, she experienced momentary panic and tensed.

She didn't know why. No one was around. But the mood had definitely shifted.

He sighed, and she felt his withdrawal even before he planted a final kiss on her belly. "Come on," he said, his breathing irregular. "I know where we can get some great room service."

7

PEOPLE CROWDED INTO the hotel elevator behind them, and Mia found herself pushed to the opposite corner of the car from David. But with David at six-two and her at five-nine, they could still see each other over most other people's heads.

Or maybe it wasn't such a good thing. All the way through the lobby he'd tried to convince her to go straight to his suite with him. She'd resisted, too hot and sticky and desperately wanting a shower. But had they been alone in the elevator, she had a feeling he might have pulled out all the stops in trying to win his argument.

God, merely thinking about how he touched her with the perfect amount of pressure, kissed her in all the right places, nuzzled her neck exactly where she liked it, was enough to make her give in. Her only viable wall of defense was Lindsey and Shelby. It was almost five, and she'd feel like crap if she didn't at least check in with them.

The elevator dinged, signaling that it was about to stop at the seventh floor and her gaze locked with his.

"One hour," David mouthed, over the head of a short, white-haired lady. "No more."

"Or?" she mouthed with an arched brow.

"I'm coming for you," he said aloud, ignoring the inquisitive looks shooting at him.

Mia pressed her lips together to keep from giggling like a little girl, and hurried off when the elevator doors slid open.

The second she opened the door to her room, her heady rush crashed and burned. Shelby was lounging on the shady balcony, alone, an open book sitting on her lap. It looked as if she might have dozed off because she jerked slightly and then swung her unfocused gaze toward Mia.

"Hi." She straightened and rubbed an eye. "Wow, it's gotten warm out here." She closed the book, rose and stretched. Then she stepped into the room and closed the balcony door behind her. "Mind if I turn up the A/C?"

"Of course not." Mia dropped her small bag and sunglasses on the bamboo secretary, her heart heavy with the possibility that Shelby had spent the day alone. "What did you do today?"

"I went to the beach, walked forever, swam in the pool, found this adorable bikini and matching wrap in the shop next door. Wanna see it?"

"Sure." Mia watched her friend disappear through the open adjoining door, and then slid a peek around the connecting room. "Where's Lindsey?"

"I don't know. I haven't seen her." Shelby reappeared with a bag. Before she opened it, she grinned at Mia. "How was your day with that tall, gorgeous hunk?"

"Great. I wish you'd come with us," Mia said breezily.

"It's like a whole different island once you get past Diamond Head. Totally awesome."

"Uh-huh."

"What?"

Amusement danced in Shelby's hazel eyes. "You seriously think I wanted the 'G' version?"

"Sorry." Mia shrugged, feeling unexpectedly defensive. They weren't kids anymore. She was not going to discuss the intimate details between her and David. "I don't have anything juicy for you."

Shelby's gaze narrowed speculatively, but she wisely dropped the subject. "Check this out," she said, dumping the contents of the bag onto the bed.

There wasn't much to the hot pink bikini. The back consisted of a thong, the legs were cut high and the front dipped into an indecently deep V bordered by a narrow ruffle. The top was a mere token. Of the three of them, Shelby was the only one who could get away with wearing something like that, or for that matter, even consider it.

Shelby arranged the two pieces on the bed and then held up the brief *pareau* cover-up apparently meant to be wrapped low around the hips. "What do you think?"

"You'll probably get arrested."

She laughed. "Hope it's by a male cop."

"You always did like a guy in uniform."

"Hey, you know…I've never dated a police officer."

Mia chuckled, and shook her head in mock disapproval. Since they'd considered the possibility that other guys might respond to their Facebook wall, Mia asked, "Happen to meet anyone?"

"A really cute lifeguard." Shelby sighed. "We're having drinks at sunset tomorrow."

"Great."

"He's built like a god. The guy has to do some serious weightlifting."

"I never knew you to be attracted to that type."

Shelby shrugged, her lips twitching mischievously. "For one night, he'll do just fine."

"God, listen to us." Mia furtively consulted her watch. Only forty-five minutes before she was to meet David. "I'm going to jump in the shower."

Shelby glanced at her watch, too. "I guess I should text Lindsey about tonight. Just to remind her." She wrinkled her nose, looking undecided, then studied Mia. "Frankly, I didn't think you'd remember."

Tonight? Mia frowned, then suddenly recalled it was their birthday night. The time they'd agreed to have a joint celebration for their January, February and March birthdays. "How could I forget that?" she said dismissively, her disappointment so acute she thought she felt her heart sink to her stomach.

She walked to the closet and rifled through the few things she'd hung up, her thoughts going to David. It wasn't as if she couldn't still see him tonight—later, after she'd had dinner with Lindsey and Shelby—but she had to call him, let him know plans had changed. She'd take her cell phone into the bathroom with her, turn on the shower so Shelby couldn't hear and call him. He'd be disappointed; so was she. They'd both get over it.

She took a couple of deep breaths, and yanked a green halter top off the hanger. She'd have to hurry and sneak her cell phone out of her purse while Shelby was busy texting Lindsey. Quietly she closed the closet door, and turned around. Shelby was sitting on the wicker chair beside the dresser, watching her.

Mia jerked. "Damn, you scared me. I thought you were in the other room."

"Before I text Lindsey I wanted to know if you're bringing David."

"No. We planned this weeks ago. Just us girls, remember?"

Shelby grinned. "You're such a bad liar."

"What?"

"Swear to me you remembered about tonight."

Mia hesitated. "I did. I—" She briefly closed her eyes and groaned. Then she stared apologetically at her friend. "I might have confused the days."

Shelby chuckled. "Look, I don't care. We're here, that's celebration enough in my book. And Lindsey, well, she's apparently forgotten, too and I'm not going to be the one to tear her away from Rick."

"Have you seen him?"

"No. You?"

Mia shook her head, and lowered herself to the edge of the bed facing Shelby. "When was the last time you heard from her?"

"This morning."

"A text?" Mia asked, and Shelby nodded. "Me, too."

Shelby sighed dramatically. "Oh, God, Mom, tell me you're not going to get all worried and screw up the evening."

Mia gave her an eye roll, but the truth was, she was a bit concerned. Of the three of them, Lindsey was the most conservative, the most sensible and really good about making sure everyone was accountable. "Okay, one question, does it make sense to you that she wouldn't make sure we knew where she was? Or not here planning every detail for tonight?"

"That's two questions," Shelby muttered crossly and straightened. "Oh, shit, now you've got me worried."

Mia wondered if she should contact David yet. She was going to be late meeting him, that much she knew, but how late? "Honestly, I'm not really worried, more curious."

"You're right. She is being weird."

"Let's text her and ask her about tonight. I'm cancelling. We can choose another night later."

Shelby dug her phone out of her shorts pocket, and her fingers immediately went to work. After she'd sent the text, she sank back and frowned. "I should've called instead."

"That's another weird thing. Lindsey doesn't usually text us as much as she calls."

"True. So why doesn't she want to talk to us?" A grin tugged at Shelby's mouth. "Unless— Did you meet him last time?"

"Nope."

"Me neither. Wonder if she's told him her real name yet?"

"I want to see him," Mia said, getting up and heading for her bag.

Shelby laughed. "Me, too. You gonna call?"

"Yes, ma'am."

"She might not answer."

"Then we both keep calling. Don't leave a message, other than to return the call. You know her, she'll be worried or nosy and won't be able to help herself." Mia withdrew her phone from her bag and stared at it. It wasn't fair to leave David hanging. No matter what happened, she was going to be late. She hadn't even showered yet.

She'd tell him she would be delayed an hour or two, give him a summary version, offer to explain later. He'd be disappointed, but he'd understand.

"She's going to be so pissed at us." A gleeful grin spread across Shelby's face as she and Mia crossed the lobby in stealth mode, alert for any sign that Lindsey had left the pool and might turn the tables on them.

Shelby wore her new bikini, with the ill-named cover-up tied low around her hips. She looked so stunningly gorgeous with her long tawny hair fluttering in the breeze, that Mia thought she just might hate her a tiny bit.

"Don't look so cheerful," Mia told her. "We have to make this look like a coincidence." She'd left on her swimsuit with the tank top, minus the shorts, as if she were making a casual trip to the pool for a late-afternoon swim.

"Do you think she suspects?" Shelby asked, oblivious to the male heads turning in her direction.

"No way. She didn't say where she was. I could hear the splashing and kids laughing in the background. For all we know she could be at another hotel and the joke will be on us."

"Oh, hell. That would be a bummer."

"Yeah," Mia murmured. Bummer for sure. She could've been with David instead of spying on their too-secretive friend. Part of Mia's motive was plain nosiness, the other part was honest concern. Lindsey was acting strangely about this dude. Twice during their brief conversation, Mia had hinted that she and Shelby wanted to meet Rick. Both times Lindsey had subtly blown them off.

They decided to go the long way from the lobby because it would give them an opportunity to scope out most of the pool area, while there would be little chance that Lindsey could spot them first. A horde of people still wet from the pool or beach were exiting the area as they approached. Made sense since it was close to the dinner hour, but that wasn't going to help their cause.

As soon as Mia spotted the familiar thatched pool-bar roof, she indicated to Shelby that they should head toward the guy signing out beach towels near the restrooms. They both wore sunglasses, but Mia knew that, like herself, Shelby was avidly scanning the groups of guests that remained poolside, lounging on chairs, reading or sipping fruity drinks.

"Oh, my God."

Mia swung a look at Shelby, who'd stopped and was staring in the direction of the giant rock waterfall. One of the boulders threw a portion of the deck into shadow and created a small semiprivate nook. Squinting behind her sunglasses, Mia caught a glimpse of Lindsey's long blond hair. The chaise on which she lounged butted up against another chair occupied by a man, stretched out on his side, facing Lindsey. He had longish sun-streaked brown hair, tied back into a short ponytail.

"Holy crap, check out his tats." Shelby lowered her sunglasses an inch and peered over them.

Mia did the same. She saw one tattoo on his upper arm, another just above his shoulder blade, though she couldn't make out what they were. The rest of him looked pretty good—lean, muscled, broad where he should be—but absolutely, positively not Lindsey's type.

Mia had to take a second glance to make sure the blonde was actually her friend.

"I don't believe this," Shelby said, shooting Mia a stunned look before resuming her openmouthed stare.

They both watched as he leaned toward Lindsey and kissed her. Her hand immediately went to her hair the way it always did when she was nervous. But she didn't pull away.

"I must be hallucinating," Shelby muttered.

Mia blinked just to be sure.

"Would you ladies like a cocktail?"

They both turned to the tall, narrow-faced waitress, who seemed to have appeared out of nowhere.

"Desperately," Shelby said.

"I'm pretty sure you have to be more specific," Mia said absently, and then advised the waitress, "Nothing for me, thanks."

"Make it a Mai Tai— No, wait." Shelby pulled a face. "We need to find a spot to sit. Catch us your next time around, okay?"

"Sure." The waitress shifted her tray, smiled and stalked off to the next guest.

Mia glanced over at Lindsey and saw her friend trying to get the waitress's attention. Mia quickly averted her gaze. "Great," she murmured. "I think Lindsey might have seen us."

Like a pro, Shelby maintained a poker face. "Okay, then let's go get our towels. And then— What?"

"I say we go over and say hi, pretend this is a coincidence. We postponed the birthday dinner. She knows we'd be looking for something else to do. Why not come down for a swim?"

"Right." They walked to the counter and each signed out a towel. "Is she looking this way?" Shelby asked.

"I haven't checked." Mia draped the yellow towel over her arm and slid a furtive look from under her lashes. "Oh, hell."

"Is she looking?"

"I don't know," Mia said, sighing. "But Jeff is here, and he just spotted me."

DAVID HAD BEEN IN THE SHOWER when Mia called his cell phone and left a message. She was going to be late, wasn't sure how long, it had something to do with previous plans with her friends, and she'd explain more later. She'd said she was sorry. Twice. And she'd sounded genuinely disappointed. But that hadn't lessened his own disappointment. Or frustration.

He put on some music while he perused the room service menu, poured himself a scotch and tried to relax. But reading the menu only reminded him that the romantic dinner he'd planned might not pan out. He eyed his phone sitting on the bar, flirted with temptation and finally ordered himself not to call her back. She would've given him the green light had she wanted to talk to him.

Instead, muttering a mild oath, he laid his head back to stare at the textured ceiling. She and her friends had planned this trip together and naturally had their own itinerary. He had no business feeling put out. He knew he was being totally selfish in wanting her to spend every minute with him, but he didn't give a damn. This could be their last chance to see if there was something there between them, figure out if the feelings he'd been suppressing were real.

His restless gaze landed on the crystal desk clock. Only twenty minutes since she'd left the message? How could that be? With the time difference, it was too late to call his office. He sure as hell wasn't about to talk to his father. He'd want to know if David had presented the offer to Mia. Which he would have done by now if he hadn't had a personal agenda.

But damn if he'd feel guilty about that, too. For three years he'd kept on blinders, concentrated on his job, refused to allow the smallest crack in his professional armor where Mia was concerned. It wasn't even just about Mia, although she'd been his ultimate test. For the eight years since he'd been out of law school, he'd always put work first. And yes, of course he was concerned about losing clients and avoiding cutbacks. The possibility of layoffs ate at him, and he was willing to do almost anything to prevent the firm from going that route. But he wouldn't sacrifice a chance with Mia.

He'd forgotten about the scotch he poured, and took a long slow sip, letting the liquid burn all the way down his throat. Thinking about the office wasn't doing him any good. The decision to extend the offer to her at the end of the trip was a good one. The right one. Tonight and the next few days had to be strictly about them.

Ironic, really, that this trip was for both personal and business reasons, after he'd prided himself in keeping those two areas of his life separate.

He inhaled deeply, then exhaled slowly. Of course this whole thing could blow up in his face if she thought his every action since arriving in Hawaii had been about luring her back to the firm and not about wanting her for himself. No, she knew him too well. He had to trust that she held him in higher esteem than to believe him capable of conning her. Mia wasn't just beautiful, she was damn smart.

Smiling, he easily pictured her lying on that crazy straw mat, her dark hair fanned out around her slim shoulders, her green eyes hazy with desire. He loved the way her lips unconsciously parted, ever so slightly, the second before he kissed her, and the way she tasted— cool and sweet and just the right amount of eager.

Well, hell, thinking about her like this and nursing yet another unattended hard-on wasn't doing him any favors, either. Not that he couldn't take care of himself, but he'd only resent her absence all the more.

Abandoning the rest of his scotch, he pushed off the chair. Waiting around the suite was a mistake. He'd have his phone with him in case she called, but he needed to expend some energy, stop doing so much thinking. What he needed was a good swim.

8

"JEFF, PLEASE, LET ME GO. I don't want to get wet." Mia tried to keep her angry voice low and not cause a scene, though luckily, very few people were close to them. But when he tightened his arms around her, his boozy, fetid breath nearly making her gag, she was sorely tempted to kick him in the balls.

"Come on, baby, for old times' sake." He drew her within an inch of the water's edge. "We had us some crazy fun in the pool last time, remember?"

"That wasn't me, you idiot," Mia growled. Thank God Lindsey and Rick had left and weren't witness to this. Shelby was getting a drink. "Now let go, or I will hurt and humiliate you."

Jeff roared with laughter. "I didn't know you were into that stuff. I like it."

Mia poked her elbow back until she made contact with his ribs, and he yelped, momentarily loosening his hold. Sure that had been enough to make her point, she stepped away. He quickly recovered, laughing, and banded his arms around her so tightly that she could barely breathe.

Damn, she didn't want to do the girlie thing and bite him, but if that's what it took…

"Oh, hell, you're gonna make me waste a perfectly good drink, you ass." Shelby stood with one hand on her hip, the other holding a pineapple-and-cherry-garnished drink that she had poised to throw in Jeff's face.

"That won't be necessary."

At the sound of David's deep, rumbling voice, Mia's pulse leaped. Embarrassed more than relieved, she turned her head to look at him. His face was devoid of expression, not so much as a brow moved, but she saw the fury in his dark eyes.

"Hey, David." Jeff blinked blearily at him, oblivious to the unspoken threat. "How's it going?"

"Let go of her." David's chin went up slightly, his jaw tight. His hands stayed relaxed at his sides.

"I was just leaving," Mia said, not wanting to see the situation escalate.

With Jeff distracted, she easily shook away from him and went to stand between David and Shelby.

Jeff frowned, glanced from Mia to David. "Hey, are you two…?"

"Yes." David tersely cut him off, and slid a possessive arm around her.

"Sorry, man." Jeff shrugged, and then set his sights on Shelby, giving her a sloppy lopsided grin.

"Yeah, that'll happen." She snorted out a laugh, and then popped the cherry from her drink into her mouth.

Jeff just shrugged before he jumped into the pool, and the rest of them moved quickly toward the bar to avoid being splashed.

"Just so you know," Mia said to David, "I totally could have taken him."

He gave a grudging smile, telling her he hadn't shaken all his anger. "I should've backed off. I would've liked to have seen that."

She bumped him with her shoulder. "How about I buy my big strong hero a drink?"

He hesitated, glanced briefly at Shelby and moved his arm away from Mia. "I didn't mean to intrude. I only came down for a swim."

"You're not intruding. We were just spying on our friend Lindsey." Shelby shrugged. "We got busted."

Mia pressed her lips together and gave her friend a withering look.

David laughed. "Spying?"

"No, not spying." Mia sniffed. "We hadn't seen her since yesterday and we wanted—"

"To check out the guy she was with." Shelby's eyes sparkled with mischief.

"That's not quite accurate," Mia said.

"And?" David was clearly trying to control a smile. "Did you approve?"

Shelby's light brows knitted. "Surprised the hell out of me. Really cute, but not what I expected." She looked to Mia for confirmation. "Not for Linds."

Mia stared back at her, dumbfounded that she'd speak so freely in front of David. "Okay." She stepped back. "I am going to my room and take a nice long shower. You two—" She waved a hand. "Do whatever."

"Wait." Chuckling, David caught her hand. "I'm going up with you."

Mia hesitated, momentarily meeting Shelby's eyes. She didn't want to ditch her friend.

"Go. Good riddance." Shelby made a shooing motion

with her hand. "You guys are screwing me up. How am I supposed to get lucky with you hanging around?"

Mia groaned, shook her head.

"Bye-bye," Shelby said, grinning, and then sauntered away, an exaggerated sway to her hips.

One of David's eyebrows went up as he stared after her. "She keeps that up and she's going to have more luck than she can handle."

"She took a hula lesson this afternoon."

"Ah."

"You're drooling."

He took his gaze away from Shelby's retreating back, and smiled at Mia. "Jealous?"

She coyly toyed with the top button of his tennis shirt. "Mmm, maybe a little."

"Just so *you* know, I wasn't drooling. At least, not over Shelby." Ignoring the few remaining guests at the bar, he slid an arm around her waist, brought her close, stared at her mouth with an intensity that sent a shiver of anticipation down her spine. "I think it's time we go to my suite."

"I still have to shower."

"Just so happens I have one, along with a sunken tub big enough for two."

"But—"

He nudged her chin up and kissed her. A firm but leisurely kiss, nothing too risqué or demanding, but still his boldness surprised her. This spot wasn't like the beach where trees or cliffs hid them. Here they had an audience. "Now," he whispered.

DAVID KISSED HER AGAIN as they waited for the elevator, then kept his distance until the couple who'd followed them into the car got off on the fourth floor. The doors had barely slid closed when he leaned against the back, taking her with him, spreading his legs and cradling her between his thighs.

"You're crazy," she whispered breathlessly, her lips damp, her eyes glazed.

He took her face between his hands, kissed her deeply and almost didn't hear the elevator signal its approaching stop on the eighteenth floor.

Mia quickly spun around to face the doors as they slid open. A stooped elderly couple, the man walking with the aid of a cane, slowly entered the car. David had immediately straightened, but stayed cautiously behind Mia to hide his aroused state. She moved back, to give the couple room, her bottom intimately bumping him.

David hissed in a sharp breath.

Mia's back went ramrod stiff. She'd clearly figured out the problem and eased away from him. Though not much. Not enough to stop his body from reacting to the snug feel of that sweet, curvy ass.

The white-haired woman considered the numbered panel, peering closely, both through and then over her glasses, while David prayed that the pair would get off on the next floor.

Her gnarled finger hovered a moment, the doors already starting to close. "Is this elevator going down, dear?" she asked, turning to Mia.

The woman blinked, then tilted her head and frowned over her glasses at David as if seeing him for the first time. Her gaze swept Mia's face, and then went back to David, her eyes narrowing in indignation.

He stuck his head out to the right so it wouldn't look

as if he were hiding. "We're going up, ma'am," he said politely, wondering why Mia hadn't answered.

With an air of disgust, the woman abruptly gave them her back. "Harold, we're on the wrong elevator. We need to get off." She stared up at the flashing floor numbers as they ascended.

"So what," the man snapped. "We'll ride the darn thing back down."

The woman stubbornly searched the panel, but by the time she figured out which button to press, they arrived at David's floor. "Excuse us," he said, his hand pressed to Mia's back as they both exited.

He walked them out of view, then stopped to look at Mia. Her face was stained a guilty red, and she looked as if she were ready to explode at any second. They heard the doors sliding close, and she burst out laughing.

"What?"

"That woman—" Mia sniffed, dabbed at her watery eyes, laughed some more. "Did you see her face? I don't know what she thought we were doing."

"We weren't exactly innocent." David couldn't help but join in on the infectious laughter, though he wasn't entirely comfortable that they'd been caught.

"We were only kissing, and not even in front of them."

"Right."

"Oh, David, she didn't *see* you." Mia automatically glanced at his fly.

He said nothing as they continued toward the suite, while digging in his pocket for his key card. It wasn't like him to behave in such an undignified manner. In fact, he'd indulged himself quite a few times today.

Funny, he'd never pictured Mia letting her hair down that way, either.

"You're not upset, are you?"

"No, of course not. No one knows us here." He stopped at his door, opened it and stepped aside for her.

Her brows had drawn together in a slight frown, but as soon as she stepped over the threshold, her pensive mood appeared to vanish. "Whoa. This is some hovel. And what a view."

She seemed to take everything in at once, her gaze sweeping the rich, dark hardwood floors, Oriental rugs, the Hawaiian artwork on the walls. At the sliding glass door to the ocean-side balcony, she paused to stare at the polished dining room table that could accommodate eight diners.

"This place is bigger than my apartment," she said, twisting around to survey the subdued tropical-print sofa and love seat. "I don't even want to know how much this sucker costs for a night."

He snorted. "Trust me, you don't. I only splurged because I haven't taken a vacation in years."

She stepped out onto the balcony, noticed that it wrapped around the corner and laughed with delight. "I could spend the whole week right here and be happy."

He came up behind her, slid his arms around her and nuzzled her neck. "Okay," he murmured against her warm sweet skin.

She laughed softly and leaned back into him, hugging his arms to her waist. "From up here you can see the ocean's different shades of blue," she said in a shaky voice. "You drive me crazy when you kiss my neck like that. But you know that, don't you?"

He smiled. "We can have dinner out here if you want. We should be able to catch part of the sunset."

She turned in his arms to face him, the bewitching green of her eyes knocking the breath out of him. "But then we'd have to hurry our shower."

"Screw dinner," he said, and covered her mouth with his.

Her eager response pleased him, triggered a need in him impossibly greater than he'd experienced on the beach. She pushed against him so hard that he stumbled back a step. She went with him, clutching the front of his shirt, returning his kisses with a fervor that matched his.

But it was no good, her arms shielding her breasts like that. He wanted to feel them pressed against his chest. He wanted to see her perfect round breasts bared again. He needed to see all of her.

With Herculean effort, he pulled away, ignoring her wide startled eyes. "Inside," he said, all but dragging her into the parlor.

He headed straight for the bedroom, unable to tamp down the pressure building inside of him like a volcano ready to explode. This wasn't him, nothing close to who he was or how he behaved with a woman. Normally he was patient, waited for the right mood. He tried to be thoughtful, even romantic at times, designing the right setting—candle, flowers, the whole thing.

But with Mia, he couldn't think straight. Around her it seemed that all he did was react, lose himself in the primal satisfaction of tasting her eager mouth, coaxing her nipples into tight buds flushed dark with arousal. The way he felt was crazy—animalistic—and he couldn't seem to do a damn thing about it.

MIA ENTERED THE BEDROOM ahead of David, both of them ignoring the light switch. The drapes to the balcony door were open halfway, and pinkish gold rays bathed the room in a sensual glow that made her heart lurch. The Asian-inspired armoire and headboard matched the tasteful parlor furniture, and the beautiful tan silk duvet that topped the king-size bed was a far cry from the floral spreads that serviced her economy room.

She was startled to discover that her legs were trembling a little when she turned to face David. Maybe because there was something different about him. Nothing scary or awful, kind of thrilling really. The way he looked as if he were doing everything in his power not to strip her naked and force her back onto the bed.

"David?" Her voice came out strange, husky and tentative.

"I know, Mia," he said quietly, brushing a gentle finger across her lips.

What did he know? She wasn't even sure what she was going to say herself. But when he drew his fingers down the front of her top and then slipped his hand underneath, she said, "Shower first."

"All right." He splayed his fingers across her belly, grazed the underside of her breast through her bikini top.

It wasn't fair that his palm could feel so dry and cool when her skin was fever hot. Nor was it fair the he smelled so clean and masculine.

"Don't."

He met her eyes, his surprised and alarmed. Promptly he let his hand drop. "Mia, I'm sorry."

"No," she said, feeling horrible for giving him the

wrong impression. "No. It's just that you've showered. I haven't."

Relief softened his mouth. "Would it help if I told you that you smell so damn good I want to—"

"No." She put a hand over his mouth, and then laughed when he nipped at her palm. "Don't you dare try to talk me out of it."

He took her by both wrists and stretched her arms over her head.

Her pulse went nuts. He had to feel it. "What are you doing?"

"Helping you undress." He yanked her tank top off before she could respond.

"I doubt that's going to work out well," she said, and gasped when he freed her bikini top and bared her breasts. The cool air danced over her nipples, and she knew without looking that they were fully extended.

He tossed both tops over his shoulder, his gaze captured by her breasts.

Then he hooked his fingers into the elastic of her bikini bottoms.

All rational thought deserted her. The trembling started in her chest and moved down her legs, and there didn't seem to be a damn thing she could do about it.

David was crouched in front of her, urging her to step out of the bottoms, and she braced a hand on his shoulder, praying hard that she wouldn't end up in an embarrassing heap.

He kissed the area just above where her bikini wax ended, and then slowly got to his feet.

At the raw hunger in his eyes, a wave of warm pleasure washed over her. He tenderly touched her breasts, and rubbed the pad of his thumb over one aching nipple.

She swallowed hard, wishing his shirt were off, wishing he were as naked as she was. It would only mean trouble. She really did want that shower before they made love, but right now, like an addict craving a fix, she needed to feel the friction of his bare, muscled chest rubbing her naked breasts.

"Go," he whispered hoarsely.

"Take off your shirt first."

"Go." He gripped her by her upper arms, his fingers digging lightly into her flesh as he held her away from him. The anguished expression on his face should have been enough to keep her at bay, but a part of her was thrilled that she'd undermined this man of iron will. "Now."

She shook free and pushed his shirt up. "Come with me."

"Mia." He hesitated, but only for a second, and then fumbled with the drawstring to his swim trunks, stopping long enough to help her pull off his shirt.

She stepped back, watched him strip off his trunks, barely able to catch her breath. He was hard, really hard, and much bigger than she'd imagined. When he kicked his trunks out of the way, a sudden and totally inappropriate giggle tickled inside her throat.

This was hardly the same man who was always impeccably dressed, never had a hair out of place, or God forbid, tolerated a cluttered desk or office.

He didn't notice her amusement. His gaze roamed her nude body, his lips damp and slightly parted, muscles tensed, like a hungry cougar ready to pounce on his next meal. His attention lingered on the recent wax job, and his small smile seemed just as predatory.

"Shower," she reminded him as she backed up, no longer feeling in control.

"Right direction," he said, "but you're about to ram that cute behind of yours into the door frame."

"Oh."

"You can turn around. I won't bite." Amusement gleamed in his eyes. "Yet."

She lifted her chin, and then her gaze snagged on his twitching penis, and she got all wobbly inside again. When he touched himself, she forgot what she was doing and stared at him, a warm flush of excitement enveloping her entire body. It took her a second to snap out of it. She continued to back up, annoyed when she bumped her hip before crossing the threshold into the bathroom. She patted the inside wall, found the switch and flooded the bathroom with a soft golden light.

The room was huge, lots of glass, brushed silver fixtures, glossy tile and granite. Her gaze went briefly to the big deep whirlpool tub. It would take too long, she promptly decided, and reached for the handle of the glass-enclosed shower.

"Be careful." David was right behind her, his hand touching her back, his thick arousal rubbing her ass, as he reached around to turn on the faucet. "The water gets hot quickly."

She smiled to herself. Who didn't?

9

IT SEEMED AS IF IT TOOK A LIFETIME for the water to adjust to the right temperature. In a small, crazy way, Mia wished that she hadn't coaxed David to join her. She wasn't sure she wanted to have sex for the first time with him while standing up. She could've taken the fastest shower in history, gotten all squeaky clean and been ready for him to do all kinds of delightful, unspeakable things to her in mere minutes.

Not that he was wasting any time while they waited. He pushed aside her hair and kissed the back of her neck, slowly moving his hips so that she could feel his need for her rubbing hot and heavy against her ass. She closed her eyes, totally forgetting where they were for a minute, and then his hands were on her shoulders and he was gently guiding her toward the spray of lukewarm water.

He let her go and, instantly feeling bereft, she turned her head to look at him. He smiled, kissed the tip of her nose, and took the big puffy lavender bath pom-pom off the granite shelf and started soaping it.

"Is that yours?" she asked, surprised.

"No." The affronted face he made was really cute. "It came with the suite. I had it unwrapped and ready just in case."

She grinned. "Just in case?"

"All right, I admit it. I knew I was getting you back here if I had to throw you over my shoulder."

"Ah, you say the sweetest things."

With one dark brow cocked in amusement, he slid the soapy, fragrant pom-pom down her back and over her buttocks, then wedged his hand between her thighs and slowly slid the pom-pom back and forth.

She gasped and turned to face the tiled wall, using it to brace herself. She didn't utter another sound, just closed her eyes and let him glide his hands down her inner thigh to her ankle. He thoroughly washed her calf and then swept up her other calf, causing her to hold her breath when he lingered at her opposite thigh. When he finally moved up higher, it was his hand he used to wash her pussy.

He slid a finger between her lips, and she tensed, then shuddered convulsively.

"Easy, baby," he whispered, slowly withdrawing his finger. "Not yet."

She hadn't come, if that's what he thought. That would be insanely fast, but that she could feel such acute arousal so quickly, that she could come so close to falling off the edge shocked the hell out of her. When he went back to scrubbing her back gently with the pom-pom, she swallowed hard, not sure if she welcomed the delay.

But it became obvious that was his intention, and she willed the quivering in her chest and legs to stop as he finished lathering her arms and shoulders.

"Turn around," he said in a gravelly voice that made it hard for her to move.

He didn't wait, but took her by the shoulders and forced her to face him. His gaze went to her breasts. Hers went to his swollen cock, and she leaned back against the cold tile wall for support. She wanted him inside her. Wanted him with a growing desperation she didn't think herself capable of.

Setting aside the pom-pom, he lathered his hands and then cupped her breasts. She looked at his face, but his lids lowered as he concentrated on torturing her tight, aching nipples. But his lips…God, his lips were damp, the tip of his tongue slowly swiping at his lower lip.

"Kiss me," she whispered.

His gaze leisurely rose to meet hers, one side of his mouth quirking up slightly. "Where?"

"Everywhere."

His nostrils flared, he flexed his jaw. He released her breasts, rinsed his hands and made sure she was soap free, as well. Then he turned off the water and grabbed a big fluffy towel off the rack.

She stepped out of the shower into the waiting towel, and he dried her off, starting with her shoulders and neck, kissing every area he dried as he went down her body. He lingered at her breasts, laving each budded nipple before circling them with the pointed tip of his tongue. She closed her eyes while he nipped and suckled and scraped with his teeth. When he got to her belly, her eyes flew open, but he startled her by not slowing. Instead, he quickly dispensed with the job of drying off the rest of her.

When she reached for the other towel to return the favor, he stopped her. Employing the same towel he'd used on her, he impatiently took on the job himself, making a swift task of it.

He surprised her yet again by slipping his arms around her, hauling her against him and kissing her thoroughly and a bit roughly, all vestiges of his illustrious control crumbling before her.

The thought that she could do that to him thrilled her. She figured it was time to give him a surprise or two, and wrapped her hand around his cock.

He jerked, uttering a guttural sound that was both primal and sexy. His already dark dilated eyes turned the color of midnight, and he stared at her as if she'd somehow betrayed him.

She didn't let up. She stroked downward, and as she came back up, found the moist crown with a sweep of her thumb. Bending to taste him, she was abruptly stopped by his hand threading through her partially damp hair. He grabbed a fistful and pulled her up, and if she hadn't willingly complied, she had a feeling he wouldn't have been gentle. The idea should have appalled her, not thrilled her.

"Wait," he said, his grip on her gradually loosening. He massaged her scalp for a moment, then lifted her chin and kissed her softly on the lips. "You're making me crazy," he whispered against her mouth. "But you know that, don't you?"

"You think I have any sanity left?" she answered breathlessly.

He smiled, his breath coming out in rasps, teasing her sensitive jaw and throat.

"Come here," he said, dragging her with one hand toward the bed and grabbing the duvet with the other.

She got the message and helped him stash the duvet then toss the myriad of decorative pillows onto a green upholstered chair. As soon as the bed was cleared off, they fell onto the sheets in a tangle of arms and legs.

"I sure hope you have condoms," she said, the thought just occurring to her.

"A whole big box." He pushed the hair away from her face and kissed her eyes, her nose, her cheeks, then rolled over and got the condoms out of the nightstand drawer and set the box next to the lamp.

Mia grinned. He wasn't kidding. It was a really big box. "Cocky bastard."

"Confident." He licked one nipple, rolled the other one around with his palm. "Big difference."

She wasn't in any mood to debate. She closed her eyes, and his hand slid to her belly, lower, pausing to trace the outline of her bikini wax as he urged her thighs apart. There was no need to ready her. She was wet and slick, and she vaguely thought to remind him again about a condom. Expecting to feel his hand, she jerked, opened her eyes when she felt his hot breath mingling with her moist heat.

When she looked down, all she saw was the top of his head. He'd forced her legs wider open without her realizing it, and maneuvered himself into position. She sucked in some air and fisted the sheets when his tongue flattened against her, then firmed and pointed to slip between her folds. He instantly found the right spot, jolting her to her core, and she bit back a cry.

She wanted to stop him. He was too good with his mouth, too precise with his tongue. She wanted them to come together. She did. But she couldn't quite make him stop, either.

As the pressure mounted, instinctively she shoved at his shoulders. He wouldn't let up. She squirmed, moaned, shoved some more, startled a minute later to discover she'd cupped her hands behind his head to urge him on.

The tremors started. Dizzying sensations shimmered through her body as the convulsion started slowly, built and built until she shattered.

He brought his head up in the middle of it, quickly sheathed himself, looming over her as he pulled her legs around his hips. He pushed into her with one deep thrust that had her bucking up to meet him. She moaned, met his next thrust by wrapping her thighs around his hips as tight as she could. He didn't stop until she begged for mercy.

MIA YAWNED AND STRETCHED, smiled when David tightened his arm around her naked waist. He lay flat on his stomach, his face buried against the side of her breast. She didn't think he was fully awake yet, kind of caught in the twilight between sleep and alertness, and she didn't want to disturb him. Neither of them had slept much.

She kept as still as possible and stared out at the clear blue morning sky. They hadn't bothered to draw the drapes. Apart from the breathtaking view, being on the top floor facing the ocean had its advantages.

Neither of the past two days seemed completely real yet. In fact, no part of her life seemed real at this point. She still hadn't accepted the idea that come Monday morning, she wouldn't be waking up at five-fifteen, donning a suit and running for the subway to make it to the office before seven. She wouldn't be seeing David, either, as she had almost every Monday for the past three years. It didn't matter that there would be no rules or ethical barrier to prevent them from seeing each other. His life was the firm, hers would be swallowed whole by Anything Goes.

It wasn't even a matter of choice on her part. The business had to succeed. It was her responsibility to make that happen after pushing hard for the idea, after convincing Lindsey and Shelby to quit their jobs. She owed them big-time.

Mia looked down at his dark, mussed-up hair, his broad muscled shoulders. How easy it had been a day or two ago to dismiss this week as a fling. No sweat, she'd reasoned. She'd been out to have a good time, a last hurrah before burying herself in work. David had blown her plans to smithereens.

God, she should have known better. Why hadn't she summoned enough good sense to run the other way? Deep down she probably had known one encounter would propel her headlong into trouble, but the temptation of him had been impossible to resist.

Silly that she'd been reluctant to have sex for the first time in the shower. How on earth had she ever thought it would only be sex? Last night they'd made love.

"'Morning," he murmured, and kissed the side of her breast.

His rough chin tickled, and she giggled. "'Morning back."

He lifted his head, and smiled down at her. "What's funny?"

She touched his face. "I've never seen you anything but clean shaven."

"You've never seen me on Sundays. I rarely shave," he said, rubbing his jaw and eyeing the spot on her breast where he'd kissed her. His gaze moved to her hardened nipple, and his face seemed to transform in a second.

Desire burned in his eyes, and he did that thing with his tongue, where the tip peeked out and dampened the center of his lower lip.

"You've got to be kidding," she said with a laugh.

"What?"

She shook her head, and curled up on her side, facing him, her thighs clamped together.

He sank back down on his pillow with a hangdog expression. "I only wanted to fool around a little."

"A little?" she asked, surprised to find that she was a bit sore. "Think we'd stop at a little?"

"I'll have you know, I have an iron will."

"Uh-huh. I'm pretty sure you lost your right to that claim last night." She caught the glint of lust and determination in his eyes just before he reached for her.

"Whose fault is that?" he asked as he wedged his knee between her thighs.

She got the giggles again. "Stop it. Right now."

"Or else?"

"Or else—" She jumped as his hand slid between her legs and accurately hit its mark. "No fair," she responded weakly.

"Tough." His mouth curved in a devilish smile as he moved in to kiss her.

She lightly bit his lower lip.

"Ouch." He ran his tongue over the abused area. "That hurt."

She knew that was a lie. "Tough."

"Okay," he said, nodding with challenge in his eyes. "You want to play rough?"

She let out a yelp and pulled the covers over her head.

He dove in after her.

DAVID FELT BADLY when he finally got it that Mia was really sore. Last night he'd been in too much of a haze to keep track of how many times they'd made love, but when he checked the box, he found there were four condoms missing.

Four times in fourteen hours. Hell, he hadn't known he still had it in him. Worse, he wanted her again. But as he'd watched her wince as she got out of bed, his conscience quelled the notion. Though he couldn't ease the absurd pride he felt, knowing that he was the first man she'd been with in a very long time.

She'd admitted as much—almost as an apology— when she begged off to take a soothing warm bath and made him promise not to bother her for at least a half hour. As much as he needed a shower himself, he wanted to give her privacy.

Coffee. That's what he wanted right now. A big pot of very strong black coffee. He yawned, rubbed his gritty eyes. Ah, hell, it was almost ten-thirty. They should probably eat, too, they'd missed dinner altogether.

He picked up the phone, thought briefly about knocking on the bathroom door to get her order, but after three years of watching her trying secretly to stash candy bars in her desk drawer, he knew she had a sweet tooth. If she didn't like what he ordered, they'd get something else.

Room service answered promptly and took his order

of coffee, orange juice, eggs Benedict and an assortment of pastries. The poor woman tried to narrow down his definition of *assortment*, but he basically told her to bring anything that was on the breakfast menu and made with sugar.

After hanging up, he moved to the patio door to look out over the ocean, stopping short of stepping onto the balcony. He didn't have a stitch on and had no desire to flash anyone. Sailboats glided across the calm water a fair distance from shore, where small waves broke gently to lap at the sand. Waikiki beach was perfect for swimming, appealing to both young and old.

To the east toward Diamond Head, a dozen or so surfers took advantage of the moderate waves. Beginners, probably. He wondered if Mia wanted to give surfing a try, although he still had quite a list of recommended sights to see on the island.

He turned around and eyed the wrecked bed, the sheets one big snarl of silk, pillows everywhere. No, they weren't going to make it through half the list at this rate, and damned if he cared. He picked up the pillows and smoothed out the sheets, trying to restore some kind of order. Room service would deliver their breakfast to the dining room through the parlor, but he didn't want the housekeeping staff to have to face this mess.

Mia's tank top and bikini bottoms were on the floor near the door, but he had no idea where the rest of her clothes—or his, for that matter—had landed. He looked under the duvet and found his swim trunks. The whereabouts of his shirt was still a mystery when his cell phone rang. He had no trouble locating it because he'd had the good sense to park it in its charger last night.

He had a strong hunch as to who was calling and

warily eyed the illuminated caller display. As he suspected, it was his father. David scrubbed a weary hand down his face. He didn't want to answer. He had nothing to report yet, and admittedly, didn't even want to think about having to talk to Mia about returning to the firm.

Aware his father wouldn't give up just because his call went to voice mail, David picked up the phone. While extending his greeting, he paced toward the bathroom door, listening to make sure Mia hadn't cut short her bath.

The pleasantries were brief. "Well, son, any news for us?"

David massaged the tension at the back of his neck. "Not yet."

A pause, and then his father asked, "Have you talked to her at all?"

"I've only been here two days."

"But you've seen her."

"Yes."

His father's lengthy silence was fraught with questions, possibly an accusation. "I hope you understand how important it is to the firm that we bank this new client."

David's patience slipped. "How can you say that to me?"

"You're right, of course." His father paused again and sighed heavily, and David pictured him pinching the bridge of his nose, frustrated and annoyed that he wasn't in control of the situation. "How's the weather there?"

David smiled. "Fine. Just fine. Look, I'll talk to her. At the right time. You have to trust me on this."

"Of course I do, son. I apologize if I seem overbearing. It's just that it's been rather tense around here lately. Peter sent out the memo yesterday regarding our decision to curtail a number of the usual amenities and the employees are beginning to ask questions. Rightfully so, but we don't have answers. No sense in further sounding the alarm."

Guilt sliced deep. He could explain that her plans for starting a new business made getting her back more complicated, but that would aggravate rather than alleviate his father's worries. Besides, that wouldn't be the entire reason behind David's stalling. "I agree" was all he could bring himself to say, especially when he didn't agree one bit. But he knew better than to try to dissuade his father from being more forthcoming with the employees. The word *layoff* wasn't in his father's vocabulary.

"Well, I guess that's it then."

"How is Mother? Everything well with her?"

"Fine, fine. She's at the Club having cocktails with Gwendolyn Mears, as we speak. Naturally I haven't burdened her with this unfortunate situation."

"No, that would be unnecessary." David smiled thinly. His parents were of a different generation, all right. His thoughts went to Mia. It wouldn't be like that with them. They'd share everything, the good and the bad. She was smart, intuitive, eager to jump in and problem-solve. He'd relied on her opinion many times; he was certain he would again.

The unbidden idea of them as a couple building a life together shocked him, but what surprised him even more was that the thought dug in to him and wouldn't let go. Longing stirred deep and fierce inside him, derailing his thoughts as they spiraled into a vortex of uncertainty and fear. He'd known for a while that she was special, and he'd long suspected there could be something big between them, but this was different, this was serious…

"David?"

He gulped in air, exhaled shakily. "Yes, sorry. I'd ordered room service. I thought I heard them knocking."

"You should go. I have nothing more." Another pause. "Before we hang up, anything I should know?"

David cleared his throat. "Everything is under control."

They hung up, and he stood motionless for a good minute, staring out at the endless sea. He finally tossed the cell phone on the nightstand and took a shuddering breath. Then he turned and saw Mia standing outside the bathroom, bundled in the thick white courtesy robe, her gaze curious. Or was that suspicion?

10

DAVID DID A QUICK MENTAL REPLAY of the end of his phone conversation and decided he hadn't said anything detrimental. He blinked away his guilt, determined that neither his father nor his responsibility to the firm was going to steal this moment away from him. Then he saw her wet, with straight hair, and her skin—devoid of makeup—was smooth and dewy. But it was her startlingly emerald-green eyes that got him every time.

"Is everything okay?" Mia cinched the belt of her robe, her gaze lowering to his bare chest, to his belly, to his cock. She moistened her lips.

That's all it took for him to start getting hard. "Don't worry, you're safe," he said. "Room service is on their way so I won't be jumping you. At least not in the next hour."

Her smile didn't reach her eyes. "You have to go back, don't you?"

He'd started for the bathroom to grab the other robe, but he stopped, frowning. "Go back?"

"To New York. The phone call, I thought—" She shrugged sheepishly. "I wasn't listening. I just walked out here, but from the look on your face I was sure your vacation had been cut short."

"No, it was my father, but—" He took her hand and pulled her close to press a light kiss to her lips. "It was nothing. I'm not going anywhere."

"Good." She looped her arms around his neck and moved her hips against him.

"Ah, being brave because you know we're about to be interrupted."

Her smile was real this time. "Uh-huh."

"You underestimate me." He jerked the robe's belt free.

She let out a shriek of laughter, gathered the lapels together and backed away. "I need coffee. I need food. I seriously need to recover. Have mercy."

"I'd rather have Mia."

"Funny."

A gap in the robe exposed the tempting curve of her right breast, and he had to hold very still. So much for his grand plan to take it slowly. "I have time for a quick shower. Room service will come to the parlor door. Do me a favor and sign for it, please?"

"I'll listen for them," she said, and gave him a pat on his ass as he turned for the bathroom.

David chuckled and shot her a warning look before he closed the door behind him. Too late he realized he should've brought clean clothes in with him. The other robe hung on the back of the door, but he wanted to be dressed and ready to hit the road as soon as they were done eating breakfast. It would be too easy to crawl back into bed with her.

He doubted she'd resist, and her being sore wasn't the issue—he knew how to please her without burying himself inside of her. But that's not how he wanted to spend the rest of their time together. Every minute counted. Once he presented the firm's offer, their relationship had to be on stable ground.

After turning on the shower, he fiddled with the spray control and waited for the temperature to be just right before he got in. He lifted his face to the jetting water. The force was harsh and stung his skin, but he left it alone. The punishment was mild, he decided, but with any luck, strong enough to wash away his lingering guilt.

BY THE TIME THEY HAD EATEN, gotten dressed and Mia had touched base with Shelby and Lindsey, it was already early afternoon. Although David had planned an outing to the north shore of the island via a picnic and swim at Waimea Falls, Mia nixed the idea in favor of sticking closer to Waikiki. She was worn out, feeling lazy and really curious why David seemed determined to fill their every waking hour with a planned activity.

When she suggested taking a long walk down the beach and then finding an outside bar to have a drink, he'd immediately countered with a proposal to first visit 'Iolani Palace and the Bishop Museum, both relatively short drives from the hotel. She agreed, and actually enjoyed the outing, especially the tour of 'Iolani Palace, the only true royal palace used as a residence by a reigning monarch and standing on American soil.

Naturally David opted for the guided tour, which she admitted was informative and fascinating, but as soon as the tour ended and they left the palace, he was ready to hop in the car and head for the Bishop Museum. She put on the brakes, grabbing his hand and forcing him to sit beside her on a shaded stone bench.

"You do realize that you're the kind of person who gives us New Yorkers a bad name," she told him, dismayed that he immediately slipped his sunglasses out of his pocket and slid them on. God, she didn't want to believe that he regretted their lovemaking, and really, there was little evidence that he did—he'd even held her hand most of the afternoon—but still, a surprising jolt of insecurity hit her hard.

"What do you mean?"

"Rushing around like you have a million deadlines."

He smiled ruefully. "I wouldn't call it rushing. Didn't you enjoy the tour?"

"Yes, but I wouldn't mind kicking back, too. We have stressful jobs. Well, *you* do. I did." She sighed, hating that she was getting flustered. But something didn't feel right between them.

She'd noticed the change in him after his shower. They'd talked some during breakfast, but he'd hurried through that, too, claiming he wanted to leave so that housekeeping could clean the suite. It was almost as if he didn't want to be alone with her, or have too much free time to talk. Was he worried that she expected they'd spend every night together? Or that she'd monopolize his time? Maybe she should've begged off doing anything with him today and given him some space.

It took a while, as if his mind was working on overdrive, but he finally responded. "Sounds to me like you have regrets."

"What?" Her heart thudded. "About last night?"

"No." He reared his head back, his furrowed brows

reflecting his bewilderment. "No, I meant about quitting the firm."

"How did you get that idea?"

His lips lifted in a weary smile. "Guess we're both too exhausted to make much sense."

She frowned, trying to think back on what she'd said. Recalling her rambling, she returned the tired smile. "I'm still trying to wrap my brain around the fact that I won't be showing up at the office on Monday. Even worse, how much unchartered, scary territory lays ahead of me." She wished she hadn't admitted the scary part, but it was already out there.

"You're going to do great," he said, closing his hand on hers and giving it a reassuring squeeze. "I've seen you in action. You put your mind to something and it's a done deal."

"Yeah, I've always been pretty goal-oriented." She made a show of unnecessarily shading her eyes, and then took her dark glasses out of her purse and hid behind them. "I'll have zero life, but I'll make the business work."

He barely reacted, only moved his shoulder ambiguously. "Didn't you just tell me you didn't have one before?"

She swallowed the disappointment that rose in her throat. "True," she said lightly, mentally chiding herself. What had she expected? For him to declare that he'd be filling her evenings with romantic dinners and tangled sheets? Nothing would change once they returned. Not only did she already know that, but it's what she wanted. What had to be. With their schedules, there could be no happy medium.

Oh, she knew they could grab a quickie now and then, but after last night, the thought was a bit painful.

"You're quiet," he said, using his thumb to trace an idle pattern against her palm.

"Just enjoying the warm breeze and flowers. Can you believe it's still March?" She abruptly stood. "Come on. Let's go back to the hotel and walk on the beach."

There it was again. At the suggestion, he'd immediately tensed. But why?

"What about the Bishop Museum?" he asked, slowly getting to his feet. "We have only four full days left and a lot more to see."

"Really?" Whether it was his unconvincing tone of voice or the way he defensively jerked one shoulder, she didn't buy it. "You're that interested in the history and culture of the state?"

He heaved a heartfelt sigh. "No."

"Then what?"

Mirroring her frustration, he said, "I don't want you to think that all I want from you is sex."

He hadn't seen the older couple wearing matching loud Hawaiian shirts approach from behind him. As if they'd overheard, they exchanged knowing smiles and, holding hands, veered toward the next bench.

Mia pursed her lips, trying not to laugh, but it turned out it wasn't hard to sober. Something about the couple's shared smiles and the familiar way they touched stirred a wistfulness in Mia's chest that took her by surprise. She looked away from them, unsettled, because she hadn't known she craved that closeness, the kind bred only by years of talking and touching and waking up together in the same bed. *Not now, for God's sake.*

Shaking his head, David groaned, and then gave a resigned chuckle.

Mia pulled herself together, looped an arm through his and steered them in the direction of the car. "Uh, excuse me, Mr. Pearson, but were you there last night?" He only smiled, patiently waited for her to zing him. "I'm pretty sure my participation was rather enthusiastic."

"What I meant was that I don't want you to think that is the only reason why I came to Hawaii."

"To get laid?" She spoke quietly so no one could hear her teasing. "Come on, if that were true, it would have been a lot cheaper to find a date in Manhattan."

David abruptly stopped, forced her to face him. He wore the most awful expression, part angry, part offended.

"Hey, I was only teasing."

He slowly removed his sunglasses, making her wait as if she were a recalcitrant child and he, the long-suffering teacher struggling to compose himself before he meted out suitable punishment. "Look, *Ms. Butterfield*, let's be clear." He startled her by plucking off her sunglasses, too.

She blinked at the unexpected glare, then swallowed at the spellbinding intensity in his brown eyes as they met hers and held on.

He touched her cheek. "I came here because of you, and only you. I won't lie, the sex was phenomenal. That's part of the problem." He smiled a little. "We need to stay the hell away from the hotel and private beaches or anywhere else where I can get away with stripping you naked and doing wicked things to you, or there is no question how the rest of this week is going to end up."

His seductive words and the dark lusty gleam in his

eyes made her body feel all warm and tingly, and her mouth go dry. Not the same predicament down south. She unconsciously squeezed her thighs together as if that would make a difference. If he wanted to get down to business right now in the convertible parked off a busy Honolulu street, she had a nasty suspicion she'd let him.

He studied her face. "You have nothing to say?"

She moistened her parched lips. "I'm still trying to figure out why, exactly, that would be a problem?"

"Jesus." He briefly closed his eyes. "Come on," he said, taking her by the arm. He was already getting hard. She could see the evidence building behind his fly.

"Where are we going?" she asked, all innocence. "The Bishop Museum?"

His smoldering gaze was all the response she needed.

THE BALCONY OFF the suite's bedroom was the perfect spot for watching the sunset. No matter how clear the day had been, a handful of clouds always seemed to gather over the horizon in time to turn the sky a vivid rainbow of pinks and oranges and salmons.

Mia lazily stretched her bare legs out to the railing as she turned to watch David, who was sitting beside her, digging the macadamia nuts out of his vanilla ice cream.

"Are you going to eat that or play with it?"

"What are you, my mother?"

She laughed. "I'm jealous. I finished mine five minutes ago."

He paused long enough to cock a wary brow at her. "I'm not sharing."

"You would if I asked nicely," she said in a sweet voice.

"Of course I would, so of course you wouldn't." He popped one of the nuts into his mouth for emphasis.

"Why *are* you doing that?" She'd watched the same ritual yesterday and it drove her crazy. "It's not as though you're not going to end up eating everything anyway."

"I know."

"So?"

"Cheap therapy. It calms me."

Mia rolled her eyes. "That's what you said about having sex three times in two hours."

He grinned. "That works, too."

She shook her head in mock disapproval and settled back to enjoy the sunset and let him finish his ice cream. After their talk at 'Iolani Palace two days ago, the frantic pace had ended, and every minute had been sheer bliss. It didn't matter if they were simply walking along the beach or making love or picking out that ridiculous souvenir for Annabelle on the couch, or just sitting here as they were now, eating ice cream as the sun dipped. It was all good. Perfect even. Better. Mia couldn't recall a time she'd felt more content.

"Here."

She turned her head to look at him. He held a spoonful of ice cream to her lips. She grinned. "Sucker."

He ate the last bite himself, and then set the empty foam cup next to hers on the small side table. "When it comes to you…"

That he was so serious, so matter-of-fact, made Mia's pulse flutter. "I was teasing," she said lamely.

He smiled, stretched back on his lounge chair

and locked his hands behind his head. "What time is dinner?"

"Dinner?" She frowned, scrambling to figure out what she'd missed. "Oh, the birthday dinner. You were still in the shower when I talked to Lindsey and Shelby this morning. Sorry I forgot to tell you, but we canceled it altogether."

"Why? I thought it was tradition."

"Not canceled, really. We postponed again."

"Hope I didn't have anything to do with it." He seemed troubled by the prospect.

Which she totally adored about him. A lot of guys would've selfishly tried to manipulate her into feeling guilty for deserting them for an evening. "Nope. We decided to wait until we go back to New York." She shrugged. "Shelby's birthday isn't until next week."

"But yours was January twenty-ninth."

"And Lindsey's was on February twenty-fifth." Mia paused, narrowing her gaze on him. "How did you know when mine was?"

"Must've heard people wishing you a happy birthday."

"No way. The admin staff celebrate with cakes or lunches out, but the attorneys—even us baby attorneys—never make a big deal out of our birthdays."

He shrugged, laid his head back and stared at the sunset. A slow smile curved his mouth. "I might have looked it up."

Mia laughed. "I didn't get flowers. Oh, wait. You just wanted to know my sign."

"Your sign?" He swung his leg onto her lounge chair and used his bare toes to torture the sole of her foot.

"Stop it," she said giggling. Damn it, he knew how

ticklish she was there. "Hey, I'm an Aquarian, which means payback's a bitch." She kicked his foot away. "Just so you know."

"Hmm, I didn't know that about Aquarians," he said, laughing.

"You apparently don't know anything about them. I lied. If anything, we're loyal to a fault."

"Okay, what else do the cards say about you?" He jerked his chair closer, and she quickly protected her feet.

"No cards. We're talking about astrological signs."

"Sorry I got my occults mixed up."

"Fine." She sniffed. "Mock me, but you'd be surprised at the accuracy of the descriptions."

"What surprises me is that you follow that stuff."

"It's not as if I read my daily horoscope. I was a kid when I learned about what the different signs mean. Naturally I was curious about mine and if the description applied to me."

"Obviously it did, hence your interest. Tell me about it."

"So you can make fun of me some more?"

Smiling, he reached over to rub her arm. "No, I won't. Now I'm curious."

She eyed him for a moment. "I'm supposed to be outgoing, amiable, highly organized," she said, and he nodded. "I'm always thinking, both a good and bad thing I've discovered. Aquarians are also humanitarians." She tried not to smile as she waited for his reaction.

He snorted. "I'll vouch for that one. You racked up more pro bono hours than any three associates combined."

"So you've reminded me, more than once as I recall. But you never said no."

"You also clocked more billable hours than the rest, and you never once let our paying clients suffer. I couldn't justify saying no." His eyes went flat, and he turned to stare at the sunset. "Your leaving is a major loss for the firm."

She'd been unprepared for the sudden change in his mood. Nice that he acknowledged her professional value, but had he forgotten that the only reason they were here now was because she was no longer an employee?

Mia cleared her throat. "I'm not sure what to say to that. Thanks, I guess."

He stretched his neck to one side, and then the other, staying silent for too long. Then he sighed and looked over at her. His smile wasn't off, not by much, but she could see it. "Tell me more about your sign."

Back to neutral territory. She could live with that. "Of course there are some gray areas. I'm supposed to be objective and not swayed by emotion."

"You don't think that's true?"

"Legally speaking, I can be very objective, but personally, not so much." Instantly she wished she could recall the admission. She hadn't meant to share that much. An hour ago, maybe it would've been all right, but she hated the way the old David was looking at her with those unreadable eyes. The mask was firmly in place, not a hint of emotion revealed.

She turned away, shrugged, tried to shake off her resentment. "I'm also supposed to be happiest when I have a goal, which is completely accurate. I'm looking forward to the challenge of Anything Goes."

His leg was still on her chaise, and he moved his foot

to stroke her calf. "I know it won't be easy, getting the business off the ground," he said, "but I admire the hell out of you for going after your dream like this. Still, it's nice that you have the side job."

It took a second to realize he meant his assumption about her working for a smaller firm. Damn, she wished he hadn't brought that up. How long could she get away with lying by omission? It shouldn't make any difference. This wasn't a romance, it was a week of fun. So why hadn't she told him the truth?

Puzzled and a little sad, she tried to pull together a smile, but she knew it would only ring false. It was time to stop playing games.

11

DAVID STARED AT HER in total astonishment. She'd quit practicing law? He had to have misunderstood. She was the smartest, most promising attorney Pearson and Stern had hired in nearly a decade. "I thought you got a position at a smaller, less demanding firm."

"I know you did." She nibbled at her lower lip. "I'm thirsty," she said, nudging his leg aside and rising from the chaise. "There still should be a couple of colas in the fridge. Want one?"

"Mia, wait." He saw that she had no intention of humoring him, so he followed her into the bedroom, through the parlor to the wet bar. "Why did you want me to think you were working for another firm?"

"I didn't." She took a long time poking around the small refrigerator before producing two cans. "You assumed, and I didn't correct you. It seemed like a good idea at the time."

Shit. His gut clenched. This was bad. For him. For Mia. But he couldn't overreact. For someone who was supposed to be quick on his feet, he couldn't think of a damn thing to say.

"I know you're disappointed." She handed him an ice cold can. Funny, he thought he was too numb to feel it. "I'm sure I've disappointed a lot of people, not the least of whom will be my parents. They won't understand how I could go through three tough years of law school and pay all that tuition, and then walk away." She pressed the can to her flushed face. "Can we not talk about this right now?"

So she hadn't told her parents yet. Interesting. He took the can from her and set it beside his on the bar. Then he sat on one of the tall stools with his legs spread and pulled her close. "You have better instincts than almost anyone I know. That quality is part of what's made you such a damn good lawyer." He lifted her chin when she tried to stare at her toes, and saw her eyes fill with glassy confusion. "Only you know what's right for you. I support your decision." Even as he uttered the words, panic rose in his throat. He forced a smile. "Not that you asked."

"Oh, David." She threw her arms around him and hugged him tight. "That means a lot," she said, her voice a broken whisper as she buried her face against his neck. "Thank you."

He closed his eyes, stroked her back, kissed her hair. Her shoulders trembled slightly, and he knew she was fighting back tears. She was a strong woman. It couldn't be easy for her to become so emotional, and all he wanted to do was ease the hurt and suffering she'd experienced in reaching her life-altering decision. As incomprehensible as it was that she could throw away such a promising career, he meant what he'd told her. He did support her.

He had no choice. Damn it, he loved her, he realized

with a sinking sensation at total odds with the discovery. Probably had loved her for longer than he cared to admit.

Now what the fuck was he going to tell his father?

MIA LET HIM SLOWLY UNDRESS HER. She closed her eyes and deeply breathed in his warm, masculine scent as he stopped to kiss the shoulder he'd exposed and then the top of each breast as he drew the cotton sundress down her body. She felt drained from finally confessing the truth, and doubted she had the energy to do much more than slip between the sheets. Until it had become clear the discussion was inevitable, she hadn't fully appreciated how frightened she was that the truth would disappoint him, make him think less of her.

She'd never dreamed he would be this accepting. It wasn't as if she hadn't seen the shock on his face. Or the pleading denial in his eyes, the moment of hope that he'd misunderstood. For someone like David, who lived and breathed every intricacy of the law, she'd been convinced it would be impossible for him to understand her decision. Smiling to herself, she realized that was absolutely true. He could make no logical sense of it, probably thought she was certifiable, but that made his acceptance all the sweeter.

With a start, she saw that he'd stripped off his clothes—she was already naked—and he was trying to pick her up. "What are you doing?" she asked, although she figured it out a second later.

She grinned, but ended up gasping when he swept her off the floor and into his arms. The trip to the bed was only a few feet, and she smiled when he laid her atop the sheets. She threaded her fingers through his hair and pulled him down for a quick kiss. "Why did you do that?"

He sat at the edge of the bed and massaged her scalp. "You look wiped out." He shrugged, a teasing smile tugging at the corners of his mouth. "I wanted to be your big, strong hero."

Mia laughed.

He feigned a pout. "Ouch."

"Ah, let me kiss it and make it better." She curled up and put her lips to the crown of his penis.

He jerked. "Hey."

"You're complaining?"

He looked serious. "Yeah, I am. I'm supposed to be taking care of you," he said, despite the fact his cock was already hardening. He glanced down, his mouth twisting wryly. "I can't do anything about that."

Mia tried to keep a straight face, remembering something her brothers used to tease each other about. "Maybe if you think about going blind and getting hairy palms?"

David smiled, touched her hair and the tip of her chin, then lightly dragged the pads of his fingers down between her breasts. But it was the tenderness in his eyes that sobered her. Warmth flushed her body, and if she had to speak she didn't think she could do it. Her mouth was too dry, her tongue felt like a lead weight. It took her a few seconds to figure out the frightening pressure in her chest was from holding her breath.

Without warning he rose. She was about to plead for him to stay when he gently nudged her to move over, and stretched out beside her. He lay on his back and slid a comforting arm around her as he urged her to lay her cheek on his chest. She snuggled close, and rested a palm on one of his flat, brown nipples, which firmed beneath her touch. She smiled when she saw that his arousal had not yet subsided. Not for a second did she doubt that she could tempt him into making love to her, but for now it was nice just to be held.

Annabelle was never going to believe this. David. Here in Hawaii. When Mia filled her in it would be the "G" version, of course.

Mia had no idea where the thought had come from, and she didn't even know when the older woman would return from her trip. No, in a way it made sense she'd think about Annabelle now, weird as it seemed. Their talks in the park had always been soothing, a balm to Mia's confused senses, and right now, she couldn't begin to explain the serenity she felt.

Listening to the steady rhythm of his heartbeat against her ear, she closed her eyes, drowsy from the heat, the comfort of his closeness, the awe of his unconditional acceptance. When he skimmed a hand down her back, over the curve of her hip, then lightly cupped her bottom, she felt a stir of excitement in her belly.

She lifted her head and moved her hand away from his chest.

His gaze narrowed. "Where are you going?"

"Nowhere." Pointing the tip of her tongue, she touched it to his already hard nipple.

He tensed. "I thought you were tired."

"I was." She kissed the warm skin right below. "Evidently big, strong heroes get me hot." She moved her mouth to his lean, taut belly, pressed a kiss there. Used her tongue to circle his navel, smiled when he sucked in his stomach.

When her exploration took her too near to his swelling

penis, he curled up, took her by both arms and dragged her mouth to his. "I want to be inside you," he whispered, his voice raw with emotion.

The intensity of it made her tremble as she automatically reached for the box of condoms on the opposite nightstand. She kept her face averted because it terrified her to witness his expression. This man, who was an expert at hiding any hint of feeling, had never sounded more vulnerable.

She tore the packet open and assumed the task of sheathing him, keeping her focus on what she was doing, knowing that he watched her, that his eyes could tell her more than she might want to acknowledge. Already on sensory overload, she refused to look up, even as she felt the weight of his gaze willing her to do so.

He put both hands on either side of her waist and lifted her up until she straddled him. She still managed to avoid his eyes—instead her gaze rested on the curve of his mouth. The smile was different than any he'd given her before, gentle yet unnervingly determined.

He touched her, found that she was wet, lingered there, teasing her, then entered her with two long, lean fingers. She quivered, let her eyes briefly close and pressed against him.

"No, inside," he murmured, low in his throat, and withdrew. He urged her into position, his cock poised to accept her as she slid onto him, slowly, taking him in gradually.

The hands that cupped her hips shook, and his face tensed. She clenched her muscles around him, and he threw back his head, the veins on his neck pronounced.

"One day," he said, his voice thin and raspy, "we

won't need condoms." And then he thrust into her, his reference to the future knocking her emotionally off balance.

A DAY LATER, Mia sat beside David, five rows from the stage, watching the hula dancers use their hands and hips to tell the story of ill-fated lovers. Great. Mia's favorite topic lately. She slumped in her seat, and ordered herself to enjoy the performance.

When David had suggested they visit the Polynesian Cultural Center on the other side of the island, she hadn't balked. Not just because they'd had quite a bit of lazy beach time, but she knew it was going to be a tough day. It was their last full day in Hawaii, and she didn't want to have too much time to think and get all mopey.

Her overactive mind had become her enemy. She still found it difficult to comprehend how graciously he'd accepted her decision to give up her law career.

Maybe he figured her disillusionment was temporary, and she'd eventually come around. There was no way to know, and she'd only make herself crazy second-guessing his reaction. One thing she did know for sure was that something was off. He was a bit quieter yesterday and today, more introspective. But so was she as the time to leave got closer.

And then there was the remark about not needing a condom one day. Yet something else to keep the wheels spinning out of control. So far she'd settled on two interpretations. One was strictly clinical, the other meant that he was thinking in terms of the long haul. Either possibility suggested that he planned to continue their affair in New York. But then again, he hadn't said a word to that end.

It shouldn't bother her since she'd already decided there would be no room in her life for a man. Except this wasn't any man. This was David. It all seemed so unfair—

Oh, God, she really had to get over herself. No, it wasn't fair. The timing was awful and who knew what she'd have done if she'd even guessed. But this was her reality, and the sooner she stopped the nonsense about fairness, the better. She had right now, and she'd be a damn fool not to enjoy it to the fullest.

She inhaled deeply, delighted with the perfumed air, and let her breath out slowly. By the time she repeated the relaxation technique she'd learned during her first court appearance, the song ended and a new set of dancers took the stage, accompanied by the heart-pounding primal beating of native drums. Three very fit, half-naked, brown-skinned Polynesian men using their open palms on the drums had pulled her back to the present.

But it was the swift movement of the Tahitian dancers' hips that had her leaning forward and staring in awe. "Good grief, they look as if they've been plugged in."

"I thought you'd fallen asleep."

"I might have been nodding off a bit during the hula dancing," she lied. Then she cast David an accusing glance. "Guess who's to blame for keeping me up most of the night."

A smile of pure male satisfaction curved his mouth. "I didn't hear you complaining."

She bit back a grin and glanced around to make sure no one had overheard them. There were about two hundred people in the audience, but the drums were loud and everyone's attention seemed to be glued to the dancers.

"I wish we could've talked Shelby into coming with us," she said, knowing that was a half truth.

As soon as the sun had gone down and the torches were lit, everything about the place seemed to change. By day, the cultural center, with its simulated tropical villages and authentic arts and craft demonstrations, was both educational and entertaining. But now that she'd started to relax, sitting in the dimness of the half-open pavilion, the warm air scented by a panoply of flowering trees that grew profusely around the grounds, she had to admit that the setting was very romantic.

He slid an arm around her shoulders, and she gladly leaned against him. "We can bring her tomorrow if you like. We only got to see half the attractions."

She pulled away to look at him. "Did you forget we leave tomorrow?"

"How could I?" He seemed to stare sightlessly at the dancers for a few moments, and then captured her gaze. "What if we stay an extra day?"

The unexpected suggestion was like a splash of cold water in her face. "How? I mean, we both have to get back. There are deadlines—"

"Understood."

She shook her head. "I don't see how it's possible."

"It is if we—"

Someone from behind shushed them. Rightfully so. Mia sent the woman a smile of apology, and turned back to stare at the dancers, her thoughts tumbling even more wildly than they had earlier.

When it finally occurred to her that she was oblivious

to what was happening on stage, she whispered, "We should go."

He nodded, and as unobtrusively as possible they slipped out of their seats and hurried to the sidewalk. When they got to a fork, she started to go right, but he took her hand and led her to the left. Within seconds she saw the parking lot.

"I hope you don't mind that I wanted to leave," she said, spotting his rental near the entrance. "I didn't even ask you."

"No, good call. We have about an hour and a half drive back to Waikiki."

"Really? It took that long to get here?"

"Yep," he said. "I guess I should've considered that when I booked the dinner show."

"No, I'm glad we came. It would've been a shame to have missed seeing what we did today."

"Next time we'll have to plan better and come early." The keys were already in his hand, and he used the remote to unlock the doors.

Mia watched him open her door, her pulse leaping, even though she was annoyed. How could he say something like that and still act so casually? Damn him. He couldn't keep alluding to the future and then let the tension hang over them like a threatening rain cloud. Finally she couldn't stand it. "There is no next time. We leave tomorrow."

He flinched, or at least she thought he had. Maybe he was baiting her, trying to force her to make a declaration. Her breath caught at the thought. When the silence got too thick, she slipped by him to get into the car.

David caught her around the waist. His arm snug around her, he bent to kiss her gently but all too briefly.

Then he gave her a tender smile that made her heart catch, and she instantly forgave him. "I'm being an ass," he said. "But I don't want this week to end."

Mia's chest tightened. "I don't, either."

"The difference is, you're not being a baby about it."

"Trust me, inside I am."

"Good." He nuzzled the side of her neck. "So maybe I can talk you into staying one more day."

She sighed. "First off, it would be too expensive to change our tickets."

"I'll take care of that."

"No," she said firmly. "Anyway, it's not only about the money." She snorted ruefully. "Although in my current position, I can't be cavalier about finances, either. Bottom line, we both have full schedules waiting for us back in New York, and that's not going to change."

But this would, she thought, when he hugged her tighter and kissed her hair. She closed her eyes, felt his quickened heartbeat against her breastbone, heard his muffled sigh. He knew she was right. Delaying the inevitable was foolish, but perhaps now was the time to discuss what would happen after they returned. At the thought, her insides coiled into one big knot.

He released her, waited until she was seated and then closed her door. His silence unsettled her.

After he was behind the wheel and started the ignition, in a light, joking tone, she said, "I can't figure out if taking this week off was a good idea or not. I'd almost forgotten that there's more to life than work."

She stared at his unyielding profile, waiting for him to respond. Whether or not he'd figured out she was fishing for a reaction, he said nothing.

AN HOUR AFTER they'd returned to Waikiki, David ordered a bottle of Mia's favorite chardonnay and chocolate-dipped strawberries from room service, while he waited for her to return with clean clothes from her room. This was their last night in Hawaii together. It should have been perfect, full of romance and promises whispered in the dark, velvety night. Instead, he had never felt more conflicted in his entire life.

Pearson and Stern needed her like a baby needed its mother's milk, and Mia wanted nothing more to do with the law. She was totally convinced she'd been on the wrong career path. He couldn't disagree more. How could she have been such a brilliant attorney? Her instincts were spot-on, every time. He'd learned quickly that he didn't have to second-guess her decisions. In that regard, his judgment had nothing to do with his cock.

Naturally, because all of that wasn't complicated enough, he'd fallen in love with her. He wanted her to follow her dream and be happy, but he owed his father and the firm his loyalty. It wasn't just a matter of the practice losing money. Jobs were at stake in a time when every job was critical. So where did that leave him and Mia?

His right hand started to ache. He stared down at it, and found that he'd clenched it into a fist. He opened his hand, flexed his fingers. He wasn't a man who sought answers in violence, but a large part of him wanted to smash every piece of art in the suite. Nice.

After staring at the city lights from the parlor window, he paced restlessly to the bedroom balcony, slowing briefly to grab the drink he'd forgotten he poured off the bar. Maybe if he put on some music he could relax.

Who was he kidding? He wouldn't relax until Mia came back, until she was in his arms. They would have a great night together. He wouldn't ruin it by thinking about work, much less laying the firm's problems on Mia's lap. After he returned to New York, he'd find a way to land the new client without involving Mia. His father would be disappointed at first, but—

He heard her soft knock and smiled. Although he'd given her her own key card, she never used it. He opened the door. She stood there with her small carry-on, her eyes bright. Too bright. Had she been crying? He drew her inside, got rid of the bag and held her face in his hands. They looked deeply into each other's eyes. Once he started kissing her, he couldn't stop.

12

AFTER MISSING THE final boarding call and being summoned by an airline employee, Mia lumbered toward the jetway with the enthusiasm of a woman about to be thrown in the slammer. She had no choice but to get on the plane and join Shelby, who'd boarded earlier, or forgo the flight, and pay a lot of extra money just to be put on a standby list tomorrow.

While the clerk validated Mia's boarding pass, Mia itched to turn around for one last look at David. He'd driven her and Shelby to the airport, even though his flight wouldn't leave for five hours. Mia had begged him not to because it was silly for him to hang around the airport when he could be sitting at the pool bar, but he'd shut her up by kissing her soundly and that was that.

The woman smiled, returned the boarding pass. Mia hesitated. As much as she wanted that last look, she was feeling ridiculously emotional, and wouldn't it be just wonderful if she got all teary. For God's sake, this wasn't a goodbye. Not really. He'd be in New York tomorrow. Poor guy had to take a red-eye flight home, which was the only last-minute seat he could get.

Mia turned one last time, to see him put his cell phone to his ear. He wasn't even looking her way, his concentration fully on the call. Smiling at herself, she kept on going. All that should-I-or-shouldn't-I nonsense for nothing.

Since she was the last passenger, some of the ground crew were right behind her, and she hurried on board. The flight was full, and she peered down the aisle toward the middle of the plane, searching for Shelby. Due to David's failed effort to get on Mia's flight, she already knew it would be a shoulder-to-shoulder ride to Dallas, where she and Shelby each had to catch separate connecting flights since Shelby had to go back to Houston for two days.

Just as Mia started to pay attention to seat numbers, Shelby put up her hand to get her attention, and bless her, she'd left the aisle seat for Mia.

"Hey, I thought for sure you were going to miss the flight," Shelby said, as Mia opened two overhead bins and, not surprisingly, found them full.

"I almost did. They were about to page the first person on standby." Mia shut the bin, and sighed, eyeing the vacancy under the seat in front of hers.

Shelby drew up her much shorter legs and indicated the empty spot in front of her. "Put your carry-on there."

"You sure?"

"It won't bother me. You'll never have room for your legs."

"Thanks." Mia stowed her stuff, sat down and buckled up.

"Well, obviously David couldn't exchange his ticket. Sorry."

Mia shrugged. "He was even willing to give up his first-class seat, but both our flights were oversold, with long standby lists. And then, the real kicker, we finally realized he'd flown with a different carrier."

Shelby chuckled. "Yeah, that would be a problem. Oh, well, it's not like he's staying and you're leaving. You'll see him when he gets back."

Mia inhaled deeply.

"Right?"

She shrugged. "Yep, he said he'd call."

"Okay, there is something hugely wrong with this picture." Shelby twisted in her seat so that she faced Mia. "An hour ago you two were all over each other, now this act of indifference. Which, by the way, I don't buy for a second."

"We weren't all over each other," Mia said crisply, though she should've known better than to let her guard down and not act as if everything were perfect. She didn't need a barrage of questions from Shelby.

Her friend settled back. "You know I would've given my seat to him," she said, "but the movers will be at my apartment early tomorrow morning, and I have to be there."

Feeling guilty, Mia smiled. "Then you'll drive to New York the day after."

"Yep, I'm still bringing my car. I know it's probably crazy, and who knows, I may end up getting rid of it. Hey, did you get another text from Lindsey?"

"No, but I assume she booked another flight before she canceled today's." Lindsey was staying a few days longer, which initially pissed off Mia, until she realized her reaction was one of pure jealousy and not because they had a lot of work waiting for them.

"One would hope." Shelby's brows arched in amusement. "I think the girl's in love."

"Seriously?"

"Have you ever seen her act like she has this week?"

"You have a point." Mia worried her lip. Lindsey had always been more shy and not as invested in the college dating scene. Mia knew she was being selfish, but she hoped their friend's involvement with Rick didn't screw up their plans for the new business.

As if she'd read Mia's mind, Shelby sighed. "I can see it now. You two riding off into the sunset with your respective hunks, and me left to juggle Anything Goes."

Mia shook her head. "Lindsey maybe. It's not like that with David and me."

Shelby's gaze narrowed in an expectant frown. She waited as if there were supposed to be a punch line. "It's not like that with you and David?" She laughed. "You are so full of crap."

"I'm telling you, it was nothing. We were in Hawaii. No obligations, no hectic schedule. We had fun. I hope we'll still be friends." She shrugged. "I think we will."

Shelby's hazel eyes darkened with concern. "You almost sound like you believe that."

"I do. We're going to be very busy. I don't have time for him, and frankly, he won't have time for me." Mia made a show of getting comfortable, laying her head back and closing her eyes. "Think I'll grab a nap."

She knew Shelby was still staring, and she could keep staring until they landed in Dallas, for all Mia cared. She wasn't ready to have this conversation. She was too emotionally raw. Despite her brave words, she was a mess.

DAVID WAS SURPRISED to see his uncle Harrison's office door open at seven-thirty the next morning. After a brief knock, he entered as his uncle's head came up. Harrison set aside the contract he'd been perusing and stared at David over his reading glasses. "You look like hell."

"Red-eye, and I haven't been home yet." He wore the same clothes he had worn on the plane, khakis along with a yellow tennis shirt under a navy sports jacket. Totally inappropriate attire, but this was too important to delay.

Harrison anxiously glanced past him. "Is she here with you?"

"No. We had different flights." It was impossible, David knew, for someone to have visibly aged in the span of eight days, but his uncle's face looked drawn, his hair thinner and grayer, the combination packing a good five years on him. Most notable, however, was his cluttered desk. The man never tolerated anything out of place.

His dark eyes grew bleak. "She turned us down," Harrison said flatly.

David chose his words carefully. "She doesn't want to practice law anymore."

"What? How could she not want to practice law? She's brilliant. She's—Jesus. This doesn't make sense." He shook his head as if the act alone would turn the tide. "I thought she signed on with another firm."

"That had been my assumption, as well."

"So she doesn't have another job?" Harrison's frown lifted with hope.

"Not exactly. She's starting her own business." David checked his watch. He didn't have much time. "Look, I've been trying to get in touch with my father but he won't pick up his cell, and I've gotten the house's answering machine twice."

"He's with your mother," he said distractedly while staring out of his large plate glass window overlooking the Manhattan skyline. "Some charity golf thing in the Caymans."

"If I'd known about that, I'd forgotten." This time David reached for hope. "I'm surprised he'd leave. Something happen I should know about? Did we land another client?"

"No lifelines. You know he doesn't want to worry your mother, so he couldn't back out." His uncle leaned back in his chair and met David's eyes. "He had a lot of faith in you getting Butterfield back, figured you'd buy us some time."

Guilt cut deep. David had a lot of nerve wondering how his father could have left. Not when he himself had been gone a whole week, cavorting with Mia. "I know." David rubbed his stubbly jaw. He desperately needed a shave and a shower. "I want this prospective client's name and number."

His uncle's eyes narrowed. "Of course, but why?"

"I want to meet with him myself. If I can't convince him that we're the best firm for the job, then I'll take another run at Mia."

Harrison shook his head. "You're wasting your time. Your father and I have both met with his current attorney. The man's quite adamant."

David hadn't slept for one minute on the plane, and he was dead tired. Briefly he closed his eyes and scrubbed at his face. "I have to try," he said, not missing the curious gleam in Harrison's eye. "Anyway, what's the harm?"

"You have to ask?" His uncle pointedly looked past him through the open door. "Time isn't on our side, David."

He looked over his shoulder. It was still early, but quite a few employees already had arrived. Even so, the place was deathly quiet without the usual Monday morning chatter. In some of their hands were cups with the corner coffee kiosk logo. Up until last week, the firm had provided coffee, Danish and bagels each morning. Obviously the cutbacks had started.

"What have they been told?" David asked, taking a deep breath as he turned back to Harrison.

"Not much. For the record, I don't agree with that approach. Your father and Peter made that call."

David agreed with Harrison. Uncertainty was debilitating. But he continued to keep his opinion to himself. At the moment, he didn't feel he had the right to weigh in. Hell, he'd been off having fun with Mia instead of having to look into the employees' faces, tense from wondering who might be laid off first.

She'd been his confidante, his right arm for a week. He'd shared more with her than with any woman in his whole life. The pull to call her was strong, but he couldn't. Not yet. Not until he made this right.

Mia splashed ice-cold water on her face, gazed blearily at the alarm clock she kept in her bathroom as a second line of defense and seriously thought about taking another shower just to wake up. It was crazy that she could be this exhausted after conking out the minute she got home from the airport the night before last, and then sleeping through half of yesterday. Apparently, she'd grossly underestimated the effects of jet lag.

Or her ability to shove David out of her mind.

"Aaargh." She squinted at her blurry reflection in the mirror. "Get a grip, Butterfield. He's only been back for one day." She dried her face and glanced again at the clock. Twenty-eight hours to be exact, so why hadn't he called already?

She muttered a curse and vigorously rubbed her eyes. This was exactly what she'd feared would happen. She was obsessing on when David would call, or if he would, or why he might not. It was insane, juvenile, completely useless, and yet her resolve melted after an hour. Of course she could always call him. No, absolutely not.

She'd given herself one day to recuperate before she had to dive into work. First, she had to purchase two new computers, go to the printers and proof the invoice and contract templates before the batches were run, and then pick up the keys to their new office and have new file cabinets installed. The place was small, configured in the shape of a shoe box, formerly leased by a dry cleaner who received and distributed laundry but did the work off premises. The cool thing was that while the front already had a counter and was large enough to accommodate a desk, a computer and the cabinets, the back led to an alley wide enough for pickups and deliveries for when they needed to transfer merchandise.

The warehouse she'd leased could've been in a more ideal location, but the price was right. While it would hold their initial inventory of bikes, power tools, sports equipment, party supplies and camping gear, there was still room to accommodate twice as much merchandise as they grew with demand.

She was excited to show Lindsey and Shelby everything. The office would be a big surprise since it was located only a block from the loft that she'd be sharing with them. Although there'd be some schlepping back and forth from the warehouse a couple times a week, more if they got really busy, she couldn't complain about the short commute.

Just thinking about Lindsey arriving tomorrow, and Shelby two days later, Mia got excited, and she decided she didn't need that second shower after all. She went to the closet and pulled out a pair of jeans and a sweater. Officially it was spring, but the March air was still chilly, which she very much resented after that balmy week in Hawaii.

Her cell phone rang. She froze for a second, trying to recall where she'd left it. The bathroom? No, the kitchen when she'd turned on the coffeepot. In her rush, she jammed her little toe on the corner of the dresser, and she limped the rest of the way.

She saw that it was Lindsey, and her heart thudded. "Hey, Linds." Mia glanced at the microwave clock. It was still early by Hawaii time. "You must be at the airport."

"Not exactly."

Mia frowned. She took another confirming look at the time. "Are you in Chicago already?"

"I'm still in Hawaii."

She leaned a hip against the counter and stifled a sigh. The hesitant tone told her Lindsey wouldn't be showing up tomorrow as planned. No sense in making her feel bad. "Bet you're having better weather than we are here."

"I'm sure," Lindsey said, with a nervous laugh, and then paused. "You're going to kill me."

Mia forgot about her injured toe, put too much weight on her foot and winced. "Promise I won't."

"Looks as if I won't be back for another two days. Is that going to totally screw up everyone?"

"Nope. I expect Shelby will be late, too. I think she underestimated the drive here."

"Then you'll be all alone. I can still get a flight—"

"Lindsey," Mia interrupted, drawing out her name in warning. "Don't you dare. I'm fine. Besides, we're our own bosses now."

Lindsey laughed. "I think we have to actually get the business off the ground first."

"And three or fours days are going to make a difference? I'm assuming you're still with Rick."

Lindsey sighed. "It's crazy, right?"

Mia smiled. "Go have fun. If you need more time, it's okay, too. I have everything covered."

"I'm sorry I didn't get to meet David. But I will when I get there."

Mia swallowed. "Yep. Now go."

After they hung up, Mia dropped her phone on the counter and stared at it as if it were the enemy. She could call him to make sure he'd arrived safely. Nothing wrong with showing concern for a friend. Right. Not a single thing transparent about that move. She exhaled with disgust, and picked up her phone. Who she really needed to call was Annabelle. Damn, she hoped she was back.

DAVID ARRIVED AT the restaurant eight minutes early. He'd never been here before and wasn't impressed with the drab decor. Heavy brown drapes, dark tan-colored walls adorned with too many autographed pictures of celebrities and tablecloths the shade of mud made the room dreary. Lit candles provided some relief, but not a single one sat straight in its holder.

Left up to him, he never would have brought a client, prospective or otherwise, to a place like this. He preferred Renae's; however, when he'd invited Mr. Peabody to dinner there yesterday, the man had flatly refused, referring to the popular Manhattan eatery as overpriced and pretentious.

This basement restaurant was Peabody's choice, a very interesting one considering the person he represented had to be filthy rich. The potential client still refused to be identified unless he decided to hire Pearson and Stern. Not entirely unusual, and in fact, such reticence often spoke to the affluence of the person, but David was frustrated and annoyed that he was forced to deal with a middle man, especially another attorney.

The blond hostess offered to seat David, but he declined, opting to wait for Peabody on an uncomfortable straight-back chair sitting against the wall near the hostess's stand.

He consulted his watch, mostly out of habit, and then checked his phone. No messages and no missed calls. And certainly no surprise. He'd been hypervigilant to the point of twice imagining his phone had rung when it hadn't. As much as he wasn't ready to talk to Mia, a part of him was disappointed that she hadn't called him, either. Hell, he hadn't been this foolish about a boy-girl phone game since middle school.

He glanced at the door, though not expecting Peabody for another five minutes. This was good timing, he thought, and pressed speed dial before he chickened out. He'd check in, explain he was at a dinner meeting and couldn't talk. She'd understand. After the fourth ring, he was sent to voice mail. In the middle of leaving a brief message, a seventy-something balding man with a thin face and a bulbous nose walked in. He wore a shabby brown suit that matched the drapes and carried a hat in his hand.

The smiling hostess greeted him by name. It was Peabody. A bit shocked, David disconnected the call and rose to introduce himself.

"Stan Peabody," the man confirmed with a firm handshake. "Heard good things about you, Pearson."

Good start that Peabody had heard of him. "Call me David."

"You call me Stan, of course."

"I have your usual table, Mr. Peabody," the hostess said, holding one red leather-bound menu against her chest, and then led the way to a corner spot oddly close to the kitchen.

It didn't surprise David when she laid the menu in front of him. Stan apparently didn't need one. "Scotch neat," she said to him, and then to David. "What can I get you to drink, sir?"

"I'll have the same."

Stan eyed him with amusement. "I drink the cheap stuff. You might want to be more specific."

David didn't know for certain, but he assumed he'd be measured by his response. "I'm not picky."

A faint smile tugged at the wrinkled corners of the older man's mouth. "You heard him, Sally."

"Be back in a jiff."

"I've got to say, David, when you called to invite me to dinner, I assumed you would've included Ms. Butterfield. I was looking forward to meeting her."

David silently cleared his throat, studied the man a moment. "I'm curious. Why specifically Mia Butterfield?"

"I have no idea." Peabody frowned. "Your father and I had this conversation last week."

"I apologize. I was away on vacation."

Stan Peabody might look like a rumpled old man, ready for his recliner and new flat screen to fill his time, but the shrewd gleam in his eye said he wasn't fooled. He knew damn well that David wouldn't be here without being fully informed.

"Look, Pearson, I don't have a team of lawyers working for me. It's me, one associate and my secretary, that's it. Both of them have been ready to retire for five years, and so have I." He paused while the hostess set down their drinks and informed them their waitress would be with them right away.

Stan took an unhurried sip of his scotch before continuing. "This is the last client I have on my books. I gave my word I would continue to administer the estate until a suitable replacement could be found. This client has been with me for thirty-three years. I take that kind of loyalty seriously," he said, settling back in his chair and looking infinitely tired.

"I understand," David said, hope surging. The man was motivated and needed a slight push. "We at Pearson and Stern also value that kind of loyalty. That's why I wanted to meet you in person and assure you that this account is important to us, and would have my undivided attention. I know my father explained that Ms. Butterfield isn't an estate attorney, but what we would bill for my time would be in accordance with what she, as a junior associate, would bill."

Peabody's eyebrows drew together in alarmed concern. "Are you saying Ms. Butterfield isn't available?"

David seriously wanted to plead the Fifth. Admitting Mia was no longer with the firm would likely end negotiations. "Not at the present time."

Peabody slowly shook his head. "I don't think you do understand. My client wants Ms. Butterfield in charge, period. If that's not an option, then we'll go elsewhere."

David's insides clenched. "Would you at least tell me why?"

"Couldn't say." He gave a weary shrug. "Now that business is over," he said, signaling the waiter, "may I suggest the porterhouse steak and sautéed mushrooms?"

David's stomach churned.

13

BY THE END OF her third day back in New York, Mia returned to her loft, feeling more overwhelmed than she'd ever dreamed. It wasn't just that Shelby and Lindsey had both been delayed, or that Annabelle wasn't around, or even that Mia had spent the day hustling all over Midtown tying up loose ends and discovering how many more frivolous details had fallen through the cracks. A big part of her problem was that she was distracted and annoyed for making stupid errors that were costing her time and energy. She was usually so organized.

She refused to think this was a result of the disjointed voice mail David had left yesterday evening. She'd just hit the shower when he called, and because he mentioned he was at a dinner meeting she couldn't call him back. What had gotten to her though, was the remoteness in his voice. But she'd heard the background noise so she knew he'd made the call in public, which could account for his curtness. As a lawyer she knew better than to make premature assumptions.

Except she wasn't a lawyer anymore. Only according to the New York Bar Association, of which she was still a member. The thought kind of depressed her, although it made no sense. She should have felt liberated, anxious to put all the planning and strategizing of Anything Goes into action, and she was eager. She was. But it was weird not having an office full of people to go to, where a stack of pink message slips collected on the corner of her desk. It was even weirder to not see David every day.

She dropped her purse and keys on the metal-and-wood console table where she stacked her mail, and then checked the thermostat. Grudgingly she turned up the heat. It was officially spring, but obviously someone hadn't gotten the memo. She had a bad feeling it would be another couple of weeks before she could store her sweaters.

After briefly considering slapping a tuna sandwich together for dinner, she decided it was too late to eat, and she wasn't hungry enough anyway. She crawled onto her bed and lay on top of the old worn patchwork quilt her grandmother had made for Mia's fifth birthday. She'd already broken down once and returned David's call, but that had been midafternoon and she decided against leaving a message. Poor guy had to be in a ton of meetings after being away for so long.

Her cell rang, and in her current state of mind, she was convinced it was either Shelby or Lindsey, calling about yet another delay. But when she rolled over and grabbed the phone off the nightstand, her pulse leaped when she saw that it was David.

"Hello?"

"Mia, I'm glad I caught you."

"I just got home, and I can finally breathe again."

"I know what you mean. I've been in meetings all day."

"I figured. Are you still at the office?"

"Oh, yeah." He paused, the silence lasting too long, long enough for a slew of bad scenarios to flit through her head, and her heart started to sink. "I miss you."

She smiled, briefly closed her eyes. "I miss you, too," she said softly, feeling the tension melt from her cramped neck and shoulders.

"I know it's late, but any chance you'd like to grab some dinner?"

"Sure." Her gaze darted to the clock, and then at her old jeans and bulky sweater. "When and where?"

"Now? Renae's?"

Renae's? She'd only been there once, with David, in fact, and another attorney from Pearson and Stern, but only because they'd taken a client there to be wined and dined. She'd thought then that the setting would have been romantic if the dinner hadn't been about business. Although she was touched that David had chosen such a fine restaurant, it wouldn't do tonight. "How about someplace more casual and give me forty minutes?"

"You got it. Name the place."

"Feel like pizza?"

David hesitated. "From Renae's to a pizza joint."

"You asked." She carried the phone with her to the closet and sifted through her clothes, looking for a pair of decent slacks.

"Mea culpa. You have a place in mind? A *quiet* place?"

Grinning, she gave him a name and address, hung up and then charged into the bathroom. She needed a quick shower and her makeup refreshed. She wanted to look nice for him, which was ridiculous on so many levels. Not only had he already seen her at her worse, but she was also not supposed to be this excited that he'd called. At this point in her life, it was supposed to be all about the work ahead. She didn't care. For tonight, she was damn happy.

DAVID ARRIVED AT the quaint neighborhood restaurant first, hoping for a secluded table. The place Mia chose was nicer than he expected, quiet and small with about a dozen tables and booths, only half of which were occupied. No hostess was in sight, so he grabbed a table that was far enough away from the kitchen and other diners where he and Mia could have a private conversation.

He sat facing the door, and loosened his tie. The damn thing felt as if it were going to choke him to death. Not wearing one while he was in Hawaii had felt odd at first, though he'd gotten used to the freedom quickly. But it wasn't about the tie. His nerves were shot. Even the infamous bar exam that put the fear of God into the most arrogant law student had been a breeze compared to his mission tonight.

The waitress showed up, and tempted to throw back a double scotch, he ordered a beer he likely wouldn't touch. He hoped like hell it wasn't a mistake to bring Mia to a restaurant to make the offer. He'd reasoned that it was as close to keeping the tone as businesslike as possible. Asking her to the office would have been awkward.

Inviting her to his apartment was out, as was going to hers. This conversation, one he'd sworn last week he'd never have with her, was going to be tough enough, and he needed to stay focused. If she showed the slightest distress, or even hinted that she thought what had happened between them in Hawaii had been a lie, he didn't trust himself not to pull her into his arms, tell her how much he loved her and damn everything else.

At least sticking to a public forum gave him a fighting chance to do right by his family and the employees who counted on the firm. Reputations, livelihoods, honor—so much more than his happiness was at stake. Either way though, guilt held him hostage. She hadn't said the words, but he was pretty sure she loved him, too. The possibility was the only thing that gave him comfort and courage. But at the same time, it was her feelings for him that gave him the power to hurt her. And if he did, he'd never forgive himself.

The bell over the restaurant's door signaled the arrival of a newcomer. But he'd been watching intently and already knew it was Mia. Something inside of him went soft as he watched her cross the threshold. Her hair was down, dark and shiny and skimming the shoulders of her red sweater. She spotted him the second he started to rise, and her lips curved into a smile that lit up her beautiful green eyes. He saw love there, whether she knew it yet or not. But did she love him enough to trust him?

MIA WAS GLAD TO SEE that there weren't many people in the restaurant. Still, she wished she'd thought quickly enough to invite him over to her loft instead. The best she could've done was tuna or grilled cheese sandwiches and the place was a bit messy, but she doubted he would've cared.

He came around the table, smiled and pulled out the chair across from the one he'd been using. "Hi."

Something was wrong. His smile seemed strained. And why didn't he want her sitting in the chair beside him? When he gave her a light, brotherly peck on the cheek, she knew she wasn't imagining things.

"Hi back," she said, trying to keep her tone breezy, even though her brain immediately went to that bad place.

She calmly sat down and stowed her purse on the vacant seat where her butt should've been. Friends, right? From the very beginning, all she wanted was a causal relationship once they'd returned, she reminded herself.

"What would you like to drink?" he asked as he reclaimed his chair.

"I think I'll stick with water." She eyed his untouched mug of beer, his loosened tie. "I have another busy day tomorrow."

"How are things going?" he asked, looking oddly serious. This was his office demeanor, from the staid expression to the polite tone of his voice. He sounded nothing like the man who called her less than an hour ago. The one who'd told her he missed her.

Disappointment rose in her throat, but she stayed cool. "It's hectic. But the cavalry arrives tomorrow, so that'll help."

His eyebrows dipped in a puzzled frown.

"Shelby and Lindsey," she reminded him.

"Ah. Aren't they supposed to be here already?"

"Shelby is driving from Houston and got slowed down by construction. Lindsey apparently is having one hell of a good time with her new guy."

"Not fair to you."

"It's not fair that they have to move all their stuff." She shrugged. "Everything works out in the long run.

What about you? Did you get dumped with a ton of motions and briefs?"

"Let's just say I don't see a vacation in my near future," he said with a wry smile, and for a moment he seemed to relax.

"I know what you mean." She got over her anxiousness long enough to notice that under his tan, he looked really tired, more than usual, as if he hadn't been sleeping well. True, they'd had a few marathon nights in Hawaii when neither of them had slept much, but there had been long, lazy afternoon naps and time spent lounging by the pool.

God, she missed those days. The memories alone made her flush with warm pleasure, and she looked into his dark eyes, willing him to remember them, too.

He smiled. "So, tell me what specifically has been keeping you so busy."

She took a long, slow sip of the water that had already been placed on the table. "A lot of running around, receiving office furniture and supplies, lining up inventory. Oh, and trying to get six crummy cabinets installed. You'd think that would be easy, right?"

"If you can get tradesmen to show up on time, I call that progress."

"See, that's the problem…they're supposed to actually show up. Silly me."

His mouth curved in a reasonable facsimile of a smile, but it wasn't right. She knew that his real smile was ever so slightly lopsided, hiking up a bit more on the right and deepening the groove in his cheek. His real smile always reached his eyes and made her gooey inside. This one put her on edge.

"What about you? Anything interesting happening at

the office?" she asked, wondering if a case had soured, which would account for his tension.

He started to shake his head, and then with a wry expression said, "Sam Glasser got cited for contempt for shooting off his mouth, and took a night in jail rather than cough up the ten grand."

"Judge Palmer, right?"

"Who else?"

Mia bit off a laugh. "But Sam? The guy is always so stoic. Palmer had to have really pissed him off."

"Palmer pisses everyone off."

"True." Mia remembered the first time she stood in front of the grouchy old judge. He looked like someone's doting grandfather but had the bite of an angry pit bull. "He's got to be close to retirement age."

"The guy needs a hobby. He's never in a hurry to get out of court. If it's a nice day, you know Lancaster and Silva will be anxious to get on the golf course."

Mia laughed, feeling more relaxed. "I'd been at the firm about a month when someone warned me about Palmer. I was so nervous the morning I was going before him, and I walked in, saw this guy who looked like Santa Claus and figured I'd been punked."

"He looks deceptive, all right, and he loves breaking in baby attorneys."

Mia snorted. "Yeah, and you said he doesn't have a hobby."

At that, David chuckled. For a second, she thought he was going to reach for her hand, but he wrapped his fingers around his mug instead.

"Yep, Palmer had a good old time with me. Fifteen minutes in, and I seriously wanted to take his head off. I just knew I'd end up fined for contempt, and you would give me my walking papers."

"Never would've happened." He looked as if he were about to say something else, but stopped and inhaled deeply. "It seems like a long time ago."

"It does." Mia felt the mood shift again and, desperate to hang on, she asked, "Hey, did Libby finally figure out how to work the new cappuccino machine?"

David frowned. He clearly had no idea what she was talking about, and of course he wouldn't. That sort of office minutia escaped his notice.

The waitress appeared and described the two specials of the night. While David listened, Mia studied him. His posture was too rigid, his features tight and a telling tic in his jaw betrayed the tension he was trying to hide. If she were to quiz him on the waitress's spiel, Mia doubted he'd have heard a word.

"Thank you," he politely told the woman. "If you wouldn't mind giving us another minute."

"No problem." The young brunette smiled apologetically. "Just to let you know, we do close in an hour."

"Thank you," he said again, and after she left, glanced at his watch and winced. "Nine-thirty already."

"I hope you don't have to go back to the office."

He gave a noncommittal shrug of one shoulder.

"Oh, David." To her shame, it finally struck her that his considerable workload had been made worse by her resignation. How hadn't she gotten that sooner? "Have you found a replacement for me yet?"

He met her eyes and slowly shook his head.

"Any candidates?"

"One."

"Good." She was glad because she hated that he had

to take up the slack. But a tiny part of her disliked the idea of being replaced. Knowing it would be someone else working alongside David. She hoped it was a guy. "How far along are you in the interview process?"

He picked up his beer and took a small sip, his gaze still level with hers. "We want you back, Mia."

She blinked, reared her head. "What?"

"Naturally, there's a promotion and raise involved."

She studied him, her heart hammering her breastbone. "Is this a joke?"

"No." He tugged at his already loosened tie. "I'm making you an official offer."

"This is insane. I have the new business to—I told you I didn't want to practice law anymore." She shook her head, saddened that he could sit there and show no emotion.

"I understand." He glanced away. "I thought perhaps a promotion and raise might give you new perspective."

She stared blankly at him, the memory of last week fading like an old, mistreated photograph. Had he listened to her at all? "Whose idea was this?"

He hesitated. "My father's. Harrison and Peter also are in agreement. We're all in agreement," he corrected.

"I don't understand." She shook her head again, overwhelmed with confusion, thoughts swirling and crashing in her head. "Why?"

"You're a brilliant attorney. We simply want you back."

The old David sat before her, professional, stoic, too rigid, as if one tiny slip would expose him, that he'd give her a glimpse of the man who'd made passionate love to her and picked macadamia nuts out of his ice cream.

"I've barely spoken to your father or your uncle in the three years I worked there."

"Trust me, they keep abreast of everything that goes on at Pearson and Stern, including associates' performances."

"I can understand offering a raise to get someone back, but a promotion? Karen, Ron and Steve have all been there longer than me. What would they say about this?"

"May I assume from your concern that you're considering our offer?" He sat there, waiting, his dark unfathomable eyes giving nothing away.

She stared back, clenching her teeth, her anger growing. "You know what, David, screw you. Or sorry, maybe I should call you 'Mr. Pearson'."

Regret flickered in his face. "Mia." He started to reach for her hand again, but clearly saw he wasn't welcome and stopped himself.

She folded her hands in her lap under the table. A horrible, devastating thought suddenly occurred to her. Fear tripped her up and she didn't know if she had the guts to ask the question. No, she couldn't ignore it. "Did you know about the offer before Hawaii?"

Not so much as an eyelash moved. "Yes."

For a second she thought she was going to be sick. Even if she wanted to hurl an accusation at him, she couldn't speak.

"My going to Hawaii had nothing to do with the firm. That was strictly personal." His composure faltered. A hint of desperation echoed in the deep resonance of his voice. "I wanted to be with you, Mia. Please believe that."

She wanted to believe him, and a part of her did. She

was a good judge of character, and she'd known him a long time. David was an honorable man. Still, he'd given up so much of himself for the firm. It wouldn't be a leap to give them up, as well. "You knew you'd eventually be making the offer, and if I were to accept, where would that leave us?"

"I admit, that's tricky. More for the sake of office morale than anything, we'd have to keep our relationship private."

"Who knew you went to Hawaii?"

"My father and Harrison."

"Did *they* know it was personal?" she asked, feeling as if she were being torn in half, and resenting his ability to keep his reactions under such tight control.

"I didn't spell it out, no."

So they likely thought the sweet-talking to lure her back was all part of the job, and for all she knew, it had been. The pain of that thought cut so deep it hurt just to breathe.

"Off the record, I didn't want to make this offer, but I virtually had no choice."

"Really?" She scoffed. He'd had a choice. They both knew that.

Yet the agony in his face looked real. "What I'm about to tell you is strictly confidential. We've had some setbacks at the firm. For reasons that have nothing to do with our performance, two of our largest clients are jumping ship."

"Who?" she asked, stunned.

"I'd rather not go into details. There's been no official announcement yet."

After all they'd shared in Hawaii, his secrecy hurt.

"Then how can you afford to offer me a raise and a promotion?"

"A potential new client has asked for you to manage their estate, which includes a very large charitable foundation."

"What? Who? I don't do estate planning."

"They won't identify themselves unless we meet their terms. Unfortunately, you're a deal-breaker."

She shook her head, still confused over who would make such a demand. "I have my own commitments—"

"What about coming in part-time?"

Mia's brain could barely handle the stream of information. But one thing registered clearly. The firm was desperate, so was David. And sadly, desperate men did desperate things.

14

"I DON'T REMEMBER THIS PLACE being so small," Shelby said, trailing Mia through the loft. "Good thing all my stuff is going straight to storage."

"Our names are on a list for a three-bedroom, but it's going to be a while." Mia sidestepped Lindsey's enormous suitcase and led Shelby into the tiny second bedroom, or so named by the landlord. Mia had seen bigger walk-in closets.

"It's not as if we'll be at home much." Shelby shrugged. "When did Lindsey get here?"

"About twenty minutes ago. She went to get us coffee."

Shelby studied the small room. "How are we divvying up space?"

"I figured we'd discuss it when Lindsey got back."

"She talk to you about Rick?"

Mia shook her head. "Like I said, she hasn't been here long."

"She's still being really secretive. I think she may be putting up a front. She say anything at all to you?"

They heard the front door open and then Lindsey call out, "It's just me. I have coffee and lattes."

"Caffeine. Good." Mia massaged her left temple as they went to meet Lindsey in the kitchen. She really didn't want to talk about their friend's love problems because that meant the conversation would inevitably turn to David, and Mia so wasn't ready for that to happen. Not that she had much choice. She had a decision to make, and it involved her friends.

Lindsey's blond hair was tied back in a haphazard ponytail, the darkness under her eyes making her look as bad as Mia felt. "Did you just get here?" Lindsey asked Shelby.

"Yep. Traffic was brutal."

"You're going to be so sorry you brought that cute little Mustang convertible of yours."

"That's right," Shelby said. "Rub it in."

Lindsey grinned, looking as if she hadn't a care in the world. So maybe everything was good with Rick. Somehow that didn't make Mia feel better, and being a bitch by not sharing in her friend's happiness made her feel even worse.

The throbbing at Mia's temple grew worse. She grabbed a coffee Lindsey had set on the counter. "Guys, I know you just got here, but there's something I have to discuss with you."

"Uh-oh." Shelby scooped up a latte. "I don't like that tone."

Mia led the way into the living room, then took the chrome director's chair and left the tan leather couch for them.

She was exhausted from staying up most of the night, weighing the pros and cons of returning to the firm, even if it was only part-time. The identity of the potential client still puzzled her. Who could possibly want her so badly that they were holding the firm hostage? She didn't know anybody with that kind of money. Not personally anyway. Unless they were already a client that she'd met at some point.

Of all the reasons not to return to the firm, the emotional toll of seeing David weighed the most heavily. She desperately wanted to believe he wasn't the kind of man who would have used her to meet his objective, but she'd be a fool to ignore how much his family and the firm's reputation meant to him.

And of course, there was the launch of Anything Goes to consider…

God, she hated even bringing up the subject. They had so much work to do before next Monday when their first ad would hit the papers and the flyers were to be distributed telling all of New York City they'd be open for business. No one, least of all her, needed to be distracted by David or his problem.

She waited until they were both curled up on opposite corners of the couch. "David wants me to go back to the firm."

"You're kidding." Shelby's eyes narrowed. "He knows about Anything Goes, right?"

Lindsey looked confused. "But if you're working for him again, then how can you see each other?"

"I'm not worried about that," Mia said, annoyed that her voice cracked.

"Meaning?" Shelby asked.

"Could we stay on point?"

Not the slightest bit deterred by her no-nonsense tone, they both said, "No."

Mia sighed, then gave them an abbreviated and less personal version of their meeting last night, careful not to give away too much about the firm's trouble or her misery. Oddly she still felt protective toward David and Pearson and Stern in general. Of course, as an employer, they had been good to her and there was no reason not to preserve their privacy.

After a long, thoughtful silence, it was Shelby who asked, "So what are you going to do?"

"I don't know. That's what we need to discuss."

Lindsey frowned. "Didn't you say he's in kind of a jam?"

"Yes, but that doesn't mean it has to be my problem." Mia bit her lower lip. She hadn't meant to sound sharp.

"Okay," Shelby drawled. "What are you not telling us?"

Damn, as good as David was at concealing his feelings, Mia was terrible at it. The stupid bastard. He even had that over her. She sipped her coffee, groping wildly for some witty, distracting remark. The only thing that emerged was a startling awareness of how much her resentment toward David had been building. "Guess I know why he followed me to Hawaii."

Shelby's eyes widened, and she seemed truly stunned. "You don't think that whole thing was a ploy to get you back."

She sighed. "What am I supposed to think?"

"I saw him with you, Mia. There is no way that man was there for any reason other than he's in love with you."

At the outrageous claim, Mia snorted, and then to

her utter horror, hope actually filled her chest. "Right. You couldn't be further off base."

"Come on, girl, you're not that stupid."

"Shelby," Lindsey admonished in a low hushed voice.

"You didn't see them together like I did," Shelby said testily. "It's crazy to think that he doesn't—Okay, look, shoving all that 'he loves me, he loves me not' crap aside, let's talk about this rationally."

The menacing look that Lindsey gave Shelby almost made Mia smile. Usually it was her and Shelby who went head to head, and Lindsey who smoothed things over.

"From what I understand," Shelby continued, unfazed, "you can go back part-time, yes?"

Mia nodded absently, her thoughts lagging. Shelby didn't know what she was talking about. Oh, for a few moments last week, Mia had foolishly thought her and David's physical attraction to each other had crossed a threshold, but now she knew better. She alone had made the leap to love. That's what had her so upset. It wasn't lust or infatuation or the thrill of finally getting something that had been withheld from her. She'd fallen in love with him. But how could she?

"Mia, are you listening?"

"Yes," she lied, and realized she'd missed a lot. Somehow, in those few moments of inattention, Shelby had swung Lindsey to her side. They both looked at her with a mixture of concern and expectation.

"If you didn't mind working a couple of days a week," Shelby said, "it would be kind of nice to have money for rent and such without dipping into savings or into the business fund."

"But only if you want to," Lindsey said, and Shelby gave her the eye.

Mia sighed. "Like I don't know you two are trying to manipulate me."

"Is it working?" Shelby asked, and then offered a faint smile. "I know you, sweetie, you're going to throw yourself into work and never give yourself the chance to find out if what you have with David is real."

"I don't see how going back to the firm will help me do that," Mia muttered crossly. "Anyway, I don't want to be a practicing lawyer."

"Hmm, I hadn't considered that," Lindsey said thoughtfully, her head cocked to the side as she stared speculatively at Mia. "But have you considered that it wasn't practicing law you were running away from?"

IT WAS AFTER FIVE when David's private line rang, and he inhaled a deep calming breath before picking up the receiver. He knew it was her. "Mia?"

She hesitated. "Yes."

"Did Shelby and Lindsey make it in all right?" About an hour ago, he'd been ready to go knock down her door. He was tired from lack of sleep and stressed to the max from the gloomy tension hanging over the office, to which he'd contributed with his foul mood. Everyone, including his good-natured assistant, had steered clear of him all day. Suited him just fine.

She softly cleared her throat. "Yes, they did."

"Good." This time he paused, tempted to tell her that he didn't want to know her answer, to forget about the job. What he really wanted was to ask if she'd catch the next flight back to Hawaii with him. "So you've thought about the offer?"

"I discussed it with Shelby and Lindsey, considering they are my business partners and will be impacted by my decision." She sounded stiff, formal. What had he expected? "I have—"

"Can we do this in person?"

"I don't see the point."

He rubbed the knot at the back of his neck. "We didn't finish our dinner last night."

After a long silence, she said, "I still don't see the point."

"Mia, please. I'm not the enemy."

"I never said you were. This is business. That's all. And frankly, I'm surprised you're not more eager to hear my answer." She paused. "This being such an urgent matter."

He squeezed his tired eyes shut, but only for a second, and then stared at his jacket hanging limply on the back of his door. He'd hoped she would have mellowed out over night, remember the things they'd said to each other in Hawaii, but she sounded angrier today. "I want to see you."

"David, please, don't make this harder than it already is."

Damn her. She should have trusted him. Obviously she didn't. "Fine. What's your answer?" His voice was all business. It seemed that's what she wanted.

"I have my own terms. I work two days a week until I familiarize myself with the client and the type of trusts that need to be established. Those two days will be at my discretion, and later, after the groundwork is complete, I come in only one day a week."

"All right," he said slowly, irritation with himself

deepening because he was already thinking ahead to what that meant for them personally.

"I'm not finished," she said, her tone equally curt.

"Go on." Probably better that they hadn't meant in person. This was intolerable.

"I won't take the promotion, but I will take the raise. And I want Karen Flint working with me. She's a good attorney and can easily replace me when the time comes that I can permanently separate myself from the firm."

Something about the way her voice lowered at the end, how she clearly enunciated each word, fed David's uneasiness. Now *this* was personal. It was him she wanted out of her life, not the firm. He went numb. "Anything else?"

"No, I—" She softly cleared her throat. He might have interpreted the pause as regret, but chose not to. "I think that's it."

"Fine. Pearson and Stern agrees to your terms. We'll draw up a contract. In the meantime, I'll need to call our new client and set up an appointment. What day can you come in?"

"I'll call and let you know."

"Great. I'll talk to you then." He started to pull the receiver away from his ear, and stopped. "Thank you," he said, his words cut short by the disconnecting click.

AS SOON AS MIA GOT INTO the elevator, she tugged at the hem of her suit jacket, then at the cuffs, and finally brushed some lint off her skirt. It was ridiculous to be so nervous. She didn't recall her first day at the firm being this bad, although in all likelihood it had been worse. Then again, she hadn't yet slept with her boss.

She groaned, smoothed back the hair that she'd rolled into a French twist, glad she'd decided to come in extra early. David would be there, but no one else yet. Any awkward moments between them would be over and done with before the others arrived.

Part of her phone conversation with David popped unbidden into her head. She'd had too many unguarded moments like that since she'd last spoken to him. Admittedly she'd been one shade short of abrupt, and she shouldn't have expected him to grovel or beg her forgiveness or make some grand, outrageous gesture like show up at her door with three dozen roses.

But a small part of her had longed for him to ignore the crap she'd dished out, ride in on a stupid horse and use his mouth, hands and body to show her how wrong she was. Whisper sweet nothings until she was convinced. She wanted her big, strong hero back. She honestly hadn't expected him to throw her coldness back at her.

The elevator dinged its arrival. God, she hoped this wasn't a mistake. Once she spoke with the new client and became immersed in work, it would be okay, she assured herself as the doors slid open.

For a split second she thought she'd pressed the wrong button. There were people, a good many of them, sitting in their cubicles or at their desks or hovering over someone else's. One by one they looked up, varying degrees of surprise registering on their faces as they watched her leave the elevator.

She knew all of the junior associates, of course, and most of the admin staff, but no one looked particularly happy to see her. Not that she expected a welcoming committee, but wow, what a way to come back. What the hell had David told them about her return?

"Good morning," she said to Laura, the receptionist, who gave her the first genuine smile.

"Hi, Mia, you're looking nice and tan—lucky you," she said, her smile turning enigmatic. "Bet you're here for your plant."

"My plant?"

Laura gestured toward the bushy green fern sitting at the end of the reception counter.

Mia recognized it now. A client had sent it to her as a thank-you last year. "To tell you the truth, I'd forgotten about it. Looks good there, though…" Her voice trailed off when it struck her that there were no fresh flowers.

No gigantic seasonal arrangement where the plant now sat, and nothing equally decadent and exotic sitting on a table in the foyer. She glanced over her shoulder. The waiting area was also bare. A few tall palms and ficus helped liven up the place, but it was obvious that just as many had been removed. And this was the main floor. No telling what the two lower floors looked like.

"Mia?"

At the sound of David's voice, she turned her head and saw him standing in the hall leading to his office, gesturing for her to follow.

"The plant looks good, Laura, better than when I had it. Keep it," she said, before heading toward David, her mind scrambling to make sense of the changes that had taken place in only three weeks and ignoring the way her heart had been crushed just by looking at him.

"You're early," he said with a scant curve of his mouth.

"So is everyone else. What's going on?"

"Let's wait until we get to the conference room," he said in a hushed voice. "You might grab some coffee on the way. There's no service set up there yet."

They got to the employee break room, and David waited outside while she got her coffee. She noticed the absence of both cappuccino machines and the hot chocolate dispenser. There was milk, none of the fancy flavored creams. No trays of donuts and bagels or fresh fruit, which in the past had been provided for the employees. Maybe because it was too early yet. She didn't think so. The firm's problems clearly were bigger and more serious than she thought.

Thank God there was still coffee, and she quickly poured a cup, eager to get out of the dismal room. That the perks had been so quickly withdrawn told her more than David had been willing to confide. The cutbacks had to really depress him. The firm had always been prosperous. This had to be hard for David's whole family to accept.

He eyed her cup of black coffee. "I've ordered some fruit, Danish and juice to be brought to the conference room twenty minutes before the client arrives," he said, his tone bordering on apologetic. "You can get something to eat then."

"I'm fine. What time is the meeting?" They'd started down the hall again, their shoulders occasionally brushing, and she vividly remembered the times when the slightest innocent touch would rattle her concentration. Now, after Hawaii, after the other night and his impersonal offer to return, she honestly didn't know what she should feel.

"Not until nine." He stopped in front of her old office, small and empty but for the desk and file cabinet. "I didn't even ask, is using your old office okay with you?"

"Of course." She tried not to feel insulted. She had taken the raise after all. Now she wasn't sure she wanted it. "Is there a specific reason we're going to the conference room now?"

"We need to talk before our meeting." He studied her face with those serious brown eyes of his, just like he had the moment before he'd kissed her for the first time. The flash of memory undercut her resolve, and her foolish heart twisted with longing. "I figured you might be more comfortable there."

She understood now. The conference room was mostly glass; his office was more private. "It doesn't matter where we are, David. I think we both know we're safe." If she'd meant to wound him, his flinch told her she'd gotten close to the mark with her sarcasm.

Then his features tightened. "All right, my office then."

She should have found satisfaction in eliciting a reaction, but all she felt was sad as she followed him. Her sense of vulnerability had prompted the needless barb. Too late to do anything about it but accept his retreat behind the mask.

He closed the door while she sat in one of the chairs facing his desk. "I had a contract drawn up guaranteeing your salary on a daily basis," he said, as he took his seat, his hand protecting his red tie as he leaned forward to open the bottom drawer. "Without obligation on your part."

"How bad is it?"

His questioning eyes met hers. "I'm not sure I follow."

"With the firm. Will there be layoffs?"

He leaned back, shoving a hand through his hair. "Obviously we're trying to avoid that."

"But everyone's worried."

His humorless lips lifted slightly, his gaze drifting toward the door. "You see how early they're all showing up. They see the cutbacks. They're wondering what's next."

"They should be told the truth." She didn't care that it wasn't her business, although to some degree she could justify her concern. "Uncertainty is far more harmful to morale."

"I couldn't agree more," he said, giving her an odd look. He took his time studying her face. "But it's not my call."

She wasn't talking about them, if that's what he thought. And even if she was, at least he'd gotten it right. "I wish you could get through to him," she said, then added, "your father."

"He's doing everything he knows how to do." David sighed, touched a finger to his lips like he did when he was trying to think something through. "Between us? Neither he nor Harrison is drawing a salary. They aren't being cavalier about the problem."

"And you?"

He drew back slightly. The question clearly had startled him. He said nothing for a long, drawn-out moment. "No."

Mia's temple started throbbing again. Damn it. "Give me the contract."

At her abruptness, his mouth tightened with irritation, but he did as she asked.

"I'm not accepting the raise," she said, and tore the contract in half.

15

THE SECOND DAY at the office Mia sat at her old desk, staring at a stack of contracts, sorely tempted to tell David the deal was off. First, she didn't like the new client. Oh, Stan Peabody was nice enough, but he should never have been overseeing this massive an undertaking, and with only an associate and a paralegal to assist him. Poor guy, he simply wanted the reins passed so he could retire. What had Mia irked was that the person he represented still hadn't revealed his identity. Pompous ass.

But that was the least of Mia's complaints. The atmosphere around the office was barely tolerable. The senior Mr. Pearson was still refusing to clue in the employees as to what was happening. With no good reason not to, everyone feared for their jobs and wondered whose job Mia had stolen by returning. She was unarguably persona non grata.

The icing on the cake? The employees didn't know the half of it yet. Unknowingly they had every reason to question why she'd been put in charge of this particular account. This wasn't her forte. She wasn't a tax attorney or an estate-planning attorney. There were a dozen other lawyers at the firm who were eminently more quali-fied to head the team, and yes, the account was colos-sal enough to require a team. Assets had been poorly managed, and the revenue pools shamefully shallow. The foundation should've been making money hand-over-fist. Pearson and Stern had more work to do than had been anticipated. The account would make them *beaucoup* bucks, and that made it even more difficult for Mia to extricate herself from her agreement.

Her prominent role also meant that once word was out about her project, Mia was about to go from persona non grata to pariah in the staff's estimation, with the exception of Karen Flint, but that was only because the woman had to work with her so if Karen did harbor any resentment, she kept a close lid on it.

The worst thing, by far, was David himself. Not that he'd done anything egregious, but working close to him was killing her. She seriously doubted if she would've agreed to return had she known he would directly over-see the account. She'd made the mistake of assuming she was in charge, but to be fair, it was Peabody who'd announced at the end of the meeting that David's in-volvement was also required. That he'd seemed equally surprised was the reason she hadn't walked out that very minute.

Well, not the only reason. Damned if she hadn't soft-ened toward David when the first retainer check had exchanged hands, and the king of stone faces had been unable to hide a flash of relief. Nothing major sure. A flicker in his eyes, a small twitch at the right side of his mouth, a slight bob of his Adam's apple. No one but her would have noticed. The knowledge both warmed her and made her want to throw her stapler at the wall.

"Knock, knock."

She looked up to find Karen standing in her doorway holding two mugs. "Come in."

"Am I interrupting? I can come back."

"No, please." Mia motioned to the plain straight-back guest chair someone had scraped up for her.

"I brought coffee, if you're interested."

"Very." She reached for the mug Karen set on the desk. "Thanks. I'm sure this is lunch."

Karen sat down. "I have some instant soup packets in my desk if you'd like." Then she added dourly, "I believe we still have hot water in the break room."

Mia glanced at her over the rim of her cup, but said nothing and sipped.

Karen flushed. "Sorry, I shouldn't have said that."

"No worries. Hard to miss the tension around here."

"Yeah, that's for sure. Look, I know that you asked me to help with this account, and I just wanted to say I'm grateful."

Mia needed to tread carefully. "Who told you that?"

The older woman's dark brows furrowed as if she didn't understand why Mia wouldn't know such an obvious answer. "David."

"Ah." That didn't make her happy. He needed to communicate better. As far as Mia knew, *everything* was hush-hush.

"He warned me not to tell anyone or discuss the account with the others, but clearly that excludes you." She shrugged. "I had to thank you. My husband lost his job two months ago, and we depend on my salary. Being involved with this account provides some job security. At least I'm hoping." She worried her lower lip. "It's just so scary around here now. The not knowing is wearing thin on everyone."

"I understand," Mia said in a slow and cautious voice.

"I'm not pumping you for information," Karen said quickly. "Please don't think that."

"Why should I? I don't know anything."

Karen looked at her with a doubtful expression. "I just figured since you and David—" She seemed really nervous now. "You know, I should go." Abruptly she stood.

Uneasiness crawled up Mia's spine. Of course she'd heard whispers, saw the accusing looks, but she didn't totally understand what chatter was being disseminated. "Karen, wait." While Mia got up and closed the office door, she motioned the woman to reclaim her seat. Maybe it was wiser to let the matter drop, but she liked and trusted Karen, who'd never been one to gossip, and if Mia were ever going to find out what was being muttered in the office bullpen, this seemed like her chance.

Mia sat down again and faced Karen, who looked as if she'd rather be stuck in an airless cab during a rush hour jam.

She cleared her throat, wondering how to begin diplomatically. "I owe you a thanks as well for not treating me like I have leprosy," she said, and Karen blanched, nervously tucking her curly auburn hair behind her ear. "I'm fully aware most of the associates are unhappy that I've returned to the firm," Mia continued. "I don't blame them, and it won't help when they find out more about this mystery account. I can assure you that I'm not here at anyone's expense. I can't be more specific, and I doubt trying to reassure the rest of them would do any good because they probably wouldn't believe me."

"No," Karen agreed softly, surprising Mia with her easy candor. "They wouldn't. Frankly, I'd leave it alone, Mia."

She wished she could, but it was eating at her, undermining her concentration. "It's needless tension. What puzzles me is that they know I'm only here on a temporary—" She stopped herself, annoyed that she'd been about to give away too much. The client couldn't know she had a finite agreement with the firm. "I'm here part-time. They all know that, right?"

Karen reluctantly nodded. "It doesn't matter."

"But it's not as if I stole anyone's account."

"There are a lot of associates who used to work on the Decker account. They're sure they'll be the first to go."

"Right." Mia drummed her fingers. "Once we have a handle on how the foundation should be administered," she said, waving at the stack of contracts, "we'll need a lot more help. I'm sure Stan Peabody did his best, but we both know he was in way over his head. I don't know, maybe you could kind of hint around that we'll be building a team—"

"It's not just—" Karen pressed her lips together and stared at the floor.

"What?"

"Landing an account like this is great, okay? Everyone is pleased, but they aren't fooled. Unless we land a couple more of these babies, or some rich schmuck is arrested as a serial killer and hires us, there are going to be layoffs. The writing's on the wall. And no one will forget that after quitting, you came back at the worst possible time and were only hired because of David."

Mia ignored the sudden cramp in her stomach. "David? What does he have to do with—?"

"Come on, Mia. You asked. I don't know how to sugarcoat it for you." Karen didn't seem nervous anymore, but was more agitated. "Everyone knows about the two of you."

"Really? And what do they know that I don't?"

Karen's eyebrows rose. "Didn't you go on vacation together?"

"No," Mia said coolly. "I went to Hawaii with my two college friends, my business partners. As a matter of fact, we'd hoped to hook up with three guys we'd met during spring break back when we were in college."

"I'm sorry." Karen looked confused and embarrassed. Very surprised.

Mia felt only mildly bad since technically she hadn't lied. "Perhaps the rumor mill should get its facts straight."

"I'm sorry," Karen said again. "I didn't participate in the gossip, but I have to admit I made the same assumption, with you both coming in tan and the way David's been looking at you…" She trailed off, clearly miserable and disgusted with herself.

"How has David been looking at me?"

Karen got to her feet. "I think I've done enough damage."

Mia clamped her mouth shut. The smart, dignified thing to do would be to let Karen go, leave the conversation as it stood, resting firmly on Mia's denial. Even though the veteran attorney wasn't normally a talker, maybe with a few well-chosen words she'd quiet the troublemakers about their suspicions.

"Karen?" Mia swallowed—hard—and she hoped it wasn't her pride that just plummeted to the pit of her stomach. "About David—" Oh, God, she really needed to shut up. "I have to know."

THE MEETING WITH HIS UNCLE and Peter ended, and David left Harrison's corner office just as Karen Flint left Mia's. He'd been avoiding Mia all morning, and if she'd noticed, he assumed she knew the reason. Or perhaps not. She was still angry with him despite the noble gesture of tearing up the contract and adamantly declining a raise.

She had no idea how much that display of concern had touched him, though he wasn't surprised. That's the kind of person Mia was in every respect. How easy it could have been for her to hide behind her anger and pain, and abuse the power she had over the firm. She was acutely aware of how much they needed her.

A lump rose in his throat just thinking about the incident. Hell, this was precisely why he had to stay away from her. Hiding his feelings for her wasn't easy anymore. Even though he knew damn well she wasn't convinced that his motive for following her to Hawaii had been pure. Sure, he sometimes got hot under the collar when she treated him as if he were a snake, but when he was in a more reasonable mood he understood she needed time.

And he needed to keep his distance.

He decided he'd been standing idly in the hall like an idiot long enough, and took a deep breath, knowing he'd have to pass her office on his way to the reception desk. Focusing on the large envelope he needed to deliver to Laura for courier pickup, he took long purposeful strides. He'd almost made it past Mia's office when out of the corner of his eye he thought he saw her packing a box.

He backed up, ducked his head in and watched her pick up a stack of file folders and drop them into the small cardboard box. "Mia, how's it going?" he asked casually, his heart damn near beating out of his chest. Had she changed her mind? Was she calling it quits?

She looked up. "I was going to phone you," she said, averting her gaze.

"I have a few minutes now." He glanced at the envelope—the courier would be stopping at reception in the next fifteen minutes—then he noticed a paralegal walk out of the next office. "Tara," he called, "mind dropping this off at reception for me?"

"No problem, Mr. Pearson." She hurried toward him and accepted the envelope, her prying eyes darting to Mia before giving him a smile and heading toward the front.

He slipped into Mia's office, his hand on the doorknob. "Open or closed?"

She moved an indifferent shoulder, and flatly watched him close the door before shifting her gaze back to her task.

In the tense quiet, he watched her set the last folder in the box, and figured the only reason he hadn't busted a blood vessel yet was because this was the calmest he'd seen her since he'd made the offer. Perhaps too calm. Maybe she'd come to a decision. About them.

Uneasiness churned in his stomach. "You should've seen Harrison's face when I gave him the check."

"I'm glad it can help," she said, distractedly.

"What are you doing, Mia?"

She looked up then, stared blankly at him and then down at the box. "I know this is presumptuous, but it dawned on me that I can handle most of this paperwork at home."

"I'm sure you'll understand why I prefer you take copies and not originals," he said, while he searched for a tactful way to find out what was wrong. Then it occurred to him what he'd just said. His admonishment wasn't simply unnecessary, it was insulting.

"These are copies." She closed the box, showing no sign of taking offense, which was disturbing in and of itself.

"I'm sure," he muttered. "Have I told you how much I appreciate what you're doing for us?"

She blinked, refusing to look up. "Several times," she said tightly. "No need to repeat it."

That she would be impervious to his thoughtlessness but annoyed at his gratitude sent a shaft of apprehension down his spine. He'd said nothing to her since yesterday, and he was quite clear that their limited contact was to her liking. So what had her suddenly packing up her work and avoiding his gaze? "Is there a problem I should be aware of?" he asked cautiously. "With Karen, perhaps?"

"No." Mia shook her head. "No. Karen's great. She should take over the account when I leave."

He should relish the thought of her eventually leaving for good because it would make everything simpler for them. But he faced the notion with certain dread.

At least now he got to see her, and if even for a second, lose himself in her beautiful green eyes. "Is this about us?"

She met his gaze, hers filled with so much confusion and anger and sadness it practically cut him in half. "David, there is no us."

MIA SAT IN THE OFFICE of Anything Goes, doing paperwork while waiting on a shipment of smartphones and BlackBerrys. With Shelby and Lindsey at the warehouse taking a final inventory before opening day tomorrow, it was quiet and the perfect time for Mia to get a chunk of work done. If only she could shut off the incessant background noise in her helpless brain.

She wished she hadn't seen with her own eyes the proof of the firm's downward spiral. In one way, it softened her to David's dilemma, but at the same time, convinced her that he would've done anything to get her back in order to buy the firm some time to recover.

Her talk with Karen last week hadn't helped. Every instinct had told Mia to leave it alone, to refrain from urging Karen to spill what was being said about Mia and David. But no, Mia had to open Pandora's box. How could she have been so dense that she didn't know people had been talking about them? Not everyone but enough of the staff. And not just since she'd returned to the firm, but for a whole year.

Cracks had been made about the many nights they'd worked late together, about how the emotionless David, man of stone, undressed her with his eyes, how she'd gazed longingly at him from afar. Stupid high school bullshit that had made her sick.

A paralegal, whom Mia knew and liked, had actually

instigated three different office pools wagering on when they'd have their first date, at what point they'd screw each other's brains out and finally, whether and when they'd announce a wedding date. It was all so humiliating, especially considering how much Mia had prided herself in being circumspect about her feelings for David. And him…oh, God, he would be mortified to hear a quarter of the gossip that had circulated.

He wouldn't ever know, of course. At least not from her. She'd spare him that, just like she was pretty sure Karen had spared her some of the details.

It wasn't fair being the topic of break-room gossip. They'd both worked damn hard and had the track records to prove it. And this was their legacy?

To top things off, now the stupid creeps were all pissed because they thought she was getting a free ride at their expense. Screw them. She was helping to save their damn jobs. But she couldn't say anything. Not even to Karen. Mia had given David her word.

What got to her the most was all that wasted time. She and David had been tap dancing around each other for nothing, and now their relationship had come down to this sad, confusing end. She was mad at him, too, damn it, for bottling up his feelings and not saying something sooner. Of course she hadn't, either, but she'd been serious about her career, and if she'd opened up and been wrong, where would that have left her?

Oh, God, it was her fault, too. She knew that. It was all such a nightmare, she wasn't thinking straight.

And yet, she still thought about him. All the time. Even though she'd been working from home for a week, balancing her responsibility toward Anything Goes and the firm and strategically planning her required trips to the office to meet with Karen. Twice she'd made the dreaded trek, timing it so she didn't have to bump into David. It was bad enough that it was impossible to avoid other employees, but Karen sympathetically met with her in the conference room on the floor below, where Mia didn't know all of the assistants and paralegals.

Sometimes when she was alone like this, with no distractions, her thoughts strayed back to the time they'd spent in Hawaii and how simple being together had seemed. It made her smile a little, but inevitably, the longer she thought about him, the more the resentment mounted. Which in turn angered her because she had no business wasting her precious energy when it was needed for Anything Goes. Although she hadn't burdened them with her trouble, she knew she was doing Lindsey and Shelby a huge disservice.

Someone opened the front door. She pasted on a smile for the delivery man before she looked up. Except it wasn't him.

Annabelle, looking sharp in a deep red outfit that matched her hat and showed off her white hair, strode into the office.

Mia jumped out of her chair. "Annabelle, I've missed you! You've been gone so long? I left messages."

"I know, dear, I just arrived today." The woman laughed when Mia hugged her as tightly as she could. "I came as soon as I listened to your message. What on earth is going on?"

"So much. I did it. I left the firm," Mia said, and then dissolved into tears.

16

ANNABELLE HELD MIA away from her to look at her. "What's wrong?"

Embarrassed, Mia waved a hand and used her other to dab fiercely at her cheeks. "Nothing. I'm tired and being stupid and— Oh, my God, Annabelle, so much has happened since you've been away."

"Apparently." She smoothed back Mia's hair, and urged her to sit down, before situating herself on the upholstered guest chair. "Tell me everything."

"I told you I wanted to stop practicing law, remember?" she said, trying gracefully to wipe away the last of her humiliating tears. "You know I was thinking about starting a concierge business. Shelby, Lindsey and I jumped in. I can't wait for you to meet them."

Her brows still puckered, Annabelle's anxious gaze rested on Mia's face. "You look terrible despite the color in your cheeks."

"Oh, I went to Hawaii for a week. See, I told you a lot's happened." Thinking about Hawaii naturally made her think of David, and she had to blink to keep the tears from welling again.

"Mia." Annabelle took her clammy hand and sand-wiched it between her much smaller palms. "Now tell me the rest."

And Mia did. Almost everything. About how David had followed her to Hawaii, how happy she'd been until she found out the firm wanted her back, apparently at any cost. How she couldn't completely trust that David hadn't come after her for personal gain. As miserable as she was, she managed not to betray the firm's con-fidentiality, saying only that there was a good reason why she couldn't tell anyone why she had returned. She faltered when she got to the part about how people had been talking behind their backs, and she had to pause for a deep, calming breath for fear there'd be more tears.

"It's awful to be in that place," she said. "I hate the looks I get. I hate that David doesn't know about those bast—busybodies, but I would never tell him, either. I'm pretty mad at him, but not that mad."

Annabelle's concerned eyes narrowed slightly. "Why are you angry with David?"

Mia gave an inelegant snort. Didn't anyone listen to her anymore? "Because I can't be sure that he didn't come to Hawaii just to hire me back."

"Hmm, I see. You don't trust him."

Mia stiffened. "Of course I trust him."

Annabelle, her preoccupied gaze darting out the win-dow, said, "You'd better think about that one, dear."

Mia was feeling edgy and defensive suddenly. "What I mean is, I trust him in every other way. He's loyal to the firm and his family, to a fault, in my opinion. Defi-nitely to his clients, too."

"So he hasn't changed his colors, per se."

Mia rubbed her forehead. Annabelle was giving her

a headache. "No, David is an honorable man. It's one of the qualities I love—" She cleared her throat. "I admire him. I'm sure he didn't want to have to trick me into going back to the firm, but he'd been backed against the wall."

Annabelle's expression grew a bit alarmed, and she fidgeted with the big, gaudy rhinestone ring she seemed to favor. "Why are you so sure he tricked you?"

"I'm not. But if you could see how dismal it is around the office— People are really scared." She shook her head. "The tension was so thick I could barely breathe."

"Imagine what it must be like for David," Annabelle said quietly, and Mia briefly closed her eyes as cold dread washed over her. "If he's the man you say he is, he would feel responsible for the well-being of those frightened people."

Mia's mouth had grown unbearably dry. "He absolutely feels that way. I know him."

Annabelle smiled a little, but she seemed clearly distracted.

"Is something wrong, Annabelle?" Mia asked, ashamed that she'd been so absorbed with her own problems that she hadn't noticed the strain on the woman's face.

"What? Oh, I'm just—" She shook her head.

Mia hesitated, unsure how hard to push. She was distracted as well.

Annabelle's remark about Mia not trusting David wouldn't leave her be. The lawyer in her fully understood the impossible task with which David had been presented. It was the woman in her who couldn't stop wondering if she'd been the sacrifice.

"You asked me once if I had any children," Annabelle said. "And I told you it hadn't been in the cards. There was a bit more to it than that. My Broadway career was more important to me than marriage and having children. You see, back then women had fewer choices. I knew I could continue to dance and act into my forties if I weren't encumbered by children, and my Herman, rest his soul, tried to convince me that he would never stand in my way, even if we were married."

The sadness in Annabelle's eyes was so real it hurt to look at her. "I didn't believe him. Bless him, he waited for me anyway. We didn't marry until I was fifty. No child-bearing years left, but we were happy for eight wonderful years." She gave a small, sad shrug. "Herman was ten years my senior. A heart attack took him in his sleep."

Mia gasped softly. "Only eight years. I'm so sorry."

Emotions clouded the older woman's eyes. "I have regretted the decision not to marry him earlier every single day. He left me a very wealthy woman, and once in a while," she said, fondly squeezing Mia's hand, "a ray of sunshine enters my life. But nothing changes the fact that I was a very foolish, self-absorbed young woman who couldn't see past her nose."

Mia sighed. "Like me?"

"Only you can answer that." Annabelle smiled. "You have a fine logical mind, something being a lawyer requires, I'd imagine. And sometimes, I'd wager you ignore logic and go with your gut. This time, Mia, what does your heart say?"

Mia's eyes blurred and she had to put a hand on the counter to steady herself. She said she'd trusted him, but that hadn't been true at all.

How would she have reacted if David had turned his back on his family firm and all the employees? She would've been horrified and convinced he wasn't the man she thought he was. She also would've been crushed that he hadn't offered her the chance to help.

He'd been pounded into a corner, and it was his honor that that kept him there. He was in hell, facing those employees every single day and unable to say a word. She'd hardly been able to handle the heat for two lousy days herself.

God, he'd practically begged her to trust him, to believe that he was still the man he'd been in Hawaii. She moaned as her body rocked with how stupid she'd been. The damn fool loved her, and instead of being a comfort, she'd made him the enemy. Why hadn't he...? No. She knew exactly why he hadn't told her he loved her. Because she hadn't trusted him.

It was probably far too late, but she had to make this right. Tell him she loved him, admit that she'd been a fool, that she'd been the one who couldn't be trusted. It would kill her to be so near him once he knew the truth, but she would suck it up and go back to work because she owed him that much. More. If by some miracle, he still loved her too, then she would fight.

Damn the delivery guy for being late. She needed to see David, the sooner the better. But she couldn't just leave the office. She jumped a bit as she realized Annabelle was still there. "Oh, God. I'm such an idiot."

Annabelle's troubled eyes looked suspiciously damp. "No, you're not the idiot. I'm afraid I am—

Mia abruptly stood. "I have a huge favor to ask you."

"Yes? Anything."

"I'm expecting a shipment at any minute." She sniffled. "But I have to see David. Now. It can't wait. I do love him, Annabelle. With all my heart—"

"Go." Annabelle spryly sprang up from her chair. "Don't you worry about a thing. Go," she repeated, practically shoving Mia toward the door. "And when you return, we need to talk. There's something very important that I must tell you."

"We will talk. I promise. And thank you." She kissed the woman's cheek. "I'll be back as soon as I can."

The door opened. They both turned, expecting the delivery guy.

David tentatively crossed the threshold.

"David? What are you doing here?"

His smile was faint as he glanced from Mia to Annabelle, back to Mia. "I have to talk to you. It's personal."

"I was just coming to talk to you," Mia said, her heart warming when she touched his arm and hope entered his eyes.

"Good," Annabelle said, startling David. "You two, skedaddle. Right now."

Mia laughed nervously as Annabelle pretty much steamrolled them out the door and onto the sidewalk.

David looked as if he didn't know what to think.

"I'll wait for Lindsey and Shelby," Annabelle said, her trembling hand pressed to her stomach. "Don't hurry back. Now get."

THEY WENT TO Mia's loft since it was close. The place was messy because, with three women and too much stuff, they hadn't fallen into a satisfactory routine yet.

Mia didn't care. She shoved aside a heap of freshly

washed towels and made room for both of them on the couch. She sat first, in the middle, forcing him to sit close. He didn't seem to mind, and made no effort to move when their knees touched.

"Ah, Mia, I have so much to—"

"No," she said, holding up a hand. "Let me talk first."

His watchful eyes narrowed slightly, but he gestured for her to go on.

"I'm not staying with the firm."

He didn't seem surprised or even upset. Disappointment did flicker in his eyes because, to his credit and to her relief, he did nothing to keep his feelings in check. Still, he only nodded.

"That's not to say I'm bailing on you. I'm not. I'll stay on, but only as a consultant." She paused, and found she didn't have to dig for courage. This was so right that it had to be said. "I admire you, David, your loyalty, your sense of responsibility. It's all part of who you are, and I love that about you. I love you. And we deserve a chance." She'd hardly dared to breathe, and it all came out in a whoosh. "I'm sorry I didn't trust you enough, but I do love you, and I hope we still have a chance to make things work."

David blinked, and then took his time studying her. "A consultant, huh? I came up with a similar solution, although I do like mine better."

She didn't say a word, just waited for him to continue, her heart beating faster and faster. He could've said he loved her, too. Was she wrong? No, not about David. She'd been confused for a while, but never wrong. He'd always been the man she thought him to be. The man she wanted.

"Yes, of course, for obvious reasons I would like it if you stayed with the firm. But if that doesn't work out, and I have to knock on every door in Manhattan to find another client, so be it. I won't let you go. I love you, too, Mia. I have for a long time. And I promise you I will never let anything come between us again." He took her hand, kissed it.

"Oh, David." Her voice broke. "I've loved you for a long time, too."

A reluctant smile tugged at his mouth. "I guess everyone knew but us."

The office gossip. Oh, God. He had to be mortified. "You know?"

He sighed. "I know. Maybe it's not too late to make my bet in the office pool," he said dryly, and Mia laughed in spite of herself. "We could make a killing." He reached into his pocket and pulled out a small jeweler's box. "Insider trading be damned."

Her heart nearly jumped out of her chest.

"I don't want you just to be part of the firm. Be part of the family, Mia. Be my wife." He opened the blue velvet box. "Marry me."

She started breathlessly at the beautiful sparkling diamond…a princess cut, at least two carats. "You aren't even drawing a salary."

David laughed. "Not the answer I was hoping for."

Mia threw her arms around him. The tears already filling her eyes. "Yes." Her voice broke. "Yes," she said more strongly. "Yes."

He buried his face in her hair, his arms tightly around her, and she felt the shudder go through his body. "I love you so much," he whispered, his voice a low, throaty murmur.

She was the one who finally drew back. She wanted to look at him, wanted him to kiss her. He took her face in his hands, and she threaded her hands through his hair. Then he pressed his firm, reassuring lips to her trembling mouth.

TWO HOURS HAD PASSED before they headed to Anything Goes. Mia hoped Lindsey and Shelby had relieved Annabelle. Although Mia knew without a single doubt that Annabelle would have no problem having been stuck there, especially once she saw the ring.

Before Mia opened the door she heard the laughter and excited chatter. Annabelle sat at the desk, Shelby was perched on the counter and Lindsey sat in the guest chair. They all turned to look at David and Mia. While her two partners grinned in unison, Annabelle looked a bit anxious.

"Well?" Shelby said. "Have you two kissed and made up?"

"Pretty much," Mia said, casually flipping back her hair making sure the rock on her finger caught the light.

Annabelle's eyes sparkled as brilliantly as the diamond. Covering her mouth with her blue-veined hand, she leaped up from the chair and fiercely hugged Mia. "I'm so relieved."

Laughing, Mia hugged the woman back.

Lindsey gasped, her hand going to her throat.

"Am I missing something?" Shelby frowned, then her eyes widened the second she spotted the ring. "Holy crap."

"Yes, indeed," Annabelle said, let Mia go and turned

to David. "I'm so happy to finally meet you, young man. "I've heard many fine things about you."

"Pleased to meet you." He extended Annabelle his hand, which she ignored, and hugged him as tightly as she'd hugged Mia.

David flushed a bit and helplessly patted the older woman's back.

Mia laughed. "I'm sorry we were gone so long. We had a lot to sort out."

Shelby had grabbed her hand and was studying the ring. "No problem. Annabelle gave us some terrific ideas, like shopping estate sales for inventory." She passed Mia's hand to Lindsey. "Good job, Pearson. You have any brothers?"

"Sorry."

"Oh, well." Shelby shrugged. "Hey, Linds, I'll flip you for Mia's room."

Lindsey rolled her eyes, and hugged Mia. I'm so happy for you, sweetie." She smiled at David. "You did good."

"I think so," he said, slipping an arm around Mia's waist.

Mia met his eyes. It didn't seem totally real yet. David. Them. She stole another glance at the ring. "Hey I'm not giving up my share of the loft quite yet, guys. Looks as if I'll have to put in more time at the firm."

"That won't be necessary," Annabelle said quietly. "Unless you want to, of course. Though certainly not on my account." She dabbed at a tear that slid down her cheek. "I am so sorry, Mia. I thought I was helping. But it seems I'm simply a foolish old woman who needs to keep her nose out of everyone's business."

Seeing that Annabelle was visibly shaken, Mia took

her friend's ice-cold hand. "Annabelle, whatever it is, it's okay."

She shifted, dabbed again at her cheek. "My apology extends to you as well, David. I hope you both can eventually forgive me."

He stared at Annabelle, his expression one of graduating awareness. "Stan Peabody?"

"A very old and dear friend," Annabelle said. "He's managed my affairs for too long. He needs to retire. If you aren't totally disgusted with me, I'd like Pearson and Stern to take over the entire estate. My late husband... he had a knack for making money."

Mia let out a short, self-deprecating laugh. Talk about self-absorbed. Her friend had given her hint earlier, but Mia had failed to connect the dots. "Why, Annabelle? Why the charade?"

She sighed. "The last time we were in the park, you sounded so miserable, and I honestly didn't believe you wanted to leave your job. I thought if I could somehow force you two together, you would stop thinking about running away from David, and he would see what a wonderful young woman you are." She cast an apologetic look at Lindsey and Shelby. "I'm afraid I didn't realize how serious you were about your business venture. And then I left on my cruise. You quit the firm, and I very nearly made a mess of everything." Her damp eyes lighting with hope, she glanced from Mia to David. "However, I dare say, it seems to have worked out."

After a brief, stunned silence, Mia gave her a mock glare. "You obviously have too much time on your hands, young lady."

"Not anymore." With hands on her hips, Lindsey snagged Annabelle's gaze. "You have some outstanding ideas, and Shelby and I shamelessly plan to keep picking your brain."

Annabelle sighed, her face looming with relief. "There's a nice, cozy little bar not far from here. I'm buying."

"I'm in." Shelby looped an arm with Annabelle and, winking at Mia, she said, "You two don't wait up."

They stopped at the door long enough for Annabelle to give Mia and David a final beatific smile. "I assume you understand that Pearson and Stern will have all of my business. I'll have Stan fill you in on the rest of it tomorrow."

Wordlessly, they watched the three of them leave the office.

"The rest of it? Mia said.

"That's what I heard." David pulled her into his arms, and she linked her hands around his neck,

"I wasn't about to ask." Mia's heart fluttered at the way the love shone in his warm brown eyes. "I wish we were in Hawaii right now."

"Hawaii was great, but it doesn't matter where we are." He kissed her gently. "As long as we're together."

She nodded. "Oh, God, they're all going to have a field day at the office when they find out."

"Don't care."

Mia smiled. "You've come a long way."

"Yes, I have," He kissed her hair, her eyelids, her mouth. "My place?"

"Definitely." Mia didn't even mind when he started kissing her, and it was another hour before they closed the office door behind them.

* * * * *

Wet and Wild

JILL MONROE

Jill Monroe makes her home in Oklahoma with her family. When not writing, she spends way too much time on the internet completing 'research' or updating her blog. Even when writing, she's thinking of ways to avoid cooking. Lately Jill has happily put to use her degree in journalism with Author Talk—where Authors Talk to Other Authors. Along with her dear friend Gena Showalter, she interviews writers, asking the questions no one else does. View these spoof interviews at www.authortalk.tv.

1

"I PROMISE I'll be good," Andrea "Drea" Powell told Kaydee as their feet sank into the warm sand of the beach. The ocean beckoned a few yards away. The waves were breaking perfectly and Drea couldn't wait to paddle out and ride them. She gripped her board tighter as they walked toward the water's edge. The waves off Oahu were legend, and right now with their high swells and consistent sets, they were living up to their reputation.

Kaydee gasped then shook her head. "You couldn't even be convincing when you told me that. It's pathetic."

Drea made a face. "I just don't know why I can't be myself to get the sponsorship."

"You *are* being yourself. We're only changing your personality. The rest is all you," her friend said with a wink.

"Thanks a lot," Drea said, as she kicked sand over Kaydee's toes.

Kaydee's expression grew serious. "Listen, bottom line is, no matter how good a surfer you are, no company is going to sink one dime on you if they think you're going to bolt at any minute. Or die out there because you took one risk too many."

Drea made a scoffing sound. "They don't give Rookie of the Year to surfers who stay back and play it safe."

Kaydee propped up her board and faced Drea. "Hey, reining in your burning desire for danger will be good for you."

"And my desperate need to prove that winning Rookie of the

Year wasn't a fluke," Drea added. "As long as my motivations are being dissected, let's go for the whole deal." This wasn't the first time her friend had brought up these points.

Kaydee braced her hand on her hip. "Okay, then, since you issued the invitation, I'm going to say it all. Enjoy. Winning the last competition may have given you the money to get to Hawaii and enter Banzai, but what if you don't win here? You'll be working at the Trading Post selling postcards to tourists while the other surfers are packing to go to the next competition. You can't surf and improve if you're counting on wins to get the money. You have to get a sponsorship. It's your insurance in case you don't win. And to get a sponsorship you have to—"

"I have to take it easier," Drea finished for her.

"Some waves aren't meant to be surfed, and I'd like to keep my friend alive for as long as possible."

"Oh, yeah?" Drea asked, feeling uncomfortable with the seriousness of Kaydee's tone. Drea liked everything in her life upbeat and happy. Hmm, she was more like her mom than she'd ever realized. It wasn't just the brown eyes that they shared. Her mom had also gone from one low-paying job to another to support her dream of singing. Same lifestyle…just different dreams.

"Of course. How else am I going to pass my marketing class if I don't have you for a case study?"

There, that's more like it. Light and funny. "Come on, let's hit the beach."

Right. With only two weeks before the competition, she needed as much time in the water as she could get. Drea pivoted toward the surf and…

There he was.

"Look at his style. His control," Drea said with awe about the tall man riding a wave with ease.

"Makes a girl wonder if he loses that control in bed."

Drea glanced sharply at her friend. Did Kaydee know Drea's thoughts often wandered in that direction?

"Come on, it's not like you haven't thought about what Kirk Murray would be like in bed a hundred times."

Try a thousand times.

She and Kaydee simply stood there and watched as the gorgeous man surfed the way surfing was meant to be done. His athleticism was clear, from the muscled strength of his legs, to the ease with which he dipped his fingers into the water.

"There you are, Drea."

Drea reluctantly took her gaze away from Kirk to see Linda coming up beside her.

"I should have known you'd be on the beach," said the friendly and now breathless brunette. Linda was second in command to Taylor Dutton with the Girls Go Banzai surfing competition. "Those waves are pumping."

Drea's fingers tightened around her board. "I can't wait to get out there."

"Well, wait until you hear this. I can't believe it, Drea. You are so lucky," Linda gushed, her tone sounding impressed.

No one could help smiling at Linda. She had the kind of enthusiasm and excitement that was almost catching. Almost.

"What's up?" Drea asked.

"I just heard Kirk Murray wants to meet with you about a full sponsorship."

Drea's stomach lurched at the mention of his name. Anyone's would. Her gaze returned to the sea. Kirk was already paddling out to catch the next wave. As a three-time Longboard World Champion, Kirk had made millions through his endorsements. A true professional surfer, he'd traveled the world and now made frequent appearances on sports TV channels. She'd heard rumors of his retirement—that he wanted to stay put on Oahu and devote more attention to his very popular restaurant, Da Kine.

But sponsorship? Of her? Her heart began to race.

"Yes, she'll take it," Kaydee blurted.

"As if there was any question," Linda scoffed, and the two of them both laughed.

But Drea didn't laugh. Obviously this was the best break she'd gotten outside of the ocean, but Kirk Murray was a man in a different league. She'd talked to him once, two weeks ago. She'd finally scrounged up enough money waiting tables and from selling her bike to fly her and her board from California to Hawaii. As she was filling out the paperwork to make her an official competitor with the Girls Go Banzai surfing competition, the man, literally out of her dreams, walked past.

Never one to pass up an opportunity, she'd said hi. He'd flashed her that fantastic smile of his that graced everything from surf fan posters to ads for board leashes. She started to stutter out something, but then his cell phone rang, and her chance was lost.

Not this time.

"He wants you to meet him at his restaurant at two. Let me give you directions."

But Drea didn't need them. She knew exactly where Kirk spent the majority of his time outside of the water. Had walked by it three times.

"Okay, gotta run. So many last-minute details," Linda said and continued down the beach.

"This is it for you. I can feel it," Kaydee said once Linda was out of earshot.

"If you thought my promise to be good was pathetic, remember how I was around him?"

Kaydee ran her finger through her hair. "Um, actually, I was embarrassed for you."

Drea grimaced.

"Oops, sorry. I'm supposed to be more supportive than that."

"Forget it, you were just telling the truth."

"Sometimes the truth shouldn't be told."

"Said like someone who plans to make a career out of marketing."

Kaydee smiled. "Let me try this again. Really, I'm a much better friend. Supportive even."

Drea laughed, then pretended to brace herself. "Fine, I'm ready."

"The last time you met Kirk Murray you were just an unknown surfer bumming her way from one beach to another. You're the celebrated Rookie of the Year now. And why is that? Because you're good and now you have the cred to back it up. Don't forget *he's* interested in *you*." Kaydee gave a gentle squeeze to Drea's shoulder. "Now is your chance to really show him what you can do."

Drea raised an eyebrow. "I'm really impressed. That was downright inspirational."

"Did you believe it?"

"No, but the hand thing you did was a nice touch."

"Wait, I want you to completely forget that if you impress this man, you could get the kind of sponsorship that would allow you to quit selling seashell necklaces, waitressing or whatever job you can find to support your sport and be on the competitive surf circuit full-time. All your dreams would finally become real."

Drea sucked in a quick breath. "Technically, that was worse."

"How about, 'put your big-girl bikini bottoms on and stop acting like an angsty teen with her first crush.'"

"Your skills at motivation leave me speechless."

"So what are you going to wear?"

Drea's eyes widened. She hadn't thought of that.

"Come on, Drea. Flip-flops, shorts and a hoodie isn't really dressing to impress."

"The only other option is a bikini. I don't have the proper clothes for a job interview." She never had. The muscles in her stomach started to tighten. She also didn't have any experience with the business side of surfing, and knew zilch about how people behaved. Did they shake hands? Dear Lord…heels?

"Don't worry about it, I'll loan you a sundress." Kaydee picked up her board. "Come on, we'll surf away those nerves."

Kirk draped his towel around his neck and peered out to the ocean one last time. The waves were breaking beautifully, and he could easily have surfed another hour without getting tired. Longer periods in the ocean helped with his physical conditioning, and his pop-up was getting sloppy, a bad habit he was determined to change.

He'd love nothing better than to paddle back out, but his day was booked with meetings. He slicked his hand down his face, removing the last traces of the salty water. Meetings, paperwork and corporate networking weren't what he'd had in mind when he realized he needed plans for when he fully retired from the professional surfing circuit. No, all that serious stuff sounded a bit too much like his dad. Kirk's idea of retirement was catching waves in the morning, playing on the beach with his nephew and spending his evenings in Da Kine, the restaurant he'd started two years ago.

Too bad his ideas and reality weren't meshing. But he'd get there. Just like with his surfing, if he put in the hard work, it would all pay off.

He was just about to reach for his board and head for the car, when the bright flash of a red bikini in the blue of the water caught his eye. Mesmerized, he watched as the surfer angled and turned, making one brash move and taking one risk after another out there in the water. He'd be horrified if he weren't utterly captivated. Just like every other man out on the beach, he noted.

"There are days when I think I'm a pretty good surfer. Then I see her, and I feel like a grommet."

Kirk tore his gaze away from the beauty in the ocean to see Taylor Dutton's second in command staring wistfully out into the water. "You're not a grommet," he told her. The term was used for young surfers.

"Thanks, Kirk," she said, smiling.

"You're too old to be a grommet."

"Whatever," Linda said as she gave him a playful jab in the ribs. "By the way, she's confirmed for two. She'll meet you at the restaurant."

His gaze returned to the woman who'd just jumped off her board and into the ocean. No smooth glide into the water at the end of her run. His muscles tensed as he waited for her to resurface. Then he saw her head pop out of the water and he could breathe again. She was paddling back out to the breaking waves when he realized Linda's meaning. "That's Andrea Powell? The woman you suggested I sponsor?"

Linda nodded.

"Are you kidding? Look at her. She's like a wild thing out there."

"Which makes her all the better match for you. You said

you wanted someone who you could help train, give pointers to. You have to admit she's got the guts, it's her style she needs to work on."

The woman took on the wave like she was challenging it to knock her off the board. He admired her determination.

"And catch the attention she's already getting in and out of the water. The other surfers are getting out of her way."

"That's not necessarily a good thing," he said drily.

"Then look at the beach. What she has grabs people's interest, and that is a win-win when it comes to sponsorship."

Linda had a point. Which was probably why she was so valuable to Taylor Dutton.

"She does look fearless," he said. And sexy.

"I knew this would work," Linda said with a laugh. "I can already hear the excitement in your voice."

"All she needs is a little technique and a little more discipline. She could be number one on the circuit in no time."

"And she can do it all while wearing a Da Kine shirt or bathing suit. No one will forget her or your restaurant. Like I said, it's win-win."

Linda was very right. He couldn't stop his eyes from drifting over the curves of the woman mastering the waves. The Pipeline was a monster, and she was handling it with skill and amazing beauty. He smiled, and his reluctance to leave the beach vanished. In just a few hours, he'd have that beauty to himself.

When he woke up this morning, the day that stretched before him meant practice time at the ocean and then a series of meetings. Now he was looking forward to two o'clock in a way he hadn't looked forward to something in a long while.

"Win-win for sure."

AN HOUR before she was supposed to meet with Kirk Murray, Drea had convinced herself that someone was playing a joke on her. No way would the great Kirk Murray actually be interested in sponsoring her. The man was a legend and he wasn't even thirty.

Someone must have discovered the secret crush and set her

up. She was an outsider, and certainly didn't fit with the close-knit group of surfers. But who would be that cruel? JC and Laci were her biggest competitors, but neither seemed the type. Besides, they'd become such good friends while sharing their rented bungalow during this competition.

Maybe it was true. Maybe Kirk Murray really did want to sponsor her. A sponsorship would mean so much to her. She could get off her diet of whatever food the restaurant where she worked didn't want. She could be on the surfing circuit from Florida to Australia, Fiji, wherever, and not have to sell off her possessions or plasma. She could make something of herself.

She sucked in a deep breath and held it, willing her nerves to settle down. She'd surfed the Pipeline, practiced in the shark-infested waters around Florida and sold absolutely everything she owned but her board to compete. But she'd never been this nervous.

She'd fallen for Kirk hard-core the first time she'd spotted him surfing in a competition in California. New to the sport herself, and supporting herself waitressing, there was no way she could afford lessons. She learned by trial and error, and what she couldn't figure out on her own, she did by observing the surfers in the water. No one was a better teacher than Kirk Murray. His style and form were about as perfect as a surfer could get.

If she hadn't already admired him for his surfing skills, seeing the man up close and personal had sealed the deal. He was tall and lean, his muscles stretched across his chest, showing his strength. He wore his dark blond hair short and spiky in a way that just made her want to mess it up. His green eyes surveyed the water so intently; she knew he was reading the ocean, learning the wave pattern so he could catch the best one. She wanted to be able to do that. She wanted him to teach her. And then she wanted him to look at her just as intently. To want to read and learn all the things about her, the way she did about him.

And she did know almost everything about him. After seeing him surf in California, she'd found a few moments alone on the Internet at the public library and searched every article that mentioned his name.

Single—yes.

Owned a restaurant—yeah, they had something in common. She'd worked in plenty.

Home base—Hawaii. And that was why she was here in Oahu at the Girls Go Banzai competition instead of staying in California and building her reputation in a place that was already familiar.

When she'd explained to Kaydee how she made it to Hawaii, the woman had thought she was crazy. But she'd lived her life flying by the seat of her pants and not taking the safe way, and she wasn't going to change now. Those very traits had won her the Rookie of the Year award and now, very possibly, a sponsorship with Kirk Murray and an opportunity to spend a lot of one-on-one time with the man himself.

She smoothed the skirt of the sundress Kaydee had loaned her, took a deep breath and reached for the door handle of Da Kine.

2

DREA HAD DROPPED blue-plate specials, spilled drinks and brought the wrong food to plenty of customers in the dozens of restaurants she'd been fired from, but none of them had possessed the warmth and welcome of Kirk's Da Kine. Donning an apron and closed-toe rubber-soled shoes might not even be a chore here. Journalists, surfers and fans all mingled together.

If the noise level was any indication, the patrons enjoyed the place as much as she suspected she would. Laughter was abundant, as was the surf paraphernalia, which wasn't surprising, seeing as Kirk had named his restaurant for the Hawaiian phrase for the best kind of wave. She expected to see more pictures of him; after all, that body could probably sell a lot of hamburgers and exotic martinis.

The broken board he'd ridden when he won his first championship was mounted high on the wall. Framed jerseys and wetsuits dotted the walls. Da Kine made her think of traditional Hawaii, minus the expected tourist tackiness. The shades of blues expressed a love of the ocean, and the traditional fare showed a love of the culture.

And Drea felt completely out of place in her borrowed green sundress and unpainted toenails. She eyed the door, ready to bolt.

"Drea."

A shiver ran down her back. She'd recognize that sexy, commanding voice above the din of a crowded restaurant or the roar and splash of the ocean. Drea had heard it often enough in television interviews and the homemade surf videos people uploaded on the Internet.

Kirk Murray.

She turned at the sound of her name and her breath hitched when she saw him. He was even better-looking up close and personal. No camera did justice to his deep green eyes, or showed the true friendliness in his smile. Wearing khaki shorts and a blue polo shirt, he looked just as good out of the water as he did wearing nothing but his swim trunks.

Well, almost. Without his shirt, he was beautiful.

"Hi, I'm Kirk," he said as he stretched out a hand. "So glad you could make it."

Good Lord, she'd have to touch him. Get to touch him. Drea stuck out her own hand, and his engulfed hers. How Kirk made her feel warm and welcome with such a simple gesture, which people did every day, she'd never know, but he did, and her nerves vanished.

"Hungry?" he asked. "The grill is up and running."

For the first time she noticed the inviting scents of roasted pineapple, banana bread and seafood. She'd had a peanut butter and jelly sandwich before she'd left Kaydee's apartment with the sundress, so unfortunately she was full.

She shook her head. "Already ate."

"Then how about a walk on the beach? One of the perks of owning a place so close. That way we can get to know each other better."

That sounded more like employment Q&A, and her nerves kicked up again. "I'd like that."

He opened the door for her, and she blinked against the brightness of the sun before sliding her sunglasses down her nose.

"So tell me about yourself. The information Linda gave me left a lot of blanks," he said once they'd deposited their shoes in the bin provided by Da Kine and their feet were firmly in the sunwarmed sand.

"I like a lot of blanks."

He smiled. "You're one of those."

She glanced up. One of the great things about surfing was that it was a sport that didn't require a participant to be tall. At five foot five, Drea was comfortable with her average height, but she had to look up, very up, for her gaze to meet Kirk's green eyes. "One of those—?"

"The kind of person that any answer has to be dragged out of them."

He had her pegged. Drea didn't like talking about herself, not because she had some big, dark secret lurking, there just weren't a lot of interesting things to tell. Surfing and waiting tables to pay for her surfing was pretty much her life. "Actually, I'm an open book. Ask me anything," she invited with a teasing smile.

"Where are you from?"

"All over."

"Originally," he said with a laugh.

"Springfield, Missouri."

"Landlocked. How'd you end up surfing?" he asked as people milled slowly around them. The pace here in Hawaii was slower, more laid-back than even California. She was used to a more frenetic lifestyle.

"My mom had what she called restless feet. All she ever wanted to do was write songs and play them on her guitar in front of a crowd. We never stayed in one place for very long. Then we ended up in Florida. She had a job waitressing in Seaside, and one day I saw someone surfing."

A slow smile appeared on his face, and he stopped walking. "And you were hooked."

"Yeah." She liked this. Drea actually liked this. The way she'd grown up, and her current nomadic lifestyle never offered much opportunity to connect with others. But Kirk's tone and expression told her he understood *exactly* what she *felt,* how she felt the first time she saw someone surf. The first time she stood on a board and rode a wave. The first time she wiped out.

A warm breeze came from the ocean, blowing through the sun-bleached tips of his hair. She sensed he was studying her face. Thankfully she was wearing her sunglasses. She'd had a crush on this man for two years, but none of that was real. This moment was real. *He* was real, and she was afraid her eyes would show just how important this meeting was to her, professionally and personally.

Kirk turned his head and began walking up the beach again. "Who'd you take lessons from? I know some trainers based out of Florida."

A question she hadn't expected. Would he still take her seriously when he learned the answer? "I never took lessons."

"How'd you learn?" he asked, surprise lacing his voice.

"Self-taught mostly. I watched some videos on the Internet and checked books out of the library."

"I'm still just amazed anytime I run into someone who's out there winning competitions and didn't even have a coach."

"If I fell off my board, I tried to figure out why, and then not do that anymore."

Kirk laughed. "That philosophy would have saved my dad thousands of dollars."

Drea joined him, enjoying the deep rumble of his laughter. She knew from Kirk's bio that his rich hotel-owning father had shelled out all kinds of cash to get his son the best instruction around. Of course, Kirk had the drive and the skill to back it up, but there were certainly no hot-dog-only days in Kirk's life as there were for a lot of the surfers on the circuit. Like her.

"The information Linda provided said you won Rookie of the Year out of California. How long did you stay in Florida?" he asked as he continued to walk down the beach. Their shoulders were only inches away from each other.

"Two years. Mostly Cocoa Beach and Daytona."

Kirk shuddered. "Sharks."

So the big strong man had a thing about sharks. Okay, very smart, but still…kind of cute.

"That just makes it more fun," she said, smiling.

"Okay, now I read you. You're a thrill-seeker. You live for danger. That explains your surfing."

"What about my surfing?" she asked, feeling a little defensive.

"The way you surf, it's as though you're daring the wave to

throw you off the board. You do realize surfing is not a contact sport?"

"The way I do it it is."

Kirk stopped and he faced her. "No, no no. Surfing is all about
becoming one with the water. An extension of the wave, even."

She kept her mouth shut and worked hard at making sure
her features didn't show him she clearly thought he was wrong.

"I can see you don't believe me," he said.

Guess she wasn't doing such a good job.

"Tomorrow," he announced, "you, me and our boards are hitting the water. I'm going to show you how to really surf."

She couldn't help the big smile spreading across her face.
"Does that mean you're taking me on? I've got the sponsorship?"

His eyes narrowed as if he were still considering it. "We'll
see how well you take instruction, but I won't keep you waiting.
I'll tell you right after we're done."

She squelched the disappointment she felt at not being offered
his sponsorship right away. Had she really expected it so soon?

"Eleven work for you?" he asked.

"I'm on dawn patrol," she told him. The phrase used by people who had to surf early because they'd be at jobs at times like
eleven in the morning.

He nodded as if he understood, but she doubted this man had
much necessity to be on the beach that early. "Okay, sunrise it is."

THE NEXT MORNING, Drea yawned as she was going through her
series of stretches on the beach. She'd hardly slept the night before. One moment she'd been in a deep sleep, the next, awake,
excited and nervous. All due to the sexy, intriguing man she'd
be meeting up with in just a few hours. To surf with a world
champion like Kirk Murray…

Even if he didn't decide to sponsor her, to get pointers from
someone so skilled was an unbelievable opportunity.

But it was the prospect of talking and laughing and spending time with a man she admired, found so sexy and wanted to
know more about that had given her sleep schedule such fits.

Sometimes when a person met a crush, they were disappointed, but Kirk Murray was very crush-worthy.

She felt a tiny prickle of awareness between her shoulder blades. She smiled, knowing Kirk Murray had to be responsible.

"Even in this dim light, I'd be able to spot you with that yellow bikini."

Kirk carried his board with ease, looking pretty good himself this early in the morning in blue swim trunks and with a bright orange-and-red beach towel draped casually around his neck.

"No one can claim they didn't see me coming with this suit," she said.

"Drea, you'd be hard to miss in anything you were wearing."

Was that…? Could that have been…? Had Kirk Murray just flirted with her? Goose bumps formed on her arms at the prospect.

"You paddle out. I want to watch you catch a few waves first."

With a nod, Drea grabbed her board and ran out into the water. She couldn't wait, longing for that first surprising splash of the ocean against her skin. Everything seemed right when she was in the ocean. She never felt awkward, and she knew what she was doing. The waves weren't too high this morning, but good enough to show Kirk what she could do.

She took on the waves, aggressively and fast, quickly getting into her rhythm.

After two runs, Kirk whistled and she returned to shore.

She paddled back, and when her feet could touch, she lifted her board from the water and walked the rest of the way toward the man waiting for her. His expression didn't tell her anything, but gone was the teasing, easygoing guy from the day before. This morning he was all business.

"Drea, when you started your set, you just picked up your board and hit the water."

She nodded. "Right." What was the problem?

"You can't do that in competition. You didn't even take a moment to observe the sets," he told her, referring to the way waves broke into a pattern.

"What's the point? I just paddle out and push through."

"Yes, but you're going to end up wasting a lot of your energy just paddling out. You can maximize your time in the water hitting waves and impressing the judges if you slow down and take a little time. Do some observation. Count the waves in the set and go before the next set starts. If you plan it right, you can diminish the water resistance."

"That makes a lot of sense," she said, nodding.

"Drea, tell me why you're drawn to surfing."

The question came so out of the blue that she answered him honestly without hiding her need to soften her desires. "I live for that rush of adrenaline. That moment right before I pop up on my board to the feel of the water rushing against my bare skin." Her fingers curled around her board. Describing her feelings to Kirk made her want to catch a wave and experience what she'd just expressed even more. "You know, the ancient Islanders surfed naked."

Kirk nodded toward the water. "Feel free."

She laughed. "Maybe another time. How about you? Why do you surf? I feel like you were looking for something in my answer."

"I was, sort of. I surf because it makes me feel like I'm part of something bigger than myself. Out there, alone on my board surrounded by the ocean, I feel at one with nature."

Yeah, no. She didn't feel any of that. She'd met a lot of Zen-type surfers, but had never figured Kirk for one of them. Interesting.

"Come on, surf with me," he said, his voice soft and inviting.

If he'd said, "Come on, let's get a root canal," in that same quiet tone he'd used just now, she probably would have offered to look up the dentist's number in the phonebook. She couldn't imagine anything better than riding the waves with him at her side.

They picked up their boards and walked together toward the water. About twenty feet inside from where the waves were breaking, Kirk sat on his board and glanced her way. "Forget what you know about speed and aggression. Instead, I want you to think about merging with the wave."

Ahh, making her see surfing his way was what he was after. Okay, she could play along, especially if it would get her that sponsorship. Rather than launch herself toward the wave, she slid from her prone position and began to paddle.

"Match your speed to the wave," he called. She glanced over, and he was right beside her. Drea felt the water against her skin, sensed the wave pattern through her board and adjusted her paddling.

"Now let the wave catch you."

This must be the oneness with the water Kirk was talking about earlier. Sure enough, the wave caught her board and began to accelerate. She popped up and began to ride.

She glanced over and saw Kirk surfing beside her. He flashed her a big smile. She'd never actually surfed with another person before. Oh, there'd been plenty of people in the water surfing next to her, but to actually surf with someone was a different experience.

They rode to shore, angling to extend the time of their ride.

"What did you think?" Kirk asked when they were waist-deep in the water.

"That was amazing," she cried. If there were ever words she wished she could call back, it would be those. It would be obvious to a three-year-old she meant the ride with him was amazing, and not the technique of becoming one with the ocean.

The smile faded from his lips, his eyes. "Yes, it was."

He didn't hide the fact that his gaze searched her face, traveled down her body. Focused on her eyes. She knew when she spotted interest in a man's expression. His body stance. Kirk was interested in her for more than business purposes.

Her whole life she'd been a risk-taker. Everything she had was because she went after it. Right now she wanted Kirk. She pushed her board out of her way, stretched on her tiptoes and reached for the back of Kirk's head, drawing his lips down to hers.

3

THE SALTY WATER of the ocean had cooled on his mouth, but his lips were deliciously warm. She closed her eyes and pressed herself against the strong, solid length of his body. For a moment he stood still. Stood still long enough for her almost to pull away. Then, with a groan, his arms wrapped around her hips and he pulled her closer to his chest.

Adrenaline rushed through her, and it had nothing to do with the beach or a wave. It was all about this man.

He wanted her.

Just like she wanted him.

Her nipples tightened beneath her bikini top and her thighs brushed against the roughness of his. His fingers made lazy patterns against the small of her back, which made her want to arch against him.

A catcall came from the beach, and they broke apart.

Kirk scrubbed his hand down his face. "One of my biggest pet peeves is people who make out in public, and here I am doing it myself."

She saw the frustration in his stance. His shoulders were tight, the muscles along his back taut. He hadn't wanted their kiss to end, and even though she was just as disappointed, she was also thrilled that he'd felt the same way.

He shrugged, then flashed her an almost chagrined expression. "Lost my discipline there. Won't happen again."

Like the ocean, like a giant wave, the words that had just come out of Kirk's mouth sounded a lot like a dare. She wanted to make him need to kiss her again and again.

"So you're a man all about control?"

He nodded. "It's what the sport is about."

"No, no. It's not control. It's chaos," she said with an excited smile.

"It's focus."

"Courage and daring."

He shook his head, but a smile tweaked at the corner of his lip. "Discipline. Something you need to become better acquainted with."

Drea raised a brow. "You going to teach me discipline, Kirk?"

"Now that one I'm not even going to touch." Kirk angled his head toward the waves. "Got time for another run?"

That sounded more like what she had in mind. Maybe he was already beginning to see things her way.

Drea looked up at the sun, the poor gal's clock. Disappointment coursed through as she realized the sun was almost directly overhead. "No, I have to get to work."

His eyebrows shot up. "You're working while in training?"

"The winnings from Rookie of the Year only covered my airfare to Hawaii. Luckily, my job at the Trading Post covers my share of the rent." Money. It all came down to money. With her nomadic lifestyle, her mother had raised her not to value it. Of course, that was not really practical when you were trying to buy things like food.

"Okay, let's process what we've done here today," he said, his tone all business.

"The kiss?"

"No, your run."

"Is this what it's like to have a coach?" she asked, as they waded up to the shore.

"I'm taking it easy on you today since you're self-taught. Tomorrow we start early. Wear a bright suit, like you did today."

"How come?" she asked as she headed toward the showers to rinse off.

"My assistant is bringing the video camera so we can film your runs and analyze them later."

"You're kidding. Like what football players do?"

"Exactly."

Drea thrust her board and beach towel to Kirk and stepped under the spray. No matter how much she prepared herself, the blast of cool fresh water was always a shock to her skin. "Yow."

She maneuvered beneath the shower, cold water sluicing down her arms and legs, as she ran her fingers through her hair.

"And to think I was going to take a few more runs and miss this," he said, his voice deep and filled with desire.

Heat warmed her cheeks. She hadn't meant to be provocative. She'd never acted coy or coquettish in her entire life, but having a man that she'd just kissed watch her shower seemed personal. Intimate. A tension zapped between them now. If they were alone, she'd tug him beneath the spray and run her fingers down his chest. His back. Sink her fingers into his hair and explore the texture. Then she'd kiss him until his skin no longer tasted of salt, but of fresh water and sexy man.

Her nipples tightened, and she only hoped if Kirk noticed he'd chalk it up to the cold water and not her naughty thoughts and what she wanted to do to his body.

When she was satisfied most of the salt was out of her hair and off her skin, she reached for her towel. But Kirk draped it over her shoulders, his fingers lightly caressing her arms as his hands fell away.

Now it was his turn, and Drea couldn't wait to watch the water slide down his back and roll along the lines of his muscles. She swallowed, and willed her voice to sound normal. "I'll hold your gear while you rinse off."

Kirk shook his head. "I shower at home."

Now that was a shame. "That's right. You have nowhere else to be until later."

Ahhh, the luxury. That's what having a sponsorship would do for her.

He picked up both their boards. "Come on, I'll walk you to your car. So how'd you do the first time you surfed Pipe?" The

Pipeline of the North Shore of Oahu was known for having some of the heaviest, most dangerous breaks in the world.

Drea laughed. "Basically a sand facial. I completely wiped out."

They approached Kaydee's blue Focus and Kirk secured her board to the rack. "Thanks, Kirk. Even if I don't get Da Kine's sponsorship, I want you to know I appreciated the pointers and your time today."

"I know I said I wouldn't keep you waiting, but there are a few details that need to be hammered out."

She nodded. "Right. Sure, I understand," she said, trying to sound blasé. Was he blowing her off?

"That kiss changed things."

Her breath hitched. Had she ruined everything with her impulsive action? She could smack herself. Of course sponsors didn't kiss their promotees.

He nodded back. "And we'll still work on your training tomorrow."

Relief poured through her. She hadn't blown everything. A minute passed without either one of them saying anything.

Okay, this was getting awkward. She needed to change, and he wasn't leaving. She looked at the black asphalt then met his green gaze. "Well, bye then."

"I was going to see you inside your car."

If this weren't such an uncomfortable moment, her heart would probably be doing some kind of melting scenario at his… she didn't even have a word for what he was doing. Gentlemanly behavior?

She wasn't one to be shy, and she wasn't going to start now. "Actually, I was going to change out of my suit."

His brows drew together. "In your car?" he asked, his voice incredulous.

"Of course, haven't you ever done the surfer's change?"

"No. Why can't you just change where you work?"

"A friend of mine got me that job, but the owner of the Trading Post doesn't like surfers. Thinks we're too transient, which is probably true. Something about we're just learning how to use the cash register correctly and then we're out of there chasing a wave somewhere else. Don't worry about me, I've had plenty of practice."

"I'll stand guard to make sure no one sees."

With a roll of her eyes, she opened the car door and draped her long beach towel over the door and to the roof. She secured it in place with the beach bag she'd kept locked in the car. Then she crouched on the seat, and began to strip. She'd changed like this dozens of times, but just like taking the shower, taking off her clothes with Kirk's back to her felt like nothing that should be done on the side of the road.

She had to lighten up the situation.

"I can't believe you've never changed like this. You talk to me about tradition of the sport, but this, my friend, is a time-honored practice that you've completely missed out on." She hooked her fingers around her bikini bottoms and lifted her hips off the seat, sliding the material down her legs.

"Imagining what you're doing right now is driving me crazy."

"Good," she said, not being able to stop her goofy grin. So he planned to keep up with her training, did his statement tell her he planned to kiss her again, too? Her top followed, and she quickly donned her panties and bra. Thank goodness the Post provided free uniforms. She slid the khaki pants up her legs and snapped the Hawaiian-print blouse closed.

She stood and slid back into her flip-flops. "You can look now."

Kirk turned and eyed her new clothing. "Pretty impressive."

She shrugged and reached for a clip out of the bag still keeping the towel in place. With a few quick twists of her wrist, she had her hair firmly secured to the Trading Post's dress code standards.

His gaze lowered to her lips, and she held her breath, wondering if he was going to kiss her this time. Instead, he took a step away from her, lifting his board from where it balanced against Kaydee's car.

With a little wave, she retrieved her beach bag and towel and tossed them into the passenger seat. She started the car, signaled and pulled into traffic.

Drea made a vow that she wouldn't look in the rearview mirror to see if Kirk was where she left him.

She even kept that vow for a good ten yards. Then she looked.

And a tiny thrill ran down her back.

He was watching her drive away.

KIRK WALKED slowly down the beach and toward his own vehicle. He'd had the best intentions when he'd come up with the idea of the sponsorship and asked Linda for a few names.

He'd had it lucky, he knew it. His father was one of the most successful hoteliers on the island and he'd never had to scrimp and save and sell his belongings the way so many surfers had just to participate in the sport they loved.

The way Drea had to.

What he hadn't expected was to be completely and totally attracted to Linda's first suggestion, but attracted he was. He'd asked Taylor's second in command to describe the sponsorship prospect, but Linda's cryptic "brown hair, brown eyes and average height" hadn't prepared him for the beat-down Drea's smile had given him.

She didn't just have brown hair, she had long flowing hair that made a man want to touch it. Wrap it around his fingers.

Drea's eyes weren't just brown, they were open and playful and naughty. What kind of man could resist that full-on sexy combination?

And while she might be average in height, when she wrapped her arms around his neck and fitted that surf-toned body of hers to his, he was a goner.

He should end this right now. What was going on between them wasn't professional. It wouldn't be good for him or for her. But how fair was that? Drea clearly needed that sponsorship, and how could he deny her the opportunity just because he didn't want to keep his hands off her?

She deserved a sponsorship. She was a good surfer, and it was no fluke she'd earned her Rookie of the Year status. She had guts

and amazing instinct. What she lacked was the style and caution
to earn the points from the judges while keeping herself safe. He
wanted to help her, he truly did, and not just because he found
her sexy, or because she kissed him in such a way that he forgot
about business or surfing or discipline for the first time since
he could remember. He wanted to help her because he liked her
and saw a little something of himself, that drive that made her
want to push and push herself until she reached the top.

He admired her and desired her all at the same time, and that
was a problem.

When he'd set himself down this path, his goal was to help
new surfers in and out of the water. Could he give her the sponsorship and walk away from training her himself?

It was three o'clock and the tourists were milling about the
Trading Post oohing over the dancing hula-girl dolls, trying on
the brightly colored Hawaiian shirts and picking out postcards.
Drea was slipping a credit card receipt into the bin below the
cash register she'd finally mastered when a large bound stack
of papers landed on the counter.

Startled, she looked up to see Kirk's smiling face.

"What is that?" she asked, excitement racing through her
body.

"A contract."

"Really?" she asked so loudly several of the customers jerked
their heads her way.

He leaned over the counter, getting eye to eye with her. "I
would have offered you the sponsorship this morning, but I
needed to do some thinking."

"About my surfing?"

His gaze lowered to her mouth. "About that kiss."

"Oh," she said, feeling warm all over despite the heavy blast
of air-conditioning.

Something fierce burned deep in his green eyes. "That kiss
changed everything. Suddenly, offering you that sponsorship
didn't seem professional anymore. Still, you need protection,
and that contract will give you that."

"Protection? Why?"

"You need to know that the Da Kine sponsorship doesn't ride on you playing in the water with the boss."

"I never thought that." She rushed to reassure him, but she'd never be able to make herself feel sorry for kissing him.

His shoulders relaxed and his smile seemed a little more easy. Had he been worried she'd only kissed him, flirted with him because she wanted his money? She'd be insulted if that weren't probably his reality. Her mother had always said being rich rather than poor only traded one set of problems for another.

Although she wouldn't mind trying out the rich-person problems for a while.

"What you're signing is an agreement between Da Kine and you. Not me. Anytime you want to leave, you can, provided you do it in writing. If the lawyers representing Da Kine want to end the sponsorship, the conditions are clearly outlined, as is the protocol. I can't fire you, Drea. The sponsorship is yours, if you want it. It's not contingent on…"

"Kissing the boss?" she asked with a laugh.

"No."

Silly as it sounded, a lump formed in her throat. Kirk had gone to this extra trouble to protect her, to make sure everything was aboveboard. He didn't have to do it. He could have given his sponsorship to someone who offered fewer…complications. If he had, she would have still wanted to see him privately. Surely she was that obvious.

Those extra provisions were the nicest things anyone had ever done for her. Drea saw a whole new side of him. Kirk Murray was a man of honor, and that would have sounded corny, but right now she'd never wanted to be with someone more. That crush was turning into something more. Way more.

Keep it light. Keep it simple.

She tapped the contract with her nail. "So, technically, once I sign this, I could kiss you whenever I wanted."

"Technically. Sure," he said with a shrug. "No one's stopping you."

"Powell, what's going on?"

Drea straightened and addressed the booming voice calling her name. "Kirk Murray, this is Larry Cronin, my boss here at the Trading Post."

Larry raised one of his shaggy brows. "Surfer?"

Kirk nodded.

"Just a few more minutes, okay?" she asked.

Her boss pursed his lips, then adjusted a display of Hawaiian coffee. "Five minutes," he agreed, then walked off.

"Interesting guy," Kirk told her.

"Not used to being so easily dismissed, are you?" she asked as she grabbed a rag to wipe the counter, hoping it would make her look busy.

"You think this is funny." His tone almost sounded accusatory.

"It must be hard to not be treated as if you're Kirk Murray, champion surfer. Or Kirk Murray, son of one of the richest men on the island."

"How about Kirk Murray, boyfriend?"

She stopped wiping and met his green eyes. "Hmmm, that has a ring to it," she said, opting for casual. But her heart beat faster.

He pushed the contract toward her. "I tried to make this as fair as possible, but still you should have your lawyer look at it."

Yeah, I'll have my whole team right on it.

She nodded as she took the papers from him. Her fingers shook. This contract represented everything she'd wanted. Worked for.

"Enough with the chitchat, Powell. Back to work," Larry called from across the store.

"Am I going to get you into trouble?" Kirk asked.

"Don't worry about it. I have a feeling I won't be working here much longer." She couldn't stop smiling or keep the excitement out of her voice.

"According to the agreement, you'll receive your first paycheck a week from Friday, but maybe we can get you a bridge loan. You'll need to get publicity shots and suit fittings before the competition," Kirk explained.

"New suits?" No more clearance rack. No more stretched-out, salt-damaged and sun-bleached bikinis.

"Featuring the Da Kine logo."

"Of course," she said, grinning.

"We can talk about that tonight. I'll pick you up at eight. My parents are having a cocktail party at the hotel lounge."

"Powell."

"He's leaving," she called good-naturedly, but right now she felt as if she were floating on a cloud. That's how good she felt.

"See you tonight, Drea."

Kirk left her with two thoughts. First, she hadn't said yes to going out with him tonight. And second…what the hell would *she* wear to a cocktail party?

4

BETWEEN Kaydee, Laci and JC, Drea was outfitted in a simple black backless dress. "These strappy heels are the perfect touch. Thanks for all your help, Kaydee," Drea said as she turned away from the full-length mirror to smile at her friends.

"The one who's going to need help is Kirk Murray. You look stunning," JC said with a laugh.

"I can't believe I agreed to go to a cocktail party," Drea said, adjusting the skirt.

"You'll do great."

Right on cue, there was a knock at the door. Drea rushed to answer it and her mouth nearly dropped open. She'd seen Kirk in swim trunks on the beach, casual at his restaurant and now in a dark suit and tie and carrying a yellow hibiscus. Talk about stunning.

After a quick round of introductions, Kirk escorted her to his car, the kind of vehicle that was probably worth more than she'd ever earned. Soft leather seats, navigation system and the kind of stereo that would have made her high-school boyfriend cry.

"Don't take this the wrong way, but your place looked kind of small. Where do you sleep?" he asked once they were on the road.

"Oh, Kaydee doesn't live there. She's a business student at the Western Oahu campus. She's been using me as her marketing project." Was he asking about the sleeping arrangements out of curiosity or for more personal reasons? Her mouth went a little dry thinking about those very personal reasons.

"Two roommates, a job and now this friend you're helping. That's a lot of distractions. How can you train that way?"

"Believe me, I've had to do a lot worse to keep my head above water," she said, chuckling.

Kirk didn't join in. "I'm not sure that you should. You're about to enter a major competition. You need restorative sleep. Time to focus."

"Is that like merging with a wave?"

"Drea, I'm serious. Things are different now. It's not just about you. You represent Da Kine. You have to be in peak physical condition. Not to mention looking good for your publicity shots. Not that you'll have any trouble looking fantastic, but bags under your eyes will not translate well onto a poster."

"I understand, but there's nothing much I can do about it." Hawaii was notorious for its high prices and sharing a place to stay came with the bargain of living on the circuit.

With a press of some buttons on the steering wheel, a phone, set on Speaker, was ringing. "Makana Hotel."

"Hi, James, it's Kirk Murray. I need a suite for the next two weeks."

"Certainly, Mr. Murray. We're booked tonight, but with a little finesse I'll have an opening tomorrow. Beachfront?"

"Finesse away. Put it under the name of Andrea Powell."

"Ahh, the daredevil rookie. Your father mentioned you might be looking for new ventures. I take it things are working out."

He smiled before he answered, and Drea felt like grinding her teeth.

"Really well."

With another push of the buttons, the call ended. Although she knew it was a mistake, Drea didn't wait to count to ten before turning on him. "I can't believe you just did that."

"Did what? James has been working in our hotel for years. It's no big deal."

"You could have asked. Maybe talked with me about it." She

took a deep breath and glanced out her window. Watched palm trees whizz by.

"The Makana is right off the beach. No surfers' changes in the car. Showers in your own place. I thought you'd be happy."

"I understand what you were trying to do, but you can't take over. *That* wasn't what I expected when I signed the contract."

With a flick of his wrist, he signaled and turned into the parking lot of a large high-rise hotel. The Makana. Her new home for the next two weeks, starting tomorrow. He pulled his car out of the way of traffic, put it in Park and faced her.

"This sponsorship thing is new to me. I saw a problem and I wanted to fix it. But Drea, you can't tell me you wanted to keep sharing with your friends. This way you'll have the quiet you need to focus, and room service."

Her eyes widened. "No more cooking? I can't remember the last time I ate something I didn't have to cook. Not that soup or macaroni and cheese is all that hard."

"Then what's the problem?"

"Laci and JC, they're part of the competition surf crowd. All those girls know each other. They're friends. I'm just…just an interloper. Which is fine, I'm used to it, believe me. I was always the new girl in school. The new employee, the new whatever. Staying with Laci and JC sort of eased my transition."

Understanding entered his eyes, and his expression softened. "The surf crowd is your crowd now. You need to start building those networks without using Laci and JC as a crutch. They won't always be there."

Kirk was right. She knew it. Drea just didn't want to start working on those friendships. She was much more comfortable with the loner role she'd cast herself in.

He reached for her hand and gave it a squeeze. "How about if I promise to not make decisions like that again, if you promise to give this living arrangement a try. If you don't like it, we'll leave."

"And you won't be weird about it?"

"I'll buy you the can of chicken noodle myself."

She squeezed his hand back. "Thanks."

"Glad we got that out of the way. Our first fight."

They both laughed. Their relationship, or whatever it could be called, was certainly on the fast track.

"Now we can get to the best part of a fight," he teased.

"The making-up part?"

He leaned over, his lips just inches from hers. "A woman who gets my meaning." Then his mouth lightly brushed against hers. She felt the warmth of his breath on her cheek. Inhaled the exotic scent of his cologne. Her mouth watered whenever she caught the scent of one of Hawaii's native plants, but the scent on Kirk made her want to close her eyes and breathe in deeply.

"I've wanted to kiss you ever since you opened the door and I saw you standing there in this dress looking gorgeous. Hell, I wanted to kiss you at the Trading Post."

"Then why are you talking?" she asked against his lips.

He didn't waste time answering her question. Instead, his fingers curved around her shoulders and his lips took hers. This wasn't the soft, exploring kiss on the beach. This was a kiss of want and desire and passion, but most especially promise. A promise of more to come. She liked the thought of it. Liked it a lot.

But slowly he pulled away. "As awkward as dragging you into the backseat would be, I'd be willing to do it if I didn't know my parents were waiting for us inside, or that there are security cameras installed throughout the parking lot."

Drea's groan turned into a giggle.

Kirk turned away and gripped the steering wheel. Had she done that to him? Made him need to wait and get himself under control? She liked that, because he'd made her breath catch, and her heart beat to the kind of level even surfing didn't match.

With a smile, she adjusted the straps of her dress. Then she pulled down the mirror to make sure her lipstick wasn't smeared.

He started the car, and pulled into the valet parking area. After handing the keys to the valet, he escorted Drea through the lobby and to a lounge.

"Spend a lot of time here?" she asked.

"I practically grew up here." He opened the door and Drea

almost lost her balance. She'd never seen such a beautiful room. One whole side was lined with doors opening up to the incredible beach view, lit by flaming tiki torches. Gorgeous chandeliers hung from the ceiling and dark Pacific wood accented the elegant surroundings.

In a word, the view, the room, the hotel was luxurious. And the people inside the room all matched. The women wore elegant updos, while the men sported suits that would pay for a new board.

And more.

Kirk must have sensed her natural inclination to flee because the reassuring warmth of his hand suddenly rested on the small of her back. "Come on, I'll introduce you to my parents."

If she thought the physical setting was intimidating, then actually seeing Kirk's family up close was downright scary. His mom had that picture-perfect elegance that appeared as natural to her as breathing, and his father wore an air of wealth.

For a moment, she wondered if she wore an air of poverty.

A waiter walked by with a tray of something that looked alcoholic, and Drea was really tempted.

His parents were all polite smiles and welcome, but then his father took Kirk aside to talk business. Drea wandered around to further check out the room. A large buffet was tucked in the corner. All kinds of fruit were on display, but she wasn't hungry.

She'd lost her appetite because she was facing the fact that she didn't belong here. She probably didn't belong with Kirk. The man was out of her league—

No. She wouldn't go there. Her mother hadn't raised her to think that way about herself. These people were rich and had probably known which fork and spoon to use since they could hold a utensil, but they weren't better than she was.

They just had nothing in common with her.

Just like Kirk. The only thing that brought them into the same sphere was surfing.

And desire.

Whenever she wanted something, she went after it full force, with everything she had, no matter what anyone said. She wanted

Kirk Murray, and she wasn't going to let money, or her lack of it, or her strange reaction to it make her back away from him now.

She scanned the room for Kirk and spotted him by an ice sculpture. He seemed miserable as he tugged at his tie, talking to two men. She wanted to take that tie off. Pull the knot apart and slowly slide the material out of the collar. She could almost hear the whisper as the fabric moved, feel the heat from the friction.

Just then Kirk glanced up. His eyes met hers, then narrowed. He must have seen the white-hot desire in her gaze. Her need. Her determination. With a quick word, he stalked toward her, leaving the man he was with in midconversation.

"Ready to go?" he asked when he reached her side.

"We've only been here fifteen minutes," she said, her tone innocent.

"I don't care," he replied, his voice rough and strained.

Excitement and desire flooded through her. Made her nipples tighten. Her panties felt restrictive. "Then let's get out of here."

"Back to the bungalow?" he asked, his face tight with tension.

"Your place?"

"Excellent idea." She felt the familiar weight of his hand at the small of her back as he gently but quickly guided her out of the room.

"Don't you want to say goodbye to your parents?"

"No."

Their rush through the hotel, into the car and to his place happened in a blur. All she knew was the second he shut the door behind him with his foot, she was putting into action her fantasy of taking off his tie.

With a push to his broad shoulders, she had him up against the living-room wall, her fingers at his tie. She tugged at the knot, not very well since she didn't have a lot of experience with men who wore the things. But finally, *finally* she had one end free, reveling in the sound of the silk sliding against the cotton of his collar, just as she imagined. She couldn't wait to get at the first button.

His warm hands slid up her legs, pushing her black skirt higher and higher. She shivered when his fingers reached her thighs, making it hard to focus on the buttons of his shirt. He hooked her leg up around his waist, and she moaned as she felt the hardness of his erection against her most sensitive place.

"Do that again," he urged, his voice husky and seductive.

"Do what?" she asked.

"Make that sound."

"Make me make it," she challenged.

Surprise darkened his eyes, then determination. Kirk seemed to be the kind of a man who always got his way, and she was just the kind of woman who'd make him work for what he wanted.

His fingers slid from her thighs to cup her ass. The heat from his hands seared her through the barely there black panties she wore. His eyes never left hers as he pulled her closer, rubbing her once more.

She moaned, and her eyes drifted shut. Drea didn't even care that he'd gotten his way. How he made her feel was just too good. Actually, she *had* made him work for it, she realized with a smile.

"What's that smile for?" he asked.

She slowly raised her gaze to meet the intensity in his eyes. "You."

He opened his mouth as if he wanted to say something, then he groaned. He cupped her face, drawing her lips toward his own.

Wild and hungry, they kissed and kissed until only the harsh sound of their breathing filled the air. She forgot everything about tonight but the calloused heat of his hands on her skin and the delicious taste of his mouth.

He broke his lips from hers. With frustration and disappointment, she tried to reach for him, bring his mouth back to hers. Until she felt his lips lower to the line of her jaw.

Below her ear.

To the soft responsive side of her neck.

"I can feel how hard your heart is beating."

He gently licked the sensitive pulse point, and her knees went a little weak. Actually went weak. She'd chide herself later, but she'd probably do it again if given the chance. And again.

He moved his hands to her hips to keep her balanced. "Check out this aerial," he said, and spun her until she faced the wall.

She'd been impressed by his aerials on his surfboard, but this move was far more thrilling. And electrifying to her senses.

Kirk placed her hands above her head. "Keep them there," he ordered.

There he went again, telling her what to do. She'd let him get away with it this time. Only because she wanted to know where this would lead.

He traced a slow path down her arms that she felt all the way to her fingertips. When he reached her breasts he lightly touched them. The wings of a butterfly would have been more forceful. She swallowed her growing need for a more powerful touch, knowing that when he finally delivered, the wait would make it all the sweeter. Then he cupped her breasts. She moaned at his touch.

"That's what I've been waiting to hear."

"Next time don't take so long," she said.

He chuckled, the warmth of his breath on the back of her neck sending a shiver down between her shoulders.

He softly caressed her breasts, played with her nipples through her clothes.

"You are the sexiest thing I've ever seen. I've thought of nothing but touching you," he said. The hard ridge of his erection grew and she arched her back to feel it more. The sound of his groan sent a wave of hot sensation all through her body, so she arched again. She loved knowing she could drive him wild.

"Then touch me. Touch me everywhere," she urged, her voice sounding achy.

A cool rush of air hit her bare legs, and she realized one of his hands had left her breast to raise her skirt. Her thighs tingled with the soft graze of his fingers. Then she felt his slow touch at the edge of her panties.

Get there, already.

Kirk laughed deep in his throat as if he understood her frustration. Wanted to prolong it. So she arched her back again, and his fingers drifted under the elastic.

He cupped her, and her knees went weak once more. His fingers lightly stroked her clit. "Yes. There," she urged.

But he slipped his hand away, and guided her to the large couch, which dominated the living room. They fell across the soft leather of the armrest. Draped over the edge of the furniture like this meant that even if her legs failed her, she wouldn't fall to the carpeted floor. His foot gently pushed her feet apart so he could have better access to her body. His hand slid into her panties once again and she moaned. She balanced on the tips of her toes and his erection once again pressed against her backside.

He stroked her clit with a light, tantalizing touch, then his fingers moved lower. Into her. She tried to bite back the moan, but why fight it? The sensations he aroused in her were not supposed to be quiet.

Kirk developed a rhythm with his fingers. Around her clit, then in and out. Over and over again. She gripped the cushion under her hands as he whispered into her ear. "That's it, Drea. Grind against me, and I'll make you feel so good."

She pushed against him hard, and he slid a finger into her while his thumb took over caressing the best spot.

"Come," he said. His voice, his hands, his warmth an invitation.

Her muscles tensed and she squeezed her eyes tight.

She gasped as she orgasmed, her whole body trembling from the force of her body's release.

Kirk licked behind her ear. "I could listen to you make that sound all day long. Let me do it again."

"No," she said as she grabbed his arm. With her wavering strength, she pulled his hand from her panties, turned and backed along the couch until she was lying fully against the soft gray cushions. "Make love to me, Kirk."

She watched as he shrugged out of his dress shirt, then the T-shirt he'd worn underneath. It probably sounded corny as hell, but he was a thing of beauty—made the way a man was supposed to be made. She'd seen his naked chest a lot, touched it even. But somehow, knowing he was about to be joined to her in the most intimate way two people could be joined, she appreciated his body on a whole new level.

"Sure you don't want the bed?"

Drea shook her head. "No. Right here." She pulled the dress up and over her head, tossing it to the carved coffee table to emphasize her point.

She watched Kirk swallow, then reach for his wallet to take out a condom. His pants and underwear joined his shirt on the floor and she watched as he rolled the latex down his hard length. That simple act alone would make her ready for his penetration. She reached up, wanting to finish the job for him. Wanting to feel the hardness of his cock in her hand.

His gaze met hers when her fingers joined his, then his eyes closed and he groaned when she slid the condom firmly in place.

"You're still wearing too many clothes."

With a smile, Drea hooked her fingers on the elastic at her hips, then slowly slid the black silk down her legs. The skin around his mouth tightened with each inch.

"You're going to pay for that," he said, his tone holding tempting promise.

She crooked her finger at him in invitation.

He lowered himself onto her, then pressed inside. Nothing felt like the weight of a man. *Nothing.* She welcomed him, wrapping her legs around his back once he was fully inside. He felt incredible. Hard and hot and just what she wanted. Needed.

He cupped her face once more and kissed her. His tongue mimicked the movements of his body as he slowly thrust into her.

But Drea didn't want slow. She pushed at his shoulders and he sat up, taking her with him. Seated atop him, she could now control the angle, the speed. His lips found her nipple, and she lowered herself onto his erection, wanting to give him a taste of his own slow performance. He gently grazed her breast with his teeth, and suddenly she didn't care about teasing him. Drea began to move.

It didn't take her long to reach her peak, and her movements became more frenzied. He cupped her backside, guiding her and bringing her down on him with force. Her inner muscles began to grip him as her orgasm took over. She held him tighter, wanting him closer. Sensation exploded inside her. Stronger, more powerful than the previous climax. She gasped for air, feeling him get harder and harder inside her. Then his whole body tensed, and he came with a deep, satisfied groan.

Drea's head lowered to his shoulder. They were both sweaty, their bodies sensitive from the rush of orgasm. After a while, he gently pulled away from her body and lowered them both to the couch. She settled against the tight muscles of his chest as he buried his face in her hair. She basked in the feel of his solid body alongside hers. How long they lay there she didn't know, but he kissed her lips and her eyes fluttered open.

"Good?" he asked.

"Very good," she told him with a slow smile.

"The couch," he said, disgust filling his voice. "I can't believe we didn't make it to the bedroom."

"Are you knocking it?"

"Never. One of my best new memories just happens to have been made on a couch."

5

If Kirk were the epitome of the fierce and tender lover the night before, under the morning sun with a surfboard under him, he'd become a tyrant. Talk about morning-after regrets.

"Make your pop-up more fluid."

"Your hands are too close to the board."

"Make your footwork more precise when you do your crossover."

And they still had the videos to analyze.

On and on it went, and to top it off, she now had some jerk paddling behind her, ready to steal her position and horn in on her wave. Surfers called these jerks snakes, and she thought that name really fit.

She managed to take care of business and ride the wave. Kirk motioned her toward the shore, and she grabbed her board and met him at the sand. She dreaded what she'd hear, hating the change in their relationship. It was as if he'd taken all that control and focus he was so fond of and directed it solely at her flaws.

His expression was harsh. "What were you doing out there? You were far too aggressive with the other surfers."

"Are you talking about that snake? You're the one who talks about being one with the water and respect for the ocean. If the water's crowded, I'm happy to wait my turn, but I'm not giving any handouts."

A series of emotions played across his face. Then she visibly saw the tension release from his shoulders. "You're right," Kirk said after a moment.

"What?" she asked, raising her eyebrows and deliberately giving her tone a touch of incredulousness. "Did you just say I'm right? After everything being wrong from my stance to how I angle, I'm doing something that works for you?"

A small smile played about the ruggedness of his mouth. "Is that how I sounded?"

That slight tug of his lips made up for a lot of his tyrannical attitude. "A little."

"A lot." His eyes narrowed. "Listen, Drea. You have amazing surf instincts. You're a winner, but you are missing the refinements, the little things that give you those extra style points from the judges. But I don't want to change you. How you handled that surfer reminded me that your style is aggressive. You don't have to do everything I say, or adopt my attitude, but I do want you to give it a try. To take it under consideration."

She met his green gaze, and nodded. "I will."

"Especially since I'm right."

She swung her head in his direction, studied his expression. Then Drea gasped. "Did you just make a joke? Kirk Murray just made a joke about the seriousness that is surfing. I can't believe it."

"I make jokes all the time."

"Are you sure? Because I think sometimes you forget that surfing is supposed to be fun."

He instantly returned to the serious trainer. "It's a sport. A very dangerous sport if you don't take it seriously. Don't forget the motto. Respect the wave—"

"Respect the sport. I remember."

He'd quoted it often enough today.

She took a deep breath, missing their special connection of the day before. And especially of the night. "I know it's Da Kine, but it's you, too. I know I can never repay you for what you've done for me. You're going to teach me style, I'm going to teach you to have a little fun in your life."

"Now that, wahine, is something I'm going to take you up

on." His voice sent shivers down her back. Here she was thinking about the fun of standing on a board, and now he had her thinking of fun between the sheets. He'd never called her *wahine* before. The endearment men used for female surfers.

She leaned against him. "I like it when you speak Hawaiian to me." She liked it a lot.

His gaze darkened, but then his expression turned regretful, and he glanced down at his watch. "Ready to say goodbye to your new roommates?"

No.

Instead she smiled and nodded.

Kirk had met her at the beach, grumbling about dawn patrol. She hadn't wanted to make a lot of noise moving out this morning, so they were waiting until after they'd completed their surfing to remove her things from the bungalow.

"You do have to admit the beach is less crowded now," she told him.

His hand slid around her hip. "I'd trade the crowds for more time in bed. With you."

Drea had spent most of the night at Kirk's, knowing her roommates, and probably Kaydee for that matter, would be wanting a full report about her date. Lucky for her, they'd been asleep when she'd finally slipped inside the bungalow. Her feelings were too new to want to talk about them.

"It's crazy you doing dawn patrol anyway."

"I told you, I can't quit the Trading Post. I promised Mr. Cronin two weeks notice, and I need to keep good relations with him in case…"

Kirk's lips tightened. "Okay, now we're getting to the real reason. You were going to say you needed to keep good relations in case your surfing doesn't take off?"

Or the sponsorship dissolves? But she'd keep that thought to herself.

"Drea, why are you afraid to think things might just work out?"

Why did everyone want to analyze her motivations?

"You have to keep a positive frame of mind at all times."

"That's easy for you to say. You've always had Daddy's money…" She let her words trail off.

"I always had Daddy's money to fall back on. That's what you were going to say."

She gave him a quick nod.

Kirk gave an easy shrug. "It's true. I've had it easier than most. That's the reason why I want to sponsor and train surfers. Give them the same kind of shot I had."

"Like what you're doing with me."

"Like what I'm *trying* to do with you. You have to start believing in yourself to make it work."

She flashed him a big smile. "I promise to try harder."

She could tell he didn't believe her for a second, but he did visibly relax. "Come on, let's get your stuff from the bungalow."

There was believing in herself and there was also being realistic. Keeping her job at the Trading Post was being realistic. Remembering that Kirk Murray wouldn't always be her financial savior was also being realistic.

Even though she'd almost put her foot in her mouth, she was glad they'd had this conversation. She'd realized something about Kirk today. Although he took her comment about his daddy's money in stride, she knew she'd struck a small nerve. Maybe that's why he was so focused and almost businesslike about his surfing. Money might have put him in the position to get his shot, but Kirk's winning was all him.

Strange that they had something in common. She wanted to prove that Rookie of the Year wasn't a fluke. He wanted to prove he was the real deal. He'd met his goal. She'd just have to think positively about hers. Kirk would be proud.

LACI AND JC were waiting for her in the living room of the bungalow. She'd met both of them briefly in California, where she'd won her title, but she hadn't hung around after the awards ceremony to chat. She just never seemed to fit in with the other surfers. But the pair had been a lifesaver when she'd arrived in Hawaii with little more than her board and no place to stay.

They'd offered her their third bedroom. She'd thought they viewed her as little more than a pest, but now that she was actually moving out, the two looked a little down. Were they upset about her leaving?

JC stood and picked up one of Drea's bags, handing it to her. "Thanks," Drea said.

"No problem."

They were about the same height, but that's where the similarities ended. JC, who had had a meteoric rise to the top, enjoyed the gorgeous, exotic looks that made her a favorite among the male surfers and potential sponsors.

"Anything I can help with?" Laci asked as she passed Drea's other bag to Kirk. She had that summery all-American girl look, with a face full of freckles.

"That's it? Just two bags?" Kirk asked.

"I'm an efficient packer," Drea said in a poor attempt at humor.

Laci turned toward Kirk. "Drea doesn't have any clothes."

"I have clothes." But that defensive statement sounded pretty weak even to her own ears.

JC flashed her a secret wink. "Not the right kind of clothes. You'll be doing interviews, community-service time. Shorts and T-shirts don't work."

"And don't forget the evening stuff," Laci added.

"I can't believe I hadn't thought of that. I've already ordered new suits and rashguards with the Da Kine logo," Kirk said.

"She's going to need the works," JC told him.

"I'm on it." Kirk grabbed his phone.

"Do I really need that stuff?" Drea just wanted to surf. Surely Kirk wouldn't want her before cameras and reporters so soon. She hadn't taken any of the publicity training Kaydee had insisted she'd need, and Drea wasn't exactly a natural with a microphone in front of her face. Memories of how she'd frozen up in front of a high-school classmate flashed through her mind. The reporter was a friend just trying to get her yearbook class assignment completed. Imagine how terrible she'd do if it were for real. She'd let down Da Kine and Kirk.

"Trust me, you're going to want all those clothes. The reporters will be all over you," Laci said with a nod.

With a click, Kirk returned his cell phone to the latch on his belt. "Okay, you're all set for four at the store in my father's hotel. I hate to rush things, but I have to get to work."

Drea nodded, but made no move. The room grew quiet. The four of them just looked at one another awkwardly.

Beside her, Kirk stood straighter, as if he'd just realized something. "I'll put these in the trunk so you all can talk. Just come out when you're ready, Drea."

"Please tell me you have hooked up with that man, because to not do so would be a sad and terrible waste," Laci said when Kirk was out of earshot.

Drea felt the heat in her cheeks and knew she was blushing. "I, uh…"

"Don't bother answering. Your face tells us nothing is going to waste. What I can't believe is that you came back here last night when you could have spent all night in bed with him," JC said. Then she glanced toward Laci. "A whole new wardrobe. Pretty slick."

"What can I say?" Laci said, grinning.

Drea leaned against the wall. "I can't believe it myself. It's like from a movie, and at four o'clock, that's where the fun, pumpy music comes in, and the girl comes out of the dressing room, flashing from one exciting outfit to the next while her friends shake their heads or smile."

"I can shake my head," JC said.

Laci nodded. "I can smile."

Looked as if she was going to have help shopping. Good. She hadn't figured it out until just this moment that she had stopped thinking of JC and Laci as competitors and roommates and now thought of them as true friends.

"I'm going to miss you guys," she said quietly, feeling her throat tighten.

JC gave her a quick hug. "Hey, it's not like we're not going to see you every day on the beach."

"And feel free to invite us over for room service anytime,"

Laci told her with a smile. "We were counting on your skills with the can opener."

Drea gave them both a hug, then quickly walked out to the car where Kirk was waiting for her.

As she shut the car door, Kirk reached for her hand and gave her a squeeze. "Okay?"

She nodded, but quickly changed the subject. "We surfing tomorrow?"

"Actually, I thought we could review the tape of today's surfing."

She raised a brow. "And where would we be doing that? Some place like, oh, your apartment?"

Kirk nodded. "My apartment works."

Drea laughed. "I'm looking forward to it."

The laughter faded from his eyes, replaced by heat and sexual tension. His fingers brushed her cheek. "If I kiss you now, I may just drag you to my apartment."

Drea leaned across the gearshift and puckered.

Kirk groaned. "Wahine, you are going to kill me. I have to go to work."

Warmth from his words suffused her body. "Drive," she said, smiling. "I can kill you tomorrow."

KIRK WASN'T SURPRISED when his dad walked into the small room Kirk used as an office at the back of Da Kine.

"You cut out of there pretty early last night. Your mother barely had the chance to say two words to you."

"Good one, Dad. Zeroed right in on the surefire guilt inducer," Kirk said as he saved the spreadsheet he was preparing and spun in his chair to face his dad.

John Murray nodded as if he was taking a small bow. "You really do need to spend more time at the hotel. Someday it will all be yours."

"You have plenty of years to run your hotel, I'm not worried about taking up the reins. Besides, I had to get Drea home. She's training."

"Very stunning young woman. You're sponsoring surfers

now?" But it wasn't really a question. His father knew exactly what his child was doing. "When you'd first mentioned looking toward ventures outside of surfing, it was only to help train other surfers. You have the restaurant, you're sponsoring and now it looks like you're still in training. What about your retirement?"

"It's buildup to the retirement. Da Kine is doing the sponsoring, and it's all part of the business plan. I've made an agreement with XtremeSportNet and the Girls Go Banzai competition. The restaurant is now the official meal provider for all the competitors, staff and other corporate sponsors."

The other man nodded. His father's unique version of "well done." "Impressive, and good experience for when you take over the hotel. But how does Da Kine sponsoring a surfer figure into the deal?"

Kirk imagined Drea in her new suit, and his body instantly became more aware. Edgy. "She'll be wearing the logo, and believe me when I tell you it will be seen a lot. Drea Powell is going to be a star. Have you seen her surf? She's amazing. Gutsy. We're training together."

Although he couldn't help noticing the panic that entered her eyes when interviews came into conversation. He'd wanted to tell her she'd be great, not just with an audience. The two of them hadn't even discussed how they wanted to proceed together in public. He would have been thrilled with showing the world she was the woman by his side, but he wouldn't without talking it over with her first. He smiled as he remembered her anger at him making the decision about where she was going to live. He wouldn't fall into that trap again.

"Surfing was always your area of expertise, so I'll take your word on it." John Murray's eyes grew concerned. "Things looked a little more...*personal* between the two of you than just a business arrangement."

Had he been that obvious last night?

Hmmm, what had given him away? The fact that he couldn't stop touching her or that they'd stayed fifteen minutes before he ushered her out of the lounge as fast as he could? The sex that had followed lived up to way more than his expectations. "Dad, I—"

"No need to explain. I was your age once. There was a time with your mother—"

Kirk held up a hand, grimacing. "Dad, these are really not details I want to know."

His dad smiled. "Probably not. As my son, I know how much you hate to take advice from your old man. But from one businessman to another, let me tell you—there's a reason for clichés like not mixing business with pleasure. It rarely works out."

"HEY THERE, surfer dude."

Kirk glanced up from the film he was watching to see Drea in his doorway.

Only it was a very different Drea. Dressed in a straight black skirt and silky, dark pink blouse, she didn't appear to be the wild and reckless surfer he knew.

The knot she'd twisted the soft, long strands of her hair into made him want to take out whatever pins she'd used to hold it in place and sink his face into the sweet-smelling strands.

The very appropriate length of her skirt made his fingers itch to find the clasp and feel the whoosh of air as the material drifted down her legs and hit the floor.

And those little tiny buttons on her shirt made him ache to undo each one and slide the material off her shoulders so he could admire her beautiful breasts.

Which was why it was a good thing he'd changed their meeting place from his apartment to his office at Da Kine.

The smile on her face was beginning to fade.

Oh, yeah. He'd been so caught up in thinking about how amazing she looked, he'd forgotten to say anything to her about it. "I could eat you up."

"Thank you," Drea said as she closed the door behind her and stalked to his desk. She wrapped her arms around his neck and leaned in for a kiss. "I've been thinking about doing this all day."

So had he. Working all day had been difficult, especially

after hearing his father's words. He bent forward, his hands already reaching for the tempting buttons on her blouse. Until he remembered *he'd* sent her to get that blouse. And the rest of her professional attire.

"Wait, Drea, wait."

Her brows knitted in confusion. "What's wrong?"

"I think we may have rushed things." He hated saying that. Wished he could call the words back, but he'd been thinking about what his dad had said ever since he'd left. His father was a successful businessman, and his advice had always been spot-on.

He was expecting her to deny it, maybe even get defensive or reassure him. He hadn't expected her to laugh. "You think? Two days…" She made a tsking sound.

"I'm serious. You're in training now and need to concentrate. This is your first major competition since winning Rookie of the Year, and a relationship between us would be a huge distraction." Hard to say when all he wanted to do was, well, her.

She backed away and leaned against the wall. He hated seeing the pain in her eyes. Experiencing the same pain himself.

"That's why we have the contract. You think I can't handle it?" she asked, her voice filled with hurt.

"I've never actually trained anyone myself. I shouldn't allow myself to get distracted, either. We both need to be focused and controlled right now."

Drea folded her arms across her chest, and he thought she was going to argue with him. He almost wanted her to. Then she nodded and he reached for the remote control.

He hated that she didn't fight harder. That he hadn't, either.

Kirk powered up the TV. "Watch your stance on this first run you did."

The next six days followed the same pattern. Surfing in the morning, followed by dissecting the films of her runs at the restaurant in the afternoon. Gone was the sexy, irreverent woman of earlier. Drea had truly become more focused and her style was improving. Cutting off the sex had been the best decision for her career.

But it was the worst choice according to Kirk's body. If he'd thought seeing her splash around in the water in her bikini was tough a few days ago, now he knew what those small triangles of fabric hid.

His body physically ached as he positioned her hips on the board. He remembered how those hips felt against him as he thrust into her.

He missed her easy smiles, their conversation and her laughter. At night he stayed away, thinking of the soft, sexy sounds she made as she came.

Kirk was at a breaking point, which was ridiculous because two weeks ago he hadn't even known who Andrea Powell was, and now he couldn't concentrate on anything but her.

"Oh, look."

He glanced in the direction she pointed to see a young boy, his longboard twice as big as he was, struggling in the water. She smiled, and his breath caught and his gut clenched. That was the first smile he'd seen since he'd told her the personal side of their relationship had to end. He'd do just about anything to keep that smile on her face.

Drea asked, "Remember your first time on a board?"

He nodded. One of his nannies had brought him to the beach, so that she could meet up with her boyfriend, and Kirk had taken to surfing right away. Much to his father's horror. But that first time he rode a wave all the way to shore had been the best day of his life.

As a child. That memory couldn't compete with his evening with Drea.

"Let's help him," she suggested, and he quickly followed.

Kirk sensed that Drea was growing increasingly frustrated with her training. She was snapping. Her teasing responses were gone. As were the heated glances from her eyes and her quick smiles aimed at him. The break might do her good.

The boy's mom was trying to give him some pointers, but it was clear she didn't know how to guide him.

"Mind if we show him a few things?" Drea asked the woman.

"Hey, I know you," the woman said to Kirk. "You're that

surf guy." A look of relief crossed the boy's mother's face. "Feel free. I'm terrible."

"Why don't you join us? You might have some fun." Then Drea turned to the boy. "My name's Drea and this is Kirk. What's your name?"

"I'm Riley."

"First thing, Riley, we're going to paddle on our board to grab that beach break. Have you ever ridden mush before?"

The boy laughed and shook his head.

"Well, you're going to."

An hour later the four of them were laughing and cheering as Riley popped up on his board and road the mushy white water of his first wave all the way in to shore. Riley hugged Drea and Kirk before they picked up their boards and made their way toward Kirk's car.

Drea handed her board to Kirk in silence, and he secured both boards to the racks on his car.

"That was a lot of fun," he said.

"Yeah, I've been missing fun."

She lifted her eyes to his, and his blood started to pound in his veins. Heat and desire were banked in those brown eyes of hers. And something else…something he could only describe as yearning.

"Have you?"

Without a thought, Kirk dragged her into his arms. His hands smoothed up and down her back. She fitted against him perfectly, so perfectly.

"I've thought of nothing else but this," she said.

Then he pushed her way. "Drea, we can't. You're supposed to be thinking of your training."

Drea glared at him. "Stop it, Kirk. Just stop it. Everything you've said to me since I moved into the hotel is about what I'm doing wrong. I can't live with my friends. I can't spend any time with you."

"What are you talking about? You're training with me."

"That's just it. Training. Your kind of training. I can't surf like this. I hate it. It's no wonder you're ready to quit. You've sucked every last bit of enjoyment and fun out of something that is supposed to be exhilarating and exciting."

Here it was, the crux of the problem between them. "And control and style. It's not about challenging the wave."

Drea made a scoffing sound. "You know what? I actually believe that part. Your whole one-with-nature, one-with-the-wave Zen thing I'm actually believing. But then I realized you don't *really* believe it. Not in your gut. Control isn't oneness, and it isn't me. I can't surf like this. And I won't."

"So what does this mean?" he asked, feeling panic. Was he losing her?

She pulled her hair from its clip, spreading it around her shoulders. Protecting herself. "I'm saying I'm releasing you from our contract. I'll put in writing as soon as possible. I think I'm just meant to go it alone."

She pivoted away, and he saw her wrap her arms around her waist. Kirk reached out for her, wanting to comfort her, but his hand fell to his side.

"I'm sorry," she went on, "I know I'm screwing up your sponsorship and publicity. I'll still wear my Da Kine surfwear if you want me to."

"Thanks," he said automatically, not knowing what to say or how to fix this. The woman he wanted, wanted to help, was walking away from him because she'd rather do that than keep working with him. It was like a kick to the stomach.

"If you'll take down my board, I'll head over to the bungalow."

"Walking?" He didn't like her walking so far. It wasn't safe. She shrugged. "I've walked farther."

He just wanted to see her succeed. To hold her. And to be with her. He'd screwed up, and didn't understand how something so right had become messed up so badly. "I'll drive you."

Drea swallowed and she nodded. "Okay. Thanks."

Something in his tone must have suggested the supreme effort he was exerting not to argue with her any longer. She walked to the passenger side and slipped into his car.

He drove her to the bungalow for the last time. She didn't pause to give him a last look as she walked inside the house.

She was making a mistake, he thought. She was making the biggest mistake of her life. Yet two days later he realized he had it backwards. *He* was making the biggest mistake of his life.

6

HER HEAT was next.

Drea scanned the surf. The very still surf. Calm ocean. Beautiful to look at, fun for families with toddlers to frolic in...not good when you planned to surf on it. A light breeze, too light, brushed her face, and she kicked the warm sand at her feet.

Frustration with the situation made her muscles knot. This was her chance, her first time to surf with the big girls and prove that winning Rookie of the Year was not a fluke.

It was also her chance to prove that turning down Kirk's sponsorship had not been a huge blunder.

For the past forty-eight hours her thoughts were filled with the idea of knocking on Kirk's door and telling him that since she was no longer his trainee, they could go back to being lovers.

Pathetic.

She still wanted him, even though she'd tried not to.

Yeah, nothing was cooperating with her. Not the sea, not the man.

She sank to the sand and pulled out the surf schedule. The next big wave of competitions would take place in Australia, but there was no way she could even get there if she didn't win this competition. Everything was riding on Girls Go Banzai since no other offers of sponsorship had come her way, which was not surprising. What little she made at the Trading Post wouldn't be enough to get her to Sydney.

She had nothing left to sell, so she was stuck here in Hawaii. Not that being locked on one of the most beautiful places on earth was a hardship, but it was not exactly what she had in mind. Drea had to put some cash together.

Maybe she could give lessons. She'd enjoyed showing Riley how to surf, and it would keep her at the beach.

"It just keeps getting worse. We'll never get any good waves out of that," JC said as she joined Drea at her beach towel. "Here's your hot dog."

It was official, Drea Powell was back on the hot-dog budget. Good thing she hadn't really started to depend on room service.

JC was antsy and ready to hit the water. Girls Go Banzai had been good for her so far. She'd won the first heat outright, and Drea found herself genuinely happy for her. With her recent drop in the rankings, JC's confidence had been taking a beating.

"At least one good thing came out of this terrible weather, if low eighties and a light breeze could be considered terrible," Laci commented as she sank down on the sand beside her room-mates. "Kirk's not here."

For the last two mornings, Kirk had surfed. He'd kept his distance, but twice Drea had thought she'd caught him looking in her direction. That wasn't surprising since every chance she'd gotten she'd been staring at him. A week ago, she would have risked it all and marched right up to him and asked why he was being such an idiot.

She was both angry and sad at the same time. A relationship could have worked between them while in training if *he'd* let it.

Yeah, a week ago she'd have confronted him. But not now. Something had changed. She just didn't want to figure it out. She stood, brushing the sand from her legs. "I think I'll go check with Linda and see if they've gotten any encouraging weather reports. Like a big tropical storm."

KIRK WAXED his surfboard as he waited for the weather to change. He'd always appreciated the familiar motions of prepping his board and stowing it away. But right now he was frustrated because he actually had the urge to rack it and head back to the beach. He truly wanted to hit the waves and surf.

Shock rocked him. He'd been feeling the drag of the professional surf circuit for a while, but he'd assumed he was just tired of the hotel rooms, the different cities and the travel. His dad convinced him he was ready to stay put in one place and do something different with his life.

And now he wasn't so sure that Drea didn't have a point. Maybe he was willing to give up his lifestyle because it wasn't fun for him anymore. Because he'd sucked the joy out of it.

Just as he'd done to Drea. His chest began to hurt.

His cell phone rang. It was Linda. "We've had some luck in the weather. The Pipeline is breaking eighteen feet, and your girl's up next."

Panic knifed through his gut. No way would Drea be able to resist eighteen feet, but it was crazy. The woman surfed like she had something to prove, and maybe he'd added to that need. He grabbed his car keys and headed to the competition.

When he arrived, large breaking waves were forming perfect barrels. Several surfers were already turning away from the lineup, intimidated by the height of the waves. Drea wasn't one of them.

THIS WAS IT. Her chance. The waves were crazy, and if Drea successfully surfed this monster, she'd win. Another sponsorship would surely be in her future then.

Daredevil.

Risk-taker.

Foolhardy.

The harsh words floated in her mind as she paddled out. The water hit her face and she arched to get a better view. More surfers were turning away. *Good.*

Control.

Focus.

She used to enjoy being alone with her own ideas on the water. Not anymore as Kirk's advice echoed in her thoughts and insisted on reminding her of his lessons.

Merge with the wave. Be one with it.

Now that was a suggestion of Kirk's she agreed with.

A huge swell headed her way. She closed her eyes and felt the vibration of the ocean through her board. Tried to be one with the wave.

She opened her eyes to see a bomb wave. And right now that wave was telling her to back off.

She had less than a second to decide.

Gripping tightly to her rails, Drea forced her weight to the side, inverting her board and submerging her head.

Her board took the brute force of the wave, propelling and dragging her toward shore.

She'd turned turtle. But that was better than being slammed and eating it.

Drea maneuvered her board and paddled back toward shore. She'd wiped out. Lost this chance to prove her skills as a surfer and an opportunity to impress enough to get a sponsorship in time to get to the next competition.

Laci met her at the shore with Drea's beach towel. "JC won."

Tired and a little beaten from the water, Drea was surprised that she felt real happiness for her new friend rather than just total disappointment for herself. This would be huge for JC.

"I'm glad you bailed, Drea. That wasn't safe."

Drea smiled because she liked hearing the relief and true concern in Laci's voice. "I think my daredevil days are over."

"Maybe you can keep just a bit. We wouldn't want you to completely change," Laci said with a wink. "I'm going to go congratulate JC. You coming?"

"I will in a minute." Right now Drea needed to be alone.

Nodding as if she understood her friend's unspoken thought, Laci waved and walked toward the competition's staging area.

Drea wrapped the towel tightly around her body like a cocoon and sank toward the sand.

"Hey, wahine."

Her body shivered. She missed his voice so much. *Great.* Kirk's appearance now just solidified her failure.

"I'm proud of you," he said quietly.

"I didn't win," she acknowledged, blinking back tears.

He lowered himself beside her, stretching out his long legs. "You did in a way. You proved something out there."

"How well I can turn turtle?"

"That you know when to back away from a wave, as well as when to take it on. That took guts and risk."

Cheering erupted and she knew they would be awarding JC her medal soon. A good friend would be there cheering, too.

"I wanted to win. I want it so bad, you don't know how much," she said, her voice thick with emotion. Her throat prickled with the effort to hold back the tears.

"Not winning is part of being a pro. In fact, you're going to lose far more often than you'll ever win. You need to come to terms with that now."

"I don't think I'll ever go pro. Not with my performance out there today."

Kirk reached for Drea's shoulders, the warmth of his fingers sinking into her skin. "That's where you're wrong. You're still Rookie of the Year, and as of ten minutes ago, you shed the one thing that was holding sponsors back. Your bad reputation."

Her back straightened. "I don't think my reputation was *that* bad."

His lips twisted into a smile. "Good. I much prefer outraged Drea over pity-party Drea."

She met his eyes. "Kirk, thank you for coming over here. I know it must have been awkward for you, and I want you to know I appreciate it. But you don't have to stay."

He leaned forward, his gaze boring into hers. "Are you trying to get rid of me?"

She'd already cried in front of the man, bared her emotions, she might as well go for the trifecta and share her feelings about him. "No, it's just hard for me with you being beside me."

There. She'd done it. Showed emotion. Given him an inkling that he could hurt her. That's why she'd never truly confronted him.

His gaze narrowed. "Why?" he asked, a strange urgency filling his voice.

"I mean, come on. What was I thinking? You don't fall in love with a person in a couple of days." *Okay, maybe not that truthful with my feelings.* She'd hide from analyzing that little gem, but she couldn't. She'd just blurted out that she'd fallen in love with him.

"Yeah, you do."

Drea's breath hitched and she glanced up. Kirk caught her face in his hands, tracing her lower lip with his thumb.

"I did," he said.

"You fell…" She couldn't finish the sentence. She wanted him to say it. To finish it.

"I fell in love with you."

Her heart pounded and she squeezed her eyes tight. Then she threw her arms around his neck. "Tell me again."

"I love you, Andrea Powell. It was the most uncontrolled, unfocused, risk-taking thing I've ever done, but there you go. Some of you is rubbing off on me."

She laughed.

"Why'd you stay away?"

He gazed out into the ocean. "At first I thought it was because you needed time. You were pretty mad and, let's face it, everything I said and did seemed to be wrong."

"Not everything," she remarked, reaching up for a kiss.

"Then I understand it was because I needed some time to adjust. I've lived my entire surf life with the same exact principles. They worked and I thought they'd work for you, too."

"Some of them did."

"And some of them did for me, too. But not all of them, and I was coming to understand that. That's why I've been so vague about my retirement. I wasn't really ready. I just wanted the fun back. I want *you* back."

"You have me."

And he lowered his mouth to kiss her. The kind of I-love-you, never-want-to-let-you-go kiss that made her ache for the two of them to be alone.

"What now? What do we do from here?" she couldn't help but ask.

He raised a brow. "What's this? Are you planning? Focusing?"

"Maybe some of you *is* rubbing off on me."

He took her hand, then stood, helping Drea to her feet. "Right now, we have someone to congratulate."

Drea scanned the podium. "I'm happy for her. She needed this win, just like I need you."

"And I need you."

"What about after the ceremony?" Drea reached for her board.

"Still more planning, I see. We have a surf circuit to do together."

"Together?" she asked, surprise lacing her voice. "So you're really not retiring. What about your restaurant?"

"Da Kine will be waiting when I return. When *we* return. The sponsorship is yours even if you kick me to the curb."

"That will never happen." Joy and excitement raced through her. She couldn't wait to start. Start her new life with Kirk *right now*. She strode toward the podium.

He grabbed her hands, his expression serious. With love shining from his eyes, he confessed, "You've given me something, Drea. Given me something back, actually. My love of surfing. I knew this morning that I'm looking forward to it again. I don't care if I win, if I lose, if my style is off. I'm just ready to surf again because I enjoy it, and you'll be right next to me."

"Being one with the wave."

Kirk draped his arm around her shoulders, and they began to walk down the beach together. "I knew you'd start seeing things my way."

"Yeah, just as much as you've started seeing mine."

He gave her hand a squeeze. "I'm going to look forward to this for the rest of my life."

* * * * *

Her Private Treasure

WENDY ETHERINGTON

Wendy Etherington was born and raised in the Deep South—and she has the fried chicken recipes and NASCAR ticket stubs to prove it. The author of more than twenty books, she writes full-time from her home in South Carolina, where she lives with her husband, two daughters and an energetic shih tzu named Cody. She can be reached via her website: www.wendyetherington.com.

To my best buds, Jacquie D'Alessandro and
Jenni Grizzle whose love, support and
interventions of champagne and
chocolate keep me sane

1

CARR HAMILTON YANKED the rope around the dock post, then stepped off his thirty-seven-foot cabin cruiser, *The Litigator*. As rippling waves of the Intracoastal Waterway lapped against the dock, the moon hung above the marina, a glowing orb casting a cool and mysterious light. The air smelled of sea life and salt.

The gloomy night and deserted dock, plus yet another solitary cruise, had put him in a rare melancholy mood. After securing his boat, he zipped his jacket against the cool March wind and headed across the creaky wooden slats, intending to circumvent the marina bar, where he'd find friends and conversation.

"...coffee is ready for distribution, so don't get jumpy now."

Carr stopped at the familiar voice, delivered in an angry and demanding tone. Coffee distribution? Jack Rafton was an insurance agent. Auto, home, life, et cetera. Mundane stuff really. But a nice guy and good business neighbor.

"This whole thing is getting dicey," another, but unknown, voice whispered harshly.

"Relax, and keep your voices down," said yet a third man.

Carr's low mood vanished. His pulse jumped. He leaped sideways and ducked behind a large storage locker at the dock's edge, realizing he probably hadn't moved so swiftly or stealthily since his days on the Yale fencing team.

"It's late." Jack's voice again. "Locals are all deep into their whiskey and beer by now."

"Let's just make the exchange and get out of here." The second unknown voice.

"You're just pissed I raised my prices," Jack said.

"Whatever," the first unknown man said, his voice deep and raspy. A smoker maybe. "That's between you and the boss. Just give us the stuff."

Carr heard footsteps on the wooden slats, then the creak of a rope tethering a boat.

He risked a glance from behind the post and saw Jack carrying a wooden crate and walking slow, balanced steps on the deck of a ski boat. By the blue and red stripes on the hull, it appeared to be Jack's boat, but it was too dark to make out the name scripted on the side and be certain.

The crate was handed over to one of the two unidentified men, then something was shoved into Jack's hand. All the characters stood in shadow, like the old black-and-white film noirs Carr enjoyed. He half expected to see Humphrey Bogart's strong-jawed profile flash before him.

No hat-and-raincoat-clad detectives appeared, so Carr concentrated on what he could see. The two unknown men scurried away from Jack and the boat. He tried to estimate their height and weight, but knew both were wild guesses based on a comparison of Jack's vital statistics.

Jack transferred the object he'd been given—an envelope maybe?—to his other hand, then, suddenly, he turned in Carr's direction. Fairly certain the angle and the width of the post kept him hidden, Carr didn't move. He barely breathed. Whatever the meeting with the two men meant, Carr knew it wasn't something Jack wanted known by a business acquaintance. The timing as well as the conversation itself spoke to that certainty.

After a few moments, he heard Jack's footsteps receding down the dock. He counted slowly to a hundred before moving and then only to take a quick look. Noting the dock was empty, he shifted from his position.

Puzzling over the discussion he'd heard, he checked his boat to be sure he'd locked the cabin door and secured the rope properly. The exchange had to be a payoff of some kind. The two men had clearly bought something from Jack. But coffee? Why would three men need to meet in the dead of night to buy and sell coffee?

He walked down the dock, stopping as he reached the boat Jack had retrieved the crate from. *American Dream* was clearly scripted on the hull in bright red letters. Jack's boat, then.

Stooping, Carr glided his hand over the dock's rough wooden planks. Something gritty caressed the tips of his fingers. He brought his hand to his face, inhaling the scent. Coffee.

With the scent, he recalled one significant reason coffee grounds might be placed in a crate, then traded for cash in the dead of night.

Drugs.

Two weeks later

FBI SPECIAL AGENT Malina Blair glared at the stack of case files on her desk and thought seriously about pulling her pistol from its ever-present side holster and firing at will.

Two computer hacking cases, one suspected drug smuggling and six complaints from helpful citizens who thought they spotted someone from the Most Wanted list hiding out behind the fake designer bags in the straw market.

How far the mighty had fallen.

She recalled fondly the business executive son's kidnapping case she'd closed three years ago. She supposed the son and his loved ones didn't remember the ordeal in a positive light, but the family still sent her a Christmas card every year, thanking her for her sharpshooting skills.

And barely six months ago, she'd led a team in solving a six-year-old bank robbery, taking down the ring of suspects as they attempted to break into the main branch vault of the Bank of America in downtown Washington, D.C.

Good times. Career-making moments.

Formally interviewing Senator Phillip Grammer's son on suspicion of securities and bank fraud hadn't gone quite so well. The powerful politician had stormed into the interview and claimed his son had fallen in with the wrong crowd briefly and that he and the SEC were working out a special process of restitution.

Phil junior was special all right. He'd ratted on three other people—who Malina considered minor players in the deal—and got away scot-free.

While a lovely city, Charleston, South Carolina,

wasn't exactly the FBI's hotbed of excitement. Getting back to headquarters in Quantico, Virginia, was imperative, especially since screwing up again was likely to land her reassigned in the desert-to-nowhere field office. Interrogating cacti.

With a sigh, she pulled out the folder about the smuggling case. Her boss had actually dropped this one on her desk that morning. At first, she'd hoped she'd been forgiven for her career-crushing mistake and assigned to the elite team that worked the harbor. With the Port of Charleston being the country's fourth busiest, illicit goods and terrorist threats were a serious possibility.

Unfortunately, the case she'd been assigned was a vague suspicion of drug smuggling based on a two-minute overheard conversation that took place on nearby—and boringly tiny—Palmer's Island. The single witness was an attorney and friend of her boss.

It seemed she had another day of tedium ahead of her.

Scooping up the documents, she headed out of her cubicle and toward the elevator.

"Hey, Malina," Donald, one of her colleagues, called out as she passed his cube. "Gonna work another dog-napping case today?"

She never slowed her brisk stride as she called back, "I'll see if I can fit it in after kicking your ass in combat training this afternoon."

"Again," several others called out helpfully from behind their own cubicle walls.

She lifted her lips in what some people might consider a sneer, but those who knew her recognized it as her version of a smile. She'd only been in the Charleston field office three weeks, and while everyone knew of her setback, most had at least come to respect her skills and determination. Hers was a cautionary tale none of them wanted coming true in their own lives.

Alone in the elevator, she allowed herself the weakness of closing her eyes as frustration overcame her. She should be in a corner office with a view. She should be solving important cases. She should be compiling letters of commendation.

She was good at her job—a few she'd worked with had even called her the best. If only she had tact as steady as her hands and as sure as her roundhouse kick, she'd rise to the top.

Donald hadn't exaggerated. Her first case since arriving at the office had been a literal dog-napping.

The mayor's prize Maltese had gone missing, and a ransom demand had been made. It had taken her all of two minutes in an interview with the dog walker to crack him and the master plot.

The mayor's kids had hugged her; her coworkers had laughed their asses off.

Minutes later, while she drove her government-issue sedan over the bridge to Palmer's Island, she cast a glance at the sun's rays bouncing off the rippling Atlantic waves in the distance. Ahead was Patriot's Point, where the decommissioned aircraft carrier the *USS Yorktown* had been permanently docked, awaiting the daily flood of tourists eager to explore her proud and massive decks.

The island that was her destination was even smaller than the one where she'd been raised. In fact, Kauai, Hawaii was as different from Palmer's Island as two floating rock and sand masses could be. And yet, they had the same effect—they calmed and soothed as no other person, place or thing had ever managed in her life.

She'd continue to resist her mother's assertion that someday she'd want to return home, but Palmer's Island did force her to remember that her life hadn't always been about ambition, power and politics.

She found the address she was looking for with little effort and pulled into the small sand-and-shell-dotted parking lot beside a large house that had been converted into a quad-plex of offices. A discreet sign announced Tessa Malone, Family Counselor; Jack Rafton, Island Insurance; Charlie McGary, Suncoast Real Estate; and Carr Hamilton, Attorney-at-Law.

Mr. Hamilton's office was on the lower left, across the main hall from the insurance agent, who was the primary focus in the supposed smuggling operation.

The whole case would most certainly turn out to be nothing. Rafton and Hamilton were probably involved in some minor quarrel, and this was the attorney's idea of revenge. Maybe Rafton had cut Hamilton off in traffic or carelessly blocked the driveway with cans on trash day or any number of other ridiculous things that people got worked up over.

For her, this trip was merely another hoop to jump through in order to get her career back on track.

She turned the brass knob on the door to Hamilton's office and entered to find herself in a small but elegant reception area. Malina's footsteps echoed across dark oak hardwood floors as a quick glance took in the emerald curtains, pale gold walls and expensive-looking antique furniture.

A woman with dark brown hair, streaked with silver, sat behind an antique cherry desk. She looked up with a polite smile. "May I help you?"

Malina pulled her badge from her jacket pocket.

"Special Agent Malina Blair. I have an appointment with Mr. Hamilton."

The polite smile never wavered, leading Malina to wonder if the cops came calling frequently or if she was simply unruffled by any visitor. "Of course." She lifted the phone on her desk. "I'll let him know you're here." After a brief conversation, she rose and hung up the phone. "This way, please."

The receptionist/secretary turned away toward the door in the back of the room. Her tailored brown suit showed off her trim figure, just as her matching heels highlighted her confident stride.

Malina had discovered she could glean valuable information about the person in charge by watching subordinates. If that observation held true in this case, she could expect Carr Hamilton to be self-assured, efficient and sophisticated. Not exactly what she'd expected from simple little Palmer's Island.

She followed the receptionist into the office and barely resisted gasping at the man who rose from behind the massive mahogany desk at the back of the room.

He was beautiful.

At a trim six foot two with wide shoulders and narrow hips, his body alone could cause a woman to wax poetic, something Malina never felt moved by but finally understood why others did. He wore an exquisite charcoal suit, and his thick, silky-looking, inky-black hair set off a face sculpted like the statue of an ancient god, even though nothing about him was cold.

In fact, he radiated heat—especially from his dark brown eyes, sharp and intelligent, standing out from that spectacular face, absorbing her from head to toe.

Moving gracefully, he rounded the desk and extended his hand, which was tanned and long fingered, elegant as everything around him. "Thank you for coming, Agent Blair."

Jolted into remembering she was there on a professional mission, she managed a nod as she took his hand. A shock of desire raced up her arm. "Sure thing."

His gaze lingered on her face, and she resisted the urge to pull her hand from his. There was something powerful, even meaningful, about that stare, and she didn't like the sensation that she'd lost control and perspective so quickly. In that moment, she was a woman, not an agent, and that was entirely the wrong tone for this meeting.

"Coffee, Mr. Hamilton?" the receptionist asked from behind Malina.

"Yes, Paige. Thank you. I imagine Agent Blair would prefer the Kona blend."

Paige turned and left the room, presumably to get coffee, and Malina forced herself to both step back from Hamilton's enticing touch and simultaneously hang on to his compelling gaze. "Kona?" she asked.

"You are Hawaiian, aren't you?"

"Yes."

She clenched her back teeth to avoid asking him how he knew her heritage, but he simply nodded in response to the unspoken question.

"I'm good with faces." He extended his hand to one of the club chairs in front of his desk, then returned to his position on the other side, lowering himself into his blood-red leather chair only after she'd done the same. "Also, Sam mentioned you'd grown up on Kauai."

Gorgeous, intelligent and honest. Three very good reasons to get to know a man. Unfortunately, he was part of her professional and not her personal life.

And never the twain shall meet.

She'd seen too many careers wither and die from office bed-hopping. And falling into the wrong bed in the world of politics landed the offenders a one-way ticket to early retirement. No way was she going down that road.

"I understand the SAC is a personal friend," she said, leaning back in the club chair and tucking her neglected libido neatly away.

He nodded. "Special Agent in Charge Samuel Clairmont." He lifted his lips in a smile that made Malina's heart jump. "He's come a long way from third string on the Yale fencing team."

"I guess you were first-string."

"Of course."

From any other man, that admission would be bragging at best, pretentious at worst. In the capable, elegant hands of Carr Hamilton, it was charming.

Paige returned at that moment with a silver tray, holding a pitcher, mugs and tiny silver spoons.

She set the service on Hamilton's desk, then turned and left the room. As he poured the coffee, Malina took a moment to let her gaze roam the office, noting the dark wood floor-to-ceiling bookcases filled with volumes, a few pictures and knickknacks. A wide-screen laptop sat on the left side of his desk. A sideboard served as a bar, displaying cut-crystal glasses and decanters filled with amber liquid.

Class, style and old money permeated the room.

"Cream and sugar?" the man across from her asked.

She almost said yes simply to watch those graceful hands move. "No, thank you."

"Strong coffee for a strong woman."

Since she had no idea what to say to that statement

without heading the conversation down a personal path, she sipped from her mug. The Kona was bold and flavorful, just as it should be.

He looked amused as he settled back into his chair, no doubt realizing she was attracted to him. A man with his looks and style wouldn't miss such an obvious detail.

Despite the near certain futility and mundane nature of her task, she had to be careful not to take the wrong step with this man. He stirred something in her better left unturned. She had a singular goal and couldn't afford any distraction.

But she so hated being careful.

"So, what do you think of my observations?" he asked.

"I'm not sure what to think at this point. I'd like you to tell me what you saw in detail." From her pocket, she pulled out a microrecorder, which she set on the desk in front of him. "For the record." She recited the standard warning about testimony and giving false information to law enforcement, then settled back to listen.

He gave a report as organized and detailed as any cop. He was careful not to speculate and left out personal feelings, as she would expect from a lawyer. From the file the SAC had given her, she'd read about his success litigating civil cases in a variety of antitrust suits, products liability and environmental issues. She could well imagine him living like a king on the proceeds of his powerful voice and structured mind.

Still, the likelihood of an everyday citizen cracking a drug-smuggling operation was about as likely as her suddenly deciding to lay down her Glock and become a pole dancer.

"Drugs are smuggled in coffee grounds," he said in conclusion.

"Twenty years ago," she said drily as she turned off the recorder and returned it to her pocket. "Things have gotten a bit more sophisticated these days."

"I don't envision Jack as a major drug kingpin. This is a small operation. Unsophisticated methods would suit them better."

Despite herself, she was impressed he'd thought through the conclusions of what he'd witnessed. "So why did you come to us? If Rafton is dealing drugs, this is a matter for the DEA."

"I have reason to believe he's smuggling more than drugs."

"How?" she asked, though she suddenly knew.

"I've been watching him."

She sighed heavily. Random citizens playing at being cops was a surefire way of getting somebody killed. "I'd prefer you leave this to the professionals."

"You mean the professionals who don't believe anything illicit is going on?"

"I haven't come to any conclusions yet."

Clearly annoyed, he tapped his fingers against the arm of his chair. His gaze locked with hers. "The FBI do investigate major thefts, don't they?"

"Last time I checked."

"And art theft would still fall in that category?"

"It would."

"Then I've come to the right agency."

It would still mean she'd have to give the DEA a heads-up, and interjurisdictional cooperation with those cowboys was one of her least favorite job requirements.

Hamilton leaned forward. "I didn't ask you here on a

whim, Agent Blair. I'm not a panicked or bored islander looking for attention. There's something to this case."

"It's not a case yet."

Those elegant hands, linked and resting on the desk in front of him, clenched. "Why are you so skeptical of my information?"

"Why do you think Jack Rafton's stealing art?"

"Because two nights ago, he unloaded a box shaped like a large painting."

She'd asked the obvious; she'd gotten the obvious answer. "Maybe he's just buying art with his drug-smuggling proceeds."

"Maybe he is. Why are you so skeptical of my information?"

Because the SAC would never, on purpose, give me anything with teeth.

She bit back that response, though, and stated facts, which she was sure the sharp lawyer would appreciate. "Drug smuggling is an extremely risky and dangerous pastime. Only the very desperate or very foolish would choose that route. The drug kingpins are protective to the death of their product's distribution and often disembowel those who cross them.

"From the quick background check I did on Jack Rafton, summa cum laude graduate of the College of Charleston and longtime insurance broker of Palmer's Island, I don't see him blending well in that violent world."

Hamilton nodded. "True enough."

"Rafton also doesn't drive an exotic car, which, if you'll pardon the cliché, is a drug dealer's biggest weakness."

"And how do you know that?"

She shrugged. "The parking lot outside. There's a

well-used SUV that belongs to the family counselor. A fairly new but understated luxury sedan for the real estate agent, a pickup truck for the insurance guy and a perfectly restored Triumph Spitfire convertible painted British Racing Green." She lifted her eyebrows. "Which I'm sure belongs to you."

"You ran the tags."

"Didn't need to."

He said nothing for a long moment as he studied her. "Well, I suppose somebody at the Bureau is taking my suspicions seriously if they sent you."

She started to argue with him, to explain that the only reason she'd been sent was because he was friends with a powerful man. But admitting that would be admitting she had no influence and simply did as she was told. Plus, despite the urge not to be, she was flattered he recognized her investigative skills.

"We appreciate the cooperation of concerned citizens and follow up on any tip that will lead to the arrest and conviction of anyone participating in criminal activity."

"Ah, the pat, politically correct answer. Not what I would have expected from a woman who risked her career by questioning Senator Grammer's son."

Malina felt the blood drain from her head as humiliation washed over her. "Agent Clairmont told you."

Hamilton nodded. "As I'm sure he mentioned, we're old friends. For what it's worth, he considers you an asset to the Bureau. He also respects your willingness to do whatever it takes to see justice served, even if your methods are sometimes rash."

"That kid was guilty as sin," she said, fighting to talk past her tight jaw, even as she felt a quick spurt of pleasure in hearing her boss respected her.

"Sam thinks so, too. Power buys silence way too easily."

"Not with me."

"So noted. But I'm guessing a drug- and/or art-smuggling case could put a nice letter of commendation in your file. Not to mention I'm suddenly moved to make a generous campaign donation to whoever runs against that idiot Grammer in the next election."

Her gaze shot to his. "Surely you didn't just attempt to bribe a government agent."

A wide, breath-stealing smile bloomed on his face. "Surely not."

She rose slowly to her feet. Who the hell was this guy?

Smart, successful and wealthy. A law-abiding citizen who took untold hours of his time to investigate a professional neighbor, then used a powerful association to see that his observations were taken seriously. Was he bored, curious or did he have a hidden agenda?

Bracing her hands on his desk, she noted he'd stood when she had and now she was forced to look up at him. At five-seven, she wasn't a tiny woman, but the height and breadth of him made her feel small and feminine in comparison. "I'm here to follow up on your information as ordered by my supervisor, Special Agent in Charge Samuel Clairmont. Do you have anything further to add to your previous statements?"

"I imagine you'd be interested in the storage garage Jack keeps under an assumed name in Charleston, which currently houses a brand-new Lotus Elise."

"How do you—" She stopped, shaking her head, irritated that he'd, yet again, managed to surprise her. "You followed him."

"I'd also like to point out that he chose Ardent Red

instead of British Racing Green for the exterior paint."
He cocked his head. "Do you think that's an indicator
of law-abiding citizen versus master smuggler?"

Temper brought heat to her cheeks. "Mr. Hamilton,
I'm—"

"Call me Carr."

"*Mr. Hamilton,* I'm advising—no," she amended,
"I'm *ordering* you to bring your amateur investigation
to a halt. Do not question Mr. Rafton or his associates.
Do not ask others about him and definitely do not follow
him. The Bureau will look into your information and
take things from here."

"But you don't really believe me."

"I do, in fact. I trust that you saw what you say you
have. What those observations mean is an entirely different subject." She reached into her pocket for a business card, which she laid on his desk to avoid touching
him again. It seemed imperative that she get away from
this man as fast as possible. "Let me know if I can be of
further assistance." She turned, then paused and glanced
back. "Or if you find Jimmy Hoffa."

With that parting shot, she headed toward the door,
longing to run when she sensed him following her. She
caught a whiff of his cologne, a blend of sandalwood
and amber, as warm and enticing as the man himself.

Her hand was on the doorknob when he spoke. "Professional considerations aside, I'd like to take you to
dinner sometime."

Swallowing hard, she forced herself to meet his gaze.
"Sorry. You're a witness. I'm not allowed."

"But you're not even certain a crime has been
committed."

Despite what she'd told him and the sheer unlikelihood of anything significant happening on Palmer's

Island, she knew there was. Her instincts were buzzing, and they hadn't steered her wrong yet.

Well, except for that senatorial questioning thing.

"I'm investigating," she said shortly, hoping to further discourage him.

Either he didn't get the signal or he didn't care, since he reached out, sliding his fingertip along her jaw, sending waves of heat racing down her body. "And I imagine you don't give a damn about what's allowed."

Her breath caught. She didn't. At least she never had.

And look where that attitude had led you.

Opening the door, she stepped out of his reach. "I also don't have time to get involved. I'm going to close as many cases as I can and get back to D.C., where I belong, as soon as possible."

Disappointment moved across his handsome face. He slid his hands into the pockets of his suit pants. "Of course," he said quietly. "Thanks for coming."

She regretted her abrupt tone but didn't see how she could change what was. "One last thing about Rafton." Though she already knew the answer, caution demanded she ask. "This isn't personal, right? Rafton didn't hit your car or steal your girlfriend?"

"No. And I don't have a girlfriend." His dark eyes gleamed with power and possession. "If I did, neither Jack Rafton nor any other man would take her."

2

As Carr sipped his whiskey at The Night Heron bar, he watched out the back windows as boats docked and launched for sunset cruises down the Intracoastal Waterway, then rounded the tip of the island and out into the Atlantic.

Had he finally spent too much time slowing down and reflecting?

Observation had become a staple. Watching other people do interesting things.

For so many years, he'd been on the fast track. He'd spent every waking moment establishing a lucrative practice in Manhattan, fighting for clients with prospects for big payoffs, dismissing others he might have helped but whose cases weren't as profitable.

He'd dispassionately profited from suffering and built a fortune and fierce reputation by doing so.

He hadn't paused to notice small, everyday things. To stroll the beaches he'd grown up on. To appreciate love and friendship. To watch the birds glide across the night sky.

It had taken the death of his uncle and mentor to jolt him.

Uncle Clinton had departed his life respected, rich and bitterly alone. He'd coldly extracted every penny from every case he'd taken on. He'd corrupted idealistic law school graduates with promises of wealth and power. Few, other than the descendants who inherited his money, had mourned him.

As Carr had watched heaps of fertile earth drop onto his uncle's casket, he knew he was destined for the same end. And he knew he had to find another path.

That had been two years ago, and while he didn't regret finding his roots again and settling on quiet Palmer's Island, the sparks of need for excitement came more frequently these days.

Dear heaven, did he have to fade into tedium? Was that his penance?

"*Hel-lo,* gorgeous."

Certain he wasn't being addressed, Carr nevertheless glanced at Jimmy, The Heron's weekday bartender, and noted his gaze locked on the door behind Carr. "What hot blonde are you fixated on tonight?"

"Brunette," he returned, his eyes following the subject in question.

Carr didn't bother to turn. Being barely twenty-one, Jimmy's taste inevitably skewed young. At thirty-five, Carr wasn't even remotely swimming in the same pool.

Instead, he stared at his whiskey.

"What are you doing here?" a familiar voice asked seconds later.

Raising his head, Carr blinked, but Special Agent Malina Blair was still sliding onto the bar stool next to him, changing his evening from watchful boredom to stimulating possibility in a matter of seconds.

"Drinking." He raised his glass as he absorbed her lovely features. "Join me?"

Her exotic turquoise gaze slid from his face to his glass and back again. "Why the hell not?"

He only had to lift his finger to get Jimmy assembling her drink. "I like you a lot better when you're speaking your mind instead of spouting Bureau platitudes." Not that he hadn't liked her then as well. His fingers tingled with the urge to pull her silky-looking dark hair from the restraining ponytail secured at the base of her neck. "How's the investigation progressing?"

"I would like you a lot better if you'd stay out of my case," she said as Jimmy set the drink before her.

"So now it's a case?"

She rolled her shoulders. "It is."

He'd had faith in her sense of justice, but he was relieved to have the instinct confirmed. Sam had been right in that she was the agent for the job.

Did his good deed erase one of the black marks next to his name?

He wasn't sure—especially since his greatest desire was to seduce her into compromising her professional code of ethics and sleeping with him.

She sipped her drink, never wincing.

Though he considered his brand of imported whiskey smooth, he knew plenty of people who found it too bracing. Women mostly. But then Malina Blair was tougher than the exotic island beauty she appeared to be.

"You like whiskey?" he asked her, fascinated by the way her pillowy lips cupped the crystal.

"Not especially." She rattled the ice in her glass.

"This is nice, though. Stop me if I lose my senses and have the urge to shoot somebody."

"I'm here to serve. Lousy day?"

"Lousy month."

"I imagine so. But do you define yourself completely by your job?"

"Yes," she said without hesitation.

That path led nowhere, as Carr well knew. She'd be so much happier if she fell into bed with him. He wondered how long it would take him to manage it.

Certainly the key to this lady's heart wouldn't be found in candy, flowers and suggestive compliments. "So I assume you've spent the last thirty-six hours pursuing the case. What have you learned?"

"That boat captains on small islands like to gossip, and your friend Jack Rafton is well liked, even if he has been coming and going at odd hours lately."

"Which you already knew by talking to me."

She shrugged. "Corroboration was necessary."

He was dying to watch that cool nonchalance fall away with the right touch. Because beneath the frustrated heat under her staid, navy-blue suit, the fire of a passionate woman lurked.

With effort, he managed to focus on their conversation. "If you need more details, you might talk to the harbormaster, Albert Duffy. He knows everything about everyone. Though you'd do better to charm him than flash your badge."

She looked at him, then glanced at her watch with a sigh. "I have a meeting with Albert Duffy in twenty minutes."

Carr tracked his gaze slowly down her body. "Not that I don't think you look amazing—and I believe

Jimmy is impressed as well—you'd do better showing Al a little leg."

She bared her teeth. "I could always show him the wrong side of a federal interrogation room."

He leaned toward her, lowering his voice several pitches. "Subtlety often works better than force."

Her gaze moved to his and held. Desire lingered in the depth of her eyes, clear as the tropical water they mimicked. Her beautiful lips parted, and for a moment, her gaze dropped to his mouth, and he thought she was going to give in to the need so obviously pulsing between them.

Tedium had vanished the moment she'd appeared, and the sensation was heady.

"Who's Jimmy?" she asked, leaning back and breaking the spell.

"The bartender." Carr inclined his head toward the young man pouring vodka in a glass for another customer. "Wave. I think he has a crush on you."

She never looked in Jimmy's direction but said, "He's too young. What are you doing here anyway?"

"Drinking, as I said earlier. But also volunteering to be your assistant, guarding your virtue, so to speak, as well as helping break the ice with Al. I'm one of the few people he actually likes."

"I thought I told you to stay out of this case."

"It's my bar."

"Literally?"

"Yes, plus I live across the street."

Admiration sparked in her eyes. "The house on the point."

"How did you know?"

She drained the rest of her drink. "It's you."

"You're hedging. You've certainly run a deep search

on me by now. You know my address, my background, my professional history and financial status. I bet you even know what grade I received on my contract law midterm my junior year of college and whether I prefer boxers or briefs. Before you walked through the door, you knew I owned this place. Why the subterfuge? Why pretend surprise at finding me here?"

"I live for subterfuge," she scoffed.

"Stop," he said quietly but firmly. The sarcasm was a defense mechanism that she obviously used to keep people from probing too deeply. A way of maintaining distance. "It wouldn't kill you to accept my help."

"No, but it might compromise my case. Plus…"

When she stopped, he prompted, "Plus?"

"I don't understand your motives. Why are you going to all this trouble? Why do you want to get involved in this investigation? What's in it for you?"

She didn't trust him. Not surprising, since he didn't trust himself. The bribery attempt, a remnant of his old ways, had been a huge misstep. But he'd wanted to know what kind of agent he was dealing with, despite Sam's assurances that Malina was fiercely ethical.

"It's my duty," he said finally.

"As what?"

"A citizen of the United States."

She shook her head. "Nobody's that committed and idealistic."

"But they should be." And he was fighting every day to be sure he could count himself among those who were. "This is my island." When she raised her eyebrows, he added, "Not all of it, though I do own a fair collection of properties. I mean, this is my birthplace, my home. It's lovely and peaceful, the place where I intend to raise my children and live until I'm ancient and dotty. I care what happens here, and I won't let smuggling or drugs or anything else ruin my community."

Saying nothing, she held his gaze. "You're—"

"Agent Blair?" a gruff voice interrupted.

Malina rose and held out her hand to harbormaster Albert Duffy. "Mr. Duffy, thanks for agreeing to meet me."

Though he shook her hand briefly, his thick gray brows drew together, and the wrinkles on his darkly tanned and lined face seemed to deepen. "I don't like working with women."

"I don't like working with anybody. Why don't we take that table in the back corner?" she suggested.

Al scowled briefly, but must have been somewhat satisfied with Malina's direct answer, because he shrugged and wandered toward the booth.

Malina turned back to Carr and spoke in a low tone only he could hear. "That was a pretty impassioned speech earlier. I can see why you were a prize to juries. I still have to ask you to keep your distance from this case." When he started to interrupt, she held up her hand to stall him. "I'd be interested in calling you for an occasional consultation, but that's where your involvement ends. Understand?"

"Since you're articulate, and I'm fairly intelligent, yes, I understand."

She narrowed her eyes briefly, as if trying to figure out if there was a loophole. Which, of course, there was.

"Your offer to help is admirable," she said after a moment. "In fact, it's—" She stopped and shook her head ruefully. "It's been a long time since I've heard sentiment like that." She brushed her hand across his arm. "Thanks."

Now she thought he was being noble.

He almost wished he could call back his words. His nobility was tainted. He didn't deserve her admiration. But he wanted her.

When she reached into her pocket and pulled out a clip of cash, he held up his hand. "I'll pay for the drinks."

"I appreciate the offer, but you can't." She took out a twenty-dollar bill and laid it on the bar.

"Generous."

She turned toward the booth Al had settled into. "My compensation to the cute bartender whose flirting I'd never consider returning."

"Why not?"

She flicked him a glance. "I'm attracted to men, not boys."

"WOULD YOU LIKE a drink, Mr. Duffy?" Malina asked as she scooted into the booth and faced the cranky harbormaster.

He pointed a knobby finger toward the bar area. "It's comin'."

Malina looked over to see Carr Hamilton headed toward them, a glass of whiskey in each hand.

He slid onto the seat beside Duffy, then lifted his drink in a toast and his lips in smirk. "I figured you'd want to abstain. On duty and all."

"Very considerate, Mr. Hamilton," she said, certain the sharp attorney caught her sarcasm. "However, I don't need your assistance."

"I'm sure you don't. However, I'm Mr. Duffy's lawyer."

"He called you?"

"No, but isn't it fortunate I was here? I'll stay on his behalf."

"I don't want to be here at all," Duffy said, glaring at her.

"Me either," she muttered. The man she had the reluctant hots for was currently sitting across from her, meddling in her case, distracting her from nearly everything. "But I have a job to do."

Duffy sipped his drink. "You should be home, cookin' for your man."

Though her muscles tensed like a coiled snake, she managed to let the anger roll off. "I'm better with a pistol than a spatula."

"Not natural," Duffy insisted.

Malina drilled her gaze into his. "Frankly, Mr. Duffy, I'd rather be anywhere else, talking to anyone else than you. And yet…" She lifted her hands and leaned back. "Here I am, striving to protect the law-abiding citizens of Palmer's Island from the criminal element. If I can make the sacrifice, so can you."

Duffy continued to glare silently at her, as if sure he'd never seen a self-possessed woman in his life.

"Al," Hamilton said quietly, "let her do this."

Duffy sighed. "Yeah, okay."

"I'd like to record the interview, if that's okay with you." She cast Hamilton a glance. "And your attorney, of course." With their verbal agreements secured, she asked Duffy, "Do you know Jack Rafton?"

Duffy looked wary. "Yeah. Slip number nine."

"Owner of a twenty-six-foot cabin cruiser called *American Dream*?"

"Yeah."

"How would you characterize your relationship?"

"We ain't got a relationship, lady. We're men."

And not homophobic at all. Malina resisted the urge to roll her eyes. She liked her job, she really did. Or, rather, she used to. "Are you friends?" she asked.

Duffy shrugged. "We have a drink together sometimes."

"Have you ever been to his house?"

"No."

"Do you have his cell phone number?"

"No."

"What do you talk about when you're together?"

"Fishing. What does that have to do with anything?"

"She's trying to determine if you're close friends with Jack," Hamilton put in.

"Are you?" Malina pressed the harbormaster.

"I guess not."

The man could give clams pointers. "But you see Mr. Rafton frequently."

"He has a boat. I run the harbor."

"Does Mr. Rafton seem under an unusual amount of stress lately?"

"How the hell do I know?"

"Have you seen him at the docks at unusual times over the last few weeks?"

Duffy's gaze darted to Hamilton. "What does she mean *unusual?*"

Hamilton's lips twitched. "Out of the ordinary."

"I know that. I don't know what that has to do with—"

"You run the harbor," Malina interrupted. "You know when people come and go. When does Rafton usually come and go?"

"Early morning, sometimes after dinner."

"When has he been taking his boat out lately?"

Duffy sipped his whiskey before answering. "Later."

"How much later?"

"Eleven, maybe twelve at night."

"So would you characterize that as unusual?"

Annoyance lined Duffy's face. "I guess so."

His statement fell in line with what others had said with less reluctance and certainly more grace. Was Albert Duffy simply ornery, or did he have some connection with Rafton that he didn't want known? With this man, directness seemed to be the only course. "Are you engaging in or helping to cover up illegal activity perpetrated by Jack Rafton?"

Duffy sputtered so heavily he couldn't speak.

"Agent Blair," Hamilton said, his gaze locking on hers, "that's inappropriate."

But it confirmed her instincts—Duffy was an insulting curmudgeon and likely not a would-be felon.

"I thought we might get to our goal more quickly with more specific questions," she said to the men across from her. "And I'm sure Mr. Duffy doesn't think the FBI engages in random questioning. I wanted to let him know that he's being watched and any attempt by him to warn Mr. Rafton of the questions I've asked would be perceived by me as the act of an accomplice." She smiled. "Everybody clear now?"

"What a man does on his own time isn't any of my bother," Duffy mumbled.

Her smile broadened. "Exactly. That's my job. Thank you for your assistance, Mr. Duffy," she added, rising and turning off the microrecorder. "I'll forward copies of the interview transcript to your office, Mr. Hamilton. Good night to you both."

"You'd do better to learn to cook, honey," Duffy said as she turned away.

Facing him, her fingers twitched as she skimmed her hand across the butt of her gun. "Would I?"

"Yeah." His gaze defiant, Duffy leaned back in the booth. "Carr here needs a girlfriend. He's rich, so he could probably even get you lessons."

"If only I'd known those options were open to me, I'd have skipped training in Quantico and raced right over to the Julia Child Institute." Her temper finally breaking, she braced her palm on the table and leaned toward Duffy, meeting his startled gaze with her own furious, narrowed one. "As it happens, I'm a pretty good ass-kicker, so I think I'll stick with what I know." She paused briefly, renewing her smile, even though it was significantly cooler. "As long as that's okay with you."

Stalking away, she didn't dare look at Hamilton, who'd no doubt find a way to warm her icy demeanor.

Chauvinistic, patronizing men who were threatened by women in general, not just the ones carrying firearms, didn't warrant any room in her thoughts. And yet, here she was, striding to her car and dwelling on the interview as if she cared whether or not she could boil water.

If Duffy owned a gun, it was doubtful he'd be able to hit the broad side of a barn with it, even with a sniper's scope and a GPS. And yet nobody was questioning his ability to be harbormaster. Though what his job had to do with weapons, she couldn't say. She just—

She ground to a halt next to her dark blue sedan. Those two didn't seriously think the investigation of this case would be reduced to gender, did they? Suspected smuggling was serious business that had nothing to do with chromosomes.

Frankly, she'd expected better from Carr Hamilton.

He caught up to her in the parking lot, bracing his arm on the hood of her car and standing way too close. "Why did you come here tonight?"

Again, she was conscious of feeling small. As an agent, the sensation bothered her. As a woman, she couldn't help inhaling his cologne's spicy scent and spending a few seconds reveling in the head-spinning that followed.

She told herself it was important that she stand her ground and resist his advances. If she let him inside, she wasn't sure how she could stay objective. Stepping back, she rolled her shoulders. "I'm here because this is where Duffy wanted to meet. He's a complete ass, by the way."

"I did advise you to show some leg."

Briefly, she closed her eyes to get a better handle on her temper. Was he really just like everybody else? "You don't honestly believe I'd resort to low-cut dresses or high heels to solve my case," she said, her gaze boring into his.

"Sure I do." He closed the distance she'd created between them. "If it solved your case, you'd do just about anything."

His assured tone angered her—or so she tried to convince herself. The fact that his statement was true was irrelevant.

Hamilton cocked his head. "As far as your personal life, though, I think you'd make a man's journey just about as difficult as you could."

Also true. Though not out of any deliberate issue with

men in general—except the chauvinistic, homophobic or idiotic ones. She simply hadn't met many men worth giving her time to lately. And if she was lonely, she had her job to focus on. The SAC respected her. For now, that would have to be enough to keep the home fires burning.

She crossed her arms over her chest. "Did they teach you how to be an egomaniac at Yale?"

Ignoring her defensive stance, he leaned into her. "No, I think that particular quality is inborn."

The challenge in his dark eyes hadn't wavered once since the moment she met him.

She liked that.

Truth told, she liked him. But he was intimately involved in her case, and she knew an attraction to him wasn't wise.

"Are you sure you didn't come here to see me?" he asked.

"I came to interrogate a person of interest in my case." If she figured the owner of the bar, who she'd learned spent many of his nights in that bar, showed up, well, that was simply a side benefit to a job that had sold her short on positive points so far.

His gaze roved her face. "And I'm irrelevant?"

"You're...distracting," she admitted, her heart racing with the crazy need that she sensed would always mark any encounter with Carr Hamilton.

"Then I'm doing my job."

She angled her head. "Is that why you followed me out here—to do your job?"

His tongue moistened his lower lip, and she barely repressed a groan. "No." He wrapped one arm around her waist. "I have other things on my mind right now."

As he lowered his head, she knew she could stop him. Should stop him.

But there were times when her instincts took over, and while those interludes didn't always end the way she'd anticipated or desired, she couldn't deny they always made things interesting.

She doubted touching Carr Hamilton would be any different.

His hand cupped her jaw as he laid his mouth over hers. As his fingers gripped the back of her head, his tongue slid between her lips, sending sparks of desire and need shooting through her body. The lustful feelings smoldering inside exploded.

Their chests met; her nipples tightened.

Her body wanted him, even if her brain warned of the danger. With a moan of longing, she ignored her conscience. She clutched the front of his shirt as he continued to devour her mouth, seeming determined to absorb every part of her into him, and she was willing to let him.

Willing? Hell, she wanted more.

Much more.

He pressed her back against her car. "I've thought of nothing but you since yesterday," he rasped in her ear.

Her pulse hammered. Her body throbbed.

Different didn't even begin to describe the hunger pulsing through her. She'd anticipated a spark and gotten an inferno.

She pressed her lips to his throat and buried her hand in the inky locks of his hair that indeed felt like silk. "You're part of my case. I shouldn't—"

He silenced her with another kiss. Her protests died in the wake of the raw emotions consuming her. Her belly tightened, craving more of his touch, knowing instinctively he could drive away the loneliness and satisfy both her body and her mind.

She wanted his skin pressed against hers. She wanted to let loose the fire behind his dark eyes.

His hand slid up her stomach, and her breasts tingled in anticipation. But before he could reach his goal, his thumb brushed her shoulder holster.

She shoved him back instantly.

In the dimly lit parking lot, white sand beneath her shoes, ocean breeze brushing against her skin, she gasped for air and watched him. He looked as dazed as she felt.

"You touched—" She broke off and slid her hands into her pants pockets. Her fingers quivered with the need to brush an errant lock of his silky hair off his forehead. She cleared her throat and tried again. "Sorry. My weapon holster. It's an instinctive thing for a cop to protect."

Still breathing heavily, his mouth lifted on one side. "Remind me to disarm you next time."

She shook her head. There shouldn't be a next time.

And yet could she really imagine resisting the beautiful man standing before her for long? If he wanted her—and by the evidence presented in the past few minutes she could only assume he did—was there any way she wouldn't be his?

She shivered at the thought.

"Cold?" he asked, stepping forward and bracing his palms beneath her elbows.

"No." She shook her head. "That's the last thing I am."

His hands gripped her waist, and she noted he was

careful to keep them away from her holster. "Come home with me."

She turned away. "I can't. I need to think." She'd never been a coward in her life, but she wasn't sure whether she should run toward or away from this man.

"Think about me?" he asked, his lips against her ear.

"Among other things. I need to go to the gun club."

"The...what?"

She glanced over her shoulder into his confused eyes. "Gun club. They have an indoor shooting range that's open twenty-four hours." Then she remembered the whiskey she'd indulged in earlier. The club would have to wait for morning. "I like to shoot to relax."

"I like to walk on the beach."

Just another way they were opposites and completely wrong for each other.

When she opened her car door, he let go of her and stepped back. "You want a ride home?" she asked him.

He started off. "I'll walk. Thanks."

"Oh, Hamilton? By—"

"Do you think you could call me by my first name?"

"No, I really don't think I can now."

He scowled. "Then when?"

She shrugged. "When it's the right time. And, by the way..." She let her gaze track down his body, long, lean and illuminated by the streetlight. "The Bureau couldn't care less whether you wear boxers, briefs or nothing at all."

"What about you?"

She had no doubt he'd look hot in anything. Or nothing. "I couldn't care less either."

3

BINOCULARS AROUND his neck, Carr leaned against the aft railing and stared at the moonlit water where his boat bobbed at the dock.

At nearly eleven o'clock on a Wednesday, the bar was the only place that was hopping. Jack's boat was still out, so it seemed the only thing to do was wait.

His thoughts returned, as they had a million times, to the night before and the kiss he'd shared with Malina Blair. Of course, describing what they'd shared as a mere kiss diminished the encounter by miles.

Touching her had been like holding lightning in his bare hands.

She—

He halted his thoughts as he sensed movement behind him on the dock. He didn't flinch or turn, but his heart rate picked up speed.

Were Jack's buddies back?

He hadn't seen them since that night he'd found the coffee grounds nearly three weeks ago.

Were more drugs being delivered? Were there even drugs involved at all? Something odd was certainly going on, but had he jumped to conclusions based on the coffee grounds? Malina had passed off the connection between drugs and coffee. Was she right, or was she simply trying to demonstrate that he had no business messing around in her case?

If these guys were drug dealers, they were certainly ruthless. And while he could hold his own in a courtroom, he acknowledged for a stark moment that he might just be out of his element in this particular world.

He could battle, but he wasn't trained in any physical combat beyond the conniving elegance of the fencing ring. Brutality wasn't part of his life. And, candidly, he was more brains than brawn.

As he heard a click on the starboard side of the boat, he spun on the balls of his feet and crouched at the same time.

"Smooth," said a familiar voice. "But I still wouldn't have missed."

The next second, a powerful flashlight blinded him. Cursing, he rose and held his hands in front of his face. Malina Blair's shadow was barely discernible. "Is that really necessary?"

The light flicked off.

He blinked and saw spots as his eyes adjusted back to the darkness. Before he'd fully recovered, she was inches from him.

She tapped the binoculars. "A little late for bird-watching."

Dressed in black, her arm was a shadow that ended in a lethal-looking gun pointed to the sky. With her dark hair pulled back tightly from her face, the first thing he could see clearly was her startlingly turquoise eyes. He had the crazy, poetic urge to drown himself in them.

"Just what the hell do you think you're doing?" she asked, narrowing those eyes as she holstered her pistol.

He wanted to see her hair loose and tangled around her beautiful face. He wanted to feel the strands brush across his bare skin. He wanted to bury his body in her softness and hear her breath catch as she lost herself in the pleasure of his touch.

"Contemplating a late-night cruise," he managed to return finally.

She shook her head in disbelief.

If he admitted the truth—that he was imagining her in his bed—would she shoot him or throw him overboard?

Or would she respond as she had the night before? With need and heat and a longing for even more?

She poked her finger in his chest, backing him against the railing. "I thought I made it clear that you should keep your distance from this case."

"Did you?" He angled his head and gave her a smile that she clearly wasn't buying. "I recall that conversation a bit differently. I remember saying I understood what you thought my involvement in the case should be." He paused significantly. "I never agreed to the terms."

She paced away, then back. "Why do you think lawyers get a bad rap when it comes to honesty?"

"Because honesty and truth are two entirely different concepts. Do you have on black underwear, too?" When she glared at him, he shrugged. "I've always wondered about the wardrobe for the undercover espionage thing."

She stopped pacing. Her fists were clenched by her sides, and he decided he enjoyed needling her almost as much as he enjoyed touching her. "How about you leave the espionage to James Bond and me to handle this case?"

"Sorry, my investment in the outcome is too great."

"What investment?"

He made a sweeping gesture to the area around him. "My island, remember?" *Among other beautiful things I want to hold close.* "I need to see this through."

"And I said I'd consult you. The stakeouts you need to leave to me."

He raised his eyebrows. "Stakeout? I'm just enjoying the night air."

With a huff that was utterly female and so unlike her, Malina leaned back against the railing next to him. "How are honesty and truth different?"

"Honesty refers to integrity, candor. Truth is answering a question without lying."

She cast him a surprised glance. "That's a despicable distinction."

He nodded, and the barb of criticism hit in ways she couldn't imagine, even though he knew she'd read his case files. "It's the law."

"According to whom?"

"Anybody who's called upon to defend themselves or someone else in court."

"Someone guilty?"

The barb turned poisonous, spreading through him like cancer. "Everyone's entitled to a defense—even the supposed guilty."

"Is that how you sleep at night?"

With fury burning inside him, he faced her, crossing his arms over his chest. The fact that part of his anger stemmed from embarrassment only fueled his indignation. "Do you want to debate legal procedures? How about the merits of tort reform?" He nodded toward her holstered pistol. "As good as you might be with that, I'm better at the law, so don't even think about screwing with me on that subject.

"A lawyer presents his or her case. A judge or jury determines guilt or the level of judgment. That's it. That's the system where we all work." He leaned into her. "If, however, you want to screw me in other ways, I'm more than happy to oblige."

Her eyes narrowed as she stared at him. And either his *honesty* or his crudeness had finally shocked her into silence.

Unable to face her or himself, he stormed across the deck and down into the cabin. He slammed the door behind him, then tore the binoculars from around his neck and flung them and himself onto the couch. Through the window above him the moon cast its haunting light.

Several moments later, the cabin door opened.

"I'm sorry I took my frustration out on you," she said, flopping against the wall opposite him and crossing her arms over her chest.

For some reason, her frustration calmed him instantly. "I'm sorry I did the same. Why are you so annoyed?"

"I didn't get much sleep last night."

"Why not?"

"The case. Concern for my job."

"No other reason?"

She moved toward him. His heart jumped.

When she stopped beside the sofa, so close their legs nearly touched, he felt the heat pumping off her, as well as a seductive scent, which could have been perfume or simply the innate lure of her skin. Both twined their way around his senses.

"You," she said. "I thought about you."

Though her tone was an accusation, he wasn't offended. She'd thrown his world off balance. Now he knew he'd done the same for her.

He also knew he should stand, but he wasn't sure his legs would hold him.

She skimmed her fingertips across his shoulder. "What've you done to me?"

Part of him wanted to tell her to run. He wasn't worthy of her time or attention. But he wasn't capable of that kind of nobility.

He captured her hand in his and kissed the underside of her wrist, where her pulse beat strong and thick. "In an effort to be truly honest, I should admit I was enjoying the night air and hoping you'd show up for a stakeout."

She slid down onto the sofa beside him. "And I knew you wouldn't give up your involvement in this case."

"Are we pursuing the case because we want to solve it, or are we pursuing it to have an excuse to be together?"

"I'm not sure."

"Does it matter which is true?"

"Honestly?" She smiled, leaning toward him, her lips an inch from his. "No."

Her tongue teased his bottom lip, then her teeth nipped the same spot. He hardened in an instant.

With a tug of her wrist, he pulled her against him, crushing her against his chest, relishing the way her heart hammered against him, as if trying to escape and join his. Angling her head, she deepened the kiss and wrapped her arms around his neck.

He breathed in the scent of clean cotton and, if he wasn't mistaken, gun oil.

She was a combination of tenderness and teeth that he found intriguing, stimulating and irresistible.

His erection throbbed. His ears buzzed.

The gentle rocking of the boat beneath them belied the electricity in the air. In the dark, shadows mingled. Hot breath and seeking hands sparked passion. Forgetting who she was and her real purpose in his life, he surrendered to the moment as he hadn't in a very long time.

But before he'd taken his next breath, she had her pistol drawn and her back plastered against the wall next to the cabin's exterior door. "Get down," she whispered.

His hands tingled. He still had the scent of her clinging to him. "I—"

"That buzzing in your ears isn't my substantial powers of seduction. It's a boat motor."

"How do you know my ears are buzzing?"

"Because mine are, too. *Get down*."

He slid from the sofa onto the floor and watched her peek between the blinds on the glass door. With a great deal of effort, he could now separate the humming in his ears from the motor outside.

She was cool, calm and in charge. He was a quivering mass of need. There was a serious balance issue with this relationship already. If there even was a relationship, which he wasn't sure about. They'd only been introduced two days ago. Didn't these things take time to develop? Didn't the fact that she was in his life only to solve a case make anything meaningful impractical? And hadn't he decided he was through with anything that didn't have meaning?

Then again, her ears were buzzing, too.

Eschewing dignity, he crawled across the cabin, then

rose beside Malina. "There are times when I feel like a freshman in the throes of my first crush."

"The throes of—" She stopped, turning her head to glare at him. "Don't throw. Don't crush. Be still."

She looked lean and sexy, her pistol raised beside her and pointing at the ceiling. Her expression was focused, her body braced. Desire tightened his stomach. "Is that thing loaded?"

She peeked between the blinds again. "Do you ever shut up?"

He pressed his lips to the shell of her ear. "If you keep my mouth occupied in some other way."

She ignored the invitation and said, "I think it's your buddy Jack."

"So we work now and play later?"

"I'm always working."

She used the tip of her gun to move the blinds aside, and he watched over her shoulder as Jack's boat puttered past and turned into its slip. "That's him, right?" she asked in a hoarse whisper.

"That's the boat."

She snorted. "You're such a lawyer."

"Unless there's now a rash of boat thieves running over the island intent on disrupting the general well-being of the citizenry, I assume Jack's the pilot."

"Hell. A wordy lawyer."

"I'm well paid for each and every syllable."

"Do you ever feel guilty for making that money on the tide of pain and suffering your clients have to weather?"

Something ugly clenched inside him. "All the time," he said lightly.

Part of the tension he felt must have slipped through

his tone, because she glanced at him. "Cheap shot. Sorry."

"I'm used to it."

"So I'm all the more sorry."

"I appreciate the—"

"Hold on. He's moving."

And Jack was.

He emerged from the cabin with a small box tucked beneath his arm. The box appeared to be made of ordinary, brown cardboard. It measured no more than half a foot wide and long. Jack was whistling as he stepped off his boat and onto the dock.

For some reason, the upbeat tune made Carr's blood boil. "Let's follow him."

Malina planted her hand in the center of his chest. "Let's watch."

After a few moments, Jack disappeared up the stairs toward the marina bar—and no doubt the parking lot beyond.

"We should go after him."

"I will. I know where he lives." Tucking her pistol back into its holster, Malina opened the door and stepped out. "Let's look around a little first."

As they moved slowly along the dock, Carr studied the bobbing *American Dream*. Something was fishy about Jack's boat—and it didn't have anything to do with nets or rods. "I don't suppose you could turn your head while I pop the cabin lock and see what old Jack had hidden beneath his mattress?"

"Not yet."

Though Malina's back was to him, Carr raised his eyebrows. "So you're not saying no? How liberal of you, Agent—"

"Hang on."

As Malina bent to one knee, Carr moved closer to her. More coffee maybe? If so, Jack really ought to find a sealed box to carry his illicit merchandise in. Didn't the man know about plastic containers? They even had fresh seal plastic bags now. Double-zippered to ensure the contents stayed tightly enclosed.

"Well, now," Malina said in a low, excited tone that immediately captured his attention. "It seems your neighbor does have a side business, though I'm not sure how drugs, art or coffee enters into it."

Carr moved his attention to her clenched fist, which she held out in front of her. "How so?"

"It appears Mr. Rafton went for the sparkle instead."

When she opened her hand, sitting on a scrap of white cloth, a large, loose diamond glittered back at him from her steady palm.

4

RISING, Malina studied the stone in her hand. Four, maybe five carats. But the thrill of discovery was rapidly being overcome by questions with no answers.

Hamilton, standing so close she felt completely wrapped in his enticing, somewhat old-fashioned sandalwood scent, seemed to realize this as well. "You make people think you're smuggling drugs, when you're really smuggling diamonds? That seems…"

"Stupid."

"And what about the artwork?" Hamilton asked. "I've bought enough paintings to recognize the crates in which they're shipped."

"Decoys? Or he's into more than gems."

"Coffee grounds and painting crates to disguise diamonds?"

Malina shrugged. "Gold and jewels are a big commodity now. With the stock market and economy shaky, tangible assets are hot. Banks, museums and collectors are being hit left and right. Smuggling stolen goods is in vogue once again."

"But Jack—head of a smuggling operation?" Hamilton

frowned. "He doesn't have the nerve or the brains. He's a nice, average guy."

"And yet he's already managed to stir up a lot of red tape. Paintings and diamonds are major theft—FBI jurisdiction, in other words. Drugs are DEA. Plus, there's local law enforcement to coordinate and possibly the Coast Guard if any of us needed to board his boat in open water. Maybe this is a more complex operation than it seems."

Hamilton shook his head. "Sorry. I can't give Jack that kind of credit." When her gaze flicked to his, he amended, "Bad guy credit, of course. He's just not that creative a thinker, not devious enough."

"Maybe you're the one who's not devious enough."

"Oh, no. I am."

How did she respond to that? His odd, self-deprecating humor had a darker source, she was sure. Were all those profitable lawsuits becoming mundane?

She knew he'd left his practice in New York City two years ago to settle on Palmer's Island, where he'd volunteered to be the unpaid staff lawyer to a variety of charities and churches. Up until they'd met, she'd been certain he was behind the scenes building a big case—tort reform be damned—that would bust out on the national scene, sending him around the talk shows and law conferences for some time to come.

But that cold-blooded plan didn't mesh with the man she'd met—and kissed.

I like to walk on the beach.

She believed those words more than she trusted the evidence she'd seen in her background check.

How far the mighty had fallen indeed.

"You observed Jack taking a payoff," she said, to get her focus back on the case as she folded the cloth carefully around the diamond and tucked it in her pants pocket. "He could be a middleman with someone more creative pulling the strings."

"True."

"Who would have the nerves and the brains around here to smuggle diamonds?"

"I can find out." A smile stretched across his gorgeous face. "In fact, we both can."

"Why am I not surprised?" Malina crossed her arms over her chest. "I should be ordering you back to your office and out of my business."

He slid his fingers down her sweater-covered arm, barely touching but easily reminding her of the intimacies they'd already shared. And the ones likely to come. Need shimmered between them like the glow of the moon overhead. "But you won't."

"No."

"Because you know I won't listen, or because you know you can use me to solve the case?"

"Both. I assume you already have an idea for finding out about the smuggling?"

"You know me well."

"You constantly think several steps ahead." She shrugged. "It's a trait I recognize."

He angled his head. "I imagine so. I've been invited to a yacht party on Friday night. All the island's elite crowd will be there, including Jack."

"How do you know he'll come?"

"I'll dangle the opportunity to mix with rich potential clients. He'll be there. And since the host is new around the island, and this recent criminal activity is new, I wonder if the two connect?"

"So Rafton and this guy don't already know each other?"

"Maybe. It'll be interesting to observe them and find out. You can go as my date."

The word *date* made her frown. "So we go undercover?"

The sensually wicked grin that never failed to make her pulse pound teased his lips. "Absolutely."

"Just remember I'm in charge."

"How could I forget?" When she flicked him a suspicious glance, he added, "You are armed, after all."

So are you, she longed to add. That smile should be registered as a lethal weapon.

"I need to get going," she said, and even she recognized the regret in her tone.

His hand cupped her jaw gently. "I was hoping you'd stay awhile."

"I have evidence to log, and I need to do some background work on the party and the guests. Can you get me the information?"

Surprisingly, he didn't press her to stay. "I'll send it over by the morning."

Why was she disappointed he'd given over to the demands of the case so easily? Why was there a part of her that wanted him to press her into staying? Into going back to his boat and finishing what they'd started?

Deliberately, she shook the idea from her mind. "Who's the sheriff on the island?"

"Tyler Landry. Former Marine. He's just been on the job a few months, but he's sharp."

"At some point I'll need to inform him about at least some of what I'm doing, what I suspect."

"Federal cooperation with the locals?" Hamilton paused, amusement tugging his lips. "How progressive of you."

"I can be reasonable…eventually. But I want to keep

this party business quiet, see what happens. I'm telling nobody but the SAC. Even though I've got probable cause for a search warrant on the boat, I'm not going to ask for it." She smiled fiercely. "I'm also not calling the DEA. This is all mine—for now."

"Ours. And you might consider bringing in Landry sooner rather than later. You'll get his support and discretion."

"You know him well."

"He's married to a good friend of mine, and they happen to be my neighbors."

"I'll think about it."

This case was pretty personal all around—not that she should be surprised on an island of this size.

She certainly hadn't anticipated being involved, though.

And, like it or not, she was involved.

Getting personally mixed up with a witness was a risky career move, but at some point during the night she'd quit pretending she could resist Carr Hamilton's allure. As long as they kept their relationship quiet and separate from the case, and as long as she reminded herself that he was simply a pleasurable means to an end, there was no reason she couldn't be a normal woman and enjoy herself.

Sex was a great stress buster, and she rarely took the time and effort to indulge in personal needs. Especially since her *last* risky career move.

She sighed.

Then again, maybe *risky* was a colossal understatement.

HE WANTED HER too much.

As Carr watched Malina walk down the pier away from him, he fought to ignore the aching need in his body.

It was better to let her go for now. He needed to re-group, and she was wise in using caution at them being seen together.

But it was hard.

Hell, *he* was hard. Perpetually, it seemed.

With no carnal relief in sight and troubled by the intensity of his attraction, he resisted the urge to slip into Jack's cabin to do a little off-the-record searching and instead headed to his own slip. He locked up and checked the dock ties before casually making his way to The Heron. There, he drank a whiskey and chatted with Jimmy, communicating to all that he was just a regular guy going about his regular routine.

Certainly not spying on a fellow islander or planning an undercover yacht party operation with the FBI.

All the while he talked and drank, however, he couldn't get Malina Blair's pillow-soft lips and vivid eyes out of his mind.

As he'd traveled his new path of redemption, he'd begun to long for a woman to share his life with. Some-one who might not necessarily have to know the man he used to be, but could appreciate the man he was trying to become.

Unfortunately, the one he wanted had instigated a deep background check on him and probably knew all his dirty secrets. One who was bound by regulations to keep her distance, as well as harboring a deep longing to escape from the island that had become his saving grace.

There was irony in that realization, as well as a hint of divine punishment.

Of course that didn't mean he wouldn't fight to make her crave him as much as he did her. Or strive to change her mind about both him and his island home. Or do his absolute best to circumvent, dodge or outwit rules and retribution, no matter how much they were needed and deserved.

Most would say the gray areas were where he did his best work anyway.

THOUGH CARR HAD spoken to Malina a few times by phone over the past two days, he hadn't seen her, and he found himself pacing his front parlor as he awaited her arrival on Friday afternoon.

The warm and sunny March day had inspired him to open his windows, so the scent of salt and sea flowed through the house. He'd called his cleaning service and had them come out that morning to polish the considerable amount of stainless steel and glass.

In a rare show of indecisiveness, he'd changed clothes three times before deciding on a pair of crisply pressed navy pants and a white oxford-cloth shirt.

His heart leaped as the doorbell rang, and he had to force himself to take a deep breath and roll his shoulders before closing the few feet between him and the door.

A curvy blonde, wearing a short, formfitting, royal-purple halter-top dress and gold stilettos, stood on his porch. For one jarring moment he thought a new form of door-to-door sales was being launched—and a very enticing one at that.

Only the tough glare in the woman's turquoise eyes gave away her identity.

"I spent two hours messing with this getup, so don't even think about critiquing."

Somehow, Carr managed to speak around his swollen tongue. "Wouldn't dream of it."

He stepped back and extended his arm to invite her in, then, groaning, watched her walk past him. Her long, toned, tanned legs had his blood running hot and his palms sweating.

He was supposed to *pretend* to be crazy about her all night?

Gee, that would be difficult.

Following her, he commented, "Why, Agent Blair, what lovely legs you have."

She cast him an amused look over her shoulder. "Cute. You look like the typical yacht-going millionaire. Where's your watch cap?"

"At the cleaners. I didn't expect you to appear incognito."

"We agreed to do this undercover, right?"

Heroically, he resisted the urge to point out that his best undercover work didn't require any clothes at all.

Especially since he'd rather demonstrate than chatter needlessly.

"We did agree," he said. "Well, given your usual choice of binding your hair back and wearing either unobtrusive navy or black, I doubt anybody would recognize you in *that*."

She glanced down at herself and shrugged. "I can't take the chance. I've interviewed several people on the island regarding Jack Rafton." She continued to walk down the hall. "Plus, the mayor's on the guest list. I met him at an event in Charleston, so he knows I'm an agent."

"I should have considered that."

"I did. It's my—" She stopped, her head twisting to scan the area around her.

The entire back half of the house where she now stood was curved in two places like towers and made up mostly of windows to take advantage of the point's majestic view. One tower even held a curved steel staircase that twined its way up three floors to a small observation deck overlooking the rippling ocean.

He watched her turn and take in the steel railing bracketing the wide, floating staircase that dominated the two-story living and kitchen areas and led to the balcony walkway and upstairs bedrooms. Her gaze flicked over the black marble countertops, the glass and stainless-steel tables, the art on the walls, the sculptures, the white decor and furniture mixed with bare splashes of red and blue.

It was quite a contrast to his conservative and comforting, antique-heavy office.

"My job," she finished finally, her gaze finding his and holding. "Do you like surprising people?"

"Do you often put on a short skirt and heels, let the bad guys take a good, long look at those fabulous legs and initiate a sting under the insignia of justice?"

She narrowed her eyes. "I try to keep the sluttiness down to once a week."

"What a shame."

"Did you design and build this house?" she asked, ignoring his come-on.

"Yes."

"So who decorated your office?"

"I did."

"Huh."

Clearly, he'd stumped her. He liked the idea. He also couldn't help his gaze dropping to her supremely impressive cleavage. "Where do you carry your gun in an outfit like that?"

"Wouldn't you like to know."

He grinned. "Definitely. Come on, where?"

"I don't. And trust me I'm not happy about it."

He closed the distance between them, bracing his

hands at her narrow waist. "You're unarmed?" he clarified, dipping his head to brush his lips across her cheek.

"I didn't say that."

"Okay." Of course now that he was touching her, breathing in a warm, floral scent that was a departure from her usual clean cotton, he couldn't care less about weapons.

"I have a switchblade strapped to my thigh," she finished.

He pressed his lips to her earlobe. "Maybe I should check to be sure it's loaded properly."

She swatted his shoulder in a totally uncharacteristic playful gesture, then stepped back. "You keep your distance."

He tried to look insulted. "I thought you were my blonde bimbo, and I was your morally ambiguous sugar daddy."

"You have quite an imagination. And you need to remember this is my op. You're the reluctant ally I'm using to close this case and get my career back on track."

Leaning back, he tried to look comically insulted, even though his gut clenched. "Being morally ambiguous, I can accept that."

She turned away. "We should get going."

"You don't want a tour?"

She cast one last and—if he wasn't mistaken—longing look around the living room, her gaze lingering on the staircase to the observation deck. "Maybe some other time."

As they headed outside, she moved toward her government-issue sedan, paused, then swore.

Since Carr could all but hear the silent argument in her head, he said nothing. He simply paused beside the garage doors. Being so close to the ocean, the house was raised above the ground and the lower level was all storage. In his case, the garage held his golf clubs, yard tools, pool and hot tub chemicals and his Triumph Spitfire.

Finally, Malina turned. "I guess we should take your car."

He pressed his lips together briefly. "If you insist…"

He pressed a button on the remote keychain in his pocket, and the garage doors slid open. After assisting blonde-but-still-stunning Malina into the passenger seat, he pulled away from the house—with the top down, naturally.

"Will the breeze upset your wig, or did you dye your hair?"

Her eyes popped wide. "Dye my—" She stopped, and her jaw tightened. "I'm not vain. I just wouldn't dye my hair for an op." She paused. "Probably. It's a wig, if you have to know. It's on, and it's not going anywhere."

"Good." He paused as he pulled out on Beach Road. "I like your hair as it is. Very Thai."

"I'm an American, like you."

"And while there's a remnant of the Scots in me, there's a world of Polynesian in you. It isn't an insult, you know. The beauty of your ancestors is renowned, and despite the chaotic mix of many island nations, differing religions and backgrounds, plus the selling of rum-infused umbrella drinks in coconuts, your culture has even miraculously survived the formidable tourist industry."

She looked over at him. "Is that your wordy way of telling me I'm pretty just the way I am?"

He chuckled. "It is."

"Thanks, but I really need to focus on this op."

"Sorry." He fought to hide his disappointment. "Just trying to stay in character."

She slid her hand across his thigh so suddenly he jolted. "I have to keep my professional life away from my personal life. When I let my emotions get mixed up with my job, I run into trouble. You know why I was sent here, so you understand."

His jaw tightened, but he nodded. Damned if he'd let her past—in which she'd done nothing wrong, by the way—dictate the need crawling through his veins. And she wanted him, too. If she didn't, he'd bow out. He'd help close the case, then move on without a word of regret. What did he have to do to—

"Whatever happens between us has to stay private and after hours."

Interrupted from his private rant, he glanced at her. "So you acknowledge there is something between us."

A rare smile bloomed on her face. "Oh, yeah."

He momentarily forgot how to shift gears. "So, after hours…when are those exactly?"

"My work is my life. I don't have hours. But I think I can fit you in somewhere."

Before he could be insulted at being "fit in" between suspects and reports, she leaned over, scraping her lips across his jaw. "This party has to end sometime, right?"

Talk about surprise.

As abruptly as the sensuous woman buried inside her had appeared, Malina leaned back in her seat, her eyes all business. "I followed up on your monthly garage tip and found Rafton's Lotus. It's shiny and obvious. I also found the record of the purchase."

"You traced it all the way back under the name John Smith? Must have been some search."

She snorted in derision. "Not that hard. You were right about his lack of creativity, and there haven't been that many domestic sales of the Lotus in the last several months. Especially not ones with Charleston as the delivery point."

Carr braked hard. "He had it shipped to Charleston?"

"Atlanta would have been wiser. L.A. or New York would have been seriously smart. But, just as you pointed out, he's not exactly a master criminal. You know how many Ardent Red Lotus Elises are registered in South Carolina?"

"Not many."

"One."

Despite his dedication to stopping whatever Jack was doing, Carr winced. Would he, even in his most morally ambiguous days, have had a defense for that purchase?

Unfortunately, yes.

"Something's certainly up with Rafton," Malina mused. "Whether he's simply a lousy money manager or a thief and/or smuggler…" She shrugged. "It's too soon to tell. What about the Kendricks? Do you know them? He has a note in our files, due to the unsolved murder of his parents."

"Aidan and Sloan. Her father was the sheriff for many years. He just retired in January, and Aidan is a successful businessman many times over. They're good friends of mine."

At her questioning glance, he added, "Yes, I know everyone on the island—the advantages of living in a small town. Despite my scheming, money-grubbing ways, even Sister Mary Katherine and I have bonded."

Malina raised her eyebrows. "Sister? As in Catholic nun?"

"She makes all the lawyers meet bimonthly."

"Wise lady."

"She certainly is." And a forgiving one, as well. She'd assured him even the worst of society had a place in heaven, should they strive to find their way. "You two are a lot alike."

"I doubt that."

"No, you are." And the more he compared the two women, the more he was convinced. "You both have a titanium center of strength. You stand on the side of what's right, no matter the risk. You're both stubborn and sure your way is the only way."

"That last part sounds just like me."

"Fortunately for both of you, I'm around to keep everyone flexible and on their toes."

Malina flicked him a surprised look. "You mean you spend all the time you're not butting into my case, following around a Catholic nun and telling her how to do her job?"

Saying nothing, Carr pulled into the yacht club parking lot. Finally, as he maneuvered the Spitfire into a space, he commented, "With conversations like this burned into my memory, is it any wonder I'm constantly trying to get you into my bed?"

"I thought my sarcasm would discourage you."

"It makes me want to shut you up by kissing you until you forget what you were talking about in the first place." He turned, bracing his arm across the back of her seat. "In fact, let's practice that technique now."

Before she could respond with more than widened

eyes, he'd captured her mouth with his. He slid his tongue into her mouth, seducing her with his touch, since his words often seemed to have an unpredictable effect. Though he'd always been enticed by her simple scent, he had to admit the warm spice radiating from her golden skin suited her, or at least suited Malina, if not necessarily Agent Blair.

The contrast between moments when she willingly gave herself over to her needs and her absolute fierceness always delighted him. Layers and layers of heat lingered beneath her tough exterior, and he couldn't wait to uncover them all.

She laid her hands on his chest, angling her head, giving back as much as he longed to draw from her. Her lips were soft and seeking, and touching her was, as always, amazing.

When they separated, each breathing hard, her pupils were dilated. She curled her fingers into the fabric of his shirt. "What was I saying?" she asked, sounding dazed.

"I recall a long discourse on my charm no longer being completely inert."

"Discourse on—" She jerked back, her eyes clearing of desire. "Hang on, didn't we agree to keep personal and professional moments separate?"

"Actually, we didn't. You requested that personal moments between us be kept private and after hours. I will agree that's wise. However, since you're currently wearing a disguise and preparing to interrogate and spy on any number of mostly law-abiding citizens for the next few hours, I figured this could actually be classified as a professional fondling." He smoothed a strand of blond hair off her cheek. "We do have our roles to play, don't we?"

Her eyes sparked with temper. "We're going to talk about the rules of engagement later, Counselor. Got it?"

"Should I put down that appointment in my after-hours calendar?"

"I'll check the ammunition in my Glock and get back to you."

Smiling, Carr opened his door. As he stood, he noticed Jack helping a buxom redhead from his car a few spaces away.

Let the war games begin.

5

"WE'RE SO HAPPY you chose our humble island to visit," Mayor Harvey Kelso said with a self-important smile belying his words.

Malina sipped from her champagne glass and tried to infuse enthusiasm into her tone. "It's such a lovely spot."

"Made all the more lovely by your presence."

Malina drank more champagne.

At this rate, she was going to be either pissed and drunk or drunk and fired when she strangled the idiotic, golf-obsessed mayor of this crappy little island she'd landed on.

"We strive to cater to both young professionals as well as families here on Palmer's Island," the mayor continued. "We're also working to attract a premier golf tournament. Unfortunately, our single course is only nine holes, so the PGA won't take us seriously. We're landlocked, and the historical society refuses to budge on their properties. Do they expect us to build greens in the Atlantic?" Shaking his head at this injustice, he smiled nevertheless. "I'm sure the tourism council would love to hear about your vacation priorities."

At least he wasn't hitting on her. Since she knew the mayor had been married for more than a decade and had four kids, she could find some comfort in the realization that he was only interested in her disposable vacation income, not her cleavage.

Still, finding out the mayor was an egomaniac but not a cheat was hardly her priority for this particular operation.

Her partner had abandoned her twenty minutes ago— leaving her safely in the mayor's company as he went off in search of Jack and the yacht's owner—the actual suspects in this little drama, the ones *she* was supposed to be observing. In return, she was beginning to wonder about the suicide rate of intelligent blondes with big boobs.

"Harvey, don't upset the new people," a smooth, unfamiliar male voice interjected. "It disturbs the tax base."

Malina looked over her shoulder to see a dark-haired man and a blonde woman. They were a beautiful couple—lovely features, lightly tanned skin, dressed beach casual and connected by more than just their entwined hands.

"Not to mention the greens fees," the mayor said, lifting his whiskey glass to the newcomers. "Have you met Sandy?"

The man extended his hand. "No, but Carr told us he'd found a gem." Shaking Malina's hand, his silver eyes gleamed. "I'm Aidan Kendrick. My wife, Sloan." He urged the woman at his side into the circle.

Sloan gave Malina a brief greeting, then a discreet sweep from head to toe, her gaze alert and curious.

"Nice to meet you both," Malina said, realizing these were the friends Hamilton had mentioned and that he'd most likely told them her true identity. She wasn't sure, however, how wise that decision was. Generally, the fewer people involved in an undercover op, the better.

Especially untrained civilians.

Dear heaven, the future of her career might hang in the balance of a nosy lawyer, a semiretired business-man, the former sheriff's daughter, who was a librarian and president of the historical society, and the general effectiveness of a push-up bra.

Before she could contemplate how she'd allowed her-self to fall into that professional pitfall, the mayor spoke. "Aidan, have you given any more thought to investing in those old properties on the north end of the island? We could really use another nine holes. We should be able to compete with Kiawah."

"We're not a resort community," Sloan said, shifting her attention to the mayor and narrowing her eyes in the process. "We have plenty of those around. And we're not interested in tearing down a seventeenth-century church to make way for a damn putting green."

Harvey lost his ingratiating politician's smile in the space of a heartbeat. "You and the historical society are always looking for a way to attract more tourists. I just don't see why we can't do that with the golfers, too. They spend plenty of money in our shops and restaurants."

"And we're grateful," Sloan returned. "But we're not destroying the history and natural beauty of this island for ready cash."

The same debate had played out for decades on Ma-lina's home island of Kauai. They needed tourists for economic survival, and, actually, most locals liked shar-ing the pride and beauty of their home. But there was the danger of going too far. Of strip malls, T-shirt shops and theme restaurants overwhelming the environment to the point of destruction.

"Regardless," Aidan said, "I was outbid on the northern properties."

Sloan scowled. "And, trust me, I'm not happy about that either."

Surprise, then speculation crossed the mayor's face. "Really? By who?"

"Our host," Aidan said.

Malina jerked her attention from Aidan's handsome features back to her job. "Why do you think he was so determined to get the properties?"

The mayor glanced at her. "You're interested in real estate, Sandy? I thought Carr said you were a model."

Malina clenched her teeth. *Of course he did.* Was her career worth this? "I won't always be twenty-three and perfect." Following this self-aggrandized announcement, she giggled.

Sloan pressed her lips together as if suppressing a smirk.

Aidan nodded sagely. "Sadly, Harvey, it's true. Diversification is essential to any portfolio."

It was no wonder Hamilton and this guy were friends. Both were slick as the ice this island might see every millennium or so.

Before Malina could probe Aidan Kendrick further about the properties, a tall, silver-haired man in an expensive-looking navy suit approached their group. Their host, Simon Ellerby, as Malina knew from the pictures she'd found during her research. "Beautiful women who laugh are always welcome at my parties," he said, his gaze locked on Malina's. "Do you mind if I join you?"

He had an exotic accent that was faintly, but vaguely, European. He was tan and handsome—which seemed to be a common trait with nearly everyone on the island— and wore a diamond pinky ring on his left hand.

As Aidan introduced him to Malina—or, more accurately, to Sandy—she watched him for any false notes in the wealthy boat captain persona. She found none. Yet the perfection itself was a fault. He seemed to be playing a part, like an actor in a play.

The FBI had suspiciously little information on the man, who claimed to be nearly fifty, and Malina sensed she wouldn't have much more luck this afternoon.

"I was telling everyone about the properties you bought on the north end of the island," Aidan said. "Do you have any firm plans for them?"

"Renovation probably," Ellerby said. "The smaller houses could be sold as is or divided into rental duplexes, and the big house could be a B and B, or maybe apartments."

The mayor frowned. "How do you feel about golf?"

"The big house was built in 1867," Sloan said after a swift glare in the mayor's direction. "It would be nice to keep the original structure intact."

Ellerby angled his head. "Was it really? My lawyer handled the transaction, so I haven't seen many of the details."

Malina widened her eyes and tried to look both confused and impressed. "You bought a house you haven't even seen?"

Ellerby laughed indulgently. "I do that quite often." He swept his hand around to indicate the deck where they were standing. "I bought *Le Bijou* here sight unseen on the recommendation of a colleague. A mere whim."

"What does Le Bee—" Malina broke off, her face flushing. "Is that French for something?"

"It is indeed." His eyes gleamed, hard as the translation she knew he was about to reveal. *"The Jewel."*

"An expensive whim, Simon," Sloan said. "The historical society would love to have your support at our next fundraiser."

"Of course, of course," Ellerby said lightly. "With such a lovely invitation, and from the president herself, how could I resist?"

"Be careful what you promise," Hamilton said as he approached. "Sloan is a shark when it comes to the society." He slid his arm around Malina's waist, and she immediately felt the spark of desire that always accompanied his presence.

It was distracting and, for a moment, she simply absorbed his elegance, the enticing scent that clung to his skin and clothes.

"Hey, all," Jack Rafton said as he and his redhead date walked up, bringing Malina's thoughts back to her job. He toasted the host with a crystal tumbler. "Great party."

Ellerby nodded graciously. "Thank you. Carr tells me you're in insurance."

"I am. Auto, home, life—the whole deal." He smiled with the winning charm of a practiced salesperson. "I handle most of the boats in the area, too."

"I've seen you around the marina a few times. I assume you keep close tabs on your clients."

"Naturally. I also have my own Sea Ray in slip twenty-three."

Without seeming to, Malina watched their exchange

closely. While Simon Ellerby seemed relaxed, she observed Rafton taking frequent sips from his drink. His gaze skipped from the group around him, to the deck beneath his feet, then the clouds in the distance.

Carr, she noticed, was left to listen to Rafton's date ramble on about the lack of decent nightclubs on Palmer's Island. Poor man.

The conversation moved on around her, and she prodded with questions from time to time that she hoped would help her get a measure of their suspects. But she was constantly aware of her partner, her witness, her would-be lover…whatever he was besides gorgeous, tempting…irresistible.

Part of her couldn't believe she was distracted during an op, and part of her was fascinated that a romantic interest could bring about such a change.

Her career was her life. No one and nothing had ever swayed her from that path.

Why now? Why Hamilton? She had no idea.

With her own motives and actions so cloudy, she decided to pursue someone else's. Wasn't it wiser, easier, to focus on others and not look too deeply inside herself?

"Why *The Jewel?*" she asked Ellerby.

He smiled, though no genuine emotion reached his cold gray eyes. "Isn't it obvious? I love being surrounded by beautiful things."

LATER, as the sun set, casting a torrid mix of orange and red light across the sky and churning sea, Carr found himself alone with Malina at the yacht's aft. The propeller churned the water into mountains of white foam.

It was a night for gazing at the moon, long kisses and breathy sighs.

Somehow, though, he didn't think the woman beside him—even in disguise—was planning that sort of evening.

"Sandy?" she asked, her tone clearly annoyed.

"Well," he began, leaning against the railing and relishing the illumination of her profile in the fading light of the sun, "the name had to fit with your character. Blonde, somewhat ditzy bikini model…Sandy seemed to fit." He angled his head. "The stereotype might annoy astronauts, doctors and nuclear physicists named Sandy, but remember I was under a considerable time constraint."

"I'm sorry I asked," Malina muttered.

"You played your part well."

"It was physically painful. Is every curvy blonde on the planet subjected to people who talk to them as if they're five years old?"

"I wouldn't know. What did you think of Ellerby?"

"Smooth." She glanced at him. "Not as smooth as you or your buddy Aidan Kendrick, of course, but good enough." Her eyes fired, throwing off the veil of her disguise despite her tight dress and golden hair. "And whim, my ass. He bought this boat for a reason. He does nothing without considering every angle, every possibility very, very carefully."

"I agree."

"And he and Rafton are more than fellow boaters who've passed each other on the dock a few times, the way they both claim."

"Yes, they are."

"That redhead Rafton brought is a complete idiot."

"Yes, she is."

"You're awfully agreeable tonight."

He stepped closer, sliding his arms around her waist. "You're incredibly beautiful."

Her gaze flicked to his and held. "Is this part of the op? Or are we after hours now?"

"I think we've worked hard enough for today."

"To serve and protect isn't a normal job."

Coming from anybody else, that sentiment would be corny. But beneath that fierce stare and drive to claw her way up the government ladder of success, Carr knew Malina Blair cared. Certainly about the citizens around her and maybe even about him.

"Serve me," he whispered, pressing his lips against the side of her neck. "And I'll serve you." He could feel her heartbeat accelerate as he moved his hands down her backside, pulling her tight against his body.

"Somebody has to keep their head and do the protecting," she said, though she looped her hands around his neck and pressed her cheek alongside his.

"You can do that again tomorrow." The floral scent of her perfume invaded him as naturally as the sun set on the horizon. His head was swimming and his body aching, and yet he knew he had to tread carefully. Seducing her was like handling unexploded ammunition. Pressing the wrong button could cause them both to implode.

"For now, I'll find somewhere safe and isolated," he said.

She leaned back. "Your boat?"

His heart thumped hard once, then again. He nodded. "Sounds perfect."

"HAMILTON…"

"Right here," Carr said, pausing to give Malina another long kiss as he spun them through the cabin door of his boat. "At your service."

"I'm really not supposed to be doing this," she muttered against his lips, even as she unfastened his belt.

"I won't tell." He grabbed the hem of her dress, tugging it up until it hung around her hips. He slid his palms across her lace-covered butt and closed his eyes as pleasure shot through his body. "I'm very good at keeping secrets."

"I'm not sure I trust you."

Even with her breath hot on his throat, he winced. "The attorney-client relationship is sacred."

"I'm not a client," she returned as she threaded her fingers through his hair, and they moved down the narrow hallway to the bedroom.

"But I've entered into a professional—" he paused to angle her face upward for his kiss "—agreement with you and the FBI to…" He sat on the bed, pulling her between his thighs, closing his eyes as she leaned over him. "To solve this case for the betterment of everyone on Palmer's Island and—"

Her fingers wrapped around his erection and, for once, he lost the power of speech.

With her free hand, she tossed away the blond wig, then ran her fingers through her long, dark hair, scattering pins across the room.

The gesture felt like a sign, the moment of capitulation he'd been waiting for, as if he wasn't sure she'd truly be his beneath the masquerade and restrictions of her job. Her eyes were dark, dark blue and her pupils dilated as she stared at him, clearly enjoying the power she held and yet needy for whatever he desired at the same time.

He caught the edge of her dress and yanked it up and

off her body, then let it drop beside them. A leather strap held a knife sheath to her thigh, making her look like some kind of ancient warrior princess.

He unhooked it himself, his fingers caressing her warm, golden skin before he let that, too, fall to the floor.

She was naked now, except for her lacy panties, and he cupped her breasts like a treasure, gliding his tongue across each distended nipple.

When she moaned softly, exhilaration coursed through him.

Her body was as trimly muscular and amazing as he'd imagined, but more than the physical, he could feel her hunger, her need for fulfillment. Her longing to share both with him and only him. He hoped he wasn't imagining the extra charge through the air, the instinctual chemistry that told him this wasn't casual stress relief or convenient proximity.

Part of him—the part he'd fought to suppress the past several years—reminded him that motivations didn't matter. His need to make reparation for past deeds was being satisfied in many ways, and, after all, desire was desire.

But he'd also learned solitude held no interest.

"You think you could call me by my first name?" he asked as he lay back on the bed, pulling her next to him.

"Maybe…" She flipped open one of his shirt's buttons. He slid his index finger between her legs, beyond the elastic of her panties. "Eventually…" she whispered as her eyes fluttered shut.

While his finger stroked the wet heat between her legs, she squeezed his erection, and he, too, closed his eyes, fighting for control.

The moment she gasped and her thighs clenched, he found a smile. He increased the pressure of his strokes on her sensitive flesh.

Her breathing hitched; her hips rocked.

As her climax burst through her, she let go of him and slumped forward, bracing her hands against the mattress on either side of his head.

The contractions subsiding, she dipped her head and gave him a long, hot, amazing kiss.

"Carr," she said like a litany when they parted.

He smoothed the curtain of her silky hair off her face. "Finally."

Her head cocked, she smiled slightly. "There's more, though, right?"

His erection pulsed. "I certainly hope so."

Leaning back, she straddled his hips and ripped open his shirt, buttons pinging against the walls. The rest of their clothes followed in a flurry of greed and anticipation.

Naked, condom securely in place, Carr rolled on top of her, his hands loving every curve and inch of exposed skin. He fit between her legs, and she wrapped them around him, inviting him into her warmth.

As he surged inside, it seemed he'd waited an eternity to be part of her. Pleasure skated down his spine, even as the urgency to move, to satisfy the clawing need deep in his gut became overwhelming.

Fancy words deserted him. Nothing but the slap of their bodies against each other mattered. Chasing fulfillment. Searching for solace.

Primal, human and instinctive, they knew they had to reach the pinnacle to survive. Maybe tenderness would come later. Maybe not. Their chemistry was as intense as she was distinctly unpredictable.

But as a man who thrived on control, he gloried in losing it when she gripped him hard with her hips, rolled him to his back and let their bodies explode.

MALINA, her body slick with sweat and satisfaction, slid weakly off Carr's body.

Every nerve tingled, vibrated…shimmered. Her skin felt alive as it never had before. She wanted to hold the feelings before they slipped away. For once, she wanted vulnerability and defensiveness to last instead of fighting to banish them, instead of considering them the highest form of weaknesses.

She did trust him, even if she might never be able to tell him.

The gentle rock of the waves beneath the boat lulled her as her eyelids drifted closed, but a nibble on her fingers brought her back to awareness.

Of what she'd done. What she'd risked. What she still longed for.

"Are you still with me?" he asked, his voice husky.

"Barely." She knew she needed to find her clothes and leave. She couldn't seem to come up with a logical reason to move, though her instincts demanded she do so. "I'll come back around," she managed to say as she rolled to her back.

He spooned his body along her side, sliding his thigh over hers, letting his fingers drift up and down her bare stomach.

Shivers raced through her, reigniting desire.

His lips brushed her shoulder. "Soon?"

A smile bloomed from deep within. She looked over at him, into the dark brown of his eyes, letting her gaze drift over the jet-black waves of hair that surrounded his remarkable face. He was beautiful. "You're insatiable," she said instead.

"Is that a crime?"

"I'll check my regulations manual and get back to you."

"I look forward to the consultation."

"That's not going to be now, is it?"

"I'm a lawyer. We get paid to talk. It's instinctive."

"And *that* is the most succinct speech you've ever made."

"You've inspired me."

Something about the tenderness in his tone, which hadn't been there before, put her on edge. "Look, this isn't going to be a thing, right?"

He raised his eyebrows. "A thing?"

She sat up, wishing she could pull a blanket over herself but not wanting him to know she was uncomfortable. "I mean, we're just blowing off steam, aren't we? This case is stressful. You're involved in an atypical situation. It's only natural we'd come together in a way that's more than a professional bond."

"And that's the longest speech I've ever heard you give," he said lightly, though he ceased his rhythmic strokes against her belly. Rising, he snagged his pants from the floor and stepped into them. "Am I correct in assuming you're committed to focusing all your energy on this case?"

What was this about? "You are."

"And aren't you concerned for your job if anyone finds out about us?"

She shrugged. "I guess. But then I don't expect you to go shouting about it all over the island or the Bureau."

"You're taking a risk being with me," he insisted.

Screw being uncomfortable. Now she was pissed, though mostly at herself.

She rolled off the bed and grabbed the first thing she found on the floor—which turned out to be his white dress shirt—and shoved her arms into the sleeves. "Yeah, I suppose I am."

"And your work is your life."

Facing him, she crossed her arms over her chest. "And so?"

"So logic would dictate that I mean something to you beyond someone to casually blow off steam with."

She heard hurt beneath the insult, which was exactly what she didn't want. This was supposed to be simple—chemistry plus hot guy times proximity equals sizzling night. Why was her life so damn complicated these days?

She wanted to run, as she never did, had never even been tempted to do. "As nice as this was, I really should go."

He grabbed her wrist and held her gently but firmly in place. "This might be a great many things, but nice isn't in the top fifty."

6

NODDING, Malina sat on the bed.

It was ridiculous to deny that sleeping with a colleague on a case was out of character. Carr was certainly too intelligent to buy that excuse.

"My life seems destined to be overly convoluted at the moment," she said. "And my work really is my life."

"You still have a right to be away from the job." He sat beside her. "I just want to be part of it. I want more than a one-night lay. Don't you?"

Hadn't she sworn to keep focused on her future? To toe the Bureau line and get her career back on track? And hadn't her mother shared her story of giving up her dreams of going to Paris to study art so she could stay in Kauai to run the family surf shop? Hadn't she vowed, to herself and her mother, that she would consider her decisions carefully and not compromise her goals?

But then nothing and no one had ever tempted her like Carr Hamilton.

"Yeah," she found herself saying. "I guess I do." She

smiled feebly. "I'd like to hang on to you for at least a week."

Thankfully, he returned her smile. "That long, huh?"

"I'm not much of a long-term woman."

An odd look crossed his face. He reached out and very gently tucked a strand of her hair behind her ear. "That's too bad. I'm a long-term man."

"But you'll settle for the rest of the night?"

He leaned toward her, his lips nearly touching hers. "For now."

She curled her hand around his neck, bringing him closer, giving over to the arousal he inspired.

Did she even have a choice in resisting him?

No matter how logically she tried to dismiss her need for him, the hunger refused to abate.

Frankly, she'd always thought the adage about not being able to help who you were attracted to was a bunch of romantic nonsense. You either chose to give in to your urges or not.

But as his mouth moved over hers, his tongue enticing and awakening every nerve ending in her body, she truly understood irresistibility for the first time.

Pressing her back into the mattress, he parted the shirt she wore—his shirt—cupping her breasts in his palms, his thumbs gliding over her distended nipples. She closed her eyes, absorbing the pleasure of him. A need she'd never felt with any other man washed over her, pulling her further under the spell of their desire.

She liked being surrounded by him. His clothes on her back; his body warm, bare chest brushing her front. As she wrapped her legs around him, the bulge of his erection met the heat between her thighs. He moaned against her lips, and she angled her hips, deepening the contact.

Even through the cloth of his pants, she could feel him pulse with raw lust, and yet, there was something inherently wonderful about holding back, taking time to let the hunger grow.

He drew his mouth down the side of her neck, leaving tingles in his wake. He moved slowly across her collarbone, sliding the tip of his tongue down, down until he reached her nipple. With barely a flick, he sent pleasure racing along her spine. She buried her fingers in his thick, silky hair, holding him against her as her heart rushed to keep up with the need building low in her belly.

Seeming to understand, he rocked his hips against hers. The friction sent a burst of pleasure through her. Still, she craved more.

She was a slave to his touch, and yet she knew he'd let her assert control in a heartbeat. There was comfort in that realization, deepening the bond she knew they already shared.

Briefly, he rolled away to ease out of his pants and take care of protection while she shrugged out of his shirt.

She sighed as his body rose over hers, as his lips glided across her cheek.

She welcomed him inside with a thrill of unfamiliar emotions and a flood of anticipation. He drew her arms over her head, his hands linking with hers as he moved in an easy rhythm, as if he could endlessly ride the waves of desire.

The tenderness in his touch was seductive, maybe even more so than the wild, aching climax from before.

As stimulating as talking to him could be, he didn't need words now. Breathy sighs and moans of longing and bliss were easy to read and respond to. As the pleasure rose and she chased fulfillment, she acknowledged she'd miscalculated. A week wouldn't be enough. Would a month? A year?

She gasped as she came, the powerful pulses draining her body and emptying her thoughts. Squeezing her hands, he followed, and she strained to hold on to the euphoria, the connection that seemed, at the moment, unbreakable.

When his breathing returned to a calmer rhythm, he rolled to his side and pulled her back against him. She shut out all questions and doubts, dragged the blanket on top of them and let sleep take her.

"OH, HELL, that's my cell phone."

Crawling to the end of the bed, Malina pawed through the heap of discarded clothes. She winced when she saw the number on the screen. "Malina Blair."

"Agent Blair, it's Sam Clairmont."

Double hell. It wasn't just the office calling, it was the boss. "Yes, sir."

"I'm interested in the progress of your case. Could you stop by the office later today and give me an update?"

"Yes, sir."

"In fact, it's curious you're not already here. You've worked every Saturday since you arrived."

The quiet, casual tone didn't fool her for a second. "Yes, sir. I know. I'll be there."

Heart pounding, she flipped the phone closed.

"Problem?"

Malina glanced back at Carr, who'd sat up, his

broad, bare chest exposed above the white sheet. "He knows."

"The SAC? About what?"

"About us." Naked, she leaped from the bed, then pulled on her dress from the night before. Damn. She'd have to go home and change first. "I gotta go."

"I'll take you."

After scooping her knife sheath off the floor, she glared at him. "I can handle this."

"I'm sure you can. I meant I'll take you to your car—it's still at my house."

"Right. Thanks."

He stepped into his pants, and she fought to ignore the fresh onslaught of lust. He did have the most amazing body. "And Sam can't possibly know about us. Don't let that silent stare of his get to you."

She forced herself back to the problem at hand—her supposedly all-important job. "He knows something's up."

"Admit nothing."

She glanced around, looking for the blond wig. "Thanks, Counselor." She didn't feel guilty about last night, she assured herself as she located the wig under the bed and stuffed it into her bag. What she did after working hours was nobody's business but her own.

Was she compromising her case by sleeping with Carr? Maybe. He was a witness. He could someday be called upon to testify in court.

And yet he was also part of the team, even if he wasn't an agent. The SAC knew she'd used Carr's connections—as well as the man himself—to work undercover at the party.

However, she didn't think he'd necessarily approve of the undercover work she'd done *after* the party.

Unfortunately, Carr was right—this thing between them was too powerful to deny. She wanted him enough to risk professional censure. There was no point pretending their relationship didn't matter a great deal.

She fastened her knife in its sheath to her thigh, then tugged her dress down to cover it.

Carr pulled the wig from her bag and handed it to her. "In case somebody's watching us."

"Right."

She should have thought of that herself. And she would have…eventually.

She needed coffee and a blisteringly hot shower before she faced the SAC.

After setting the wig, she headed through the cabin and outside. It was breezier and cooler than the day before, and Carr laid a jacket around her shoulders as he joined her on the dock.

She thanked him, and he smiled, looking a little distracted, as if he, too, was lost in thought about the turn their relationship had taken. He'd zipped up a black leather jacket over his own chest. No doubt the now buttonless shirt he'd worn yesterday would have been a bit exposing.

They didn't talk on the drive to his house, but Malina didn't find the silence uncomfortable. Carr might be able to discourse with the best of them, but he apparently knew the value of quiet as well.

As a woman who lived alone, had few female friends and worked in a male-dominated industry, she appreciated his restraint, or maybe, knowing Carr's successful record in court, his instinctive ability to read his audience.

"Would you come in a minute?" he asked as he helped her from the car.

"I still have to go home and shower and change."

"Please? I have something I'd like to give you in private."

She narrowed her eyes in suspicion, but nodded, then followed him inside. Truthfully, she was afraid of going back inside his spectacular house.

She might never want to leave.

As soon as she stepped across the threshold, she turned to him. "So?"

From his jacket pocket, he pulled out a plastic Baggie, which he handed to her. Inside the Baggie was a fingerprint card.

"They're Simon's," Carr said before she could ask. "He was very careful to hold on to the same glass all night. Did you notice?"

"I did." And she'd cursed the fact that she had no cause for a search warrant on Mr. Mystery and his floating cocktail party.

"I slipped into the master suite and lifted these off his hairbrush."

"You—" She ground her back teeth against the spurt of annoyance. "You could have been caught."

"But I merely wanted the full tour. I'm thinking of buying a similar boat myself."

She hated to admit he was so damn smooth, he'd probably pull off such a convenient excuse. She slapped the card against her palm. "This is also not admissible, Counselor." In fact, she was more than surprised he'd cast aside so many investigative rules—ones he had to be aware of.

"It doesn't have to be. I'm sure you're clever enough to get a warrant for prints and/or DNA if you need them later. Besides, I'm just an innocent and concerned civilian, offering my assistance to the overworked members of law enforcement."

"You think a judge and/or jury will buy that?"

"I can practically guarantee it." He grinned. "In the meantime, wouldn't it be interesting to see if Simon Ellerby is who he says he is."

"Have I mentioned this is my case?"

"Several times."

She glanced down at the card, then back at him. He'd done what she couldn't—or rather *wouldn't*—do. She was sticking hard and fast to the rules these days.

As unfamiliar as that idea was.

"Thank you," she said simply, tucking the prints in her bag.

"Good. I want payment."

FOR THE FIRST TIME since he'd met her, Carr knew he'd caught her completely by surprise.

Her eyes lit like blue flames. "No kidding. Payment?"

"Definitely." Before she could give in to the obvious urge to slug him, he grabbed her by her waist and pulled her against him.

He kissed her with an effort to remind her of what they'd shared and all that he wanted beyond the now.

Her body molded to his, her heat infused his veins.

Dear heaven, he wanted her, and the idea that she didn't want him as much was torture. He'd have to find a way to reach her, to convince her that a successful career didn't always lead to a happy life. That giving up everything for one thing was too great a sacrifice.

As he knew all too well.

Aware of her other obligations, he pulled back before

he wanted to, but he kept his hand against her cheek, knowing she'd retreat quickly.

She knocked his hand aside as she stepped back. "A kiss as payment?"

"Sure. I have money."

When she sighed, he closed the distance between them. "Take your evidence, talk to Sam, then come back here for dinner."

She looked skeptical. "You cook?"

"I'll make sure dinner is available," he clarified. "Come on. I'll be waiting all afternoon, wondering what you get from the print."

"Your larcenous print, you mean."

"Technically, larceny is taking something with the intent of depriving the victim of that item permanently. Simon still has possession of his fingerprints."

Saying nothing, she crossed her arms over her chest.

He was so crazy about that slightly annoyed, secretly amused look, he nodded. "Yes, that print."

Was he actually stooping to using the case as an excuse to see her?

Though, given the depths to which he'd stooped in the past, this one was positively virtuous.

"I'll be hungry later," she said finally.

"I'll be here."

In the open doorway, she turned back. "When I get brought up on charges of trespassing and tampering with evidence, I'm calling you to defend me."

"Naturally. It would be my great pleasure."

"SHE'S COMING?"

Nodding, Carr set his cell phone on the kitchen counter. "Finally," he said to his friend and neighbor, Andrea Hastings Landry.

Her husband, Tyler, sat at the chrome-and-glass table beside the house's rear windows. Beyond him, the landscape lights illuminated the pool and palm fronds blowing in the strong wind.

A storm was coming, and Carr would be glad to have Malina safely here with him. How he could be worried more about wind and rain and not diamond-stealing, gun-toting bad guys was a puzzle he ought to consider assembling.

Most likely, it was simply the fact that he was separated from her and the fear she wouldn't come back, which haunted him.

"You sure she's not a figment of your imagination?" Tyler asked, leaning back in his chair.

"Funny," Carr said, moving toward the windows to watch the dark clouds gather. "You should have gone into show business instead of law enforcement."

As Tyler opened his mouth to retort, Andrea interrupted. "Don't antagonize him, honey. I'm dying to meet this mystery woman who has our unshakeable Carr so twisted up."

Carr frowned. "I'm not twisted up."

Andrea patted his hand. "Oh, you so are." Her head angled, she regarded him thoroughly. "It's kind of cute actually."

"Oh, yeah, he's adorable," Tyler said as he grabbed his wife's hand and tugged her into his lap.

Tyler had once considered Carr a rival for Andrea's attention, even though she and Carr had never been more than friends. It seemed Tyler still hadn't let go of his jealousy completely.

As unsubstantiated as Tyler's feelings were, Carr

finally understood them. He wouldn't want another man near Malina either.

Hell, he *was* twisted up.

"She's not a figment of my imagination. She's…" How did he describe Malina in a way that was logical? He wasn't yet prepared to share the confusing and unfamiliar feelings he had for her. "Interesting," he said eventually. "Smart, resourceful, tough. You'll like her."

"Uh-huh," Tyler said, raising his eyebrows. "I didn't hear *hot* anywhere in that sentence."

"Of course she's—" Actually, *hot* seemed too tame. *Beautiful, exotic* and *compelling* were more to the point. "She's more than hot. That's too—" He broke off, shrugging.

"Oh, my," Andrea said, her eyes wide. "Carr, you never stumble over anything. What's going on?"

"Well, I'm not—"

"She obviously has a demanding job," Tyler broke in, directing his comment to Andrea. "And she doesn't live on the island."

"He's pretty much trolled the availability of all the women here," Andrea agreed.

"Maybe she's resistant to meeting Carr's friends. Maybe she's not that into him."

"She didn't show up for dinner. Maybe she has food issues." Andrea looked at Carr. "Does she?"

Carr made an effort to tuck his aggravation away and feign surprise. "Oh, you're going to include me in this psychoanalysis?"

Amused, Andrea nodded. "Sure. The patient is usually the best source of information."

"Usually," Tyler said, seeming skeptical.

And no doubt enjoying the digs at Carr's expense.

Carr leaned back against the windowsill. "Malina does have a demanding job, she doesn't live on the island. I have no idea whether she's resistant to meeting my friends, since I didn't tell her you were here. I also don't know if she has food issues—we've never shared a meal."

Speculation slid into Tyler's eyes. "And is she really into you?"

"I think so, but I don't think she's all that happy about it." Carr lifted his hands, then let them fall. "I'm not sure."

Andrea stared at him in shock. "You think so? You're not sure. You have no idea?" Her tone rose dramatically with each word.

"What the hell has this chick done to you, Carr?" was Tyler's pointed question.

Carr shook his head. "Realizing I'm repeating myself, I have no idea."

"So what does she do?" Andrea asked, compassionately passing over his out-of-character uncertainty.

"She's—" He stopped, realizing suddenly that his friends could help him figure out why he was so fascinated with Malina. A few days ago, he simply wanted to seduce her, and now he wanted a relationship. A serious one. Possibly.

Maybe Andrea and Tyler would understand the attraction in a way he couldn't. Hadn't they jumped quickly into their relationship? Hadn't it led to love and happily ever after?

He desperately wanted to know what it was about this woman that made her different from all the others he'd ever known.

Why was she so important? Why her? Why now?

She wasn't at all like a woman he envisioned himself

getting serious about. She was too direct. Though he was sure she understood and appreciated subtlety in other people, she didn't bother with it personally. Her toughness was sometimes harsh and unyielding. Necessary for her job, but could she turn it off and be tender? Would her sense of justice stand in the way of understanding his past, the way he used to live? And last, but certainly not least, she wanted off this relaxing island as fast as possible, and he wanted to be nowhere else.

He liked swords, and she was a .357 Magnum.

He refused to explain to Andrea and Tyler about who Malina was, what she did and what she represented in his life beyond what he'd already told them—she was a woman he'd recently started seeing whom he'd invited to dinner. He would explain to Tyler about the case if Malina wanted him to, but for now, he was keeping silent. Understanding the turn his life had taken in the past few days was essential, and he knew of nobody better to help him figure out the cause and consequences than his friends.

When the doorbell rang a few minutes later, he was grateful, as Andrea wasn't wildly patient when her curiosity was aroused.

She was, in fact, so inquisitive that she followed him down the hall to the front door.

Malina stood on the doorstep wearing the traditional government employee uniform—blue pantsuit, pressed white shirt, polished dark shoes. She'd pulled her hair back in a low ponytail, but she'd clearly been agitated at some point, since several strands had escaped to hang around her face, as if she'd run frustrated fingers through many times over.

"Sorry, I—" As her vivid turquoise gaze found

Andrea, her exhausted posture stiffened. "I'm clearly late. Too late."

She instinctively doubted him. Maybe she always would.

But as much as that possibility bothered him, he knew she had reason to doubt. She'd given the Bureau her blood, sweat and maybe even tears, and when she'd needed them most, they'd cast her aside to save face.

Before she could turn away, Carr wrapped his fingers around her wrist and tugged her inside. "I'm glad you're here. This is my friend and neighbor, Andrea Landry."

"Neighbor?" She directed her attention to Carr for a second, an apology clearly evident. "The sheriff's wife." She extended her hand to Andrea. "Malina Blair. Nice to meet you."

Andrea shook her hand, then her gaze flicked to Malina's side holster, exposed as her jacket fell open. "You're a cop?"

"FBI. Your husband's here?"

"He's in the kitchen."

"I'm going to need to talk to him," Malina said to Andrea, though she looked at Carr.

"I haven't said anything," he returned defensively.

She surprised him by sliding her hand down his arm. "Then it's time we did."

As Malina headed down the hall, Andrea gave Carr an elbow nudge. "FBI? You're dating an FBI agent? What's going on?"

Since he wasn't about to repeat the humiliating mantra of *I have no idea,* Carr shrugged and continued down the hall.

Tyler rose as they approached. In worn jeans and a red T-shirt, he didn't look much like the chief law enforcement official on the island at the moment, but then Carr was wearing nearly the same thing, except his T-shirt was white, so he probably didn't look much like a high-powered lawyer. Well, formerly high-powered.

The expression in both Tyler and Malina's eyes was all cop-to-cop as they exchanged introductions. Even without the sidearm, it seemed that Tyler would have certainly recognized her for what she was.

"We saved you some manicotti," Carr said as he joined them. "Are you hungry?"

Malina's gaze swept the room, full of chrome and glass, the black marble bar separating the kitchen from the dining area, then finally the backyard, ocean waves churning in the distance.

She assessed and evaluated with lightning speed, but Carr, used to reading people quickly, saw the pleasure and comfort that washed over her even before she smiled at him. "Starving. Thanks."

"Wine?" he heard Andrea offer as he headed to the fridge.

"Sure."

"Working on Saturday?" Tyler asked her.

Malina sat in the chair that faced the back of the house—and the ocean. "I've got a case that needs the extra time. Thanks," she added as Andrea set a glass of Chianti in front of her.

"You're not from South Carolina," Andrea said.

"No. Kauai."

"Yeah?" Andrea said. "I've always wanted to go."

"You've been to Prague and never to Hawaii?" Tyler asked, eyeing his wife with skepticism and pulling out the chair opposite Malina for Andrea.

"Anytime you want to take me, Sheriff, say the word." Andrea said sassily. "You look Hawaiian—sort of."

"My father's family goes back six generations. My mother's a California blue-eyed blonde, so I'm a mix."

"You work out of the Charleston office?" Tyler asked, returning to his seat on Malina's left. "You must know Rick Holly."

"Sure," Malina said. "He works Cyber Crimes. He's a good agent."

"What makes a good agent?" Andrea asked, her nosiness in full force as she leaned forward.

Carr set a plate of manicotti and salad in front of Malina. "Don't take offense. She's been trying to psychoanalyze me all night."

"Thanks," she said as she followed his movements. He sat next to her and saw her caution drop briefly. The connection between them sizzled, sparked to life by a glance. As much as he wanted Andrea and Tyler's opinion, he also wished—at that moment—that he was alone with Malina.

He probably shouldn't have unexpectedly thrown the friends in with their dinner date. His idea had been to get her to relax, not see him as the guy who simply wanted her in his bed, but as a whole person, one who wanted her in his life, not just his bed.

"We have an entire department at the Bureau dedicated to human behavior," she said as she turned back to Andrea. "They're way smarter than I am."

"So how did you get in?" Andrea asked, completely unabashed in her abrupt personal questions. "Federal law enforcement is extremely competitive."

Malina paused with her wineglass halfway to her lips. "Is it?"

"Sure."

Carr nearly intervened and explained about Andrea's

exposure to the police, beyond her husband, but he wanted to know the answer to the question. Sam hadn't given him Malina's recruitment history.

Malina's gaze never shifted from Andrea's. "See that landscape light in the top of that palm, third from the right on the left side of the pool?"

Andrea turned to view the light in question. "Yeah."

"I could draw my sidearm and shoot it out in less than fifteen seconds."

Everybody—with the exception of Malina, who continued to hold her wineglass casually in her left hand—jolted in surprise.

"Years ago," Malina continued, "one of the Bureau directors was on vacation in Kauai and happened to attend a bow-marksman tournament I participated in during high school. After I won, he gave me his card and said I should call him after I graduated from college. I did."

"So your greatest skill is shooting things?" Andrea asked slowly.

"No," Carr said automatically.

"Yes," Malina insisted.

Carr shook his head. "You're more to the Bureau than hired muscle."

"I have no problem being muscle," she said, shrugging. "That's where the action is. I spent the nearly five years of my career assigned to HRT."

"Hostage Rescue Team," Tyler supplied before his wife could ask. "The tactical division. Badasses."

Malina nodded—no arrogance or bragging, just acceptance of the truth. "Carr said you were a Marine. You worked with our guys at some point, I'm sure."

"Many times," Tyler said, his gaze intensifying in

his scrutiny of Malina. "They're a valuable asset in a crisis."

"Same to you." She toasted him with her wineglass. "Mostly we show up with storm trooper uniforms, a lot of firepower and attitude and scare the living crap out of the bad guys without a shot ever going off."

Carr found irrational fear blooming in his chest. Picturing Malina in black fatigues and a bulletproof vest wasn't exactly a comforting image. "And if the bad guys don't scare so easily?"

Malina forked up a bite of manicotti. "We're prepared for that, too. This is great, by the way," she added, glancing from Tyler to Carr to Andrea.

"Thanks," Andrea said. "I've been learning, since these guys would eat fried fish sandwiches and burgers at Coconut Joe's every night otherwise."

"Coconut Joe's?" Malina asked.

"The beach bar near the main pier." Tyler stroked his wife's cheek with his thumb. "We had our first date there."

Andrea's eyes widened. "We did *not*. That was a professional consultation."

"Really?" Carr put in. "He was certainly territorial. He didn't like that I was there."

While they launched into a discussion over just how shameless Tyler had been in his pursuit of Andrea the previous fall, Malina watched them curiously and finished her dinner.

Carr was distinctly aware of her and the information he'd learned about her past. A quiet island girl comfortable with extreme tension and the probability of violence. A woman raised in paradise who chose grit.

The contrast intrigued him.

Was it this contrast that drew him to her in a way

he'd never experienced before? Was it the unlikelihood of their contrasting paths ever merging that worried him?

He'd wanted to escape his quiet island life as well. He had enjoyed it with relish for a time, but he'd broken with his past and never wanted to go back.

Returning to the pulsing excitement of the city was her greatest ambition.

"Sorry, Malina," Tyler said, bringing her into the conversation. "It's an old argument."

"I wouldn't get too worked up over it, Sheriff," Malina said. "You obviously won."

Tyler nodded. "True. So...hot tub?"

"Smooth segue," Carr commented.

"We fed you women and sat through a polite chit-chat," Tyler said. "Don't we get a reward?"

Malina's lips twisted as she glanced at Carr. "Like a payment."

"I didn't say anything," he reminded her.

Andrea narrowed her eyes in her husband's direction. "What reward?"

"You two in bikinis in the hot tub," Tyler said, nodding for emphasis.

Malina leaned back in her chair. Carr was sure she would fire back at Tyler quickly. After all, he and the sheriff had done nothing but find glasses and open the wine for dinner. "I happen to have a bathing suit in the car, so I'm game for the hot tub on one condition."

"Name it," Tyler said as Carr recovered from the surprise of her response.

"I want to swim twenty laps in the pool first."

Tyler rose and held out his hand. "Deal."

As Malina reached out her hand, Andrea held up her finger. "I want to go to Hawaii."

Carr cleared away Malina's dishes and headed to the kitchen while Tyler sputtered in shock. "You have to admire her sense of timing."

Malina stood. "It's settled then. The hot tub is a perfect place to talk about stolen diamonds."

7

"DIAMONDS?" Andrea asked.

"Stolen?" Carr asked.

"Beer?" Tyler asked.

After Tyler filled beer and water orders from the poolside bar—complete with fireplace, wicker lounge chairs, full kitchen and giant grill—Malina let the warm water pound over her aching muscles while she gave the sheriff and Andrea the rundown on the case so far.

"You're right about Jack Rafton," Tyler said. "He doesn't have the balls for smuggling or theft."

"I'm not sure that Simon Ellerby does either," Malina said. "He's crafty enough, I guess, but major jewel thefts are generally instigated by organized crime groups, which are intricate, organized and brutal. Career thieves, on the other hand, are loners, resourceful and rarely violent. This gang—if there even is one—seems to fit with the latter profile."

"And yet you said stolen diamonds, plural," Carr pressed. "That seems to be a major theft."

Malina nodded. "It does. It turns out a remote diamond mine in Australia is missing a cache of stones.

No official report has been made to international authorities, but my boss made some calls to colleagues and learned that the theft is being kept quiet because a government official is suspected of being involved—in fact, they're all but positive it was an inside job. Law enforcement has the guy under surveillance and doesn't want anyone to know there's even been a theft, hoping he'll try it again." Malina could all but see giant rolls of red tape unspooling all over yet another small island. "So there's an internal investigation within the government and another one by the company that owns the mine."

Tyler sipped his beer. "Meanwhile, a whole lot of glittery stones are in the wind."

"And for more than a month," Malina said.

"They'll never recover them after all that time, will they?" To Malina's surprise, Carr directed this question to Andrea.

"I wouldn't think so," Andrea said. "I could check around about under-the-table diamond sales."

"You can, huh?" Malina asked, her surprise evident.

Andrea smiled with confidence. "I know some people, who know some people."

Malina's gaze sharpened. "No kidding."

"Andrea is an expert art appraiser," Carr said. "She works for a global insurance company and is often called in to determine the veracity of forgeries in theft cases."

Malina had easily determined that Andrea was intelligent and successful within five minutes of meeting her. She could also see the delicate-looking blonde wandering among dusty old art in museums, but it took a great deal of knowledge as well as technical skill and equipment to find fakes. "Are these thieves in jail? We don't want word leaking about the theft."

"They prefer the term *alternative architects*," Andrea said with a mischievous glint in her eyes. "And, no, they're not."

Malina glanced at Carr, who shrugged and drank from his water bottle. "Terrific. Thieves catching thieves." Surely her sarcasm was clear. "My job would be so much simpler if people either wore black or white."

"But it's the shades of gray that keep life interesting," Carr pointed out.

She pointed at him. "Don't think I don't realize you own a lot of gray suits." She let the jets massage her back for a few minutes in silence, then she inclined her head. "Sure. Why not. Ask," she said to Andrea. "I assume these guys are pros at being discreet."

"Definitely. I assume you can get me a list of the carats involved and the specifics of inclusions for each missing stone?"

"I'll copy it down for you," Malina said. "I'm pretty sure the SAC would object to me forwarding official, but secretly nonofficial, government reports."

"You could always transfer to the CIA," Tyler suggested.

Malina toasted him with her water bottle. "There's an uplifting thought."

"Any way to connect our local yacht captain Simon Ellerby to Australia?" Carr asked.

As he spoke, he slid his finger down her thigh. Even here, in the middle of crime solving—as unconventional as the setting was—he seemed to feel compelled to remind her of his physical presence.

As if she could forget.

Just as the rain overhead held off, the storm seeming to gather its strength before bursting, she sat beside him in a churning, intimate world of repressed need. With his flushed, handsome face close enough to touch, his husky voice sending shivers of anticipation rolling down her spine, she had to fight to concentrate, to hold off until she could find their intimacy again.

Unfortunately, she had a job to do. One that had never felt a burden until now.

She cleared her throat self-consciously, certain it had been a while since Carr had asked his question. "Simon Ellerby has several aliases—most of which are linked to minor jewel or art thefts."

"Oh, really," Carr asked, his tone full of innocence. "How did you learn that?"

Under the water, she grabbed his seeking hand, which had been wandering its way up her leg to her crotch. "I have my sources, too."

Tyler held up his hand. "I hate to throw cold water on such a warm night, but a theft in Australia linked to our little island here? What're the odds?"

"Really, really long," Andrea said.

Seeing as she was the expert, Malina accepted that assumption. But something about this case had her senses tingling—and not just because the object of her personal desire was within easy reach. "We can find no travel to Australia by Ellerby or any of his aliases."

"He could have sent an associate," Tyler said. "The guys you saw with Rafton."

"The thief could have sold them to somebody who sold them to Ellerby," Andrea added. "The farther down the line away from the origin the gems go, the less likelihood of tracing them to their source."

"But more people are brought into the fold," Carr said. "The chances of getting caught rise."

"What do your instincts tell you, Malina?"

Malina glanced across the bubbling water at Tyler as she considered his question. The immeasurable, undetermined, indistinctive evidence of a cop's gut. Only somebody who's looked into the eyes of a victim, then sat at their desk and stared at their computer late into the night, drinking bad coffee and praying for a break, could understand the trust and results that an instinct could bring.

It was drive, experience and desire rolled into one.

She trusted hers implicitly. "Australia and Palmer's Island shouldn't be connected, but I think they are."

"What do you want us to do?"

No hesitation, no question of support, no paperwork or official requests. There were big advantages to a small town that Malina had forgotten in the huge ocean of bureaucracy she'd chosen to wade through.

"Do you know a gem expert who could evaluate the one Carr and I found?" Going through Bureau channels could take weeks, and there was no way they had that kind of time. The diamonds would be sold soon, if they hadn't been already. To solve this case, she had to move fast.

Andrea nodded. "I know a guy in Charleston."

"I'll get you the evidence." Malina gave her a significant look. "To maintain the chain of evidence, you'll have to sign a statement, and I'll have to accompany you on the trip. Will that be a problem?"

"Nope." She high-fived her husband. "Back in the game."

Just as Malina was wondering if "the game" was a code word for illicit merchandise exchange and wondering how in the world Andrea and Tyler might be involved, Carr leaned over and whispered in her ear, "There's not a lot to do on this island."

"So, they—"

"They just want to help."

Malina shifted her gaze from Carr, to Tyler, then finally Andrea. "You people are strange as hell."

"It's part of our charm," Carr said.

Tyler toasted her with his plastic beer cup. "We also throw a great luau."

Thunder rolled in the distance, but everyone ignored it.

Malina was grateful. People—regular, ordinary people who wanted to protect their friends and neighbors—were a valuable commodity for a cop. A rare occurrence. It was almost comical in its honesty.

There were many who wanted to be "in the know" or to observe or speculate. But to participate in the process was rare.

"The cooperation isn't what you're used to, I guess?" Andrea asked.

"Not in D.C.," Malina acknowledged. And for the first time in a long time, she didn't feel the longing for the city she'd adopted and fought so hard to reach. The Bureau pinnacle. The escape from simple sunny days, mediocrity and obscurity.

Why couldn't she remember why that goal was so important?

She lifted herself out of the bubbling water. Sitting on the side of the tub, leaning back on her elbows, the stormy wind rolled over her, and she craned her neck back to stare at the tumultuous sky overhead.

Her gut, that infallible sense of right and wrong, was still talking, and she wasn't sure she was happy with the conversation. "But I understand island community all too well," she said, still watching the clouds sweep and gather overhead. "My childhood was full of it. I guess I just forgot how good it felt."

Warm, wet fingers linked with hers.

Carr.

She knew his touch as surely as she did her investigative instincts. That knowledge was both comforting and disturbing. She wasn't sure whether to clutch him like a lifeline or run as far and as fast as her feet would carry her.

"We're going to get through this," he said, his voice low and confident. "The case is as good as closed."

"My office may seem casual," Tyler said, "but we're serious about anybody who messes with us."

"As long as we're on the subject of true confessionals…" This time it was Andrea speaking. "How many calories does shooting burn?"

"Does that really have a place here?" her husband asked, clearly exasperated.

"Are you going to deny the power of those abs of hers?" Andrea returned. "Besides, I'm just trying to break the tension."

Clearly hearing them, Malina continued to watch the stormy sky. The blues, grays and shades of the blackest night swirled together. She wanted to make sense of it all. She wanted to prove herself more than anything, but not only to the Bureau brass. She wanted to close this case for the people of Palmer's Island. They wanted nothing more than a safe, happy, quiet life, and yet she knew they'd defend themselves and their neighbors at any sacrifice. They were the community every law enforcement agency wanted to be a reality, the one Malina, for one, had forgotten still existed.

Squeezing Carr's hand in silent thanks for giving her this moment, she pushed herself off her elbows and sat up straight. Her gaze moved to Andrea and Tyler. "Welcome to the team."

CARR HELD Malina's hand as they walked on the sand, their bare feet enveloped in rhythm by the rising and retreating Atlantic surf. With the cool air whipped up by the coming storm, he'd put on jeans and a white T-shirt, but she remained in her turquoise bikini, only adding a silky wrap around her waist.

Her indignation and determination no doubt kept her warm enough.

"Did you make the calls to Australia or did Sam?" he asked.

"He did. I'm too low on the bureaucratic pole to have powerful international connections."

"But he made the calls because you asked him to."

She slowed her stride. "Where is this going?"

"Just tell me. What led up to the calls?"

"I didn't think it was likely this was simply about smuggling diamonds. They're not illegal. The only reason to smuggle them is to avoid customs fees, like duties and tariffs, and they aren't large enough to warrant going outside the law. They're generally considered a cost of business and passed on in the price to brokers and end consumers. Diamonds are a valued commodity, transported with relative ease. Why take the chance of smuggling when you can simply add the cost into your selling price?"

"Unless you don't own the diamonds in the first place."

"Exactly."

"So you started researching diamond mines."

"It seemed the most logical place to start."

They walked on in silence a few minutes, then she glanced at him. "Your friends are really great."

The feeling was apparently mutual, since Andrea's parting whisper had been the same compliment for Malina. At least he knew for certain now that he wasn't crazy in noticing how special she was. "All part of the Palmer's Island package."

"You have something rare here."

He didn't think she was talking about herself, but the island. Still, he recognized both were true. "I know."

"I really appreciate your help with this case."

"You do?" At every opportunity, she'd told him he was interfering.

"I like to work solo, so I'm doing a lousy job of appreciating your insight. And I'd never understand this island so well without being part of it."

"It's important to understand the island?"

"Sure." She shrugged and he found himself distracted by the muscles that contracted at her shoulders. Andrea hadn't exaggerated—Malina's physique was lined with lean muscle.

Which he definitely wanted to get his hands on before the night was out.

"Basic victimology," she continued. "Know your victims, understand the guys targeting them."

Carr had employed the same tactics once in targeting juries. Life was indeed very ironic. "And what does our island tell you about the thief?"

"That he wanted somewhere quiet, completely unsuspecting. These gems are seriously hot, and he needed to get them as far away from their source as fast as possible. Also, this isn't a network of people who're used to working together."

"Jack Rafton."

"Exactly. He's drawn attention to himself. He's a wild card, one I'm sure Simon Ellerby aka Paul Galbano aka Stuart Costas, is kicking himself in the ass for bringing into the mix."

"Even though you gave us the information about violent, organized groups usually involved in jewel thefts, you think Simon is responsible?"

"I do."

"The cop's gut."

"That, plus the victimology I've already pointed out. Simon's a small-time thief who's branching out."

"And completely screwing it up."

"I don't know about that. We've got nothing on him yet, including his true identity."

"He has a lot of diversity in aliases."

"Smart. Most stick to one nationality. He works that silver hair, tan and vaguely European accent to his advantage." She stopped, staring at the storm clouds overhead. "And he just annoys the hell out of me."

"I can't imagine what that's like."

"Seriously." She turned to face him. "He likes doing all this under the sheriff's nose. He likes being mysterious. He absolutely loves having the president of the historical society on his yacht, asking him for donations, as if he's a member of legitimate society. *I bought Le Bijou here sight unseen on the recommendation of a colleague,*" she mocked, cocking her head from side to side. *"A mere whim.* What a lot of blowhard crap. He makes me want to shoot something."

He winced. "Sorry to be a downer, but I'd rather this didn't come down to who has the most firepower."

"Yeah." She sighed, visibly bringing her anger

under control. "I'll do my best, but I'm not promising anything."

"Speaking of firepower...HRT?"

For the first time, he saw a hint of uncertainty in her eyes. "Yeah. Not too sexy, I guess."

"It is. And yet scary at the same time. You're not..." He slid his hands down her arms, then gripped her hands. "Is that why you want to go back to D.C.? To be part of HRT?"

"No way. I want to run the place." She grinned suddenly. "It's about time a woman was in charge."

"Of the entire Bureau?" His tone climbed in surprise.

"Sure. Why not?"

'Cause that's too damn far away. "I—" He cleared his throat in the face of that fierce stare. "No reason. I just...if you were HRT, you must be good at working on a team. Don't you like that?"

"I was in command most of the time."

His heart sank. "Oh."

She scowled. "Still, the leadership has to deal with politics as much as procedure. I'm lousy at that part."

"True. I can't imagine you networking at cocktail parties and making under-the-table promises to special-interest groups." How shameless had he become? Discounting her abilities so she wouldn't leave him? It was pathetic. "Your strength of character is one of the things I admire most about you," he added at the urging of the little conscience he had left.

"Uh-huh." She slid her hands up his chest, wrapping her arms around his neck. "You're not just saying that to get me in bed, are you?"

"Certainly not."

"No way, Counselor. That righteous indignation may impress juries, but I know you too well."

With her pressing her nearly naked body against him, Carr found it hard to concentrate, much less lie. A feat he previously considered impossible. And though he'd done some despicable things in the past, he considered trying to lure her and hold her to his side—when he didn't remotely deserve a hero like her—one of his worst.

Considering how instinctively she kept pulling away, she must suspect his stellar record in court had come via both fair means and foul. But if she knew everything… if she realized his worst…she'd sprint in the opposite direction.

He wrapped his arms around her. "Is it so devious to want you with me? To want to spend time with you?"

"No, and I'm done questioning how right we are together, even though we seem to be on different paths." When he frowned, she added, "You want to understand why I want to go back to D.C. so badly, and I want to know why you left Manhattan."

He stiffened.

"Or maybe not so different." She pressed her lips against his, gently seeking. "Enjoy now. Today. This moment. You never know when you'll have another chance."

How well he knew that truth. Hadn't the realization of limited time changed his life?

Repent of selfishness, Sister Mary Katherine was always saying. Wasn't that his desperate goal? Didn't he want Malina to have everything she wanted, even if the result came at his expense?

Yes. But he wasn't about to give up easily on the

dream that he could have it all. Even if he deserved nothing.

Regardless, he had no chance resisting her touch.

Her mouth moved over his; her tongue slid past his lips to entice him beyond reason. He cupped the back of her head with one hand, the other gripping her backside, molding every part of her to his neediness.

His erection pulsed against his jeans. He could hardly believe this beauty, this extraordinary woman, wanted him and allowed him to touch her. And yet, his body overrode any sense his mind might have made of reality.

Addiction came in all forms, and she was his.

Her hands moved to the hem of his T-shirt, which she drew over his head. With him naked to the waist, she pressed her cheek briefly to his bare chest. The simple intimacy had him coming unglued on many levels, not the least of which was sexual.

Then she kicked her heel against his calf.

They both fell to the sand below with an abrupt thud, and by the time he'd recovered his breath she was already stripping off her bikini top. She leaned down, kissing him again, and her bare breasts teased his chest, sending a shot of acute hunger through his body like a rocket launch.

With a lift of her hips, she'd shimmed out of her suit bottom and wrap, then, straddling him, she unfastened the buttons on his jeans. Her hand found his erection, and within a stroke he'd flopped back on the sand, completely helpless to her needs, like a fish waiting for the surf to take him under.

Thunder rumbled overhead. She moved her hands over his body, up and down, over and across. Kissing him with the same wild urgency, the very elements heard her call as raindrops plopped hard and insistent against their skin.

A storm on the coast gathers and builds as no other place on earth. It draws from land and sea until the water seems to boil with its intensity and the sand on the shore contracts, bracing itself for the onslaught.

She arched her back and glanced at the sky. The rain fell harder, and when her gaze found his again, she was laughing.

"Back pocket," he managed to gasp.

She found the condom and applied it with haste, then she lifted her hips over his erection and plunged down before he could fully acknowledge the wet onslaught from the heavens.

With an intense rhythm, she pumped her hips against his. His heart raced, seeming to want to jump out of his chest. Her breathing hitched.

Gasping, she climaxed, her inner walls gripping him, urging him to follow. As he instinctively closed his eyes to absorb the spike of pleasure, he buried his hand in the glossy wetness of her hair and brought her face to his. His kiss was grateful and desperate at the same time as he followed her into the glory of completion.

8

THEY RAN through the storm into the house, water dripping everywhere, sand grating in a variety of crevices.

Carr insisted on a shower to warm up and clean up, and Malina could hardly resist. With water dripping off his lashes, his brown eyes full of satisfaction and laughter, she was certainly willing to go with the suggestion.

"You know the only bad thing about you in a bikini?"

"No."

"I kind of like disarming you."

He shampooed her hair, then pressed her against the tiled wall, her legs wrapped around his hips.

His erection pressed between them, rocking against her, never entering, teasing her to near madness. He kissed her neck, brought her nipples to painful buds with his thumbs then completed his pleasurable torture by yanking a towel off the rack outside the shower and drying her from head to toe.

Drugged with need, she let her head drop back

over his arm as he lifted her and carried her to the bedroom.

She was a slave to the wild desire he inspired. Did he even have to touch her to make her come? Probably not, but his touch was pretty damn amazing, so she wasn't about to question success.

Lying on his bed, she watched almost in slow motion as he loomed over her. Something primal and possessive flashed in his eyes. When he entered her, it was apparent he'd already taken care of protection.

When he'd done that, she had no idea. He had a way of overwhelming, exciting and caring all at the same time. And never had she been so happy to lose control.

He'd left the windows open, and rain lashed at the glass, spraying through the screens. Lightning flashed in unexpected bursts as the wind howled, tossing the white gossamer drapes back and away from the walls. She was at the center of a maelstrom, one only they could feel but that nature had provided a backdrop for.

Wrapping herself around him mind and body, she met each thrust with the realization that the acceptance she craved was fulfilled in these intimate moments with him. She wanted the building and heightening to go on and on, almost fearing this time would bring even more pleasure than the last, and she'd become dependent. But his skill and their chemistry were too powerful to deny for long. All too soon, the spiral of need deep inside tightened, then burst, casting rhythmic pulses over them both until he collapsed on top of her, his breath coming in satisfied gasps.

"If the storm takes us, at least I'll die a happy man," he said after a time, flopping on his back next to her.

She found the energy to pat his bare chest. "Same goes."

He made her feel fluid and womanly and vulnerable in a way she never had before. She'd never let anyone so close, and the idea of him being the one who could affect her so strongly worried her. They were going in opposite directions; their goals—other than closing this case—weren't remotely similar.

They could never last.

To distract herself from her troubling thoughts, she glanced around the bedroom. It was somehow warm and modern at the same time. The wood floors were stained a dark cherry, and an antique settee rested in one corner. The walls were pale gray, the bed frame a streamlined polished steel and the comforter light blue.

Through the skylight overhead and the windows along the back wall, the unrelenting rain continued to pound.

An elaborate sword in a glass case, hanging on the wall by the door, attracted her attention. She turned on her side and propped her head in her hand. "Where'd you get the sword?"

"An auction in New York."

"Any particular reason it attracted your attention?"

"I like swords," he said, his gaze riveted to the object in question.

"You were a fencer, right?"

"I was."

It was rare for Carr to be uncommunicative. She wasn't sure whether he wanted her to be quiet or to leave, or whether he was simply tired.

He seemed to come out of his silent trance and pushed off the bed. "You're probably getting cold." He pulled back the bed covers, then swept her up in his arms, sliding her beneath the sheets with all the ease of a father and child's bedtime ritual.

It was oddly comforting and arousing at the same time.

Joining her, he tucked her against him and kissed the top of her head. "You prefer guns, I guess."

"Damn straight."

"They're cold and not very pretty."

"They're functional. Appearance doesn't apply."

"You have a Glock nineteen, polymer finish. No stainless steel?"

She snorted. "Flashy. Nobody with any decent skill carries one of those things."

"But appearance doesn't apply."

Caught in her own judgment, she asked, "This relates to swords how?"

He turned his head to meet her gaze. "Have you noticed we're very different?"

"Have you noticed we have some very unusual conversations?"

"I thought I was the only one who'd realized it." He returned his attention to the sword. "It's called a *jian,* a double-edge sword known in Chinese folklore as the gentleman of weapons. The earliest records have them mentioned as far back as the seventh century BC. This one was made nearly two hundred and fifty years ago. I thought it was historic and lovely, almost mesmerizing."

"But still deadly."

"Certainly." But he frowned, as if he hadn't considered the brutality of the weapon. "I think of it as elegant."

"I do, too. I mean, I don't think I'd hang a gun on

the wall of my house as a decoration. It's a tool I need to do my job effectively, not a piece of art."

"You don't have a gun collection?"

"No. Do you have a sword collection?"

"Just the one."

"Ditto." She paused, reconsidering. "Well, I do have a clutch piece I used to wear back in my HRT days, but I haven't carried it in years."

"Why not?"

"Haven't needed it," she said slowly, realizing she'd been so busy chasing high-profile offenders and trying to make a name for herself in the Bureau, she'd stayed off the streets and out of the action in other ways.

She liked investigating, solving the puzzles. She liked the heightened awareness she always experienced in those last moments of tracking down and arresting the subject who'd caused so much turmoil. She was proud of the way her mind and body went eerily calm in the middle of a crisis.

That sense of adventure was what had drawn her into law enforcement in the first place.

Her marksmanship had simply been the ticket.

But she couldn't deny she missed HRT. The sheer physicality of the constant training was always a challenge. Keeping mind and body in top shape was essential, and she was skilled at both.

"Still think this is an unusual conversation?" Carr asked.

"Ye— Maybe not. At least not for us. You're telling me we're not so different. We just use different methods to get to the same place."

"Ah...actually, I was trying to point out I'm subtle and you're obvious."

"You're..." She sat bolt upright. "I'm what?"

"Not that obvious is a bad thing," he hastened to explain. "You look pretty damn cute in your blue suit and sidearm."

"Cute?" She was sure her blood, literally, was on the verge of boiling. "I've never been cute at any time in my life."

"Even when you had braces in middle school?"

"I didn't have braces."

"Really? Well, nice teeth, then." He cleared his throat. "I actually like your assessment of our situation much better than mine. We're different simply because we go about things in a different way."

"Exactly." She narrowed her eyes. "You talk things to death, and I—"

"You stare people down until they crack under the pressure."

"Now you're just trying to suck up."

"Is it working?"

"Not really."

"Then you must be missing something in the delivery." He wrapped his arm around her waist and tugged her down to lie alongside him. "You challenge me in ways I've never experienced with anyone else. I rarely find myself caught off guard and yet you always surprise me."

"You do read people well."

"But you're a tough one." He kissed the corner of her mouth, and she breathed in the now familiar sandalwood scent of his skin—so seductive, easily soothing the ragged edges of her temper. "I want to know you, to understand you."

"As much as you want me naked in your bed?"

"As much as."

Definitely scary. She'd stepped into completely unfamiliar territory, an area where her training held no power.

She stared into his eyes, dark, probing, unfathomable. And leaped into the abyss. "Then it should be obvious what I need right now."

CARR WOKE to ringing.

As Malina groped for her cell phone on the bedside table, he commented, "Is this going to be a thing?"

She jabbed him briefly with her elbow before answering, so when he realized the caller was business—obvious by the sudden formal clarity of her voice—he took great delight in placing lingering kisses against her neck and shoulders while she talked.

He was entirely annoyed, however, when he heard the words "I'll be right there," which caused him to clutch her back tighter against his chest.

Their stormy, sensual night couldn't be ending. The reality of the case they'd yet to solve, the possibility that she'd—again—find a reason to pull away from him wasn't something he wanted to face.

He was in serious trouble with this woman.

"Do you have any idea who that was?" she asked as she sat up and snapped the phone closed.

Not only didn't he know, he didn't much care. It seemed selfishness wasn't an impulse that could be easily cast aside. "Do you? I was hoping my distraction was actually distracting you."

"The freakin' mayor."

"Harvey?"

She nudged his shoulder before leaping from the bed. "Not yours, Counselor. Mine." Naked, she strode into the bathroom. "Well, mine for now."

Carr buried his face in his pillow. After his blundered

attempt last night to get her to talk about their differences, which was supposed to lead to a discussion of their future and feelings, he hardly needed a reminder that she was only his temporary lover.

When he heard the shower running, he knew his fantasy of making love, followed by omelets and a bareskin swim in his heated pool was just that.

Rolling out of the bed, he snagged his pants off the floor and put them on before walking into the bathroom.

She was already in the shower.

He literally clenched his fists at his sides to keep from reaching for the shower door and joining her. "It's Sunday morning. Doesn't he have babies to kiss, lies to tell and preachers to impress?"

"Probably. But his dog is lost. Again, I might add."

Carr, his mind supplying vivid images of Malina's amazing body under the stream of hot water barely two feet away, braced his forehead against the wall and fought for control. "His dog?"

"Pooky. The family Maltese. He's been kidnapped before, so the kids are a mess." She paused, then the water shut off and the towel hanging over the shower door disappeared. "Seriously, they couldn't possibly have hired another dog walker with a record, could they?"

"I, for one, have no idea. But I'm about to make it my mission in life to be sure they never do again."

The shower door popped open, and Malina's head poked out. A fog of hot air billowed around her. She'd piled her hair on top of her head, but her face and body were dewy with steam.

He closed his eyes. The things he did for his soul's respectability.

She grabbed him and kissed him at the base of his throat, then wrapped the towel around her body. "You should come. You charm everybody within miles, and a puffy white dog shouldn't be a stretch to find."

"Can I ask a very obvious question?"

"Ha," she said as she stood at the bathroom sink and pawed through her bag. "I thought you were the subtle one."

"How can I charm a dog that's missing?"

Pausing in the process of applying mascara, she looked at his reflection in the mirror. "No, you're charming the kids—twins, a boy and a girl. You know, good cop, bad cop."

"You're the bad cop, I take it."

"Definitely," she said, snagging her suit off the hanger she'd hooked to the towel rack the night before.

All in all, he preferred the blue bikini, but she was inviting him along on this odd quest and, by definition, inviting him into her life, so he'd be crazy to argue.

"Why are we doing the good cop, bad cop routine with a couple of kids?" he asked as they climbed in her car a few minutes later.

"Because they kidnapped the dog."

"You think so?"

"Pretty sure. Their parents are fighting. There was a rumor of their dad cheating, which I personally think is crap, but they decided to take drastic action. A lot of attention focused on them, the family gathered around, sticking together to find sweet little Pooky—it's a pretty smart way to have some family-bonding time, if you think about it.

"Anyway, I gave them my card and cell phone number when I found the dog the first time, so—"

"Hang on." Carr held up his hand. "The first time

you found him? *You* solved the case of the mayor's kid-napped dog?"

"Yeah. The dog walker did it. Though that butler did have some beady eyes, so I kept a close watch on him, too."

Carr remembered reading about the feel-good story in the newspaper. The FBI had been called in, and the case had been solved within hours. Now he knew why the agent in charge had refused to be interviewed for the story. "Sort of a step down from interrogating a SEC-violating senator's son, wouldn't you say?"

She winced. "Thanks for reminding me."

"So you want to explain why you're so happy to save little Pooky again?"

"Hey, I might have suffered great humiliation in front of my shortsighted colleagues, but having the mayor on my side can only be a good thing. Besides, it'll be fun." Looking gleeful, she exited the Ravenel bridge and headed into downtown Charleston. "Interrogating a couple of ten-year-olds, causing a scene in the neighbor-hood. I can't think of any better way to spend a Sunday morning."

"I can."

"Men," she sighed, "always thinking with their pe-nises."

"I didn't hear many complaints from you last night."

Smiling, she glanced over at him. "Good point."

Carr might have wanted sex, but he knew when to play the cards he'd been dealt. While the mayor and his family were bonding, Carr would be doing some bonding of his own. The fact that Malina trusted him enough to bring him into her work without him having to beg, cajole or insist was definitely a positive sign for their relationship.

When they turned off King Street into the gated driveway of the mayor's historical three-story mansion, complete with impressive Venetian-style palazzi at each level, it was apparent that he hadn't called the cops or the press this time. After all, one dog-napping was a feel-good story, but a second was an embarrassment.

The security detail met them at the gate, checked their IDs, then allowed Malina to park before they were escorted to a side door.

Just inside, Mayor Don Parnell paced the hall in a rumpled charcoal suit. "Thank goodness you're here, Agent Blair." The mayor shook Malina's hand, then his tired gaze moved to Carr. "And Mr. Hamilton, good to see you again."

"Carr happened to be with me when your call came in, sir," Malina explained as the security guards closed the door behind them.

The mayor nodded. "Excellent. He helped out First Presbyterian last year when some jerk staged a fall down the front steps, then tried to sue the church for ten million dollars. Mr. Hamilton cleared the whole thing up nicely."

At Malina's impressed glance, Carr nodded modestly. His charity knew no bounds—and it shouldn't, according to Sister Mary Katherine. Still, he didn't think it was wrong to take some credit in front of the woman he was trying to romance.

"It's hard to believe we're back in this position so soon," Parnell continued. "My wife is a wreck."

"And the kids?" Malina asked.

"They can barely stop crying, and they won't let my wife and me out of their sight. They're afraid one of us is going to be next."

Malina exchanged a knowing look with Carr.

Clearly frustrated, the mayor speared his hand through his wavy brown hair. "The only way they'd let me leave the room is because I told them it was you. How could this happen *again?* We don't even have a dog walker anymore."

"Well, I'd like to talk privately with you before we go back to your family." Malina slid her hands calmly into her pockets and faced the mayor. Her voice was confident and quiet. "When did you notice Pooky was missing?"

The mayor stopped pacing and mirrored her pose. "This morning," he said, his tone more controlled than before. "I got up about six-thirty. Pooky always hears me and comes out of one of the twins' rooms, meeting me at the top of the stairs. This morning, no Pooky. I looked everywhere, had the security detail hunting through the bushes, driving down the street.

"When it was apparent she was gone, I had no choice but to wake up my wife and the twins. Madison and Edward insisted I call you. What else could I do? They were hysterical."

"I'll bet," Malina said. "When was the last time you saw Pooky?"

"Sometime after dinner last night." He waved his hand vaguely in the direction behind him. "The kids took her out to play in the backyard."

"Did you see them come back in?"

"No, but I heard them."

"You heard the dog bark?"

Parnell looked thoughtful. "No, she's not much of a barker. I heard the kids come back in."

"Has it occurred to anybody that Pooky might have simply gotten out and run off?" Malina asked.

Parnell shook his head. "She can't. We have an

electric fence, remember? As long as she's wearing her collar, she can't cross the property's barrier without getting shocked. You've seen her, high-strung, tiny little ball of fur. She won't go anywhere near the edge of the yard."

"Oh, right," Malina said. "I'd forgotten."

But it was apparent to Carr that she hadn't overlooked that detail at all. She was leading the mayor somewhere, and Carr, for one, couldn't wait to find out how she'd get there without insulting him and jeopardizing her powerful connection.

Crossing her arms over her chest, Malina stepped closer to Parnell. "Besides the fence, Mr. Parnell, you also have a security detail with you twenty-four hours a day. How do you suppose the dog-napper got access to the property, not to mention your kids' bedrooms?"

Parnell stiffened. "Agent Blair, I'm not sure I like your tone. What are you suggesting?"

"An inside job."

"Not me certainly."

"No, the twins."

Her flat delivery was a wake-up call to Parnell. His head snapped back, and he rubbed his temples as if he could reach inside his head and physically clear his thoughts.

"I don't hear you arguing against that theory," Malina said after a few seconds of silence during which the mayor returned to his pacing.

"They're not really criers," Parnell said with a sigh. "Especially not Edward. But every time he looked at his sister and saw her crying, he started up, too. It seemed strange."

Malina angled her head. "Kids do strange things to attract attention sometimes."

The mayor's face flushed with embarrassment. "I'll bet most of them don't involve calling the FBI, though."

"I don't see any reason to make an official report, but I think they ought to try excelling at baseball or soccer or singing in the choir rather than learning to cry and manipulate on command."

Parnell smiled weakly. "How about the drama club?"

"There you go." Malina's gaze locked on Parnell's. "How do you feel about letting the consequences of their actions play out?"

The mayor looked from Malina to Carr. "How?"

After a minute or two of whispered planning, the mayor led them down the hall to the den, where the kids and their mother were waiting.

"Excellent work," Carr whispered in Malina's ear as they walked. "The everything's-under-control tone and the composed body language were nice touches."

She shrugged away the compliment. "Don't even think about stealing my technique for your next appearance in court."

"I'll do my best."

"One last thing…" Malina said as they approached the doorway. "Where's the butler?"

Parnell angled his head. "Stevens? Sunday's his day off."

Malina patted his shoulder. "Just checking."

When they entered the posh den, Madison and Edward Parnell, both blue-eyed blonds and still wearing pajamas, sat on either side of their mother on the sofa. Their faces were red and puffy from crying, but Carr was certain he saw little Madison's eyes gleam as she noticed Malina.

"I'm sorry we have to see each other again under these difficult circumstances," Malina said formally to Mrs. Parnell, who rose to shake both Malina's and Carr's hands.

"I really don't understand how this could happen again," she said somewhat desperately, her gaze seeking out her husband's.

Uncertainty and fear permeated the room, and the mayor, either from embarrassment or lack of compassion, didn't seem to sense his wife's anxiety. He stood apart from the family.

"I have a pretty good idea," Malina said to Mrs. Parnell. "I've examined the crime scene thoroughly, but I'm going to need to talk to the kids now."

"But, I—"

"It's okay, Lorene," Parnell said, interrupting his wife. Somewhat hesitantly, he extended his hand to her. She grabbed it like a lifeline, and they retreated to the other side of the room.

From their gestures and expressions, Carr assumed the mayor was explaining the plan.

Facing the kids, now alone and uncertain, Malina wasted no time in putting on her bad cop gear. "I brought an attorney with me," she said, jabbing her thumb over her shoulder to indicate Carr. "You should have one present when you're questioned by the police."

In sync, two pairs of bright blue eyes widened. "Q-questioned?" Madison ventured to ask.

"Sure," Malina said, placing her hands on her hips. "You wanted the cops, you got 'em."

Carr acknowledged that Malina looked wildly intimidating in her dark suit. Plus, when she moved her hands to her hips, she revealed her holstered pistol.

This isn't a woman to mess with was clearly the message.

Understanding his role, Carr stepped aggressively between the kids and Malina. "There's no need to intimidate my clients, Agent Blair. They're cooperating, aren't they?"

As he looked back toward the kids for confirmation, they nodded slowly.

Sitting next to Edward, knowing he was the weak link in this conspiracy, Carr glared at Malina. "Please continue, Agent—as long as you can keep your questions soothing and nonthreatening."

Malina looked disdainful. "I'd certainly hate to be threatening when there's a criminal to be unmasked, Counselor."

Carr forced himself to appear appalled. "An innocent dog's life is at stake, Agent Blair. Surely you don't intend to—"

"Where were you two last night at seven-thirty?" Malina demanded, her glare jumping to Madison.

"W-we took Pooky in the backyard to play," the little girl said, reaching out to clutch Carr's hand like a lifeline.

How Malina continued to glare into that innocently beautiful—and now terrified—face, Carr had no idea, but he supposed they didn't let wimps into HRT.

"Did you see anyone in the backyard?" she asked.

"Well, we—" Madison glanced over at her brother. "No, no we didn't."

Malina, not missing a beat, loomed over the girl. "That, Madison, is a big, fat...lie."

As Madison burst into tears, which may have actually been genuine this time, Edward leaped to his feet.

"Pooky's fine! Nobody kidnapped her. We gave her to my friend Alan to take care of and pretended she was missing and it was all Madison's idea and she made me do it so it's not my fault!"

9

MALINA WALKED with Carr and the mayor to her car.

"Thanks for all your help," the mayor said. "I certainly hope this is the first—and last—stunt the twins pull."

"Anytime, Mr. Mayor." With the door open, Malina braced her foot against the frame. "And I hope you and your wife work things out. You make a nice couple."

Parnell nodded and turned away, but before Malina could drop into the driver's seat, he'd faced her again. Uncomfortable and hesitant, he asked, "How'd you know we were having problems?"

"You asked your security detail to help you look for Pooky, which tells me you're not in the habit of turning to your wife in a crisis. You don't want to bother her or worry her, or maybe you simply don't want to include her." Malina shrugged. "Plus this stunt the twins pulled was a big neon sign."

Parnell ducked his head. "I stay pretty busy."

"Of course. You have a high-pressure—"

"I didn't have an affair," Parnell interrupted defiantly.

Malina held up her hands. "None of my business." She lowered her voice, partly because she was in no position to give advice and partly hoping surveillance on the grounds wouldn't pick up her words. "But you have a nice family. I'd find a way to hang on to them."

As she settled into her sedan, Malina glanced at Carr. Her family was nearly five thousand miles away, and she could think of nobody she'd rather spend time with than the man next to her. "It's not every day you open and close a case within two hours. I say we celebrate. How about lunch?"

He leaned across the console and kissed her softly. "Sounds perfect."

At the all-you-can-eat crab-and-oyster bar they found in downtown Charleston, they talked about their child-hoods, the singularly unusual bond of growing up on small-town islands. They had the same experience of littering tourists, rowdy tourists and tourists in search of historical and naturalistic experiences—as well as the unmistakable knowledge that those tourists kept their economy in the black, whatever the drawbacks.

Once, Malina tried to broach the subject of why Carr had left Manhattan, but he brushed over his move from high-powered litigator to partially retired defender of churches and charities as if it was simply the natural evolution of a lawyer's career.

She'd faced too many cold-eyed sharks in court to know that wasn't remotely true, but she didn't see how she could probe him for answers when she was deter-mined to hold back herself.

As they rose to leave the restaurant, Malina linked their hands. "So, Counselor, got any ideas on how we could spend the rest of the afternoon?"

Grinning, he held open the door. "A few."

Outside stood a woman, about sixty, with silver hair and wearing an expensive-looking plum suit. She thanked Carr for holding the door open, then paused, staring at him. "Carr Hamilton?" she asked, her face going white with shock.

"Yes, ma'am, are you—"

She slapped Carr across his face. "You killed my husband!"

Malina's instincts kicked in the next instant. She jumped between them. "I'm sure there's been a mistake."

The woman moved forward as if she wanted to hit Carr again, and Malina snagged her arm, pressing her gently but firmly against the wall outside the restaurant. "Don't even think about touching him again."

"Malina, please." Carr grabbed her waist from behind and pulled her away from the woman. "She—" His voice broke. "Just let her go."

Stunned, Malina turned to watch her lover head down the block toward the parking lot where they'd left her car.

"He killed my husband," the woman in front of her insisted.

Malina stepped back and eyed her with distinct suspicion. Carr had been a profitable litigator in New York. He'd successfully argued many cases against big corporations throughout the country. There were bound to be people who didn't like the outcome of the judgments.

"I'm not sure what happened to you," Malina said finally, backing away, "but Carr wasn't the cause."

The woman lifted her chin. "But he was. *Aberforth versus Bailey Industries,* here in Charleston, five years ago. Look it up."

Then, with regal bearing, she headed into the restaurant.

Malina fought to calm her racing heart.

She braced her hand against the restaurant's brick wall. Carr's hurt and guilty eyes flashed in front of her.

There were plenty of horrors in her past. All of them job-related. Justice was sometimes bloody, often unpleasant, but Carr would never knowingly hurt anyone.

No way.

But then why had he gone from the glory of being on the short list as the attorney most feared by global insurance companies and high-powered consumer products corporations to defending churches against fraud?

Honesty and truth are two entirely different concepts, he'd said. And once she'd asked him, *Do you ever feel guilty for making that money on the tide of pain and suffering your clients have to weather?*

As her stomach clenched, she spun around and headed toward the car. There had to be an explanation. A man who'd gone to so much trouble to stand against smugglers and thieves wouldn't—

He stood for justice and integrity.

A sense of righteous assurance filled her, driving her to the parking lot.

Carr stood by the passenger door. His expression was closed, remote, unapproachable.

Malina swallowed the lump trying to form in her throat. "You can't please everybody, I guess."

All the way back to his house, she kept a running, inane and one-sided commentary going on cases she'd worked where the victim whose ass they'd just saved wanted to sue the Bureau. People were odd, blah, blah.

You just can't predict what somebody who's been through a traumatic experience will do afterward, et cetera.

Carr said nothing. He stared out the passenger side window.

She knew she was bungling the situation badly but had no idea how to adjust. It gave her a whole new respect for people who had to deal with her when she was moody and distant. No wonder they annoyed her further by babbling like idiots most of the time.

When she shifted the sedan into Park in Carr's driveway, he got out and came around to her side to open her door. He held out his hand to assist her but immediately let her go when she'd gained her feet.

Fear and uncertainty consumed her as she followed him inside.

He strode straight to the living room and poured a crystal tumbler of whiskey, no ice.

"It's only three o'clock," she said, her nerves clanging with alarm. "A little early for that, don't you think?"

He shrugged, sipped and headed over to the windows at the back of the room.

She approached him, having no idea what she was going to say but knowing she had to do something. "Look, Carr—"

"Have you ever killed anyone?" he asked, his back to her as he stared out the windows.

The knots in her stomach twisted tighter. "I have."

"Shot, I guess."

"Yes."

He downed the whiskey in one gulp. "I've killed, but with nothing so clean as a bullet to the heart."

Malina laid her hand on his shoulder, rubbing the knotted muscles, wishing she could find the right thing to say to comfort him. "Whatever happened, I'm sure you did what you could."

He shook his head. "Do you remember their faces, the ones you've killed?"

"No," she said, mirroring his quiet tone. "The lost innocent haunt me, not the dead and the guilty."

"What about the guilty who continue to live?"

Had one of his clients died over the stress of a trial? Had one of the defendants? "Whose—"

"Me!" he shouted, spinning around, his beautiful face harsh with anger and pain. "*I'm* guilty."

"Of what?" Malina demanded. "Everybody's done things they're not proud of, Carr. You learn from your mistakes and move on. Trying to change the past is futile. Look at me, nearly ruining my career because of blind ambition. So I get dumped in Charleston, and I start again. Whatever that lady thinks you did, you have to remember all the people you've helped, all the good you've done."

"It'll never be enough." He stared at her, his eyes bleak. "I so obviously ruined her life, and I have no idea who that woman was."

Malina sucked in a quick breath. Her belief in him faltered, then solidified even more strongly. Whatever injustice, real or imagined, Carr had caused, she didn't care. She'd insist he purge this toxin and forgive himself. *"Aberforth versus Bailey Industries.* Five years ago in Charleston."

Carr sighed. "I don't remember that one." He stared into his empty glass. "There are so many to pick from."

That's it. Malina plucked the tumbler from his hand, set it aside and dragged him to the sofa. There, she kept a tight hold on his hand, even though it hung limp and lifeless. "Spill it. So many what?"

"People I've destroyed."

"Oh, cut it out. You're not in a daytime melodrama."

His head snapped up. "You don't know what I've done."

She much preferred the temper to the hopelessness. "You just said you don't remember either. How can you blame yourself for something you can't even recall?"

"I don't have to know specifics. Don't want to." He pulled away from her and rose. "I need you to go now."

Her heart contracted. "Carr, I—"

"Please. You need some rest, and I need to be alone for a while."

She'd never been good at comforting people. She had few friends and certainly hadn't inherited her mother's compassion. She was terrible with victims, since her instinct was to tell them the truth—your life's going to suck for a long time, and nothing I say is going to change that.

Apparently her abilities were just as poor with lovers. "Fine," she said as she stood and buttoned her jacket. "But no more booze."

Listless again, he shrugged. "Yeah. Sure."

She stepped close and laid her palm against his jaw. "I don't care what you've done in the past. I care about who you are now."

Then she kissed him and left.

In the car, she called Andrea. After arranging to meet her at the jewelry store the next morning, Malina told her about what had happened with Carr and asked his friend to check in on him later.

"What happened in this woman's case?" Andrea asked, her tone full of worry.

"I don't know, but I'm damn sure gonna find out."

MONDAY MORNING, Malina walked into a slightly shabby jewelry store on the edge of a respectable neighborhood in downtown Charleston.

She found Andrea Landry already inside the small, dark place, talking to an elderly man in a baby-blue cardigan. He held a jeweler's loupe up to one eye. He looked like somebody's birdhouse-making grandfather.

This case got weirder all the time.

"Malina," Andrea began with a twinkle in her eyes, "meet Bill Billings."

I rest my case.

Malina shook Billings's hand, then wasted no time in pulling the evidence bag from her jacket and handing over both the diamond and the list of stolen Australian gems.

Billings examined the stone, then, within moments, he was lowering his loupe and studying the list. "It's this one," he said, pointing at the seventh diamond on the list.

Malina exchanged a startled look with Andrea. "You're sure?"

"Gemology isn't an exact science, yet each gem is unique. Gems are identified by their weight, color and number and location of inclusions—naturally occurring flaws."

"Right," Malina said, nodding. "Like the fewer the imperfections, the more the stone's worth."

Billings smiled. "Exactly. If I was going to name the characteristics of this particular stone, this—" he pointed to the list "—is how I would catalog them. To be more certain, I'd need a microscope or a refractometer."

Malina angled her head. "A what?"

"It measures the refraction of light in a gem—the angles," Andrea explained. "I can get the diamond to someone who has one if you need."

"Yeah, that would be good." Malina directed her attention to Billings. "But you're reasonably confident even without this refractometer thing, right?"

"Hmm…reasonably confident," Billings said, as if testing both the idea and the words.

"As in, could you testify in a court of law regarding your findings if you were ever called on by the government to do so?"

"Court, huh?" He chuckled. "Sure, honey. Be glad to."

Malina returned the diamond to its envelope, thanked Billings for his time, then strode outside with Andrea.

"It looks like you found part of your Australian cache."

In the face of the bright sun overhead, Malina put on her sunglasses. "Looks like."

"So what's the next step?"

"Did you give me Bill Billings for fun, or does he really know what he's talking about?"

Andrea grinned. "Both."

"Thanks, I needed a laugh today." Malina shook her head ruefully. "People do some crazy-ass things to their kids."

"Don't they? He's got brothers named Will and Phil, if you can believe it."

"Absolutely bonkers."

Andrea shifted from one foot to the other. "Are you going to ask me about Carr?"

"He sent me home to get some sleep, and I didn't close my eyes all night." Malina sighed, exhausted and beyond worried. She was scared. About Carr's reaction to that unstable woman's assault, about the information she'd learned and about how much she cared concerning both. "Do you have time for some coffee?"

Andrea linked her arm through Malina's. "There's a shop two blocks over."

Tucked into a corner booth with caramel mocha lattes—way too sweet, but Malina hadn't wanted to be shrill and ask for plain coffee—they sipped and watched shoppers pass by the window for a couple of minutes before Andrea broke the silence.

"I've never seen him like that."

The guilt Malina had been battling back all night washed over her anew. "I shouldn't have left him." She bowed her head, massaging her temples. "I didn't know what to do. I've *never* not known what to do."

Andrea gripped her hand and squeezed. "It's harder to react when you care so much about the one in pain."

Malina managed to nod. Keeping the professional and personal separate. That had been her plan. What a joke.

"Do you want to hear it all?"

Malina lifted her head to stare into Andrea's understanding eyes. "I have to."

"I called him and asked if I could do anything. He blew me off, but I brought him dinner around six anyway. He refused to eat."

"Was he drinking?"

"No. Given his state, I was sort of surprised he was stone sober."

"He threw back a whiskey at three in the afternoon. I asked him not to have any more."

"Well, despite the pain he was in, he kept that promise."

"That's something, I guess."

Andrea glanced out the window before looking back at Malina's face. "I think he was punishing himself by not drinking. He was forcing himself to face what he'd done without anesthesia, as if he deserved to suffer."

So many what? she'd asked.

People I've destroyed, he'd answered.

"Yeah." Malina sipped the overly sweet coffee to burn away the emotions clogging her throat. "I can see that."

"When I refused to leave him, he stormed outside onto the beach."

"He likes to walk to relax," Malina mused, curling her hands into fists.

"I sent Tyler out to talk to him, but they nearly came to blows, so we pretended to go."

"Pretended?"

"Tyler and I waited until he'd set the house alarm and gone upstairs, then we spent the night on his sofa. We have each other's alarm codes in case there's an emergency while one of us is traveling."

Never before had Malina felt so powerless, ashamed and yet so grateful at the same time. "Thank you. I should have been there. He needed me, and I ran."

"Maybe so, but I think you're the one person he doesn't want to see. He doesn't want to face you. Why? Because of something in his past? Because some nutty woman clocked him?"

Malina shifted her gaze to Andrea's. "Did he say anything about her?"

"No. The only thing I got out of him was *he died because of my greed.* Do you know what he meant?"

"I do."

And she realized she and Carr had followed similar paths last night, though they'd been miles apart physically. He must have looked up the case he couldn't recall, just as she'd done.

So she told Andrea about *Aberforth versus Bailey Industries.*

Bailey manufactured kids' toys, mostly cheap, plastic wagons and indoor riding scooters for toddlers. Sandra Aberforth had tripped over her son's scooter and broken her hip. She'd had several surgeries, but would still walk with a slight limp the rest of her life. She was pissed and on the verge of bankruptcy, so she sued.

The court found in her favor and awarded her an astounding ten million dollars. Bailey Industries went belly-up six months later, and Charles Bailey killed himself a month after that.

The newspaper accounts of the trial credited the plaintiff attorney's impassioned closing statement with the unusually high judgment.

"Carr was the attorney," Andrea said, her eyes full of bleak understanding.

"I think we can assume the widow, Coraline Bailey, was the woman in the plum suit with the swift backhand." Malina cupped her hands around her coffee cup, hoping for warmth that didn't come. "She took up tennis and a crusade for tort reform after her husband's tragic death."

As awful as the case sounded in black and white, did the knowledge really change Malina's opinion of Carr? She wasn't naive. She'd always known a lawyer didn't get to his level of success without working a lot of different angles, cultivating a wily personality and pushing the boundaries of right and wrong. Saturday night she'd even teased him about owning lots of gray suits.

She hadn't cared then, when she was using his clever brain to help her solve her case. She had absolutely no right to judge him now.

And she found talking with Andrea made her understand the desire she had for him was as strong as ever. How many deals had the Bureau made with low-level criminals in order to get the guy at the top? How many times had she swallowed her personal opinions and followed orders she thought either overenthusiastic or impotent?

Justice wasn't always pretty.

As Carr had once told her, honesty and truth were two different concepts. So, whatever he'd done, whatever the lingering consequences of his actions, at some point he'd decided…

"That's why he defends churches and charities," Malina found herself saying aloud.

Andrea sipped her coffee. "Carr does work pretty closely with Sister Mary Katherine. They're an odd pair in a way, but—"

Malina grabbed Andrea by her wrist. "He's trying to make up for all the things he's done in his past. From the beginning, I thought his interest in the possibility of smuggling was too much. I could never figure out why he wanted to devote so much of his time to this case."

"Oh, come on. I think you probably had something to do with that."

"It's not just about me." Though Malina acknowledged that their desire was powerful, maybe even life-changing—at least for her. "He's repenting."

"Repenting?" Andrea flicked her hand to the side as she leaned back in the booth. "That's a bit dramatic."

"But he believes it," Malina insisted, hunching forward. "Absolutely."

For a few minutes, Andrea said nothing. Then, "Well, he *is* Catholic."

CARR FLUNG open his front door only after the patently annoying person on the porch apparently didn't get the message that he didn't want to be disturbed. Didn't a man have the right to refuse company anymore?

He was going to make damn sure that piece of legislation was on the next senate bill.

"Look, I don't—" He stopped, clenching his fist by his side.

Malina was on his porch. She was wearing the familiarly staid navy-blue suit, white shirt, sidearm and fierce expression.

He nearly fell to his knees.

"You don't want to see me?" she asked, her gaze and tone challenging. She grabbed his hand and tugged him outside, where the sun blared down on him. "Too bad."

He dug in his heels. He outweighed her, was certainly stronger physically. "I'm sick."

"So I noticed." She jerked him forward a few more steps, belying his confidence in his power. "Your secretary was helpful in telling me you haven't failed to show up at the office a single weekday in two years."

"Everybody's entitled to a day off."

"But not you. You're on a mission."

Despite his reluctance to leave, he found himself standing next to her sedan. "I'm sick."

"Bull." She pushed her face near his. "You're not a wallower, Hamilton. You're strong and crafty and determined. Sure, you've got issues. Don't we all?" She flung open the passenger door and pushed him inside. "Me, I'm terrified by you and what we become when we're together, but here I am anyway."

Slamming the door closed, she rounded the car with resolute strides, giving Carr his first hint of hope since yesterday. He'd been so sure she'd run from him after learning the ugly truth about his past.

There was no way she hadn't gone home and re-searched the case Mrs. Bailey had shoved in their faces. And still she was here.

Despite her need to get ahead and her desire to push at the strictures of justice, she'd never gone outside that barrier. He had. So many times.

And yet she was here; she hadn't turned away.

He wasn't sure whether to be grateful or angry. "Where're we going?"

"The shooting range."

Disbelieving, he stared at her profile. "The—"

She threw the car into Reverse, did a quick turn, then shot out onto the road. "You like to walk on the beach. I like to shoot. Let's try my way this time."

_10_

BEFORE CARR COULD blink, he found himself standing in an indoor shooting stall with a pistol in his hand and a target in the distance.

He felt ridiculous. How was this supposed to help him deal with the fact that he'd spent most of his life as an unconscionable leech?

With a sigh, he fired. Again. Then again.

Each time, the kick from the pistol jolted him back, and he found himself wanting to overpower the urge to recoil.

Malina laid her hand on his back and shouted over the other shots echoing through the range. "Relax your fingers! Keep your shoulders and stance strong."

Taking her advice, he found his rhythm smoother, his shots more accurate. At some point, the world around him fell away and all he saw was the target.

When the clip was empty, she reloaded for him, and he set off again.

He pictured nights he'd toasted victory with colleagues in Manhattan. He remembered the cold satisfaction he'd felt the first time one of his clients had received a judgment that was way out of proportion with the damage done. He recalled the times he'd smiled over companies driven to their knees or out of business entirely as a result of cases.

At the end of the fourth round, he was exhausted and oddly cleansed. The exercise had been brutal but absolutely necessary.

He and Malina might be different in many ways but she understood, as no one else could, that he needed a safe way to expend his anger. He'd spent the past few years hating himself, and he needed to kill his old life before he could truly move ahead to the new future he was embracing.

Not a therapy the good Sister might advocate, but one he supported anyway.

"Don't even think about doing that in reality," Malina said, snagging the gun from his hand and holstering it.

"Why?" He pulled off his headphones. "I didn't do so bad."

She glanced back at the target and winced. "Firearms are for trained professionals, which you most certainly are not."

He'd hit, well…something most of the time. "You do it," he challenged.

"Nah. Too easy."

"But you come here a lot."

Her gaze searched his, and whatever she found had her turning. "Come on."

After a walk down the hall, through a door and yet another hall, he found himself in a stark room with dark walls extending in a box in front of him. Malina walked to the far end of the room, where a computer rested.

She tapped the keys, then pulled a pistol, not from her holster, but a bin beside the monitor.

As she approached him, he noticed both the challenge in her eyes and the gun in her hand.

"It has the same weight as a real pistol," she said, shoving not an ammunition clip but a tiny card, like the ones in digital cameras, into the butt of the gun. "Ready?"

After a mesmerizing pause as he was captured senseless by her turquoise eyes, he nodded.

She pressed another button on a tiny black box against the wall.

The simulation began.

It was sort of like shooting ducks with a rifle at the fair, only the scene was a computer-generated, 3-D, all-too-real video game. The bad guys jumped out from all angles, firing at will. People screamed. The report of guns ricocheted. And, near the end, the lights went out and Carr heard random fire from seemingly all directions.

Malina simply closed her eyes and continued to knock off targets.

"How'd you do that?" Carr asked as they walked out of the gun club a while later.

"Arrange for you to shoot inanimate objects and save yourself thousands of dollars in therapy? I called and made a reservation."

"I got that." Carr slid his arm around her waist as he steered her back against the car. "How can you close your eyes and still hit all the targets?"

"I practice."

"Uh-huh." He pressed his body the length of hers, and she let out a quiet moan. He was alive again, and she was the reason. He skimmed kisses along her neck. "How?"

"You're certainly back to normal."

"Thanks to you. How?"

She met his gaze. "Your vision isn't as acute as your hearing in the dark. Closing my eyes helps me to focus. What you hear is just as important as what you see."

"Mmm…and what do you hear?" he whispered in her ear.

"You. I hear you…constantly." She wrapped her arms around his waist and laid her head against his chest.

The helplessness that had invaded him so thoroughly had lifted, and he knew both Malina's unusual brand of therapy, as well as the woman herself, had caused the change. What he didn't know was why she'd decided to help him.

She seemed to use any excuse to discount or outright avoid their relationship, and yet she was beside him. Holding him.

"How about dinner? I'm fairly certain there's a roasted chicken with vegetables in my fridge that's completely untouched."

"You're on."

THEY MANAGED idle conversation during dinner, but the moment the last plate was in the dishwasher, they grabbed each other.

Covering her mouth with his, he backed her against the kitchen counter as she attacked the buttons on his shirt. He cupped her cheek in his palm, angling her head, deepening the kiss with needy desperation. He slid his tongue against hers as they continued to fumble with their clothing, their fingers clumsy in desperation.

She got his pants and shirt unfastened, then rolled

a condom in place. He got her shirt off, her front-clasp bra unhooked and her pants and panties off. Just enough access so that when he lifted her onto the counter, he was able to enter her in one, smooth, deep stroke.

"Oh, man," she moaned. "Please do that again."

He obliged her until she'd wrapped her legs like a vise around his waist and her breathing grew choppy, frantic. She came on a hot groan of surrender, squeezing with potent, seductive pulses, bringing him to his own breath-stealing climax.

She collapsed against him. "I feel so much better."

He chuckled, stroking the silky length of her hair. "Hey, I was the one suffering."

She placed a kiss against his heaving chest. "Not the only one," she said so softly he could barely discern the words.

"Why are you here?" he asked reluctantly, not sure he could have if she'd been looking at him with those intense ocean eyes. "You don't want to be with me. Why should you?"

She clutched him tighter, with both arms and legs. "But I do."

Closing his eyes, he kissed the top of her head. He had no idea where they were headed, but he knew the journey was one he couldn't miss. "I never knew about Bailey's suicide until last night."

"I know."

"And you think that makes me better?"

"It makes you human."

"There are dozens, maybe hundreds out there like her. You've done a background check on me. You know what I was."

She finally lifted her head to look at him. "I know

you're a great attorney. You've won hundreds of judgments for your clients."

"And I never cared about one of them," he said harshly, turning away and fastening his pants. "I smiled at them, wined and dined them to get their lucrative cases, then I cashed my checks and never gave them another thought. I didn't take on small cases, ones with true injustice done."

She walked around him, still wearing only her unbuttoned shirt, unashamed in her nudity.

But then, she wasn't the one exposing her humiliating past.

"So you decided to make it your mission to beat yourself," she said. "That's why you defend churches, charities, anybody who's weak, underfunded or just has a righteous cause. You didn't want somebody like you coming along to subvert justice." She studied him as if seeing him for the first time. "Why? What changed?"

He grabbed her hand like a lifeline. "Come on. I'll tell you."

They settled on the sofa in the living room, and though she said she wasn't cold, he certainly was, so he settled at one end, tucking her back between his legs and a blanket on top of them both.

"My uncle died," he said into the silence. "If he hadn't…" He shook his head humbly. "Well, I might still be a shark with no soul or conscience."

She said nothing, simply rubbed her hands over his, where they rested against her stomach.

Who would have believed tough, decisive, my-way-or-the-highway Malina Blair's well of compassion was so deep and strong.

In that moment, he knew he loved her.

However illogical or ill-fated, she was the one he'd been searching for, hoping and praying for.

He leaned his face into her hair, breathing in the clean scent, wanting to remember her long after she left him for bigger and better things in Washington. In many ways, it was right that he should love but not have.

"He was an attorney in New York, too," he continued. No secrets could be held between him and this woman now. He couldn't protect his heart anymore, after all. "He was my mentor and had a lucrative practice in products liability. He taught me the ropes, sponsored me at his country club in the Hamptons, introduced me to fine wines and beautiful women.

"Other than my years at Yale, I'd spent my life on Palmer's Island, and I was dazzled by all of it."

Carr forced himself to look back and remember expensive dinners, flashy nightclubs and meaningless nights with vapid women who couldn't care less how he paid the bills, as long as he did.

"I learned the game quickly," he continued. "I helped us expand to environmental disasters and class action suits. And the money rolled in...."

"Okay, stop." Malina held up her hand and twisted around to glare at him. "A lot of those companies deserved judgments against them. I read your file. Chemical spills. People with chronic pain and cancer. Blatant plant safety violations. You aren't the only villain here."

"You think I'm a villain?"

She looked exasperated. "You seem determined to cast yourself in that role. I was merely helping."

When she settled back against him, he continued. "We took only cases that were capable of bringing in big judgments. I protested that policy at first, then as I made more money and our firm's reputation rose higher and higher, I bought my luxury uptown apartment and didn't much care how I'd arrived there.

"I'd sold out. I knew it when it was happening and chose to ignore the warnings my conscience tried to occasionally instill. I used my brains and charm without scruples, and I became a huge success."

Malina clutched his fingers, as if she was afraid of the scene he described.

"Only my uncle's sudden heart attack jolted me back to reality, made me face what I'd become. I swore I wouldn't die as he had—rich, bitter, unconscionable and alone. So, I closed the practice, packed up and came home."

She turned. "That's it? You didn't kick kids or dogs or homeless people?"

"Kick—" What was she talking about? "No, of course not."

She laid her hands against his cheeks. "I have a thing for dogs—golden retrievers in particular, and I don't care about the rest of it. I didn't know you then, and the man in front of me now is the one I'm interested in."

The look in her eyes was steady, unyielding and vividly blue. She should be running from him, and she wasn't.

Grateful beyond words, he leaned forward and kissed her.

She returned his touch ardently, straddling his lap and parting his shirt, then pushing it off his shoulders. Within moments, they were naked and she was beneath him, moaning his name, giving him solace and understanding with strokes instead of words.

As they lay on their sides, satisfied and replete, he continued to slide his hands up and down her warm, bare back. He wanted to say things, pretty words that spoke to the depths of his emotions. But he knew she wasn't ready to hear them, and he wanted to hear her rejection even less.

Pushing her tangled hair off her face, he brushed his lips across her cheek. "Would you be so understanding if someone else, not me, admitted they'd done all those things?"

She winced. "Probably not." When he grinned, she asked, "How is that a *good* thing?"

"It makes me special."

She rolled her eyes, but she was clearly holding back a smile.

"Let's do my favorite thing now," he said.

"I thought we just did."

He slapped her backside lightly. "I meant walk on the beach."

WEARING HER NAVY SLACKS, which would never be the same after the salt water dried on them, and one of Carr's old Yale sweatshirts, Malina kicked through the cold surf. "Chicken," she said when he jumped out of reach of the spraying water.

He stretched out his arm and grabbed her hand, dragging her onto firmer, drier sand. "If you want a swim, the pool's heated."

"I didn't bring my suit."

Pulling her against his side, the expression on his face became decidedly lecherous. "That won't be a problem."

She drank in the hungry look in his dark eyes. He did have a way of making her heart race and her knees weak. "I'll bet."

"After we walk, okay?"

She nodded mutely. Falling under Carr's potent spell was like falling asleep, fast and natural. It was no wonder the man had made millions off juries.

Hand in hand, they continued walking down the beach, which was surprisingly peaceful. Malina only had the urge to take off in a sprint once. It wasn't 3-D hostage takeover simulations, but it wasn't half-bad.

"So how did things go with the jeweler this morning?" he asked.

Oh, right. She was here only long enough to solve a boatload of cases so she could hightail it back to D.C.

And why did that suddenly seem like a lousy plan? Why did part of her long to walk with Carr up and down this tiny stretch of beach in the middle of nowhere for years on end?

But was she really considering giving up her career dreams for a man? Didn't she want to move up the Bureau's elite ladder? Didn't she want to make Director?

Shaking aside her internal questions, she recounted her and Andrea's encounter with Bill Billings, finding it hard to believe that had only occurred this morning.

"So Simon, Jack, plus associates really did steal diamonds from that mine in Australia and bring them to South Carolina to unload."

"Sure looks that way."

"I actually stumbled onto an international jewel theft ring."

That would certainly go to his head. "Yep."

Carr stopped suddenly. "And we have absolutely no proof."

"We've got a stolen diamond."

"Found on a public dock with no fingerprints or any other forensic evidence."

"We witnessed Jack carrying a box on the dock just before we found the diamond."

"But we didn't see the diamond fall out of the box. Theoretically, it could have already been there."

"You witnessed an exchange of merchandise for money between Jack and his cronies."

Looking wildly frustrated, Carr kicked sand with his foot. "They could have been buying and selling candlesticks, baseball caps, shells from the seashore."

"Shells from the seashore?" Malina repeated. "Do you ever stop being a lawyer?"

"No, it's instinctive—like you and your little gun games. And it's a good thing for you that my instincts are finely honed. We know what happened, we know pretty much everybody involved in the crime, but we've got nothing to prove it in court."

"We have Simon and his varied aliases."

Carr waved that away. "From prints obtained illegally. It's not enough."

"No, it isn't."

"You don't seem worked up about that little reality." When she shrugged, he seemed to finally realize her calm had a reason. "You've got a plan."

"I've got some definite ideas."

Laughing, he grabbed her and swung her into his arms, heading back toward the house. "All in all, I usually like your ideas."

"Usually?"

"I seem to recall you ordering me off your case several times."

"Even the best agents can make mistakes."

"You admit making a mistake? Remind me to note this date and time in my PDF."

Part of her wanted to tell him to put her down, she

could walk herself. But the house's landscape lights glowed in the distance, accenting its round, modern features, and Malina sighed against his shoulder instead.

She was pretty crazy about that house.

Promising they'd talk through her ideas after their swim, Carr set her down by the pool. She was in the process of, yet again, unbuttoning his shirt—really, the man should just walk around bare chested—when she noticed movement from inside his house.

Cursing the carelessness that had her leaving her Glock on the kitchen counter, she stepped between him and the windows. "Get down."

"Wha—"

She grabbed his arm and jerked him to a crouch. "Be quiet. Stay here."

Careful to keep to the shadows, she inched closer to the windows. Carr, naturally, ignored her order and followed.

"This is Palmer's Island," he whispered when they stopped behind a shrub underneath the kitchen window. "I leave my doors unlocked all the time. It's probably just some lost tourist."

Malina looked at him in disbelief. "This is Palmer's Island, home to an international jewel theft ring."

"Hmm, good point. Still, you did that yesterday with Mrs. Bailey—jumped between me and her. I can handle myself, you know."

"Whatever."

"Do you really think Jack or Simon is on to us?"

"Obviously I didn't, since my pistol is inside."

"Are you always this cranky during missions?"

"Are you always this chatty?"

She needed to know what they were facing so she could decide if they should head for the car or if they could handle whoever they'd encounter inside. She risked a peek at the corner of the window.

After a quick glance, she sighed and dropped next to Carr. "You can handle yourself, huh? How about a nun sitting at your kitchen table?"

11

"THANK YOU so much, Carr," Sister Mary Katherine said as she accepted a china teacup and saucer. "I'm sure this will warm me right up."

Malina kept her distance. She felt as if her usual control had flown the coop on angel's wings. Andrea had confided all about the case to the good Sister, which was enough to make Malina grind her teeth, but she also found herself hanging on to her edgy mood at being caught unaware and unarmed.

"Surely you don't think you'll need that, Agent Blair."

Malina jerked her hand back from her holstered pistol, which she'd been about to put on. "Of course not," she said, facing the smiling nun. "Sorry. It's an instinct when I'm working."

Carr moved behind her, laying his hands on her shoulders and rubbing lightly, as if he knew how tense she felt. "We thought you were intruders when we first saw you through the window."

"It's no wonder," Andrea said, sitting beside the Sister with her own cup of tea. "The front door was unlocked.

Really, Carr. There are jewel thieves running around the island."

With a significant look, Malina glanced back at her lover and felt much, much better.

"You didn't come to church yesterday," the Sister began, her tone holding just the right amount of accusation. "I couldn't reach you on your phone all afternoon, and when I dropped by this evening, there was no answer at your door. I became concerned and went to Andrea's."

"She was convinced something horrible had happened to you," Andrea said, picking up the story. "Given yesterday's events…" She glanced briefly at Malina. "Well, I felt it was best we come check."

Carr cleared his throat. "I'm sorry to have worried you ladies. We just went for a walk on the beach."

"He got over his virus pretty quickly," Malina added, proud she could keep a straight face. "Nothing some TLC couldn't cure."

Andrea's lips twitched. "I'm so glad to hear it."

"I think I'll have some wine." Malina patted his hand. "Carr?"

"Love some. In fact, I'll help you open it." He was right behind her as she opened the fridge. "Okay, so this is all my fault," he whispered in her ear. "I was looking forward to a swim, too, you know."

Malina pulled a bottle of Pinot Grigio from the fridge. As she set the bottle on the counter, Carr handed her a corkscrew. "Did Andrea have to spill about the thefts? I didn't really have a role for a nun in my plans."

"She probably did. The Sister can be pretty persuasive."

"How quickly can we get rid of them?"

"The Sister will expect us to tell her how we're going to stop these guys."

"I thought Tyler was the sheriff."

"Sure he is."

Malina poured out two glasses of wine, then tapped hers against Carr's. "Fine. I'll bring her in." She met his gaze. "On a consultant basis only."

"We could always send her over to the SAC—that would keep her occupied."

"I'd like to actually keep my job, if you don't mind." Glancing at the Sister, Malina sipped the crisp wine. "She's kind of cute, though."

"Malina, no kidding, you can't underestimate her."

"Fear, huh?" She shifted her gaze to his, then grabbed him by the collar of his shirt and jerked him toward her. "Makes me want to be naughty."

"You've lost your mind." Still, as she nibbled at his lips, he pressed himself against her.

"No, I just feel like breaking the rules a little."

"Agent Blair," the Sister said quietly, making Carr's body jolt. "I'd very much like to hear how you're going to rid this island of its most recent criminal element."

"Yes, ma'am," Malina said, releasing Carr and reluctantly dragging her gaze away from the sexy need in his eyes. "I've got some definite ideas on how I want to handle things."

Carr groaned in her ear, stroked his hand discreetly down her backside, then they headed toward the kitchen table.

Everybody sat but Malina, who preferred to stand and occasionally pace.

She wished the sheriff could have been present, since she admired Tyler's decisiveness and she'd need him to help keep an eye on their suspects before she launched her plan. But he'd been called to duty for a case of teen-age vandalism—the local high school baseball team had stolen the rival school's pig mascot—and he had to work the interrogation before the co-conspirators—the cheerleaders—followed through on the threat to have a beach barbecue.

"My idea is relatively simple," Malina began. "Though it requires lots of bad cops and one good one." At this, she looked to Carr. He was as good as they came. And in a variety of ways.

"We confront Jack with the diamond—actually a simulated one, since the real one is on its way to Andrea's expert for analysis. I'm hoping you and your pal Billings can help with the fake, Andrea."

"Of course," she said. "We can come up with something."

Malina stared out the window, but she could see the scenario in her mind as clearly as the people in front of her. She could only hope the reality would be as effective. "We go at Jack hard and fast, busting into the office in the middle of the day, shouting about who we are, who we want, with guns drawn, Kevlar vests on every agent—the works."

"This sounds very violent," Sister Mary Katherine said, clearly wary.

"It won't be." Malina turned from the window and faced the delicate-looking nun, who probably had more spine than half the Bureau. "It's the shock of the moment that'll spook Jack Rafton. He thinks he wants to be a bad guy, but he's really only after the cash and the excitement."

"And the hot cars," Carr added.

Sister Mary Katherine nodded. "He's a lost soul."

Malina shrugged. "If you like. We interrogate Rafton at his office and pray he doesn't ask for an attorney."

"And if he does?" Carr asked.

"Then we're screw—um, out of luck. But I don't think he will at first. He'll think he can talk his way out of anything. So I push him—we know what you're up to, we know about the robbery, you'll be charged with an international felony. The Australian government, Interpol, the FBI, etc. We all want you.

"When I've got him on the ropes, then you come in, Carr." She shifted her attention directly to him. "You have to be careful not to agree to be his attorney—you don't do criminal cases, but maybe you could recommend a friend. You're just there to hold his hand."

"My favorite role," Carr returned, setting his wineglass on the table with a snap.

"But it's a critical one," Andrea said before Malina could. "You'll be his lifeline among the chaos. He'll relax and tell Malina what she needs to know." Andrea looked at Malina. "That's the goal, right? To get him to roll over on Simon."

Grateful for Andrea's support, but worried about Carr's strained expression, Malina nevertheless nodded. "That's the only chance we've got."

Carr said nothing for several minutes. He stared at the stem of his wineglass, which he turned round and round on the kitchen table. "It skirts the line of an attorney's role and allegiance. By standing with Jack, I'm implying I'm on his side."

Malina had been worried about this obstacle. After Carr's recent confessions, she didn't think he'd particularly like her tactics. But the plan had been brewing ever since she'd met Simon, or whoever he really was. He was the kind who used weaker people, over and over, while he slipped away like a snake in the night. She wanted him behind bars and his pretend lifestyle of respectability exposed.

Carr's problem was that he saw too much of himself in Jack and Simon. He saw himself as the villain. Malina was going to make it her personal mission to prove him wrong—to prove that though his decisions had caused heartache in some, his talents had changed the lives of others.

He may not have intended to do good, but he had.

"Would you rather the thieves get away with their crimes?" Malina challenged. "Maybe they'll think Palmer's Island is a nice, quiet place to set up shop permanently?"

Carr scowled at her, then directed his attention to the nun. "Sister Mary Katherine?"

Regally, the Sister nodded, then her steadfast gaze moved to Malina and held. "Do you often feel forced to lie during the course of investigating your cases, Agent Blair?"

"No," Malina said coolly. "I lie by choice in order to put people behind bars, people who corrupt and taint the lives of ordinary citizens who simply want to live free and happy. Do you have a problem with that?"

The nun blinked, probably not used to people who met her challenges head-on. But Malina believed in degrees of right and wrong, and intention was a critical element. She hoped the good Sister had some sense of that philosophy.

Finally, she linked her pale, vein-covered hands in front of her on the table. "I certainly don't. Do you think Carr is essential to your capture of these men?"

"Yes. Without him there, I'm the enemy, and he'll

clam up and hire a guy who'll tell him to keep his mouth shut while the lawyers haggle the details for days."

Andrea sighed. "And the real thief—Simon Ellerby— slips quietly away."

Malina had no intention of letting that happen, but she knew it was a possibility. "Exactly."

"Do you want to do this, Carr?" the Sister asked him.

You decided to make it your mission to beat yourself. You didn't want somebody like you coming along to subvert justice.

Malina could all but see her words from earlier zipping through his brain.

"Very much," he said.

"Then I think you should," the Sister concurred.

Carr absorbed this verdict with a nod. "Is this the plan the SAC would recommend?" he asked Malina.

"Hel—" Glancing at the nun, Malina cleared her throat. "No, I don't think so. He'd recommend watching the suspects a while longer, seeing if we can find out more about all the members of the group. Jack might not be the most vulnerable link."

"But the diamonds are gone already," Andrea said. "Or nearly are."

Malina was really starting to like that woman, even if she didn't get the whole thieves-as-friends concept. "Exactly. We don't have the luxury of surveillance and research time."

"After we confront him, Jack could run," Carr warned, who seemed to be as committed to his role as devil's advocate. "Or, worse, rat us out to Simon."

"The minute he agrees to talk, I'll put him in protective custody."

Carr lifted his eyebrows. "Won't Simon be suspicious

if Jack suddenly disappears? And if the SAC doesn't approve, how are you going to get authorization for the deal?"

"The SAC will approve," Malina insisted. *I just have to do a better job selling this to him than I am to you.* "And we'll be watching Ellerby. Losing Jack will make him panic, do something stupid, then we'll have him."

We could always send her over to the SAC, Carr had said about Sister Mary Katherine. That wasn't a half-bad idea. But the *her* Malina wanted to send wasn't the nun, but Andrea. Her expertise and neutrality would go a long way to getting Sam to approve the operation.

"If he does, then fine, I'm in." Carr rose and faced Malina. "I have one suggested change."

"Naturally."

"Get Jack to make a call to Ellerby and set up a meeting between him and me. I'll get corroborating evidence out of him."

Malina had no doubt that he could, but it wasn't him she was worried about. Okay, maybe she was. There was no way Simon wasn't a smart, dangerous guy. He'd pulled off quite a few jobs over the years. Though most thieves weren't violent, most were into burglary, not major thefts. Simon Ellerby was a different animal. "Jack couldn't pull off a call like that," she said. "He'd panic."

"His very real panic is what will make the sting work," Carr insisted. "We get him to tell Simon that he wants out. He doesn't have the nerves for the business, so he broke down and blabbed about the thefts to a colleague—me. He sets up a meeting between me and Simon. During that meeting, I offer to take Jack's place." When Malina stubbornly shook her head, he added mockingly, "If he looks at my background, he'll easily believe I could fit right in with the gang."

Malina glared at him. He was going to use his past mistakes to close this case? More punishment and retribution?

She didn't like it. Not one bit.

She felt as if agreeing would be sacrificing her lover for her job. Something she'd have done a few months ago without question. Now, the whole idea made her sick.

"He's right, Malina," Andrea said, and Malina suddenly liked her less than before. "Jack's testimony against Simon may not be enough. And what if losing Jack doesn't spook Simon into doing something stupid?"

Carr nodded. "If I could get Simon to spill details about the operation, however…"

"I don't like it." And Malina liked even less the way her gut tightened. It wasn't just the idea of a civilian going undercover with a major case on the line. She didn't want her lover caught continually in a cycle of retribution. She didn't want him thinking it was his sole duty to right this wrong. She didn't want Carr within a hundred yards of Simon Ellerby.

Sister Mary Katherine pursed her lips. "This addition to the plan does seem a little dangerous. You will be careful, won't you, Carr?"

As Carr closed the front door behind Andrea and Sister Mary Katherine, Malina rounded on him. "Were you trying to show your balls are bigger than mine or were you deliberately trying to piss me off?"

"Neither. My plan is better."

"You think a *nun* really understands the danger you'll

be in?" Malina stormed down the hall. "You think she has any idea that if you stumble over any word, phrase or gesture, Simon Ellerby could put a bullet in your head and dump you overboard from his cozy little yacht?"

Finding her anger oddly comforting, Carr followed her. "I thought you said most thieves aren't violent."

"He's not most thieves, and he'll probably have some weak-minded associate do the actual deed."

Much as that idea wasn't remotely appealing, Carr knew he had to do this. He'd dragged all of them into this mess. It was only right he be there to wrap it up. "I won't stumble."

Malina pointed at him. "Next case, Counselor, you're riding the bench."

He grabbed her by her wrist and pulled her into his arms. "Oh, so you think you'll be around beyond this case?"

"Sure. This whole thing is going to blow up in my face, and I'll be stuck here forever." She caught the spasm of hurt that crossed his face. "No offense. But nuns, neighbors with thieving friends and an idiotic insurance agent whose biggest goal in life is to be a criminal? I've lost my mind thinking this is going to work."

"You forgot the morally ambiguous attorney in your cast of characters."

She sent him a defiant stare. "You're not morally ambiguous."

Not anymore. He laid his cheek against the top of her head. The love he had for her was the reason he was fighting to get his life back. He hadn't started out knowing she was there to fight for, but now that he did, he finally understood the power of redemption.

"You shouldn't worry about me," he said. "I can

handle this. I'm an expert at charm and lies—in case you hadn't noticed."

Her toughness finally gave way, and Malina clutched him against her. "I don't want you to do it."

"But I need to do it."

"It's part of your punishment?"

"No. It's me using my talents for something good and true, something that matters." Her heart thumped against his chest, and he drew a bracing breath. She was everything. How could he not help her—and make up for the past a bit more in the process? "*He's after the cash and the excitement,* you said earlier. I was Jack Rafton."

"Oh, please. You've never been that weak and stupid."

"I need to do this."

She said nothing for a moment. Then, "I'm going with you to meet with Simon." When he frowned, she added, "You're an expert at charm and lies. You'll think of an excuse for me—or rather Sandy—to tag along. There's no way you're doing this without backup."

"I hadn't planned to, but I was thinking I'd wear a wire and you'd be listening in, ready to burst onto the scene, armed and dangerous, if things got dicey."

"I'll be with you, and a team of agents will be ready to burst onto the scene."

"Fine," he said, though the idea that she would also be in danger didn't exactly thrill him.

Her job, however, involved considerable risk, and if he wanted to be with her, he was going to have to get used to that idea.

"Oh, good. We're even. How about a swim to burn off that tension?"

His whole body went hard. "You fight dirty."

She slid her cheek across his chest, then sank her teeth, ever so lightly, into his earlobe. "I know you're committed to the straight and narrow these days, but I bet you can remember how that works."

In answer, he swung her into his arms, strode out the back door and dumped her into the pool.

He knelt on the smooth stone deck as she popped to the surface, spitting water from her mouth and rubbing it from her eyes. "Come to think of it," he said, reaching out to stroke her cheek. "I do remember how to fight dirty."

Naturally, she jerked him in.

By the time he found his feet, she'd already shed her sopping clothes and was plowing through the water making laps.

Naturally, he chased her.

He caught her and dragged her to the shallow end next to the waterfall that flowed over the rock formation that was part of the pool area landscaping.

Their verbal battle had heightened his need, which he'd once considered impossible with Malina. In addition, a bone-deep fear of the upcoming plan had settled into his bones. Logically, he knew she could handle herself, but love wasn't reasonable.

Caging her against the side of the pool, he moved his mouth over her slick skin, glorying in the way she clutched him against her body. She angled her head, giving him better access to the delicate skin between her neck and shoulders.

With her help, he managed to peel off his clothes. Thankfully, the vacuum-packed condoms had fared better than his pants and shirt.

He teased her, pressing at the entrance of her body,

and she moaned, grasping his hips. How long she'd need him was uncertain, but all he had was the moment.

Knowing he couldn't hold her forever, he pushed inside her, and she gasped, meeting his rhythm, and the panic of losing her burst through him with sudden intensity. Why couldn't this go on? Why couldn't she stay?

Why wouldn't she love him?

Her body tensed, and he forced his dread aside. He sought only pleasure now—hers and his.

What else did he have?

"You don't trust your own judgment anymore?" Malina asked him as they sat, wrapped in a blanket, on the sofa beside the outdoor fireplace a while later. "You have to ask the Sister?"

He kissed her temple, breathing in the clean, refreshing scent of her hair. "Not in some cases."

"I think that's stupid."

Leave it to Malina to not hold back. "It's not."

She craned her neck around to stare at him. "I'm also not crazy about you confronting Simon."

"I've been there from the beginning—even before you arrived, by the way. You won't deny me the reward of seeing this through to the end."

"You're not a trained agent. You could get hurt."

Smiling, he asked. "Worried about me?"

"Yes."

"I can handle myself."

"Doesn't mean there's not a risk."

He stroked her cheek, taking great pleasure from the concerned look in her eyes. "I need this, Malina. You know I do."

"Fine," she said, turning back toward the fire.

"Are your parents proud of you?"

She glanced briefly. "That's some segue."

"Sorry. I'm a little rough around the edges lately." As happy as she made him, in some ways he felt as if his life were falling apart, bit by bit, and while he recognized what was happening, he had no way to stop its progression. "Are they?"

"I guess. Yes," she admitted, somewhat reluctantly it seemed. "They don't really understand why I do what I do, but they support me."

"What do they do?"

"They run a surf shop."

For some reason, that made him smile. He'd imagined Malina with stern, exacting parents. "No kidding?"

"My mom paints, too. I've tried to get her showings in a gallery in Honolulu, but she doesn't think anybody would be interested in her work."

"So, she's…"

"The complete opposite of me, yes. She has zero ambition beyond keeping a leaky roof over her head. She wouldn't know a pistol from a crossbow, or a con man from a tourist in flowered shorts. Who are sometimes the same person," she added drily.

The exasperated affection in her voice was so normal, so lovely, so completely different from his feelings about his own parents, it made Carr's smile broaden.

"They wanted more kids," she continued, "but it never happened for them. These days, they bring in foster kids, which, on Kauai, usually turn out to be lost college students on spring break. Are your parents proud of you?"

"I have absolutely no idea."

That had her turning her whole body around to face him.

Faced with that forceful gaze, he had a hard time pulling off a casual shrug. "They think I was crazy to leave Manhattan and come here."

"Didn't they raise you here?"

"No, my grandmother did. She passed away when I was in college."

"You weren't raised by your parents," she said slowly, as if needing clarification.

"They never planned to have a child. My mother had family money, so they've always moved around Europe and the Caribbean."

Pinched annoyance drew her brows together. "They abandoned you."

He kissed away the wrinkles. "I was better off, believe me. But genetics do tell occasionally, so I'm assuming that's where I get my selfishness."

"A soulless, money-grubbing uncle and idiotic, narcissistic parents. How'd you turn out so great?"

He leaned in, nibbling at her lips. "You think I'm great?"

She laid her hand in the center of his chest, pressing him back. "Seriously, that's a pretty sucky childhood."

"Was it? I grew up in paradise and was raised by a woman who loved me. I always had the beach, friends, and plenty of material things."

"But, essentially, you were alone."

"True. You were, too. Do you feel deprived?"

"No." She sighed. "Though there were moments of teenage rebellion and back talk that I'm sure my parents wouldn't be too anxious to revisit. We were talking about you."

"Actually, we initially began the discussion about you and whether or not your parents are proud of you. So we seem to have come full circle. Want to share some more childhood trauma?"

"Not really, no."

"You sure you don't want to talk about when you decided that bow marksmanship was preferable to waxing surfboards?"

"Look, Counselor, you're the one with damaged moral issues. And, can I add that you're a lot more forthcoming when we're having sex?"

He moved his lips across her feather-soft cheek. "Oh, that can be easily arranged."

She pressed her finger into his chest. "The question is, why did you bring it up?"

"Sex? I always—"

"No, your parents."

"Starved for conversation?"

"Ha! You're never at a loss for words, at least not until yesterday."

It was his turn to sigh. "I find myself having a hard time just now."

"Well, stop it."

"Okay." With that fierce blue gaze boring into his, how could he not? With her warmth so close and accessible, how could he let the past turn him cold?

"Though you're liable to use my words at some point to boost an ego that already seems inherently healthy, hear this, Carr Hamilton." She held him in her sights as surely as any target at the end of her pistol, and her voice was as hard and true as any bullet. "You're a good man. And though your parents may be idiots and your grandmother gone and your moral advisor a bit too committed to black and white, I need you. I've needed your help with this case. I've needed you to introduce me to your sort-of-law-abiding friends. And I've especially needed you to challenge me and remind me of what's at stake."

With that pronouncement, she wrapped her arms around him and hugged him tightly against her.

"Glad to be there," he managed to say gruffly into her hair.

The one person's approval he wanted, he had. What else was there?

The future would come, and choices would be made, but right now he had it all—the way he dreamed he might if he changed his life for the better.

"You're taking a big chance," he said a few minutes later, "moving on Jack like this."

"Sure, but my way is the only way, remember?" She leaned back and planted a firm kiss on his lips. "Besides, I'm tired of playing it safe. I may even wear a red suit."

12

"COME ON, Rafton." Malina spoke harshly, shaking her head as she stood in front of the terrified insurance agent. "We know you're in this up to your greedy, bloodshot eyeballs."

"I—" Jack Rafton cast a panicked glance around his office, where several armed FBI agents, sheriff's deputies and crime-scene techs were milling around, talking in low tones while they either studied him or gathered evidence in plastic bags and packed up all his computer equipment. "You're wrong."

"Judge North feels differently," Malina said, waving the search warrant.

"Y-you could be bluffing."

"Could be." Malina laid her hand deliberately on the butt of her gun. "But I'm not."

"But I—"

"Do you honestly think that I'd bring my team in here without cause? You think the Bureau is just sitting around, waiting to pounce on private businesses 'cause we got nothin' better to do? We have terrorists to hunt. And, yet, we came in here, armed and ready, bulletproof vests in place, because we know you've hooked up with some seriously bad dudes. We were ready to shoot if provoked." Malina lurched forward, bracing her hands on the desk chair where he sat. "Do you have plans to provoke me, Jack?"

"N-no."

"I understand you've got a nice island here, lovely vacation spot. How do you think your fellow citizens are going to feel when word gets out that you've brought these thieving scumbags to their shores?"

"Agent Blair," Carr said, his tone disappointed, "you said you'd keep this matter quiet."

"And I will." Never looking Carr's way, she sent Rafton a glare. "As long as I get what I want."

"B-but…" Rafton blustered. "I have rights. Don't I have rights, Carr?"

Carr laid his hand on the other man's shoulder and returned Malina's glare. "Of course you do."

"Please, Hamilton." Malina rolled her eyes, and though they'd agreed to this plan of action it still bothered her to see the hurt briefly cross Carr's face. "Don't give me any of that bleeding-heart crap."

Carr had offered moral support, not legal representation, but it was clear Rafton relied upon his judgment anyway. Malina had a team of agents watching Simon Ellerby to make sure he was on his yacht and wouldn't pop in to find one of his compatriots was being interrogated by the cops and thereby ruin the operation. Everything was moving along as they'd anticipated. If only they could drive Jack to the edge where he'd turn on his boss.…

"We know about the Lotus, Rafton." Malina shook her head as if disappointed. "Pretty reckless. Didn't you go to any of those helpful classes at the last Smugglers International Convention?"

"I'm not a smuggler!" he squeaked.

"Oh, yeah?" Malina pointed at the landscape painting on the wall beside his bookcases. "What's that?"

Rafton turned sheet-white, and Malina's heart jumped. It had been a wild stab, but after Carr's observations of the crates coming off the boat, plus Andrea's speculation that Rafton had to be passing over more than diamonds, Malina had begun to wonder just how long the list of stolen goods was liable to wind up being.

"Well, well," Malina chortled, pacing around him. "The gang's just floating in illicit merchandise."

"There's no gang," Rafton said desperately. "I didn't steal any diamonds—or paintings. I don't know what you're talking about."

"Be smart, Jack," Carr said in a low, soothing tone. "If any of this is true, your cooperation could go a long way to keeping you out of federal prison."

"Prison!" Rafton jerked to his feet. "You're out of your mind! I'm not going to prison."

Malina leaned back against the desk and made an effort to look bored. "Sure seems that way to me." She paused significantly. "But then it's not you we want."

"Who then?"

Approaching him, Malina stopped mere inches away. "Simon Ellerby."

Based on Rafton's reaction, she decided—though she'd already suspected—that the insurance agent would make a lousy poker player.

She angled her head. "Listen, Jack, you don't have the stones for this. You're drowning. And when we offer a deal to Ellerby, you can bet he'll jump on it and screw you to the wall."

Rafton drew his shoulders back. "I have no idea who you're talking about."

"You went to a party on his yacht last week," Carr interjected.

"No kidding?" Malina forced surprise. "Isn't that interesting? What exactly went on at this party?"

Rafton winced. "Carr, please."

Carr shrugged. "You can't pretend you don't know him, Jack. Lying to the federal authorities isn't going to help the situation."

They worked him for more than an hour, but he simply alternated between panic and denial.

He admitted nothing.

Malina took to clenching the butt of her pistol. Her finger twitched many times toward the trigger, and she silently recited federal penal codes as a way of distracting her from her instincts to break ninety-nine percent of those codes.

While Rafton bent his head, Carr, who stood just behind him, looked at Malina and lifted his eyebrows.

Time for the secret weapon.

Since she could hear the words as clearly as if he'd spoken them aloud, she scowled.

But what choice did she have? Moving quickly on Ellerby was essential.

She turned away from the two men and started out of the room. "Mr. Hamilton, get your friend a glass of water. I'll be back."

Outside in the bright sunshine, a brisk wind whipping off the Atlantic, Malina walked to her car, parked at the curb. The idea had come to Carr in the middle of the night—he'd literally woken Malina up out of a dead sleep to give her this last, fail-safe tactic.

If the dog-napping case had given her office ridicule, she couldn't wait to find out what humiliation this latest, unconventional strategy was going to bring.

As she opened the passenger side door, she noted the woman inside was knitting, gathering together strands of blue and green yarn from opposite sides of her lap. "We're going to need you."

Sister Mary Katherine glanced up, her expression calm as she nodded and set her yarn aside. "I anticipated as much. Jack was in Sister Agatha's Sunday studies during high school, and she assured me he was an attentive student."

"Yeah, he's a prince, all right," Malina said as she helped the nun out of the car.

Sister Mary Katherine pursed her lips. "The Church can redeem everyone who's lost, everyone willing to change their life."

"As Carr will undoubtedly attest."

"Are you angry with me, Agent Blair?" the Sister asked as they headed toward the office door.

"No. No, of course not," Malina added, barely suppressing a wince. She wasn't exactly religious, but she had great respect for those who willingly devoted their lives to the greater good. "I just—" She stopped and whirled to face the nun. "Carr's a good man." She flung her hand in the direction of the office. "He's not Jack Rafton or anyone in his gang. He tried to help people. Is he a criminal because he made a lot of money?"

The nun folded her hands in front of her. "No one said he was a criminal."

"But he thinks he is!" When a couple of guys who were hauling computer equipment from Rafton's office paused on the sidewalk, Malina ground down on her temper. "I don't appreciate you, or anybody else, putting him down."

"You are angry."

She was. At least part of her. She knew the good Sister wasn't the villain here, but she didn't appreciate anybody who didn't see Carr's need to help others. And she wasn't exactly sure where Sister Mary Katherine stood. "Do you know his parents abandoned him?"

"I do."

That wasn't a surprise really. It was a small island after all. But the sadness in the nun's eyes took Malina aback. Her vision of nuns was tough love and rulers smacking on knuckles. Clearly a stereotype that wasn't worthy of the woman before her.

How many times had Malina busted stereotypes of snipers and marksmen? *Ahem, women.*

Well, hell, she and the Sister had something in common.

Okay, maybe not hell, exactly.

"He's not morally ambiguous," Malina asserted, still uncertain where the Sister stood regarding Carr.

"Well, no." The Sister laid one hand over her heart. "He's the exact opposite. At least now. There was a time…"

Malina pressed her lips together to keep from shouting. "Do you honestly think the people he won cases for cared about his motives for helping them?"

"I have no idea. But *he* cares about his motives. Carr feels the need to make up for his past." Sister Mary Katherine held up her hand to forestall Malina's interruption. "Whether or not it's required by you, me or anyone else doesn't matter. This is something he's compelled to do."

"Something you encouraged him to do," Malina insisted.

"My only goal over the last two years has been to help him find a way back to his roots and the reason he started off for the glories of city in the first place."

Well, hel—er, dang. The Sister knew what she was about, and it was very clear she had deep affection for Carr. "To prove to his parents that he was worth something," Malina said on a sigh.

"You understand him so well."

"Same goes."

"Frankly, I could use four dozen exactly like him."

"Me, too."

Sister Mary Katherine reached out and grasped Malina's hand in her own. "I've been trying to soothe his soul, but you've healed him."

Malina found the sensation of holding the nun's vein-covered hand disconcerting, but she felt pulling away would insult her. "Oh, ah, well, I don't know about that."

The Sister's face broke in a wide smile. "How lovely."

Malina glanced behind her, and the Sister laughed. "Me? How?"

"That's not what I meant—though you're very attractive and have remarkable eyes. I meant how lovely that you don't yet realize how much you mean to him."

"Who?"

"Carr. He's in love with you."

There was absolutely no answer to that absurd statement.

Sister Mary Katherine tilted her face upward and kissed her cheek, a surprising gesture that brought a glow to Malina's heart. "You'll see. Now, should we go take care of this thieving ring?"

In a fog, Malina led her to the door. Carr loved her?

No. No way. They were having a simple, fun affair, which was bound to end when she was transferred back to FBI headquarters in Quantico, back to the excitement of Washington where she belonged. The good Sister might know her Bible verses and soul-soothing, but she was completely off base about this conclusion.

Wasn't she?

While Malina pondered the implications, she led the nun into Rafton's office. She had no idea if this "secret weapon" plan would work, but she figured they had nothing to lose by trying.

Sister Mary Katherine walked serenely toward their suspect, who immediately stiffened. "Jack, I think we should talk."

AS HER COFFEE MUG CLANGED against the others, Malina smiled. "He cracked like the proverbial egg."

Andrea nodded. "The Sister has always had a way about her."

"Her way," Tyler asserted.

Carr sipped from his mug. "Which has worked, by the way."

Sometimes Malina worried that those three were just a bit off center, but since the SAC had complimented her operation and had approved laying a trap for Simon Ellerby, she wasn't about to criticize her investigative team, as unconventional as they might be.

They'd gathered at Andrea and Tyler's house, just down the beach from Carr. Like Carr's place, the back side of the house was mostly windows, but the design and decor were completely different. The modern steel and cool colors were replaced by shades of gold and wood floors, and the curves became more angular and traditional.

The resulting effect was more casual and homey, but Malina greatly preferred Carr's house. Because it was both welcoming and lonely? Or simply because it belonged to him?

She was fighting not to think about Sister Mary Katherine's assertion on Carr's feelings for her. Part of her wanted to panic; part of her wanted to smile.

The rest of her knew she was completely out of her element for the first time in her life.

"So, this ends on Wednesday?" Andrea asked.

Malina nodded. "Based on Jack's information, another shipment of stolen gems—emeralds this time—is coming in early Wednesday morning. After Jack makes his panicked call to his leader, we'll intercept the gems and take them to Simon Ellerby. Ellerby will be forced to deal with us because we have the merchandise."

"Which we'll part with for a small handling fee," Carr added.

"The whole exchange will be recorded by the FBI, who'll be holed up in a van in the marina parking lot." Malina saw twenty different ways the plan could go wrong, but it was still the best opportunity they had. "The merchandise exchange and Jack's testimony will be enough to make an arrest."

"So you'll have Rafton and Ellerby," Andrea said. "But what about the rest of the gang? There are more than two people involved in this operation."

"Oh, we'll get Ellerby to tell us about them. He'll never go down alone. His ego's too lofty."

Andrea looked doubtful that everything would be so simple.

Carr laid his hand over Malina's. "She's pretty fierce in an interview. I don't think getting Ellerby to rat out a few colleagues will be much of a stretch."

Malina shifted toward him and let her gaze linger on his. "We all have our little gifts."

"Great." Tyler stood. "The island will be safe for nuns, children and democracy. Who's up for video games?"

Since Andrea and Carr simply exchanged a silent glance, and Malina had been on this end of one of Tyler's abrupt segues before, she felt it was up to her to ask, "Ah…what?"

Tyler clapped his hands together and headed toward the living room. "Video games. You know, preloaded disks, plastic controllers, simulated action on a TV screen."

"Uh-huh." Sipping coffee, Malina leaned back in her chair. "You guys have fun with that."

"You don't know how to play, do you?" Andrea asked, clearly amused.

"I don't play video games," Malina said, barely resisting a sneer.

Carr cleared his throat.

Knowing he was thinking of the shooting range, Malina glared at him. "I don't play. I train."

"How disappointing," Andrea said as she rose to follow her husband. "Tyler was bragging the other day about this military mission game, and how he could totally kick your butt on it."

Malina flicked a glance at the woman she'd been bordering on considering an actual friend. "Are you trying to distract me from the semidangerous operation that'll take place in less than two days, or are you seriously challenging me?"

Andrea spun, moving her head right, then left. Her blond ponytail swung with each twitch. "Both."

Malina set aside her mug. "I've killed people cuter than you, you know."

"Oh, yeah?" Andrea pulled a plastic pistol—eerily similar to the ones Malina used at the driving range—from a box beside the TV. "Let's see it."

Between her and Tyler's skill and wildly competitive instincts, the game was the most fun Malina had had in a very long time. She didn't relax often. She worked, she thought about work, she slept, ate, then worked again. She couldn't remember the last time she'd done something so normal as play video games. She'd never do this in Washington. She had no friends to play with.

"You're very scary," Carr said as they left via the back door and headed down the beach toward his house.

"The Bureau has an excellent training program."

"And very hot."

"Only for you, Counselor." Grinning, Malina hugged him to her side. "Now let's nail these jerks."

WHEN CARR and Malina stepped aboard Ellerby's boat, the yacht captain was considerably less hospitable than he'd been the first time.

Gone was the mask of the charming party host. In its place was the cold-blooded criminal Carr knew he really was. He'd lost control of his operation, and he wasn't happy about it.

"I thought we agreed you'd come alone," Ellerby said, his annoyed gaze scraping the blonde and disguised Malina.

"Did we?" Making an effort to stay calm and not let

Ellerby's attempt at control rattle him, Carr smiled. "I notice you're not alone either."

Two beefy guys stood a few feet away, looking as if they'd like nothing better than to start the morning with a murder or two.

Carr was counting on both the busy marina and Malina's expert assurance that thieves were generally not killers—except out of panic.

Ellerby wasn't *most* thieves, but if he was panicked, he was hiding the emotion very skillfully.

Their suspect extended his arm to invite them to sit at a small table that was set up on the rear deck of the yacht.

Bold egomaniac.

The FBI's assessment of Ellerby's character was dead-on. Most people conducting an exchange of money and stolen property might do so under the cover of darkness, or at least inside the cabin. Even Jack had made his deals late at night.

Either Ellerby had more ego than sense, or he'd simply been a criminal for so long he'd forgotten his business was completely illegal.

As Ellerby pulled out a chair for Malina, his gaze lingered on her trim, sun-darkened body, encased in a yellow tennis dress. Though Malina smiled brightly at their host, she hadn't been thrilled with Carr's wardrobe choice, but he'd assured her the exposure of her legs was just the sort of distraction they could use.

The dress's short length also meant Carr had to carry her backup pistol strapped to his ankle, which certainly annoyed her more than flashing a lot of skin.

Ellerby sat opposite Carr and next to Malina at the table. "Much as I enjoyed your company at my party, I must admit your call came as a rude shock."

Carr nodded. "I can assure you Jack's blubbering confession about being involved in a major diamond theft provided me the same response."

Ellerby's lip curled in a sneer. "Jack has no appreciation for the subtleties of business."

"You've got a sweet setup here," Carr commented, glancing around.

"Yes, well…" Ellerby's gaze again drifted toward the lovely blonde Malina. "Due to recent events, I'm afraid I'll be moving on soon."

"You're not afraid Jack will go to the cops?" Carr asked.

"And say what?" A hint of a smile appeared on Ellerby's lips. "He has a handful of stones he's trying to liquidate? No, I'm well insulated."

Unfortunately for Ellerby, what he didn't know was that yesterday afternoon, his contact at the diamond mine had been arrested by Australian authorities and was even now spilling all kinds of details about Ellerby's connection.

The FBI was still tracing back the emerald theft that was the source of today's exchange, but when the middle of a structure started to crumble, the rest couldn't be far behind.

"Smart," Carr said.

In response to the compliment, Ellerby merely inclined his head.

Carr had known getting him to talk wouldn't be easy, but he'd anticipated a bit more bragging. Certainly the FBI listening via the recorder Malina was wearing was hoping the same thing. He also noted that the other man kept his hands out of sight, probably folded in his lap. Body language, hands specifically, revealed emotions.

He glanced at Malina to see she was playing her role as vapid girlfriend and simply staring at Ellerby as if he'd recently hung the moon. The devoted look on her face was frankly disturbing.

"As we discussed on the phone," Carr said to Ellerby, "I'm here to merely help out a friend who's gotten into a situation he's unable to handle."

"Yet you expect to be paid for this favor."

Carr nodded. "Naturally. I'm well paid for my expertise in handling troubling situations."

"You have an impressive track record in court."

"Products liability is a lucrative if somewhat mundane field."

"Oddly enough, though, the last few years you've taken on the peculiar challenge of defending churches."

Carr made an effort to look embarrassed. "Yes, well, I got involved in a few projects that weren't altogether legitimate. I thought I ought to lay low for a while. And consulting is both profitable and mostly effortless."

The ease with which Carr slipped into the role of the bored, depraved lawyer made his stomach tighten. After all this time, had he really changed? Was he any different from Simon Ellerby, profiting from the effort and suffering of others?

Malina, as if she guessed his thoughts, distracted him by laying her hand on his thigh. "Baby, are you going to talk boring business all day? You said I could have an emerald."

He let her warmth infuse him. What would he ever do without her? "Of course you can, darling. Let me work out the details, okay?"

As they'd hoped, the idea of selling them one of the gems pleased Simon. The transaction would draw them firmly into the illegality of the operation—they wouldn't tattle to the cops because they were guilty, too.

"Beautiful women are often high maintenance, aren't they?" Ellerby commented.

Malina's fingers dug into Carr's leg, and he picked up her hand, bringing it to his lips. "They're worth it."

Judging by the lightning-quick gleam in Malina's eyes, Carr knew he'd pay for that quip later. Even if it was in character.

With his other hand, Carr reached into his pants pocket and pulled out a small jeweler's pouch, which he dropped in front of Malina. "Pick the one you want." Carr shifted his gaze to Ellerby. "Unless you have a preference, Simon?"

Seemingly indulgent, Ellerby leaned back in his chair. "Be my guest."

With an expression of pure joy, Malina spread the bag's contents on the table. The glittering green stones looked unreal, spread out at random like pieces dumped from a children's board game.

Malina oohed and aahed over several of them, showing each one in turn to Carr. As the indulgent lover, Carr encouraged her to choose the largest, which appeared to be nearly five carats.

Ellerby happily provided a jeweler's loupe for both him and Carr to examine each stone more closely. They haggled back and forth on the price of the stone for "Sandy," then about the transfer fee to give Ellerby the merchandise.

Business complete, Malina leaned toward their suspect, drawing her finger down his forearm. "Did you really steal all these beautiful emeralds?"

Carr's heart slammed against his ribs. That wasn't part of the plan. She was trying to get a confession and cement the case.

Ellerby went statue-still for the space of two of those heartbeats. "Better. I had somebody else do it."

"Wow." Malina's eyes sparked. "That's so cool, isn't it, baby?" she said, rising from her chair, then shifting to Carr's lap. "Thank you for my pretty emerald."

While Carr was fighting the instinctive arousal he always experienced when Malina touched him, she was making a big production out of kissing his cheek and stroking his chest.

With her other hand, however, she was reaching down his leg for the pistol holstered at his ankle.

Almost casual, she rose and turned, pointing the weapon at Ellerby. "FBI. You're under arrest."

In a way, it was all rather anticlimactic.

"Come on, Ellerby," Malina said, her own, commanding voice in full effect instead of the role she'd been playing. "Hands up."

True to the order, Ellerby pulled his hands from under the table and lifted them. In the right one, he held a snub-nosed revolver.

Which he pointed, not at Malina, but Carr.

"You don't want to do that," Malina said calmly, taking a step toward Ellerby before Carr could do anything other than blink.

Ellerby's eyes flashed cold as ice. "Oh, yes, I do. And if you move another step closer, I'm shooting him."

Malina's hot stare seemed to burn right through Ellerby. Then, for a second, she shifted her aim to the guards, who were reaching into their jackets, presumably for weapons. "Don't even think about it."

They ignored her warning, but before they could fully draw their guns, Malina fired off two shots and both men went down.

The whole exchange hadn't taken more than ten seconds.

"You want to try me, Ellerby?" Malina asked, her even-toned voice nevertheless threatening.

True concern crossed the thief's face for the first time. He'd clearly underestimated her.

His hesitation was all Malina needed. She kicked the revolver out of his hand, then jerked him from the chair and forced him to lie facedown on the deck.

Carr rushed over to help her put cuffs on Ellerby, then hauled their prisoner to his feet. Resentfully staring at them, Ellerby groaned in disgust. "A damn blonde bimbo and a puffed-up lawyer."

"Come heavy," Malina said into the watch on her wrist, communicating with the team that had been waiting and listening from a van in the marina parking lot.

"Heavy?" Carr asked.

"You'll see."

Moments later, Carr heard heavy footsteps on the gangway, then a group of agents, dressed in black fatigues and helmets, guns drawn, stormed onto the deck.

Simon Ellerby fainted.

Smiling, Malina jerked off her wig and pushed the thief into the waiting arms of a colleague.

His heart racing both with pride and leftover adrenaline, Carr stared at her. "Thieves aren't violent, huh?"

"He panicked." When Carr continued to gape silently, she added, "He didn't shoot you, did he?"

13

Much to Malina's surprise, less than a week later, the call from D.C. came.

They wanted her back at headquarters in Quantico ASAP, and Carr took her to The Night Heron marina bar to celebrate.

Andrea and Tyler came, as well as Sloan and Aidan Kendrick. Even Sister Mary Katherine stopped by briefly to congratulate her before heading back to the rectory. Carr seemed to be the only one who wasn't in a party mood.

For the past several days they'd lived in an insulated world of accomplishment and blissful satisfaction, and now the bubble had burst.

Malina kept telling herself she was thrilled about the transfer, but part of her was determined to mourn. Carr was a remarkable man, and Palmer's Island felt like a real home for the first time since she'd left Hawaii. She was surrounded by both nature's beauty and people who had carved out their very own slice of heaven.

But her work was her life, and the only way to advance her career was to go back to Washington. She wanted to run the Bureau someday, didn't she?

And yet she only knew two things for certain—she wanted to go, but she didn't want to leave. Since those two states completely contradicted each other, she was pretty well screwed.

Glancing around the table at the people who'd so quickly become trusted friends, dread settled in her stomach. She didn't want to break the bonds she'd made.

But the Bureau would demand a psych evaluation if she turned down this transfer to stay in piddly Palmer's Island.

Plus, in a whole different area of concern, she was desperately trying to convince herself she wasn't turning into her mother.

They were nothing alike. Malina didn't compromise her dreams for men. She wasn't about to settle for ordinary assignments and waste her considerable skills.

She and Carr were only having a fling. The intense feelings would pass—on both sides. Sister Mary Katherine and her vision of love was just that—a hallucination.

But will your skills make you happy?

Carr had spent years using his, and the results made him miserable. Could she really go back to playing the hated game of politics? Had anything really changed except the Bureau's favor?

She glanced at Carr sitting next to her, his thigh pressed against hers as they sat in the booth. He immediately slid his hand over hers, bringing her wrist to his lips, where he pressed a gentle kiss.

But there was no hiding the anxiety in his eyes.

"So, Malina, the bad guys are all safely locked up?"

Sloan Kendrick asked, reaching for another helping of the hot wings in the center of the table.

Focusing on the question instead of Carr's brooding expression, Malina nodded. "The judge even denied Ellerby bail. With his resources and connections, he's considered a major flight risk."

"And the stolen goods?" Andrea asked.

"We found both Jack and Ellerby with paintings, sculptures and gems in their homes, boats and warehouses," Malina said. "We think we've gotten most of the items except the diamonds. There were several that had already been sold to distributors. We're still running them down, but we're not hopeful they'll ever be recovered."

"Are those two goons really threatening to sue the FBI for police brutality?" Tyler asked, looking amused.

Malina snorted a laugh. "I glanced their shoulders. They're lucky to be walking. Drawing down on a federal cop isn't wise."

"I believe you were wearing a skimpy tennis dress at the time, Agent Blair," Aidan pointed out. When Malina's pleased expression turned to a scowl, he added, "But they're obviously sore losers."

Carr squeezed her hand. "She was amazing."

Tyler grinned. "I, for one, admire your accuracy. Sure you don't want to hang around the island and help me scare off the riffraff?"

The casual question evoked an odd response. Every gaze at the table whipped to Carr.

"I belong in Washington," Malina found herself saying after an uncomfortable silence.

Completely contrary to her fearless facade, though, she didn't look at Carr as she said the words.

"Come with me," Malina said to Carr when they were alone in his car—the party pretty much breaking up after her confirmation that she was leaving.

Carr kept a tight hold on her hand, but his gaze was directed at the steering wheel. "I can't."

Her heart lurched. She'd been too impulsive. She'd pushed this too far, too soon. A fling, right? Hadn't she told herself a thousand times that's what this was? Why would he—

"I lost my soul in the city," he said before she could finish her thought. His tortured gaze found hers. "Now that I've found it again, I can't ever go back to that life."

Pulse pounding, she turned toward him, laying her hand alongside his jaw. "Washington isn't Manhattan. It won't be the same. I'll be there for one."

To her heartbreak, he shook his head. "You didn't know me before. You don't understand. I won't be able to resist making connections, working the system."

"It won't be the same," she repeated, though she saw the resignation in his eyes and knew her plea wouldn't help. She even understood why.

He hugged her against his side, as much as the gearbox in the center console would allow. "I was both terrified and hopeful you'd ask this question, but my answer is no. I can't leave this island."

She tucked her head against his shoulder. Their feelings weren't strong enough to make this last. She hadn't done enough to nurture their relationship, and she was choosing advancing her career over his sanity, after all.

But there was one thing she had to know. "Do you love me?"

"Very much," he said without hesitation. "But if I go back, I won't be a man worthy of love."

She wasn't sure a heart could literally break in two, but hers did anyway.

She wanted to tell him she'd stay with him, that she loved him in return, but everything inside her was at war. Her past and present; her career and her life.

"I don't know what I want," she said, knowing she could give him nothing less than her absolute honesty. "I've never loved anybody but my parents. I don't know how it's supposed to feel."

He pressed his mouth against her cheek. "I could give you a demonstration."

SHE LEFT in the early morning, leaving him sleeping in the bed they'd shared the past few weeks.

Leaving the house he'd built, which was so much a part of him, both traditional and modern, warm and cool, past and present, was nearly as hard as slipping from between the sheets and abandoning his body warmth for the unknown future.

She went home.

What choice did she have? Who else could give her answers? Where else could she reflect on her options and choices?

She found her island birthplace the same as always—tourists taking Zodiac raft trips around the cliffs, the annoying buzz of helicopter tours overhead and her parents, welcoming her with open arms, then handing her a surfboard.

Since it was March, the end of winter surf season, the north shore was full of tourists, locals and professionals alike. But, typically, after three days absorbed in the mundane task of renting boards and teaching vacationers to ride the waves, Malina grew restless.

And, though she rarely smiled, her mother telling her she should smile through her sorrow was becoming annoying.

Late in the afternoon of her fourth day home, she walked alone on the beach, watched the deep blue Pacific surf crash against rock and sand, all the while wishing she was at another beach, on another coast and certainly not alone.

Her and Carr's end had been inevitable.

Yet, there were parts of her that were screaming about what a horrible choice she was about to make. Instead of hiding in the bushes, she should be drawing her weapon and firing. Moving forward instead of going back.

"If you wanted to run, you should go over to the track at the high school."

Stopping, Malina turned to see her mother rushing to catch up to her. "I'm not running."

"You're walking too fast to catch all this," her mom said, gesturing at the beauty around them.

"I see it."

Breathing hard, her mom finally reached her. "Do you?"

They were as opposite as night and day—Malina with her dark Thai coloring and her mother's sunny California beauty. Where Malina was edgy, her mother was calm.

Only their eyes were the same. What did her mom see that Malina didn't?

"I met a man in South Carolina," she began abruptly.

"I figured as much."

"You did?"

"Only love can put a look like yours on a woman's face."

Malina cleared her throat. She wasn't sure what to say to that. "Yeah, well, if I accept this transfer, I'll leave him behind. Didn't you say you always regretted giving up Paris and staying with Dad and the surf shop?"

"No, I didn't."

"But—"

Her mom grabbed her hand. "I told you about giving up Paris because I wanted you to think hard about your decision to leave home, to realize that certain life choices can change your path forever, and I didn't want you to feel obligated to stay in a place you obviously longed to escape. I've never regretted my decision. I wanted you to have that same peace."

Peace. Malina was sure she'd never find the same state of mind.

"Besides, my paintings look better on the walls around me than in fancy city galleries. Why do I want to work that hard for someone else's pleasure?"

"A woman shouldn't give up her career for a man," Malina insisted.

Her mom shrugged and hooked her arm around Malina's. "Why not? You break up with a man who makes you unhappy. Why shouldn't you keep one who does?"

"It's not that simple."

"Sure it is. Do you love him?"

"I suppose so."

"Ah, Malina." Her mother shook her head. "You don't suppose anything. You *know.*"

Malina stopped and sighed, staring at the retreating waves against the shore. "Yes, I love him." Nothing else could be causing this crazy mixture of pain and pleasure. "But I asked him to come to D.C. with me. He refused."

"Because of you, or because of something within himself?"

How had her mother gotten so wise and perceptive? Artist equaled psychic apparently. "Because of him."

"And Washington is the only place you can serve justice?"

Serve justice. Leave it to her mother to romanticize the FBI, a feat previously thought impossible. "It's the only place I'll move up in the Bureau."

"Do you really want to sit in an office and run the place? No, Malina, you'd be miserable."

"But I want more than..." She trailed off, knowing her thoughts were disrespectful.

"Spending your life managing a beach shop? Oh, honey, there has to be a middle ground between FBI director and surfing instructor."

As she said it, Malina smiled, feeling silly. "Sure there is." And she'd been there for years, but that hadn't made her happy either. Being with Carr, feeling his hand squeezing hers as they walked the beach, as they challenged each other, debated and made love—that had been happiness. "Why can't ambition and love co-incide?" she asked on a sigh.

"They can. The FBI isn't the only place you can right wrongs."

"Leave the Bureau entirely?"

Her mom put her arm around her waist. "You come from a long line of entrepreneurs. Work for yourself. Do what you want, rise as high as you desire instead of going where they send you."

"I could do security consulting," Malina said slowly,

the idea taking on shape and appeal. "That mayor could stand to update his equipment and procedures."

"Sounds like a career to me."

Was her mom right? Was she holding on to false perception? Why was she so determined to look at her mom's decision to give up art school and stay on the island for love as a mistake she'd never make?

Was she really giving up anything? Maybe, instead, she was choosing love over another path.

As for seeing Palmer's Island as mundane, that perception was also off. Her few weeks there had certainly provided plenty of adventure. Working for herself, there was no telling what kind of cases she could get into.

But, more than the excitement, she'd enjoyed getting to know the people affected by her case. She could make a difference to those who mattered to her instead of nameless strangers.

Watching the sun dip closer to the bright blue ocean, she realized something had definitely changed.

She had.

"I'M RESIGNING," Malina said, laying her badge on SAC Samuel Clairmont's desk.

Sam looked up at her, then nodded at the chair in front of his desk. "Have a seat, Agent Blair."

Reluctantly, Malina did as he asked, although even to the end taking orders was difficult for her. Her way was the only way, after all. With a smile, she remembered Carr's accurate assessment of her philosophy.

"Are you looking forward to leaving that much?" Sam asked.

Malina forced a sober expression onto her face. "Sorry, sir. It's been a difficult decision."

"In less than a week, you've gone from the promise

of glory in Quantico to unemployment." Clearly curious, he leaned back in his chair. "Want to catch me up?"

She glanced around his office, the walls full of pictures and commendations. Framed, signed photos of the last three presidents held a place of high honor directly behind his desk.

She didn't envy him anymore. She couldn't care less about glory or running the Bureau.

"I want to open my own security consulting firm." She smiled again. "I'm pretty good at finding lost dogs."

"You're—" Sam shook his head. "You're not serious."

"The dogs would only be an occasional thing, I guess. By staying here, I'll never be anything more than an agent. My career will never advance beyond what it is now."

"It's still a pretty damn good job, and you're one of the best. And stop smiling like that. You're scaring me."

"I'll try." And she did. Mostly, though, she wanted to get this meeting over with and go see Carr. She needed this part of her life finished, so she could start down her new path. "I appreciate your confidence in me, sir, but I don't have the patience for politics anymore."

"And this has nothing to do with Carr Hamilton?"

"Oh, it has everything to do with him."

"If you're staying here for him, you can still work for me. I'll talk to the director about canceling the transfer."

She let her gaze rove the wall of honors. "The Bureau doesn't hold the appeal it once did."

Sam turned briefly to see what held her fascination. "I

know you don't need us, our commendations or probably our paycheck—you'll have a wealthy husband."

Malina's heart jumped at the idea of marrying Carr. She hadn't gotten *that* far planning her new path.

Still, the idea didn't seem as crazy as she might have considered a few weeks ago. She pressed her lips together to keep from grinning.

"I'm asking you to stay because *we* need *you*," Sam said forcefully.

"You didn't like my plan for catching Simon Ellerby," she pointed out.

"I reluctantly approved the operation, but since it worked, you seem to have been right. I'm not going to say we'll always agree, but give me a chance to make it work. And here in Charleston we're not as backwater as you might think. We have the harbor assignments and a SWAT team, you know."

Either of those assignments would certainly feed her desire for adventure. But she wasn't sure Carr would love the idea. She'd have to consult with him before she could agree to join the team.

Wow, they really were a couple.

"You're doing it again."

She bit her lower lip. "Sorry."

"At least give it a few months."

Maybe she was being rash in leaving the Bureau. She did respect and admire Sam. And since closing the Ellerby case, her coworkers had abruptly cut off the ragging about dog-napping.

As if sensing she was wavering, Sam leaned back in his chair. "I notice you didn't turn in your gun."

Malina laid her hand protectively over her Glock. The sidearm was as much a part of her as her hand. She could buy her own, but how many opportunities other than the firing range would she have to actually use it in the private sector?

As she started to slide the weapon from its holster, Sam held up his hand. "Keep it for now. I want you to talk to some people before you decide." He picked up the phone and said, "Send them in."

Malina glanced out the office windows to see the mayor and his twins walking through the bullpen.

What the— She whipped her head back toward Sam.

"The mayor asked me to contact him the minute I heard from you," he said. "I called him and told him about our appointment today."

Malina rose as Mayor Parnell walked into the office. "Good afternoon, sir, I—"

Madison and Edward threw themselves against her sides. "Don't go!" they cried in unison.

"Well, I don't—" Malina began.

"What'll we do if somebody runs off with Pooky again?" Madison asked, blinking tears from her bright blue eyes.

Malina thought it would be churlish to point out she and her brother had been the last ones to roll out that dastardly plan.

"There's this big kid at school that threatens to punch me if I look at him," Edward said, his voice desperate. "Who's going to help me with that?"

Ah, your dad's big, bad bodyguards?

Malina looked desperately at the mayor for help.

"Sorry, Agent Blair. I told them about your transfer to Quantico." He sighed. "I had a moving speech all planned to convince you to stay. It appears that won't be necessary."

Sam rose, and now he was smiling. "I'm sure it was

an excellent speech, Don. Maybe you can use it at Agent Blair's commendation ceremony."

Good grief. Malina finally understood how Simon Ellerby had felt being taken down by a bimbo and a lawyer.

"Look, kids," she said, kneeling between them. "I'm not going anywhere. I'm still deciding my career plans," she added, her gaze flicking to Sam. "But I promise I'll be around to protect you guys and Pooky."

Then, contradicting her uncertainty, and in between patting the twins on their backs, she caught the badge Sam tossed her.

"CARR, YOUR BOAT'S BEEN broken into."

Prior to picking up the phone, Carr had been seated at his desk, staring out his office window. At this news from the sheriff, however, he jerked to his feet. "When? How?"

"I have no idea," Tyler said. "Al Duffy just called me. I'm headed over to the marina now. Why don't you meet me?"

"I'm coming."

He hung up the phone and strode from the office, telling his secretary that he had to go out for a while.

Since waking up last week to find Malina gone, he'd been going through the motions of waking, working, sleeping. He'd struggled over the promises he'd made to himself—and Sister Mary Katherine—and the irresistible lure of being with the woman he loved.

Could he really live in a city like Washington, full of high-profile clients and power brokers, and not indulge in old habits? Was there any lure left in trying to prove his parents had been short-sighted in leaving him behind?

Yes. And no.

Besides, Malina was assigned to Bureau headquarters in Quantico, Virginia. He could buy a house with a farm, grow peaches or cotton and retreat to the beach on weekends.

Peaches or cotton? he asked himself as he pulled into the marina's parking lot.

Okay, maybe not.

But there were certainly plenty of charities and foundations in the Washington area that could use his expertise.

Bypassing The Heron, he jogged down to the pier. At four-thirty it was a bit early for after-work cruisers to be about, but he did expect Tyler and Al. He saw neither of them. He could see the tip of *The Litigator* bobbing in the water some distance away.

What in the world was going on?

Could the would-be thief have actually overpowered both men? And why? Still, the whole incident had Carr's nerves clanging with alarm. Was there another member of Simon Ellerby's thieving ring that they'd been unaware of?

His body braced for anything, he moved closer. He wished like crazy for a weapon and paused as he realized he'd left his phone in the car. But then, Tyler had undoubtedly been wearing both his police radio and his pistol, and he didn't appear to have fared so well.

Two slips from his own, he saw the smoke.

A stream was billowing out an open window, so, thief or no thief, he broke into a run. He leaped onto the deck, flung open the door and nearly plowed into Malina, who was frantically waving a towel over a pot on the stove.

His heart literally stopped. "*You* broke into my boat?"

he asked, his gaze frozen to her trim figure, encased in jeans and a cherry-red shirt.

She scowled. "I was trying to make you a romantic dinner."

She was? He could hardly believe she was real.

"Al Duffy is an ass." She stalked across the cabin to open another window. "He claims he saw me sneaking around. He knows I know you. But does he walk up and ask me what I'm doing? *Nooo*. He calls the sheriff. Then Tyler shows up, gun drawn I might add. We nearly shot each other!" She pointed at him, as if the whole mess was his fault. "I spent fifty bucks on seafood at your buddy's shack in the marina's parking lot. He's wrong, by the way. You don't just throw everything in the pot and let it boil."

Carr had barely heard her rant and continued to stare at her as if she were a mirage. "You were making me a romantic dinner?"

She flopped on the sofa. "As you can imagine, Tyler laughed like a loon about that before he left. He offered to send Andrea over to help. I probably should have taken his advice."

Now that Carr was convinced he wasn't hallucinating—'cause, hey, in his fantasies he always pictured Malina in a bikini and her deep blue eyes full of lust, not frustrated and upset—he caught the implications of her appearance.

She was back.

But for how long? Was she making him a goodbye dinner? If so, she was going to find losing him much more challenging than she'd expected.

Carr leaned over the pot. He saw crabs, shrimp, sausage, corn, potatoes and onions, but no liquid. "Did you add water?"

She looked puzzled, then rueful. "I was so distracted by nearly murdering the sheriff, it's entirely possible I screwed up the instructions."

"We can probably salvage it." He dumped the food into another pot, tossed out the burned bits, which turned out to be mostly potatoes, then reached into the fridge for a beer. He poured the contents of the can into the fresh pot, along with several cups of water.

Turning to face her, he leaned against the counter. "When did you get back?" he managed to say.

"Late last night. I slept all day, then came here."

A bout of nerves he hadn't experienced since his first middle school dance washed over him. "Oh, yeah?"

Her eyes cleared, the anger gone. She blinked as if just realizing he was there. Standing, she moved toward him.

He noticed she wore not only her pistol and holster, but her badge, which was tucked, shield out, in the front pocket of her jeans. "Is this an official visit?"

"Sort of."

He frowned. Something about her was different, not the least of which were her vague answers. "When do you go to D.C.?"

She stopped inches away from him, and his heartbeat picked up speed. "I'm thinking of doing an HRT refresher course next month."

"I see." But of course he really didn't. "I wasn't sure you were coming back here."

"You're here," she said simply.

He finally realized what was different. The change was subtle, but up close he could see the distance in her eyes was gone. The vague suspicion and doubt she'd used as a barrier between them had disappeared. Hope sparked deep inside him.

"I learned something important at home." She curled her arms around his neck.

"The weather's too perfect in Hawaii?"

"No, but it is."

"The surfing is lousy."

"No, it definitely isn't." She laid her finger over his lips before he could ask any more inane questions. "I learned this is how love feels. At least for me."

He crushed her against him so hard that tears exploded behind his eyes. "You're not going."

"I resigned."

"But you're wearing your badge."

"The SAC talked me into staying, at least for now. We'll see how things go, then decide together what to do."

"My money's on Sam."

She leaned back. "Not we—Sam and me. We, as in you and me."

Carr planted a hard, relieved, hopeful kiss on her lips. "I love you."

"And I love you. Nothing in my life is as important as you."

Carr searched her gaze, seeing the truth of her conviction. He knew the happiness flooding him was only beginning, and the future would be faced, not alone, but with her. "I thought your job was your life."

"Not anymore."

"Does my house have anything to do with your decision to stay?" he teased.

"I *do* love your house," she hedged.

Laughing, Carr hugged her. "We'll move you in tomorrow. And remind me to call Charlie McGary and have him call off the Virginia search."

"The Virginia search?" Malina asked.

He moved to the couch, where he sat and tugged her into his lap. "Charlie's my real estate agent."

Her eyes widened. "Wow. You weren't afraid of the temptation to go back to the Dark Side?"

"I figured I'd have a high-ranking federal law enforcement officer to keep me on the right path."

"Yes, you would."

He cupped her cheek in his hand. "You're my life. I couldn't let you go without me."

"Carr?" she asked as he brushed her cheek with his lips.

"Yeah?"

"You still talk too much."

"I bet I can fix that." As he kissed her, he poured all the love and promise he'd been holding quietly inside for so long. Neglected as it had been, his heart overflowed with gratitude.

Unfortunately, the next thing he heard wasn't a chorus of angelic approval, but Al Duffy's scratchy voice.

"No more mopin' around. You hear, boy? Ain't dignified for a man to be so depressed about a woman who can't even cook."

LATER, LONG AFTER DINNER and sunset, Malina lay in the master cabin's bed, her head pillowed on Carr's bare chest just as she had the first time they'd been together.

That night the sea had undulated beneath them, rocking them in a steady cradle of contentment, even as she'd convinced herself she was simply releasing stress from her demanding job. Tonight, the waves continued their relentless motion, and she was completely different.

She could finally appreciate fulfillment with the love of her life. She didn't have the constant drive to wonder what professional challenge might be over the next horizon. She didn't worry about what compromise might cost her.

At last she understood her mother's internal peace.

Still, she wasn't her mother in many ways.

She turned on her side and propped her head in her hand. "I still think Al Duffy was being difficult, not—as you so innocently believe—trying to get us together."

He mirrored her pose. "It seems imminently obvious that he saw you, worried you wouldn't stay long enough for me to see you, knew how much I needed to see you, so he took matters into his own hands. Drastic matters maybe, but still pure of heart."

She snorted in derision. "Oh, please."

"You two are going to have to find a peaceful middle ground eventually. Al's a good guy down deep."

"Way down."

"Maybe so, but he does know everything about this area. He can navigate through these waters, under any weather conditions, with his eyes closed."

"I can shoot accurately with my eyes closed. Who'd you rather have in a fight?"

He paused. "I think you've won your argument, Agent."

"Of course, I have. But do you know what became of Simone Anderson?"

"The abrupt segue of the day award goes to..."

She slapped his chest lightly. "Come on, Simone Anderson."

His eyes darkened with regret. "She was my client for the case against Nelson Chemicals. Most of her family was poisoned by the runoff water from their plant."

"You remember her?"

"I've had a lot of free time on my hands the last week. You might say I took a walk down memory lane."

"And did your stroll reveal where she is today?"

"No." He slid his hand across her hip, drawing her closer and confirming what she'd thought—he was afraid to know too much. Another case like Bailey Industries was too painful to face.

"Simone works for an international peace organization that strives to eliminate river and stream chemical poisoning produced by industrial plants in third-world countries."

Carr went still, then shook his head as if trying to clear his thoughts. "She what?"

"You heard me. She credits you with opening her eyes to the neglectful policies that run rampant in countries without a legitimate legal system. How about Bruce Carmandy?"

"Who? I—" He stopped, and Malina could clearly see his brain straining to switch gears. "He was paralyzed by a bus hitting him on Seventh Avenue in New York City."

"By a bus driver who had a serious history of drug abuse. With his settlement money from the city, Carmandy got a great apartment overlooking the East River and paid for the driver to go through rehab yet again. Apparently the treatment stuck this time. The two men started a company that builds motorized wheelchairs."

His eyes full of wonder, Carr stared at her. "How did you find out all this?"

"I investigated. I'm highly trained, you know."

"I know. But why?"

"To show you that your debt is paid. You don't have to redeem yourself anymore. You've made mistakes, but the good completely outweighs the bad." She slid her fingers through his silky hair, letting her gaze rove his beloved features. Beaches, oceans and sunsets included, she'd never tire of that view. "You're a great man. Not just in my eyes, but many others."

"Thank you." As she felt a deep breath of relief escape his chest, he kissed her lips, then trailed his mouth along her jaw.

Carnal sensations that had shifted briefly into dormancy reasserted themselves. She inhaled his sandalwood-scented cologne and knew this was the place she belonged for the rest of her life.

"Is this 'you're redeemed' thing just a ploy to keep me from butting into your cases?" he whispered between kisses.

"I refuse to answer that question on the grounds it might incriminate me."

He held her tightly against him. "I love you."

"Same goes, Counselor. Same goes."

* * * * *